Dug fled.

He'd had a go at rallying them, shouting that they couldn't lose if they just held the badger-fucking line! He'd grabbed a spear off a passing man and tried to push to the front. He'd thought, *Coward*, but knew he was no braver; he just knew that his best chance of survival lay in the line holding. "Cavalry can't charge a spear line!" he'd shouted, but in vain. Barton was beaten before the armies even met. So Dug turned and ran as fast as a fit but mildly overweight forty-year-old man wearing ringmail can run through a panicking army. He could have stood like a hero of old and met the Maidun force, he thought as he ran, but there were old soldiers and there were brave soldiers. You can't be both.

AGE of IRON

Iron Age Trilogy: Book One

Angus Watson

orbit

www.orbitbooks.net

For Nicola and Charlie

———————

Copyright © 2014 by Angus Watson
Excerpt from *Arcanum* copyright © 2013 by Simon Morden
Excerpt from *Malice* copyright © 2013 by John Gwynne

Orbit
Hachette Book Group
237 Park Avenue, New York, NY 10017
HachetteBookGroup.com

Printed in the United States of America

RRD-C

First US Edition: September 2014

10 9 8 7 6 5 4 3 2 1

First published in Great Britain in 2014 by Orbit

Orbit is an imprint of Hachette Book Group, Inc. The Orbit name and logo are trademarks of Little, Brown Book Group Limited.

The Hachette Speakers Bureau provides a wide range of authors for speaking events. To find out more, go to www.hachettespeakersbureau.com or call (866) 376-6591.

The publisher is not responsible for websites (or their content) that are not owned by the publisher.

Library of Congress Cataloging-in-Publication Data/Control Number: 2014933835

ISBN: 978-0-316-39978-4

In 55 BC, ten thousand Roman soldiers commanded by General Julius Caesar invaded Britain. They advanced no further than the Kentish beach they'd landed on before returning to Gaul.

A year later Caesar crossed the Channel again, this time with twenty-five thousand soldiers, plus cavalry, in six hundred newly built transport ships. This huge force certainly intended to conquer and occupy Britain. Yet a few months after landing, the mighty Roman army fled back to Gaul with nothing to show for its expensive venture.

The Romans did not return until AD 43, almost a hundred years later.

History has always accepted the only surviving account of the 55 and 54 BC invasions—Julius Caesar's diary—which says that the Romans won every battle in Britain, had never intended to stay anyway and departed in triumph with their forces intact.

The following is what really happened.

Part One

Barton and Bladonfort
61 BC

Chapter 1

"**M**ind your spears, coming through!"

Dug Sealskinner shouldered his way back through the ranks. Front rank was for young people who hadn't learned to fear battle and old men who thought they could compete with the young.

Dug put himself halfway in that last category. He'd been alive for about forty years, so he was old. And he wanted to compete with the young, but grim experience had unequivocally, and sometimes humiliatingly, demonstrated that the young won every time. Even when they didn't win they won because they were young and he wasn't.

And here he was again, in another Bel-cursed battle line. Had things gone to plan, he'd have been living the respectable older man's life, lord of his broch, running his own seaside farm on Britain's north coast, shearing sheep, spearing seals and playing peekaboo with grandchildren. He'd been close to achieving that when fate had run up and kicked him in the bollocks. Since then, somehow, the years had fallen past, each one dying with him no nearer the goals that had seemed so achievable at its birth.

If only we could shape our own lives, he often thought, rather than other bastards coming along and shaping them for us.

Satisfyingly, the ragtag ranks parted at his request. He might not feel it, but he still looked fearsome, and he was a Warrior. His jutting jaw was bearded with thick bristle. His big head was cased in a rusty but robust, undecorated iron helmet. His oiled ringmail shone expensively in the morning sun, its heaviness flattening his ever-rounder stomach. The weighty warhammer which swung on a leather lanyard from his right hand could have felled any mythical beastie.

He'd been paid Warrior's wages to stay in the front rank to marshal the troops, so arguably he should have stayed in the front rank and marshalled the troops. But he didn't feel the need to fulfil every tiny detail of the agreement. Or even the only two details of it. First, because nobody would know; second, because there wasn't going to be a battle. He'd collect his full fee for a day standing in a field, one of thousands of soldiers. One of thousands of *people*, anyway. There were some other Warriors – Dug knew a few of them and had nodded hello – but the rest were men and women in leathers at best, hardly soldiers, armed with spears but more used to farm equipment. Quite a few of them were, in fact, armed with farm equipment.

What, by Camulos, is that doing here? he thought, looking at a small, bald but bearded man holding a long pole topped with a giant cleaver – a whale blubber cutter, if he wasn't mistaken. He hadn't seen one of those for a while and wanted to ask its owner what it was doing so far inland. But an interest in fishing equipment wouldn't help his battle-hardened Warrior image.

He pushed out into the open field. Behind Barton's make-shift army, children in rough wool smock-frocks ran across the bright field, laughing, fighting and crying. The elderly sat in groups complaining about the army's formation and other things that had been better in their day. To the left, sitting in a heap of rags and shunned by all, was the inevitable drunken old druid, shouting semi-coherently about the imminence of Roman invasion, like all the other dozens of drunken druids that Dug had seen recently.

Over by the bridge were those others who escaped military service – Barton's more important families. A couple of them were looking at Dug, perhaps wondering why their expensive mercenary was taking a break.

He put his hands on his hips in an overseer pose and tried to look like he was assessing the line for weaknesses. *Very important, the rear rank of a defensive line*, he'd tell them if they asked afterwards.

Dug hadn't expected to be in the Barton army that sunny morning. He'd been stopping in Barton hillfort the day before when word came that the cavalry and chariot sections of King Zadar of Maidun Castle's army would be passing on their way home from sacking the town and hillfort of Boddingham.

Boddingham was a smaller settlement than Barton, forty miles or so north-east along the Ridge Road. It had stopped paying tribute to Maidun. Perhaps Boddingham had felt safe, a hundred miles from the seat and capital of King Zadar's empire, but along good metalled roads and the hard chalk Ridge Road, that was only three days' journey for Zadar's chariots and cavalry – less if they pushed it. It would have taken much longer to move a full army, as Dug well understood, having both driven and hindered armies' movements in his time, but everyone Dug had spoken to said that Zadar's relatively small flying squad of horse soldiers was more than capable of obliterating a medium-sized settlement like Boddingham. If that was true, thought Dug, they must be the elite guard of Makka the war god himself.

The Maidun force had passed Barton two days before, too set on punishing Boddingham to linger for longer than it took to demand and collect food, water and beer. Now though, on the way back, swords bloodied, slaves in tow, the viciously skilful little company might have the time and inclination to take a pop at weak, underprepared Barton.

"You!" A man had shouted at Dug the night before. So courteous, these southerners.

"Aye?" he'd replied.

"Know anything about fighting?"

You'd think his dented iron helmet, ringmail shirt and warhammer might have answered that question, but southerners, in Dug's experience, were about as bright as they were polite.

"Aye, I'm a Warrior."

And that was how he'd ended up at the previous night's war council. He'd actually been on his way to sign up with Zadar's army – finally fed up with the strenuous life of a wandering mercenary – but he saw no need to mention that to the Barton defenders.

Fifty or so of Barton's more important men and women, the same ones who weren't in the battle line, had been packed into the Barton Longhouse for the war council. Calling it a longhouse was pretentiousness, another southern trait that Dug had noticed. First, it was circular. Second, it was only about twenty paces across. At most it was a mediumhouse. It was just a big hut really, made of mud, dung and grass packed into a lattice of twigs between upright poles. Four wide trunks in the middle supported the conical reed roof. Dug could have shown them how to build a hut the same size without the central supports, thereby freeing up space. Perhaps the hall predated that particular architectural innovation, but there was a wood at the foot of the hill and plenty of people, so rebuilding would have been a doddle.

This tribe, however, was clearly neither architecturally diligent nor building-proud. One of the support posts leaned alarmingly and there was a large, unplanned hole in the roof near the door. At the end of a long hot day, despite the hole, the air inside was thick and sweaty. It could have done with double ceiling vents. Dug could have shown them how to put those in too.

King Mylor of Barton sat on a big wooden chair on a platform in the centre, rubbing the back of his hand against his two remaining rotten teeth, staring about happily with milky eyes at his visitors and hooting out "Oooo-ooooh!" noises that reminded Dug of an elderly seal. He looked like a seal, now Dug came to think of it. Smooth rings of blubber made his neck wider than his hairless, liver-spotted skull, which was wetly lucent in the torchlight. Whiskers sprayed out under his broad, flat nose. Dug had heard that Barton's king had lost his mind. It looked like the gossipy bards were right for once.

Next to Mylor sat the druid Elliax Goldan, ruler in all but name. You didn't cross Barton's chief druid, Dug had heard. He was a little younger than Dug perhaps, slim, with tiny black eyes in a pink face that gathered into a long nose. Rat-like. If you could judge a man by his face – and Dug had found that you could – here was an angry little gobshite. Dug had seen more and more druids as he'd migrated south. There were three basic types: the wise healer sort who dispensed advice and cures, the mad, drunk type who raved about dooms – almost all Rome-related these days – and the commanding sort whose communes with the gods tended to back up their plans and bolster their status. Elliax was firmly in this latter camp.

On Mylor's left was the druid's wife, Vasin Goldan. Her skin was shiny and mottled. Big eyes sat wide apart, far up her forehead, very nearly troubling her hairline. Frog-face, Dug had heard her called earlier. *Spot on*, he mused. Seal-head, Rat-nose and Frog-face. Right old menagerie.

Behind Elliax and Mylor were four Warriors in ringmail. It was never a great sign, Dug thought, when rulers needed protection from their own people.

Elliax silenced the hubbub with a couple of claps, interrupting Dug's explanation to a young woman of how he'd improve the hut's roof. "The meeting is convened!" he said in a surprisingly deep voice. Dug had expected him to squeak.

"Could we not do this outside?" asked Dug, pulling his mail shirt away from his neck to get some cooler air down there. Spicily pungent body odour clouded out. The woman he'd been talking to shuffled away. Blooming embarrassment made Dug even hotter.

"Barton war meetings take place in the Barton Longhouse!" Elliax boomed, also reddening.

"Even when it's hot and there's plenty of room outside? Isn't that a bit stupid?" Several people around Dug nodded.

"Hot-t-t-t-t!" shouted King Mylor.

Mylor, it was said, had lost his mind along with Barton's wealth and position ten years before, when he'd bet his five best against King Zadar's champion. The champion, a massive young man called Carden Nancarrow, had slaughtered Barton's four best men and one woman in a few horrifying moments. Barton had paid painful taxes to Maidun ever since.

By persuading Mylor to accept the five-to-one combat rather than defend the highly defendable fort, Elliax claimed he'd saved Barton from annihilation. Over the following decade he'd continued to serve his town as Zadar's representative and tax collector. Zadar's taxes would have starved Barton in a couple of years, said Elliax, but he was happy to mislead Maidun about Barton's assets and collect a little less. All he asked in exchange were a few easy gifts like land, food, ironwork or the easiest gift of all – an hour or so with a daughter. While others became steadily malnourished, Elliax thrived, his wife fattened, and unmarried girls bore children with suspiciously rodent faces. Anyone who complained found themselves chosen by Elliax's druidic divinations to march south as part of Zadar's quarterly slave quota.

"We have nothing to fear," Elliax continued, ignoring Dug and King Mylor. "I have seen it. We pay our dues and it's in Zadar's interest that we keep paying them. He will not attack."

"But Zadar can't be trusted to act rationally!" shouted a young woman at the back. "Look what he did to Cowton last year."

Dug had heard about Cowton. Everybody had. Zadar had wiped out the entire town. Men, women, the elderly, children, livestock . . . two thousand people and Danu knew how many animals had been slaughtered or sold to Rome as slaves. Nobody knew why.

Elliax looked sideways at King Mylor. The king was picking at the crotch of his woollen trousers.

"Who is your chief druid?" Elliax asked. Nobody had an answer. Elliax smiled like a toad who'd caught a large fly. He held out his arms. "This morning, on the wood shrine, I sacrificed a seabird from the Island of Angels to see its tales of the future. As the bird quivered in death, I was distracted by a sound. I looked up and saw a squirrel hissing at a cat. The cat passed by, leaving the squirrel unharmed." Elliax looked around smugly, eyes finishing up on Dug's.

Most people looked at each other and nodded. More often than not the gods' messages were too cryptic for Dug to grasp immediately, but he got this one.

"Can't argue with that!" said a stout man.

"Yeah, if it was true. Ever heard a squirrel hiss?" muttered a woman behind Dug.

"No one would dare lie about something like that!" whispered a man who, by the frustration in his voice, Dug took to be the woman's husband.

Elliax continued. "I looked into the bird's viscera and found Danu. She told me we had nothing to fear from Zadar. Next I found Makka. He outlined our strategy. The weather has been dry, so Zadar will leave the Ridge Road and take the quicker lowland road, as he did on the way to Boddingham. Makka told me that we should gather everyone on the valley floor and form a spear and shield line between the two curves of the river on the other side of the bridge. Cavalry and chariots cannot charge a spear line."

"Unless the spear line breaks," said Dug. He wouldn't have usually challenged any god's proclamations, especially Makka's, but these people didn't know battle and needed to be told. A few older voices murmured agreement, which encouraged him to continue: "In which case you might as well have a row of children holding wet reeds. Why not bring everyone up into the fort? Do a bit of work on the walls overnight – sharpen the angles, tighten the palisade, few spikes in the ditch – and they'll never get in."

"And leave all our farms, homes and crops to the whims of Zadar's army!" Elliax spat, his voice becoming steadily higher. "You're as stupid as you look, northman! You shouldn't be in here anyway. You're not from Barton. There's no reason for a spear line to break. I think two gods know a little more than some shabby has-been Warrior. And actually I have the advice of three gods, because further into the guts of the bird, I found Dwyn."

"Pretty crowded in that bird," said the woman behind Dug. Her husband shushed her again.

Elliax ignored the interruption. "That cunning god perfected the plan. He told me to send a rider to Zadar to tell him that we'll be lining the route to celebrate his passing with a ceremonial battle line. We'll defend our land with something that looks like a show of respect. That's the sort of strategic thinking you won't have seen much of where you're from."

"Are you sure that's what Dwyn told you?" Dug had never questioned a druid before, but Elliax's plan was madness. "Forewarned, as most kids where I'm from know, is fore-armed."

Elliax sneered. "We have slings, many more than Zadar can possibly have. His troops will be on horseback and in chariots, we'll be behind shields. If Zadar tries to attack, our shields will protect us and we'll send back a hailstorm of death. Zadar is not stupid. He will not attack! He knows how futile it would be. Besides, the gods have spoken to me. Perhaps if you'd listened to them more, you wouldn't be walking the land begging for work. At your age too. It's shameful."

Dug's ears were suddenly hot. Elliax turned away from him and outlined his plan in detail. Irritatingly, thought Dug, the jumped-up prick's idea made some sense. Charging a line of spears on horseback or in a chariot was indeed suicide. Horses knew this too, so it was also near impossible. He was right about projectile weapons as well. Barton's more numerous slingers and shields should neutralise any projectile threat.

Geography also favoured Barton. To get from Zadar's likely route to most of Barton's land, you had to cross a river. The only bridge for miles was in the centre of a long bend. The best way for cavalry to beat a line of spearmen was to gallop around and take them on the flank or from behind. With the army bracketed by two loops of the river's meandering course, that would be impossible. But there was still one big, obvious flaw.

"Why don't we stay this side of the bridge?" Dug asked. "We can hold the bridge with a handful of soldiers, protect most of the land and you can still have your wee procession. If Zadar attacks and your long line of bakers and potters doesn't hold, which it probably wouldn't, then we're trapped between him and the river and in all sorts of bother."

Elliax grimaced as if someone had just urinated on a relative's funeral bed. "Still you challenge the gods? They know, as you don't, that there's valuable property just the other side of the river."

"This property wouldn't happen to be yours, would it?"

"Why don't you shut up and stop embarrassing yourself? We share property. It's *everyone's* land, you northern fool."

Elliax stared at him furiously, but then, as if recalling a pleasant memory, smiled. "Or maybe you'd like a stronger reading? Why don't you come up here and we'll see what your spilled entrails say about Zadar's intentions? We'll see the next ten winters in your fat gut! Bob, Hampcar, why don't you find out just how much this know-it-all knows about fighting?"

Two of the four guards stood forward and slid swords a couple of fingers' breadth from scabbards. They were both big men. One had a long face with a pronounced muzzle and drawn-back lips showing uncommonly white teeth. The other was beardless, with a scar soaring redly from each corner of his mouth into his shaggy hairline. That injury was caused by making a small cut at each corner of a person's mouth, then hurting them; an iron auger screwed between wrist bones was one method Dug had seen. The victim would scream, ripping his or her flesh from mouth to ears. If the wounds healed and they didn't die of infection, they were left with a smile-shaped scar. Way up north this was called a Scrabbie's kiss, after a tribe keen on handing them out. Men generally grew beards to cover the scars, but this guy had shaved to show them off. It was, admittedly, quite effective, if you were going for the scary bastard look. His mate looked even tougher.

Dug decided not to take them on.

"Are you coming? Or are you a coward?" Elliax sneered.

Dug stared back in what he hoped was a cool, Bel-may-care manner. He didn't need to take on four Warriors to prove a point. Or even two. Besides, if Dwyn, god of tricks, Makka, god of war and Danu, mother of all the gods, had all been involved in the planning, who was Dug to argue? He might as well negotiate a decent fee for standing in the line, then leave the following evening a richer man with his guts still in his belly.

"Are you coming, I said?"

"I'll stay here."

"Stupid, fat and cowardly too. Some Warrior!" Elliax looked around triumphantly and seemed to grow a little. "Ignore this oaf's ignorant comments. I have been shown the way. The plan is made and King Mylor agrees." Mylor looked up and smiled at hearing his name, then returned to plucking at his genitals. Elliax continued: "Have no fear. Zadar hasn't got where he is today by attacking against impossible odds. We are completely safe."

So the following dawn everyone who wasn't too young, infirm or important to hold a weapon, around four thousand men and women in all, wandered at first light across the bridge to the big field and gathered between the two river bends. The mixed bunch of farmers, crafters and woodspeople from Barton village and its outlying hamlets and farms shuffled about confusedly but good-naturedly as Dug and others formed them into an as effective a line as possible, putting those with relatively decent shields and spears at the front. Dug herded a few people with longer spears to the rear, going by the theory that if those in front were engaged in a hand-to-hand mêlée, the back rank could still thrust their long weapons at the enemy. He knew it was futile – if this front line engaged with even half-trained troops then they were all fucked – but it kept him busy and showed that he knew his game.

The children and the elderly crossed the river and gathered behind them, standing on carts, boxes and barrels to watch Zadar's army pass. The chief families arrived last, dressed in well-worn finery. Mylor, Elliax and his wife Vasin arrived last, with their chairs from the longhouse mounted on the biggest cart.

As the day warmed, a carnival atmosphere developed behind the spear line. The crazy druid stopped shouting, children played less frantically and the elderly forgot their gripes as they drank and talked of battles past. Puppies scurried between feet. Older dogs padded around looking for pats and scraps. The line grew ever more ragged as its members left to grab a drink, find somewhere to squat or just wander about.

Dug was pushing back through the line to say hello to some old boys with a gigantic barrel of cider that he'd spotted earlier when Zadar's army rode into sight from behind a stand of trees some four hundred paces away. A few shouts got everyone's attention and silence spread through the crowd like blood soaking into sand.

"Lift me up, please?" It was a small, skinny boy with huge brown eyes and a tuft of hair the red-brown of freshly ploughed earth. He stared up at Dug. "Please?" The boy's eyes widened ever further.

Dug sighed and hoiked the boy onto his shoulders. He hardly weighed a thing.

"Is that Zadar?!"chirped the child.

"Probably. Yes." A lone rider headed the procession. He wore a huge, golden, horned helmet, a shining black ringmail jacket and black leather trousers. His black horse — by far the largest Dug had ever seen — was similarly attired in a golden-horned pony cap and a draped sheet of black ringmail protecting its rump.

"What's he wearing on his head?"

"Can't you see?"

Dug felt the boy slump a little. Dug could see well over long and short distances, but he knew that a lot of people had trouble with either or both. As a young man, he'd made no allowances, convinced that everybody could see just as well as him but pretended not to be able to for perverse reasons. Age had made him more tolerant.

"His helmet has horns on it."

The boy perked up. "Why?"

"Maybe to make him look scary, or maybe he's trying to

persuade people that he's Kornonos, the horned god of animals. Probably he's not very tall and he thinks people will think he's taller if he wears a big hat. But of course people will think he's just a wee man in a big hat."

The boy giggled. Zadar in fact looked like quite a big man, but Dug was never one to let truth get in the way of belittling people he suspected to be puffed up.

"That coat he's wearing – and that rug covering the arse of his horse – is ringmail. That's hundreds or thousands – probably thousands in this case – of rings of iron all linked together. It'll protect you from slingstones, a sword slash, that sort of thing. But it's not much use against this." Dug raised his warhammer. The boy jiggled with glee. The hammer was an effective but simple weapon, no more sophisticated than the rock-tied-to-a-stick design that had been popular for aeons. An iron lump the size and shape of a large clog was moulded around a shaft of fire-hardened oak a pace long and held in place by a tight criss-cross of leather strips. Both ends of the handle were sharpened into points.

"Only kings and Warriors are allowed to wear ringmail."

"But you're wearing ringmail!"

"Aye. That's right. I'm a Warrior . . . Mine is more the hundreds of rings type, though not as supple or as light as his'll be."

"And is his horse a Worrier? Or a king?"

"Uh . . . neither. Thing about rules is that if you become powerful enough, you get to break them. And make them."

"Your voice is funny."

"I'm from the north."

"What are you worried about?"

"What?"

"You're a Worrier?"

"A Warrior. It's a title, like king. But this one you earn. You have to kill ten people in a battle. If five people who are already Warriors agree that you've done that, then they

say you're a Warrior, and you get one of these." Dug tapped
the crudely made iron boar that hung on a leather thong
around his neck. "And you're allowed to wear ringmail, which
is a neat way of making sure fewer people become Warriors
and making life safer once you do. Being a Warrior also
means you can claim a certain price as a mercenary. And
people treat you better, like you might be given food at an
inn on the understanding you'll protect the place."

"Can I have a boar necklace?"

"No. You've got to earn it."

"But our smith could make one for me?"

"Aye, he could, but the punishment for pretending to be
a Warrior is death by torture."

The kid mused for a few moments on Dug's shoulders.

"Probably not worth it."

"No."

"And the man dressed in black behind Zadar?"

"That must be his head druid, Felix." Dug spat for good
luck. They said that Felix, Zadar's Roman druid, could
command the gods' magic like nobody in Britain had for
generations. Dug had heard tales of Felix thwarting enemies'
plans by reading their minds from afar, and other stories of
him ripping souls from people's bodies or tearing then apart
just by looking at them. You couldn't believe all, or even
most, of what the bards said and sang, but Dug had heard
so much about Felix's powers that some of it must have been
true. He shivered despite the warmth of the day.

"And who's that next lot? Oh gosh!" squeaked the boy.

"Aye." Following King Zadar and Felix were fifty mounted
men and women. Their helmets were hornless, their mail less
polished and their horses' spiked pony caps were dull iron.
"Those are Warriors."

Two hundred paces away they rode by, eyes front, not
deigning even to glance at Barton's suddenly pathetic-looking
spear line. They'd obviously been ordered not to look to the

side for effect, thought Dug. That told him two things. One, that Zadar was a showman, and two, that discipline was strong in the Maidun army. Worryingly strong.

The chariots came next.

"The chariots are built with wooden struts under tension so they can bounce over bumps, narrow burns, corpses . . . Two people in each, a driver and a fighter. See that first lot, with the armoured soldiers?"

"Yes!"

"Those are the heavy chariots – less bouncy, more solid. They'll drive up to a battle line. The fighter will lob a javelin at the enemy. That probably won't kill anyone, but it might stick in a shield, making it useless or at least difficult to use. Or it might go through two overlapping shields, pinning them together when the iron spearhead bends. Then two soldiers have the choice of fighting joined together or chucking—"

"What would you do?" the boy interrupted.

"The only time it happened to me I chucked the shield away. There's something to be said for using a sword without a shield. It can free your senses, changing the whole direction of your—"

"What do the fighters do after they've thrown their javelins?" said the boy.

Dug nearly dumped the boy off his shoulders, but he remembered that his daughters had always interrupted his advice and stories, so, in their memory, he decided to give some leeway to the impertinent wee turd.

"Javelins away, the soldier usually leaps off the chariot and wades in with sword, hammer, spear – whatever. Most people down here use swords, great iron double-edged swords, for swinging. The Romans use shorter pointy swords, for stab—"

"Have you got a sword?"

"Me? No. I had one. I've had a few, but I'm a hammer

man now. So, the soldier starts killing people and trying not
to get killed, while his charioteer mills about in the background keeping an eye on things. When the guy on foot
gets tired or hurt, he retreats or waves to the chariot, which
picks him up and they shoot off to safety. They'll have a
snack and a piss, maybe take a shit, grab a drink, and then
head back to the battle. Brilliant way to fight if you have
the means."

"Why do they have those big swords sticking out of the
chariots?"

Dug had been trying to ignore the curved blades that
protruded a pace from the boss of each of the heavy chariots'
wheels. He shuddered at a memory. "If your enemy runs,
you chase them. Those blades are sharp. One moment someone's running, the next they've got no legs from the knee
down."

"What are these other ones? They're smaller."

"Light chariots. Unarmoured or lightly armoured driver,
plus a slinger or sometimes an archer. No blades, thank Danu,
but they're still nasty. They're all about speed. They fight
from a distan—"

"My mum said that the bravest fighters go naked into
battle to show how brave they are not needing armour."

"That does happen. But it's not bravery. Battles are
dangerous enough. You don't have to be naked to appreciate
that. It's mostly because they've drunk way too much, or it's
men showing off; usually a mix of the two. And it is always
men. Women are cleverer than that. Nobody likes the naked
ones they always get killed the quickest. Often by their own
side."

"Have you ever gone into battle naked?"

"I have not. But there was one time a whole gang of naked
men charged a group of us. It was a cold day, and their wee
blue cocks were pointed straight at us, like mice looking out
of hairy holes, somebody said. They were still a way away

and a girl on our side hit one of them in the bollocks with a slingstones. The noise he made!" Dug chuckled. "We were laughing almost too much to fight. It was up on the banks of the Linny Foith, a great channel miles north of here but way south of where I'm from. I'd just sworn a year's service to a—"

"What about going into battle painted blue?"

"I've done that, but I don't like it. When I was with the Murkans I was in a battle and each side had blued up, trying to intimidate the other. We all felt like arseholes, and it was hard to tell who was on which side. I'm pretty sure I killed a friend that day. Sometimes your blood gets up. I was lashing out at anybody blue, forgetting . . ."

"Will you kill me if Zadar attacks?"

"I will not."

"Will Zadar's army kill us both?"

"No, no. They can't do a thing. They may all be Warriors but it's just a small part of his army, and we outnumber them ten to one. They can't outflank us because of the river, and they can't attack us head-on because we've got spears and they've only got horse troops. If we stay in this line we're fine. Although if they get off their horses we might have problems, and if we break we're in all sorts of bother, whereas if we'd stayed on the other side of the river or, even better, in the hillfort. . ."

"What?"

"Don't fuss. We'll be fine."

The procession continued. After the chariots came the cavalry, again in heavy and light order. Those fifty horsemen who had followed directly after him were plainly Zadar's famous elite, but the couple of hundred heavy cavalry didn't look much less useful. Dug wouldn't have been surprised if they were all Warriors too.

Most interesting to Dug were the light cavalry – one section in particular. On the near side of the procession were six mounted female archers with long hair and bare legs. The blonde one at the front was staring at the Barton line. She was the only soldier in Zadar's army who'd turned her head.

"Are they goddesses?"

"Aye, son, I think they might be."

"And what are these?"

"Musicians."

As if to prove his point, the men riding at the rear of Zadar's army raised brass instruments to their lips and blared out a cacophony. The wooden clackers fixed on hinges in the instruments' mouths added a buzz like a swarm of giant bees.

"I say musicians, but that's no music!" chuckled Dug.

The men and women in Barton's battle line looked at each other then back to the horn blowers. Other than thunder, this was the loudest noise that most of them had ever heard. The boy's legs tightened around Dug's neck.

"Don't be scared, it's just noise!" Dug yelled over the increasing din, for the benefit of those nearby as well as the boy. "We'll be fine! Can you loosen your legs?"

Zadar's army was all in view now, stretched out to match precisely the length of the Barton line. *That probably isn't an accident*, thought Dug. The cavalry and chariots wheeled as one to face them. The trumpets screamed louder. Mylor's ramshackle pseudo-army took a step back. The horns ceased. A gap opened in the centre of the Maidun line, and a lone chariot wobbled slowly towards Barton. Instead of horses, it was drawn by two stumbling, naked, blood-soaked men. They were harnessed to the chariot by leather thongs attached to thick iron bolts that had been hammered through their shoulders. Standing in the chariot, whipping the men forward, was a young woman with large, wobbling bare breasts.

Chatter spread through the Barton line like wind through

a wheat field. Someone said one of the men drawing the horrific chariot was Kris Sheeplord, king of Boddingham. The other was the messenger sent by Elliax to Zadar to tell him about the parade plan.

The king of Boddingham toppled forward, pulling the messenger down with him.

"Big badgers' balls," said Dug. "I don't like the look of this."

Chapter 2

Zadar's army stood motionless. Dug took the boy off his shoulders, squatted and drew him in close.

"Run," he said. "Back over the bridge, up to the ridge."

"To the fort?"

"No. Stay on the ridge and watch. This may be a display. But if Zadar's army attacks, run along the Ridge Road, away from Barton. Don't stop until you reach another fort."

The boy stared at Dug.

"Go!"

He went. Dug stood.

Zadar's army remained motionless, other than the troop of six female mounted archers, who trotted forward. Just within range of Barton's slingers, they reined back their horses and halted, perhaps ten paces between each. The horses' tails swished and the mild breeze played in the women's hair. The metal tips of the heavy bows that each held in her left hand glinted in the bright morning sunlight. Most bows were no more powerful than slings, but these looked different. They had the double arc of a gliding seagull and were made of much thicker wood than the slender, single-curve bows Dug had come across. Probably nothing to worry about. Over-elaboration made a weapon weaker in Dug's experience. He tapped his hammer.

The women reached for arrows, nocked them, pulled back bowstrings, aimed high and shot. The six arrows went much higher and further than arrows were meant to go. Five sailed over the Barton line and landed harmlessly in the gap between army and spectators. One flew a little further and speared an elderly man through the chest. He squawked, dropped his cider and fell backwards. The six women lowered their bows and sat on their horses, looking calmly ahead as if appreciating the view.

"Prepare to shoot!" came the order from somewhere in the Barton line. There was a pause while a couple of hundred slingers fumbled in their bags.

"Shoot!" Hundreds of little round missiles flew in graceful parabolas. They would have landed on or near enough the six Maidun horse archers had the riders not galloped forward, hooves drumming on the hard ground. By the time the salvo landed where they'd been, the archers were twenty paces from the spear line. As if it were a synchronised dance, the women lifted their bows and pulled arrows from the quivers on their backs. They nocked the arrows, drew, aimed and loosed.

Six arrows thrummed into the Barton line. Four smashed into shields with explosions of splinters. Two of these held in the thick wood, two passed through and spitted the shield holders, one in the chest, one in the stomach. The arrows that missed shields hit the faces of two men who'd peeked round their wooden protection to ogle the women. Their heads burst in sprays of blood and brain.

The dead men fell. The injured men shrieked. People screamed. Six more arrows hummed through the gaps left in the shield wall by the fallen. More screams tore the air. Wails of panic drowned out the howls of the wounded. They'd never seen missiles like these.

The six Maidun horse archers, driving their mounts with their legs, long hair streaming behind them, charged up and down, pumping arrows into the line of Barton spearmen.

The line reeled, then crinkled. The better shields did stop the arrows, but these were few. As men and women fell, more gaps opened in the shield wall and more arrowheads ripped through leather, wool, linen and flesh.

The Maidun women turned and swooped like a flock of birds, pounding arrow after arrow into the Barton ranks. The Barton army seemed to wake from its torpor and several people ran at their attackers, only to be impaled by arrows before they'd gone a few paces.

Dug watched, eyes narrow, stomach somersaulting.

The Barton slingers couldn't get a clear shot at the archers past their own spearmen, so they pushed forward. Shields were moved aside to give them a clear view, but it was as if the women knew where each breach would appear before it did. They shot through the gaps. Slingers died.

"Concentrate!" Dug shouted. "Have courage! If you all shoot together you'll take them out!"

He managed to gather a gang of slingers. With shouts, pushes and a couple of punches, he primed some men to drop their shields on his command, and readied his slingers. The women headed towards them. Just a few more heartbeats . . . As he drew in breath to shout the command, the archers spun their horses and galloped back to Zadar's lines, kicking up soil at the shocked people of Barton.

"Badgers' cocks," said Dug.

Barton's men and women breathed a collective sigh of relief. The dead and wounded were dragged back, and people began shouting, trying to reorganise the line. Their shouts were drowned out by cries of terror as Zadar's heavy cavalry trotted, then thundered towards Barton's right flank, spears lowered. On the left, Zadar's fifty elite cavalry charged, brandishing long swords in circles about their heads. Leading them, swinging his heavy sword around his horned helm as if it weighed nothing, was King Zadar. His musicians, still blaring a throbbing storm wave of sound, followed behind.

"Hold! Hold! Hold!" shouted a few in the Barton line including Dug. But before Zadar's cavalry had covered half the distance between them, more than half of Barton's forces turned and ran. The line collapsed. What should have been a parade and could have been a battle became a rout.

Those who didn't flee were impaled by spear point, slashed open by swords, trampled under hooves and separated from their lower legs by chariot blades. Those who fled didn't fare much better. Zadar's men slowed into a trotting line of hacking and stabbing butchery.

Elliax Goldan stood on the cart next to King Mylor, his mouth widening. *What the Bel was Zadar doing?* He looked at Mylor. The king gulped up at him smilingly.

"Back across the bridge!" Elliax shouted at the carter.

The carter whipped the oxen, which lumbered forward to begin a wide turn.

"Can't you go backwards?"

The carter looked him in the eye and shook his head with what looked like disgust.

"Fuck this shit!" said Elliax. He leaped off the back of the cart and headed for the bridge.

"Elliax!" He spun round. It was his wife Vasin, looking after him from the back of the cart, hands on hips. "Where do you think you're going?" she boomed at him.

Cromm Cruach, he thought. *Why am I the only one who can think?*

"Come on!" he shouted. Then, much more quietly, "You silly bitch." Splinters exploded as an arrow hit the cart next to her. She seemed not to notice. Another zipped into the ground not three paces from him. *"Come on!"*

"But you know Zadar! We won't be harmed."

"Yes, but I don't know the arrows, do I?"

"Oh really, Elliax. Come back here and—"

"This is happening *now*! Stop complaining about it and *fucking come on!*"

Finally she began to climb heavily from the cart, which had now trundled about a tenth of the circle that would bring it back to the bridge. Not waiting for her, Elliax sprinted across the bridge and didn't stop on the other side. He didn't turn until he was a good way up the slope to the hillfort. Vasin was panting her way towards him across the riverside pasture, a beacon of brightly dressed fatness in the muddled stampede of young and elderly who'd been nearest to the bridge. She stopped, bent over with her hands on her knees and panted. She looked behind her, seemed to be reminded of her predicament, and lumbered on as tiny children raced by.

Cromm fucking Cruach, thought Elliax.

The cart was halfway across the bridge. King Mylor was still sitting on his chair and looking about smilingly as if on an outing to view autumn leaves. The carter was whipping the oxen like a madman, but if they felt his urgency, it didn't show. The vast majority of Barton's people were stuck behind the cart on the wrong side of the river. Zadar's forces were advancing steadily, slaughtering as they came.

The six horse archers who'd started the battle broke from the Maidun line and wheeled in a wide galloping loop around the fleeing Barton people. Reaching the river, they raised their bows as one and shot the oxen. The beasts bellowed and bucked, kicking chunks of flesh out of each other and smashing the cart's front wheels to pieces. The cart pitched forward. The oxen panicked and surged, trampling several children. The splintered axle of the cart jammed into the stonework, pulling the cart sideways and blocking the bridge.

With the bridge jammed, it was safe for Elliax to wait for his wife. He watched Zadar's forces advance in their organised line, chopping Barton's bakers, fieldworkers, chandlers, smiths and bards into piles of meat.

Chapter 3

Ulpius brushed a lovely tress of hair from his face as he watched the Maidun troops' massacring advance through the population of Barton. By Mars it was a sight. Was there a better way to spend a day than sitting on a sunny hillside with his brothers in arms – well, brothers in thievery, rape and murder – and watching a battle? It was as if it had been arranged for their entertainment. Ogre had been right, as usual. Ulpius normally loathed authority figures, but Ogre was like some druid with his ability to foresee opportunities and sniff out pickings. He'd known not only that this battle was going to happen, but he'd also worked out a great place to watch it from. The others said Ogre was a living legend. Ulpius wouldn't go that far – about anybody, ever – but he was prepared to allow that the man had some talents. He was content to be in his gang, for now.

The sounds that drifted up to them – the cries of the horses, the screams, the clang of metal on metal, the chop of iron through old wooden shields – made his arm hair stand up and sent shivers of glee up his back. Best of all was watching some fleeing fool being run down by a chariot. It was like someone trying to escape a wave on a beach. "Oh oh oh ooooooh!" they'd all shout together as the pathetic figure was running one moment, disappeared the next, then reappeared as a corpse. Best of all were those who sat up with their lower legs missing, looked around, spotted their own feet some distance away, then collapsed. Such fun. The gang loved it too. They whooped and cheered and pointed out bits that the others might be missing, and acted out amusing little skits of life without feet. It was this sort of fun that brought them together.

All of them apart from Spring of course. Ulpius looked around. Yes, there she was, lying on the grass and staring at the sky while a once-in-a-lifetime spectacle took place below them. How could she not watch? Some people had no idea how to enjoy the world.

There'd be rich pickings tomorrow. But not as rich as – *Mars! Where was it?* Ulpius patted himself like a man with a wasp down his toga. Ah, relief. His mirror was exactly where he'd put it, like it always was.

Aulus Ulpius Galba had been known as Ulpius for so long that he hardly remembered his full Roman name. He was a short man with a triangular, pox-cratered face which rose from a minute goateed chin into a broad forehead crowned with a voluminous, flowing display of lustrous, excellently coiffed, obsidian-black hair. Unlike any other outlaw he'd met since leaving Rome, he owned a mirror. Wealthy people, some Warriors and some druids had mirrors, but nomadic bandits, as a rule, were not so vain.

Ulpius' mirror, until recently at least, was the most important thing in his life. Much of his leisure time was spent gazing into its polished silver surface and styling his hair. He spent hours formulating the finest styling creams and lotions. Current favourite was a few gobs of his own saliva mixed with a smear of clay, a squirt of beery piss and plenty of blood. Didn't matter what kind of blood; human was the easiest to find, so he used that mostly. He'd lost his sheep's bladder, so now he stored his hair goo in a girl's bladder that he'd picked up after another of Zadar's actions.

When he wasn't perfecting the peaks and troughs of his bouffant halo, Ulpius liked to polish his mirror. The repetitive circular movement with the metal cradled in his lap calmed him, even if some jealous onlookers likened it to masturbation. One ill-mannered fool had paid for a wanking jibe with a cut that she'd be reminded of if *she* ever saw a mirror.

Ulpius reckoned he was about thirty-five years old, although he told everyone he was twenty. (The truth, for him, was what he thought other people would believe.) He saw his existence as two lives separated by the incident caused by the mirror. The first was, by a long shot, the happier.

He was the only child of a couple who owned an upmarket butcher's shop in Rome. Had owned, at least. He didn't know whether either was alive still. They were first cousins, both single children who'd felt neglected by their own parents and envious of others' siblings. They wanted nothing more than to marry early, trot out a multitude of children and lavish love on a happy brood. So they'd married at sixteen and taken over the butcher's shop left to Ulpius' father by Ulpius' paternal grandfather, who'd died, wailing in despair at the unfairness of it all, when a Cimbrian spear severed his femoral artery during the Roman defeat at Arausio. The shop had been one of the best in Rome, pandering to the tastes of the rich with a bewildering range of animal flesh. Ulpius' parents improved it and were justifiably proud. But they still, more than anything, wanted children.

After seven miscarriages and most of the profits of the business going to Rome's wide range of fertility experts – from sensibly bearded Greek bloodletters to raving barbarian chicken-wavers – Ulpius had been a gift from the gods. Tiny, sickly Ulpius with his funny-shaped head. When he'd almost died of smallpox, they'd almost died of worry. When he recovered, they focused on making him the happiest child in the world, despite his pox-scarred face. It was no surprise to their few friends when total indulgence and no discipline turned a mildly eccentric capricious child into a nasty self-centred oddball.

At fifteen, when most Romans were as good as married, Ulpius showed no interest in girls. He liked only his own company. His parents didn't push him. He spent long hours learning how to butcher the various animals whose parts they sold: goats, sheep, horses, cats, dogs, bees, hippopotamuses, ocelots, rhinoceroses and more. At first it had bored him into raging furies. He'd swear, hit, bite and often run away from his despairing parents. Slowly though he learned to love the trade. He became proficient, then good, then obsessed. A well directed obsession, his parents used to tell each other, is a blessing.

The only cloud in the bright sky of butchery was the deep smallpox scarring that covered his body and face, which the unsporting gods had seen fit to interweave with a virulent case of pustular acne. Ulpius didn't mind that he looked so unappealing because he didn't know. His parents were careful to keep the shop and their flat above it clear of reflective surfaces. Fortunately, there was a backlash against elitism and a championing of the downtrodden in Rome at the time, so the customers took his physical repulsiveness as a cue to be more kind and friendly.

So Ulpius was happy. He loved chopping up animals and talking to customers, and if you love your work, then it's not work, right? That was what his dad used to tell him.

Then, the mirror. It was a typical Day of the Moon morning. He could remember it as if it were last week. He was preparing a boned jaguar's head stuffed with various animals when a beautiful girl called Sulpicia walked into the shop. While waiting for Ulpius to sew up the head, she produced a hand-held mirror to check her make-up. He couldn't remember how it came to pass, but one moment he was noticing the mirror, the next the jaguar's head was spilling its filling onto the counter, and he was holding Sulpicia's mirror, looking into it and looking at himself, really looking at himself, for the first ever time.

Ugliness looked back. His face looked like a sponge that had mopped up watery blood, been dipped briefly in molten cheese, then had a pair of eyes daubed on by an inept painter. But there was one good thing: he did have almost unnaturally black shiny hair. Seeing his face was a shock, but there was the compensation that he could use his hair to distract people from it. Unfortunately, like someone who likes the effect of one mug of beer so drinks another fifteen, he went too far.

Every Roman man that Ulpius knew had short, regularly trimmed hair, while the fashion among smart Roman women was to curl their hair in piles on top of their heads. Loads of barbarian slaves, tourists, merchants and immigrants, however, strolled around with long, unkempt hair. Ulpius believed that if he could combine the best aspects of barbarian men's and Roman women's hair fashions to produce a clean, managed wildness, it would look magnificent.

To his parents' slowly burgeoning dismay he forsook the barbers, and slowly, slowly, his wonderful mane grew. While others his age were reading, running, going to the games, loitering in forums and visiting places like Capri, Athens and the ruins of Carthage, Ulpius was in his room, styling his hair. He concocted a range of hair unguents from herbs and animal fluids. He polished the shop's knives to use as mirrors.

But Sulpicia's mirror was the best. He looked forward each week to the Day of the Moon, when she'd come to the shop and let him look into it. Its polished silver surface reflected his tresses in much higher definition than knives and puddles, and its gold frame surrounded them with an appropriate degree of splendour. He began to obsess almost as much about that mirror as he did about his hair, and Sulpicia would have to spend longer and longer in the shop waiting for him to give it back.

Initially, Sulpicia thought he was sweet. As time went by, however, the purer emotions of her youth gave way to the insecurity of young adulthood and the compensatory desire to mock others. So she found the situation increasingly hilarious. She'd take friends to see the strange little butcher's "tonsorial fetishism", as she cleverly called it. When she married and had a son, she often interrupted her morning walks with her baby through Rome to visit the butcher's.

Ulpius was blind to mockery and his parents' increasing confusion because he was deeply in love with his own hair and Sulpicia's mirror. He knew he could never hope to afford such a mirror, but he had to have it. That was why, one morning when Sulpicia had come to the shop alone, he found himself standing over her with the mirror in one hand and a paring knife in the other. Sulpicia was lying on the floor, blood jetting from her neck, staring at him with increasingly glassy eyes.

He'd fled to Ostia, then to sea.

At sea long spells of boredom had been broken by terrifying, exciting and shameful adventures. His self-obsession and growing penchant for brutality suited marine life. Soon he'd risen from junior deckhand to junior pirate. He did well. He killed a lot of people. Butchery skills, he discovered, lent themselves well to knowing how to finish a knife fight. A shipwreck on Britain's south-west Dumnonian coast had put paid to piracy for a while, and Ulpius, via a host of ugly events that he'd pushed to the recesses of his memory (the men who'd rescued him, half-drowned, from the beach had pretended that they didn't know he was a man, which wasn't a great start), had ended up where he was now. Still with gorgeous, heavily styled but manly hair, he was stuck on the Hades-blighted isle of Britain, earning a performance-related wage as a land pirate in a small band of bandits run by a man called Landun Ogilvie, who went by the name of Ogre.

Ulpius suspected that he'd been recruited to bring some beauty to the gang since Ogre had a large nose, no hair and no ears. He'd lost them in a torturing incident that he didn't like to talk about. He could still hear through the puckered clumps of gristle that he had instead of ears, but he didn't like talking about them either. Very few who mentioned waggishly that his ears looked like cats' bumholes got away with their lives.

Ogre was not just the most uncannily perceptive gang leader; he was also the cruellest man Ulpius had ever met, which was saying something. The depravity visited on the gang's victims kept Ulpius very happy. Until his new obsession arrived. An obsession to rival or even supplant the mirror. This was Spring. A girl called Spring was ruining his life.

Spring was the newest member of Ogre's gang. They'd found her working in a drinking house and Ogre had taken a liking to her, Pluto knew why. They needed a replacement for Farrell, who, to everyone's surprise, particularly Farrell's, had been killed by a bear earlier that year.

Ulpius knew that all women were trouble and Spring was no exception, even though she couldn't yet be ten years old. She'd seemed fine to begin with, a quiet girl who sat on her own and was small, flexible and useful for burglary. But slowly, somehow, Spring had done something despicable and unforgivable that nobody else had ever done. She had made Ulpius feel embarrassed about his hair.

She had a way of looking at him when he was combing it.

Yesterday he'd asked her straight out, "Are you trying to mock me?"

"No," she'd replied. "Why would I mock your hair?"

It was an hour later, running the exchange back in his memory, that he realised what she'd done there. He decided to kill her at the next possible opportunity.

Sitting on the hill, drinking cider, watching the massacre below and looking forward to the next day's battlefield looting, Ulpius silently practised tomorrow's potentially tricky conversation. "That's right, Ogre. Bugger was still alive! He stuck a knife in her when she tried to take if off him. A terrible shame. Such a sweet child, cruelly taken."

Chapter 4

Dug fled.

He'd had a go at rallying them, shouting that they couldn't lose if they just held the badger-fucking line! He'd grabbed a spear off a passing man and tried to push to the front. He'd thought, *Coward*, but knew he was no braver; he just knew that his best chance of survival lay in the line holding. "Cavalry can't charge a spear line!" he'd shouted, but in vain. Barton was beaten before the armies even met. So Dug turned and ran as fast as a fit but mildly overweight forty-year-old man wearing ringmail can run through a panicking army. He could have stood like a hero of old and met the Maidun force, he thought as he ran, but there were old soldiers and there were brave soldiers. You can't be both.

He almost tripped over the boy who'd been on his shoulders.

"Help meeee!" squealed the boy, reaching up for Dug. His spindly shin was broken into a right angle.

Dug stopped. "Why didn't you run? I told you to run!" The boy tried to get up but fell, faced twisted in agony and slimy with snot. Dug looked back. Zadar's heavy cavalry were a hundred paces away and coming fast.

He stooped to pick the boy up, then remembered the mantra that had kept him alive since he'd left the north, since the day he'd lost everything. Never help anyone. He glanced up again. The cavalry were closer. If he picked the boy up they'd both die. If he didn't, he might make it. And it wasn't his fault that the boy hadn't done what he was told.

He ran on, telling himself to ignore the boy's screams.

He hurtled across the flood plain towards the river, ring-mail jangling. A woman was ahead of him. Suddenly an arrow shaft was jutting from her neck. She crashed to the ground, right arm flapping like an angry chicken's wing. He jumped over her. More missiles fell all around. One moment someone would be running headlong, the next, falling. An arrow or a stone ricocheted off Dug's helmet with a loud *spang*. It was like being whacked with a cosh. He stumbled, half-tripped over a corpse and ran on.

If he could make it to the bridge, he might get away. He looked over at it. A fan-shaped crowd of waving, shouting, screaming, pulsating humanity spread back from the crashed cart that blocked it. *Badgers' arseholes!* There was no escape.

He was in the reeds before he saw that the river was too deep to wade. Dug could swim, but not when he was wearing ringmail. A green-headed mallard broke cover, padded along the water's surface and took off, banking and flying away in the very direction that Dug would very much have liked to have flown. Was there time to pull off his mail before the enemy was on him? He turned. *No.*

The heavy cavalry had slowed and was wheeling towards the bridge. Chariots came on in its wake, killing those who hadn't fled fast enough. Two were slicing towards Dug like hot cleavers through warm blubber. They'd spotted his mail shirt and they wanted it. This, thought Dug, was the down-side of being better dressed than the rest of the army. There was no hiding. Four pairs of enemy eyes fixed firmly on his as the chariots bounced along towards him. Javelins were raised. Dug looked around for a weaker, more lucrative target to point out to them, but saw only dying people with in-effective weapons wearing nothing anyone would want.

He was a big man and a good fighter. He knew he wasn't the biggest or the best, but he was bigger and better than most. Although well past his best. He'd taken on and beaten a chariot before, but that had been up north and he'd been ten years younger. And it had only been one, while here came two of the famous Maidun Castle teams, drilled to a level of gung-ho military perfection that Dug had never had the time or character for.

Why oh why had he got himself into this? He'd been too stupid, and too drunk, let's face it, to realise that taking on Britain's most powerful and notoriously vicious army was a bad idea, no matter how safe the plan had sounded. He should have been on his way to Maidun right now to sign up with the very army that was about to kill him. But it was too late to explain that to the oncoming charioteers.

"Badgerfucktwats," he muttered, feeling sick and sorry for himself. He sighed, stood square and readied his hammer, preparing himself for the final action of a long and tarnished military career. Bouncing on your toes from one foot to the other was meant to make it easier to dodge javelins. He gave it a go. His heels squelched in the riverside mud and it didn't really work.

"Praise you, Danu! Praise Bel! Praise Toutatis! Praise Makka! Praise Camulos! Praise Lugh . . . Praise Cromm Cruach!" He wasn't sure whether he was pleading for rescue or thanking the gods for death.

Chapter 5

Lowa Flynn sat naked on the hearth edge, her usually pale skin golden in the firelight. She frowned as she scraped blood and soil from her fingernails with one of her beautifully forged, cruelly sharp iron arrowheads. She looked about, scowling. Was it the *hut* filling her with this annoying, unprecedented feeling of dread?

She looked around. Nothing seemed unusual. The packed-earth floor was strewn with clean reeds and the hut filled with the well ordered if meagre belongings of a poor but proud family. The circular wall was made of mud, dung and vegetation packed around twigs latticed between wooden posts. It led up to a conical reed roof with a central chimney hole.

There were four rolled-up sleeping mats next to the central hearth and a smattering of tools and toys arranged neatly on shelves. A shoddily made three-legged wooden dog with nails for eyes looked at her reproachfully in the firelight. Eight clean leather indoor shoes – two big, two medium-sized, four small – were arranged neatly in the doorway. Poignantly awaiting owners who'd never return, she found herself thinking.

Where was this sentimentality coming from? Life had beaten mawkishness out of her a long time ago, yet she'd been feeling distinctly odd since the end of the battle. She kept jumping at things in the corner of her eye that weren't there. When a spider scampered across the floor, she almost cried aloud. Something was very wrong. Or maybe this was what happened when you got older? Maybe old people felt like this the whole time? That would explain a lot about their behaviour. She cursed her weakness, shook her head and returned to cleaning her nails with the arrowhead.

Usually the shaft was the most valuable part of an arrow. The fletches – feathers that straightened the path between bow and target – could be plucked from ducks, and ducks were easy to find and absurdly easy to shoot. Too easy. Unlike almost everybody she'd met, Lowa saw no reason to believe that gods existed. However, if there were proof that they did, then surely ducks were it. Only the protection of the gods could explain why an animal as delicious, fine-feathered and easy to catch as a duck could not only avoid extinction, but survive in huge numbers and myriad variations.

A standard arrowhead was easy enough to knock from iron, knap from flint or cast from bronze, and could be dug out of flesh to use again. Shafts, on the other hand, had to be dead straight, a pace long and made from a light wood like ash, birch or poplar. A good shaft was difficult to make and tended to snap if an inconsiderate target pitched forward onto it, wrenched it from his leg or mistreated it some other way.

Lowa's iron arrowheads were different. Each was lovingly forged, beaten and sharpened by Elann Nancarrow, Maidun's chief weaponsmith. They were sharp and perfect. Just one of them could be exchanged for ten of the finest fletched shafts. She had a few different types: slim bodkins for distance and penetration, barbed broadheads for short-range damage, blunts for small game and even half-moons for cutting ships' rigging. She knew that they were an affectation, little better than standard arrow heads, and that she'd never have a reason to use the half-moons. But they looked fantastic. As one of Zadar's top soldiers, she'd amassed more riches than she knew what to do with, so she could easily afford them. And she liked beautiful things.

Her longbow leaned against the wall of the hut next to

the shorter, less powerful recurve that she used on horseback. The longbow was no affectation. It was the culmination of years of learning, practice and experimentation – mostly Elann Nancarrow's and her ancestors'. Elann had air-dried and cured a whole yew tree for five years, then rasped and sanded it into a two-pace-long bow limb. Stiffer heartwood made the bow's belly so the draw was more resistant, adding more power. Springier external wood made the bow's back, making the release quicker, adding even more power to the arrow. Most men couldn't draw the bow properly, but after years of practice Lowa could shoot an arrow from a fully drawn bow every three heartbeats. Each arrow could pierce iron a finger's breadth thick at close range or, at eight hundred paces, knock a ringmail-clad man off his horse.

The bow's tips were fire-hardened aurochs horn, its string rawhide, the handle soft but tough foal's leather. It had no decoration. It was gnarled and knobbed like a freakishly long badly stuffed sausage. Drawing it fully was an inelegant manoeuvre of squeezing the shoulder blades together and wrenching the chest open. Ballistas and other horse- or ox-drawn weapons aside, it was probably the most powerful bow in existence. Equal most powerful anyway. Its twin sat proudly in Elann Nancarrow's hut on Maidun Castle, and she was making more. Many said that these longbows must have been made with magic, and that Lowa herself must be a powerful druid to be able to use one. That annoyed her. The bow and her skill were the product of a lot of hard work and nothing else.

Looking at her longbow now, then down at the beautiful iron arrowhead, its deep contoured hues even more lovely in the flickering light of the fire, didn't give Lowa its usual warm pleasure. They were just things, she found herself thinking. She cursed and tossed a slingstone at the toy dog. The stone ricocheted off a wall upright and skittered into a dark corner.

Unlike her to miss. *What the Mother was up?* Must be hungry, she told herself. If Aithne hadn't forgotten to collect their lunches from the food wagon that morning, or if she could be bothered to head to the main camp to forage, then she'd feel fine, she told herself. Much more importantly than hunger or paranoia, what was she going to wear to the after-battle party?

She rifled through a chest of clothes tucked into an alcove. Peasant threads. She lifted out a leather waistcoat. It still smelled of the dog shit it had been tanned with. You'd expect people with a well made hut like this to have better clothes. But Barton had been crippled by Zadar's taxes for ten years. The structure of its prosperous past remained, but the luxuries were gone. She tossed the waistcoat back into the chest and pulled a crumpled red linen dress from her own leather bag. It was all she had for the evening's festivities, but she'd worn it two nights ago. It had a mild body odour hum and a grass stain on the bottom. She smiled in memory of the grass stain.

She'd only planned for one victory party on this sortie. The red dress would have to get a second outing. In her teens that might have upset her. Now she'd reached her grand old mid-twenties, it still worried her, but she knew it shouldn't. Men didn't care if you wore the same thing ten times in a row, as long as you looked good. There were women who would notice, but the opinion of women who cared about shit like that meant almost nothing to her. Besides, as she'd decided years ago, and almost convinced herself, most people would be far too busy worrying about themselves to notice her outfit.

Ducking into the porch and reaching for the door, she remembered how cold she'd been the other night. She dug her leather riding trousers out from her pile of battle clothes and pulled them on under the dress. So what if she wafted an equine aroma at the party? She'd still smell better than

any of the men. She had a final look around the roundhouse
and spotted a woollen shawl stashed on a high shelf. She
reached it down and held it up to the firelight. It was better
quality than the crap in the chest. There was a picture of a
. . . badger perhaps . . . maybe a dog, embroidered on it.
Unsophisticated and ill woven as it was, the lady of the hut
had clearly been proud enough of it to keep it out of her
children's reach. It would be dark by the time it was cold
enough to need it, so nobody would see the shitty design.
Yeah, she'd take it. She reached into her old saddlebag and
pulled out the gold brooch that Zadar had given her after a
previous triumph. That would smarten it up a bit and *might*
please Zadar. He certainly wouldn't say, so she'd never know.

She slipped on her light leather shoes, then changed her
mind. Iron-heeled riding boots would tackle the hill better,
particularly on the way back, when it would be dark and
she might be a bit drunk. *Good*, she thought. Thinking about
something as mundane as her outfit had dispelled the dread.
Unless she thought about it. *Danu!* Now she'd picked off the
scab, the stomach-lurching unease came spilling out again.
Nothing she could do about it though, it would seem, so the
only course was to ignore it and get on with things. Drinking
would help. She tucked the shawl under her arm, shook her
head and stepped out of the hut into the bright evening light.

The hut was one of twelve similar huts in a circle around
a central green, all surrounded by a low bank and shallow
ditch. A spiked palisade topped half of the bank. It wasn't
newly cut wood, so some time ago someone had built half a
palisade, which was about as useful as half a bucket. They
must, she guessed, have started it ten years ago just before
Carden Nancarrow defeated Barton's champions, then
thought, *Why build defences when you were already conquered?*
and stopped. They'd found out why today. The Maidun army
was unpredictable.

East of the huts, glowing golden in the low sun, the land

swept up to Barton's hillfort. From the west came the noises, smells and smoke of the rest of Barton's spring-line village, now the Maidun army's temporary camp. Raucous laughter and the clang of iron from practice bouts reminded Lowa of a simpler time when she would have been billeted with the body of the army. The evening would have been drinking games to cheat at and sexual advances to avoid or enjoy, rather than a poncey party to endure. The smoky aroma of roasting meat from the camp made her stomach lurch with hunger, even though it was mixed with the sweet reek of horse shit.

"Lowa! Lowa Flynn!"

It was her sister Aithne and the rest of her girls, waiting for her. Aithne had one hand on a meaty hip, a no-complications grin on her freckly face. The girlish circlet of flowers in her hair clashed nicely with her absurdly short leather skirt. "Little more than a belt!" at least five unimaginative dullards at the party were bound to say. As if reading Lowa's mind, Aithne turned and waggled her arse at her little sister. A good thumb's breadth of bare cheek showed on either side. Lowa felt a small smile escape from under her previous gloom and she raised a hand in greeting.

Usually only Lowa was invited to Zadar's upper-ranks after-battle party, but because of their success in opening up Barton's lines that morning, all six of her squad of mounted archers had been asked along. It amused Lowa that they'd waited for her. On the battlefield they'd charge anything, but the idea of walking without her into a party full of Maidun's elite terrified them.

"How's Findus?" asked Lowa.

"Out to pasture, happy. He was such a funny pig this afternoon. Grabbed an apple out of my bag when I wasn't looking then trotted away like a prince, farting with every step!" said Aithne with a sing-song chuckle. Lowa's sister loved horses. Lowa thought they were useful. "How's the smarter end of town?"

"Clean. Quiet."

"Opposite of ours then. What's up? You look . . . troubled?"

"Nothing. Hungry, I think."

"Ah yes, sorry about that." Aithne shrugged. "Good thing is, now I've forgotten our lunches once, chances are I won't do it again."

"You did it last year at Thanet."

"Doubly likely not to do it again then."

Aithne took Lowa's arm and led her to the track running up to the hillfort.

The four other women smiled hello and fell in behind. Cordelia Bullbrow had biceps that made men envious, olive skin, a forehead like a shield boss and a beard that she was apparently unaware of. Maura Drunkstotter was small and angry. Seanna Applehead was the oldest and tallest. Her small head sprouted a massive bush of curly blonde hair. Realin Ghostfeet was the group's beauty, with a voluptuous figure, a bell of thick, dark red hair and green eyes that seemed to catch any light, focus it, and twinkle it out in such a filthily flirtatious way that anyone talking to her – man or woman, young or old – was convinced that she was keen to perform any number of depraved sexual acts with them right there and then. She was very popular and possibly the most chaste woman in Zadar's army.

They were dressed in a mixture of scanty battle garb and scraps of cloth they'd plundered from the village. They wouldn't look out of place, thought Lowa, in Maidun's whorepits. Knots of soldiers and camp followers stopped to watch the heroes of the day's battle pass. Lowa's gang. She felt her dread lift a little. Pride was a defensive pretence of the weak, so she wasn't proud of her gang as such. They were just better than everyone else, and she was the best of them and their leader. That was how it was, and how it was felt good.

Chapter 6

Smoke drifted across the field and reached in misty fingers up the steep escarpment that led up to Barton's hillfort. The usually white chalk-cut walls of the fort were tender pink in the sun's low rays. Light glinted off the bronze torcs, bracelets and other jewellery of the straggling procession that zigzagged along the path up to the hillfort and Zadar's victory party.

Lowa recognised most of Maidun's luminaries. There was Atlas Agrippa, the huge ebony-skinned Kushite, his mighty double-bladed iron axe strapped to his back — a party accessory that would have looked ridiculous on many, thought Lowa, but it suited Atlas. Talking to him was almost-as-big Carden Nancarrow: Zadar's champion, the blacksmith Elann Nancarrow's eldest son and the man responsible for the grass stain on Lowa's dress. Lowa smiled. Alongside Carden was the rangy figure of Deirdre Marsh, or Dionysia Palus as she now, Roman-style and very annoyingly, called herself. She was a head taller than Lowa but looked small next to the two men.

The track crossed a broad meadow of grazing land. Over to their right junior chariot drivers were practising dashing and turning, running up draught poles, jumping from one horse to another and other tricks that *might* be useful in a battle but were mostly about showing off. Evening light flashed off wheel hubs and horses' flicked saliva.

Over on the left, atop an ancient burial mound, Zadar's head druid, Titus Pontius Felix, known as Felix, was disembowelling children.

He had selected nine of the youngest new captives, nine being an auspicious number, and had them tied to wooden crosspieces hammered onto uprights to face the setting sun, which meant they also faced those heading to Zadar's party. Felix was circling them widdershins, with the children always on his right, as the gods preferred. Three of the Barton kids, slumped in the ropes next to piles of their own entrails, had already served their purpose. Six were yet to help.

Felix waggled an iron rod encrusted with tiny bells at the children as he walked. He stopped, then shouted, "Eenha, meenha, minha . . . mo," pointing his stick at a different child with each syllable. The rhyme finished on a boy and Felix advanced. Lowa and her gang stopped. The chosen boy stared past the druid straight at the women. He was thin, with a tuft of red-brown hair. Seven years old, Lowa guessed. The lower half of his left leg jutted at a strange angle from his knee. Part of her wanted to intervene, an old part that had no say any more.

"There have to be nicer ways of talking to the gods," said Aithne. "And it's not like it works. He never even gets the weather right."

They watched the druid. A wood pigeon hooted in a nearby tree. Felix raised his balding head to the darkening sky, drew a silvered bronze blade across the child's taut stomach and shouted, "Bel, show me!" The boy gasped, then screwed his face into a ball of silent agony. A slimy sac bulged from the slit in his stomach. Felix ran his finger along the protruding offal. The child tossed his head from side to side but made no sound. Felix punched the child in the chest. The boy convulsed, the slit in his stomach burst into a broad gash and a bloody gloop of intestines slopped out. Felix deftly stepped clear, then squatted and stirred the shining pile with the iron rod. The boy stared down at his own intestines, then closed his eyes and cried wobblingly but silently.

"That was a brave one," said Aithne as they walked on.

"He had guts," said Lowa.

The other women laughed but Aithne raised an eyebrow. "You don't ever think . . . ?"

"What?" Lowa sounded testy.

"That it's wrong?"

"Wrong?"

"Felix seems to kill a lot of kids for no reason?"

Lowa sighed. "Zadar could have philosopher druids, teacher druids, storyteller druids, but Felix the cruel dark mystical druid suits our image better, so it's him we have. The enemy don't run screaming because they're terrified we're going to lecture them on the properties of herbs. And besides, we do have healing druids. You just notice them less because they don't torture people in public."

"But, children . . ."

"Look Aithne, the best place to be in Britain is in Zadar's army. There's nowhere safer or more lucrative. Until that changes, I agree with everything Zadar says and does. And so do you."

Up ahead a vixen broke cover from a patch of bushes and streaked downhill. The women watched her run. She'd have a fine night feasting on the day's battlefield.

As they walked Lowa could feel Aithne brooding next to her and knew there was more whingeing to come. A scream rang out from the sacrifice mound below, seeming to prompt her: "But there was a time it wasn't like this. When murder and torture were unusual. When druids were good. You don't remember – you're too young."

"You're two years older than me."

"Exactly. I heard more about it before Mum died."

"If it wasn't for me we'd still be peasants, like Mum. So how about you remember how quickly we could go back to that, or end up like those children or much, much worse, and shut the fuck up? And besides, we lived across the sea.

How could you or Mum possibly have known what it was like here?"

Aithne looked away. Lowa felt guilty, but her sister had to be told, partly because it was deeply irritating when she made up stories about their shared past, but more because talking like this was dangerous. Remembering what had happened to the last woman who'd been reported for gossiping about Zadar and imagining it happening to Aithne made Lowa shiver. Few lived a happy or long life with their tongue split in two by red-hot liars' scissors.

The sisters trudged in silence up the steep slope to the hillfort, up the switchback path which finally curved onto the ridge. To the south — their right as they reached the scarp top — a rough road ran gradually downhill. To the north, carved in a circle from the escarpment promontory, was Barton Hillfort. Its four-pace-high gates were gaping open, as they had been when Lowa and others had ridden up to claim it that morning.

It was a standard medium-sized hillfort. Nothing compared to Maidun Castle — few were — but still a useful gain for Zadar, and totally defendable if you didn't do something really stupid like pour all your people out of it into a weak line of inexperienced infantry in a field perfectly suited to your mounted enemy. Its white chalk-hewn ramparts rose from a ditch as deep as the walls were high. There were tufts of vegetation on the wall and too much scree in the ditch, Lowa noticed. That would have to be fixed. There should be as few handholds as possible on the rock-cut walls, and a hillfort should have nice clear ditches, preferably with sharpened stakes dug into the bottom, or at least a liberal sprinkling of large caltrops to make anybody leaping into it regret that they had. The spiked oak palisade that crowned the rampart was in reasonable repair, but it was vertical, which irritated Lowa. The palisade should have been canted back to the same angle as the bank, so that attackers couldn't shelter in its lee. Fort builders should *know* that.

Rather unoriginally, fresh heads had been impaled on some of the palisade's spikes.

"Is that King Mylor, do you reckon?" asked Aithne, pointing at a big head in a plain, rusty iron helmet with a swollen black tongue resting on stiff beard bristles and something stuffed into its mouth.

"Doubt it. That's a boar necklace in his mouth. He's one of the few Warriors they had. Mylor was captured. Zadar'll probably sell him. Although you can't get as much for a king as you used to be able to." *Or he'll keep him as a pet*, she thought.

Lowa surprised herself by shuddering at the idea. Aithne's doubts about the murdered children had begun to get to her too. What *was* wrong with her? Why should she suddenly care anything for a bunch of loser kids and their moron king? If they'd stayed in their stupid fort, she thought, Mylor would still be ruling happily, those heads would be attached to their bodies, the nine sacrificial children would be a great deal happier, and the people whose hut she'd taken would be settling down to their evening meal. Last night they'd been a family. Now they were carrion.

As they passed through the gates, Lowa was convinced that the four heavily armoured guards looked at her and her girls like foxes might look at chickens behind a badly made fence. She thought she saw one whisper something to another, then look at her and smirk. But Lowa had seen people who panicked about things that weren't there, who had the arrogance to believe that everyone was out to get them. There was no way she was becoming one of them. Food. Food would help. Booze would help more.

Aithne took Lowa's wrist and pulled her closer.

"Lowa, surely it's not right that we're killing all these people. They say it wasn't like this before Zadar. They say it was so peaceful that hillforts were falling apart. It can't be right that everyone needs to build them again. It can't be right that we're sacrificing children. The Earth Mother cannot approve."

"If Danu doesn't like it, why doesn't she do something?"

"Maybe we should do something for her?"

"Aithne, seriously, stop this. Unless you really, really want to end the evening impaled on a stake?"

Aithne smiled saucily. "Well, I sort of do . . ."

"That's better."

The gateway opened up into the wide hillfort interior and chattering knots of conquering Maidun soldiers. Lowa fixed on her party face and plunged into her least favourite form of mêlée.

Chapter 7

Dug Sealskinner ran. He knew it was too late. His feet sank into sand and marram grass cut his hands as he hauled himself up the dune. The dune shouldn't have been that high. A small part of his mind realised that he was dreaming, but it couldn't make itself heard over the much larger part of his mind which was gibbering in a rolling boil of horror because it knew what he was going to find on the other side of the dune.

He paused when he reached the summit. His broch stood firm by the burbling burn, peaceful as a sleeping dog. Maybe he was wrong. Its circular stone wall was so solid, everything looked so quiet, surely this time all would be fine? Brinna would be waiting for him, Kelsie and Terry playing nearby? Kornonos had only blessed Brinna once with pregnancy, but Danu had given them two in one go and he loved them so much that just saying their names in his head almost made him weep.

He jumped down the dune in two huge leaps, sinking knee-deep in sand, like he'd done so many times with his wee girls whooping in his arms. He ran across springy estuarine turf, splashed through the burn's stony ford. Geese scattered on the bank, honking angrily. Geese that should have been fenced into the walled yard. Horse hoof marks in the mud. They didn't have any horses. No twin tots running out to meet him. No squeals of joy with the sunlight shining in their beautiful red hair. No noise from the broch. The door open.

He felt his bowels slacken as he walked in. He knew he'd find Terry first. They looked identical, Kelsie and Terry, but he always knew who was who.

There was Terry, the tiny thing, four summers old, slumped against a wooden pillar, as always. One eye staring at him, as always. One eye part of the pulp that the other side of her face had become. A mace blow, Dug thought, as he always did, as his knees buckled.

Chapter 8

Lowa Flynn sank her teeth into a gooey venison haunch. She was standing on her own, but not so far from the throng that people might ask what was wrong. She came to Zadar's after-battle parties for the food. She stayed for the booze. Small talk she could do without. Chat at the beginning of parties was not conversation, it was just people making noises at each other. Lowa preferred to stand, watch and think.

She could hear Aithne's honking laughter from over by the fire, above the minstrels' cacophony. Her sister had shed her misgivings about the regime quickly enough once Atlas the Kushite showed her some attention. Shaking her hair and inflating her chest, she put a hand onto his broad, dark-skinned shoulder. Of Lowa's mounted archers, Aithne was the keenest to leap into bed with pretty much anyone who asked. Actually, leaping into bed was rare. Nipping round the back of a hut, tumbling into a defensive ditch or simply shuffling a little further from the firelight was more her style.

People were always surprised that they were sisters. Aithne was big-boned, big-arsed, busty and tall with hair the colour of piss-soaked stable straw, while Lowa was average height, slender, with hair so blonde it was almost white. Admittedly she was on the stocky side of slender. Riding and archery had built muscle, and a keen observer would have seen that her right shoulder and arm were bigger than her left from drawing the longbow, but she was slim-waisted and supple, with a bottom that lobbed slingstones would have bounced off. Aithne had the small-featured, freckled face of a milk-maid. Lowa had the pale skin and high cheekbones of a fairy princess. Aithne had dark, bovine eyes with long heavy lashes. Lowa's eyes were blue, pale-lashed and slanted like a wildcat's. Aithne was gregarious while Lowa watched from the edges. Aithne was confused and idealistic where Lowa was logical and pragmatic. Aithne was a glutton for food and booze, often to be found vomiting before bed, while Lowa never overate and had never been sick after drinking. Aithne was two years older, but Lowa had been the leader as long as she could remember.

Lowa had no memory of her father, but she was pretty sure he wasn't the same guy as Aithne's.

Her other four archers stood by the blazing fire, in a circle talking to each other, as they always did at the beginning of any social gathering. Lowa felt a swelling of affection. *Must be the booze*, she thought. Part of her wanted to join them, but she couldn't be both friend and leader. Yes, they'd been together for years. Yes, they'd become Zadar's most favoured fighters – right now more favoured than the Fifty. And yes, she loved Cordelia, Maura, Seanna and Realin like daughters. But that was exactly it. Lowa loathed mothers who got drunk and shared smutty jokes with their daughters. Too much familiarity cheapened and weakened the bond. So, even though she was younger than at least two of them, she kept a maternal distance.

Looking around at the chatting, laughing throng, it was odd to think that these people had spent the morning up to their armpits in gore, slaughtering the massively more numerous but woefully inferior foe. *Ah, not all of them had fought*. There was Keelin Orton, Zadar's latest mistress, standing on her own because none of the men dared talk to her and none of the women wanted to. She was a beautiful girl, about fifteen years old, with come-and-get-it eyes, a two-handspan waist, an equine rump, tits the size of her head and a pout pettish enough to sour milk. Her white linen dress and broad leather belt would have looked virginal on most other girls. On Keelin, it had Lowa questioning her usual preference for men. She was typical Zadar fodder. When Zadar announced that she would open the morning's battle by driving the gruesome man-drawn chariot, Keelin had squealed with delight. Once the draught-men were mad with the agony of a thick piece of metal hammered through each shoulder, she'd teased them coquettishly. She was no sweetie.

Lowa could see a little smile playing on Keelin's lips as she looked at Mylor. Next to the fire, where all could see, stood a wooden-fenced pen of pigs. Barton's king was inside, chained to a wooden upright. The former ruler didn't seem to mind. He was sucking his thumb and stroking a big hairy boar. The boar was enjoying the attention and grunting encouragingly. It looked like it was thinking about mounting Mylor. That would please the spectators.

She saw Keelin stop smiling as the druid Felix oozed up to her. He'd clearly finished the sacrifices quickly, or maybe he was saving some for later. He stood too close to Keelin, took both her hands and looked up at her like a half-bald puppy. If Felix noticed her cringe, he didn't show it. He barked out a joke and laughed roaringly as she looked over his head for a rescuer. Lowa was not going to help.

The party was in the lower section of the hillfort, where buildings were sparse and livestock should have been corralled in times of danger. Long tables had been piled with Barton's food reserves. Near the fire the revellers' cheeks were bronzely aglow with health and happiness. Further away, soft starlight painted people gentle silver in the moonless night. It was vastly more pleasant than Zadar's usual hellishly smoky hall-based shindigs. On summer evenings like these it was impossible to remember the winter.

But still Lowa couldn't shake her unease. *What the Mother was it?* Booze and food hadn't helped much. She thought about going back to her hut, but she couldn't face the inevitable door-hanging, arty dickheads, whose role was to drunkenly and belligerently demand where you were going and why, take personal offence that you could think of leaving, then splatter you with spittle as they demanded that you stay. She didn't want to talk her way past them just yet, and she couldn't kill them. Even in Maidun's army wanton murder was frowned upon. Unless it was Zadar's idea.

She turned her attention to the band. Five men in brightly patterned outfits were playing brass instruments on a platform extending from the rampart at the side of the enclosure. The blaring of bronze instruments died in a long, ugly blast, and the men sang unaccompanied in a rumbling bass,

> There was a mad king called Mylor
> Who took Zadar on in a war.
> As they were routed,
> Mylor's people all shouted,
> What a stupid old king to die for.

"The weakest section of the army, I've always thought."

Lowa jumped. For such a huge man it was uncanny how Carden always managed to creep up on her.

Carden Nancarrow, Zadar's champion. As a teenager ten years before, he'd beaten Barton's five best with ease. At the celebrations two nights before, and several times before that, he and Lowa had ended up together.

She smiled. "My horse farts a better tune."

Carden leaned his head back and laughed like a god. His thickly muscled chest heaved as he guffawed, then he shook his long dark locks as the laugh became a chuckle. Lowa's reply hadn't been that funny. He was clearly after a shag again. Maybe that was what she needed? She felt a quiver in her groin. Yes, Carden was exactly what she needed.

"Lowa, you do know that women aren't meant to be witty?" His dark eyes sparkled with mischief underneath the strangely protruding brow that stopped him from being typically handsome, and a spasm shot across his cheek. Even his *face* was muscular.

"And men are. Topsy-turvy situation we have here." She raised an eyebrow.

Carden chuckled but less enthusiastically. He wasn't a massive fan of having his own qualities brought into question, which didn't, thought Lowa, make him particularly unusual.

"How was your battle?" he asked. "You and your girls opened up very quickly in the face of such stiff opposition."

She ignored the innuendo. "You're right to mock, Carden. Six archers attacking a few thousand soldiers is nothing to be impressed by."

"The Fifty started the rout."

"Yes. You came in nicely behind my archers."

"Perhaps you'll show me exactly how that manoeuvre works later on?"

This time, she smiled.

"Yes, that's why it's such a shame——" He stopped mid-sentence and shook his head sadly. The band's song ended and trumpets blared a high-pitched fanfare. Lowa turned, expecting to see Zadar borne towards them on his golden shield. Instead, she flinched as Carden grabbed her from behind. Strong fingers dug painfully into her arms.

"What the Mother . . . ?"

She watched as men and women near Cordelia, Maura, Seanna and Realin grabbed swords from hiding places under tables and behind screens. A sword lashed out and Seanna went down. The others saw it wasn't a joke and formed a circle around their fallen comrade, brandishing nothing more than wine horns.

"Carden, what the fuck!?" Carden didn't answer. She struggled ineffectively. The partygoers were advancing on the archer girls with grim-faced, united purpose.

"Carden! What the fuck is going on?! Let me go! Let me go!" she screamed. No response.

The attackers closed in and swords came down. A severed hand flew high, spraying an arc of blood. One of the Fifty – a man with a large head called Aydun who Lowa had never liked much – stumbled back, blood spurting from his neck. Cordelia Bullbrow hacked her way out of the circle. Somehow she'd got hold of a sword.

Lowa shouted and struggled, but Carden's grip was iron and her legs were clamped between his knees. She slammed her head back, but it thumped harmlessly on his chest.

"Give it up, Lowa," he said through gritted teeth. "I'm sorry. We have orders."

Cordelia turned back on the circle hacking at her friends. Lowa felt hope surge. The big woman sliced a man two-handed across the back. He went down, limbs flapping. Another came at her with an upward sword thrust. Cordelia parried and slashed her blade across his face.

Weylin Nancarrow, Carden's younger brother, son of Lowa's friend and weaponsmith Elann Nancarrow, strode up behind Cordelia. He swung his sword and slashed the backs of her knees open. Lowa's strongest horse archer, the last hope for all of them, collapsed like a sack of mud. Weylin raised his sword matter-of-factly, swung it down, and chopped her head off.

Lowa tried to wrench herself free again and failed. She was still holding her venison bone, a potential weapon, but her arms were pinned. She looked for Aithne, but all she could see was Atlas walking away from where he'd been talking to her, wiping his war axe on his sleeve.

Carden shifted one arm to grab Lowa's hair. Atlas walked towards her.

"Atlas!" she shouted imploringly.

He shook his head with a sad smile, like a child rejecting a fat friend when picking teams for a running game.

"Atlas, what are you doing? Why . . . ?"

Atlas raised the axe. Carden twisted his hand in her hair to expose her neck.

Atlas pulled his axe back. Was this really happening? *It must be a dream*, she thought.

A shape rose behind Atlas. It was Aithne. She grabbed his dreadlocked hair and swung a fist into his ear. Atlas stumbled, the axe fell and Carden had to step away to avoid it. His knees loosened their grip. Lowa wrenched a leg free and stamped on his foot. Bones crunched under her iron heel. Carden fell back, clutching at her dress. She spun and smashed her right elbow into his temple. He went down. She grabbed a stool and flailed it at Atlas, who'd broken free of Aithne. He ducked. She rammed her venison haunch up, into the soft flesh under his jaw, and on. He dropped to his knees. She twisted the bone then let go. Atlas clutched his face with both hands and fell with a bubbling scream.

Aithne was kneeling behind him. She looked up at Lowa, brown eyes full of pleading and terror. She tried to say something, but blood spilled from her slit throat like water from a kicked bucket and she pitched forward.

Lowa whipped a dagger from Atlas's belt. A slingstone whistled past. Armed men and women were coming at her from all directions – apart from where Keelin Orton stood blinking in shock. There was her only way out. Lowa ran at her and whacked the stool backhanded into her chin. The girl crumpled. Lowa leaped over her onto a table. She sprinted along it, stamping through plates and drinking horns, kicking clay amphoras in all directions. People clutched at her legs, but she was too strong and too fast.

She jumped from the table, grasped the edge of the minstrels' platform with both hands and swung herself up. The musicians shrieked and fled, leaving Lowa among their instruments. She grabbed the nearest, a horn with an end twisted and hammered into a horse's head. The entire throng was coming at her, swords and daggers raised. She knew them all. Many, she thought, had been friends. They were all in it. They'd all known it was going to happen, and they'd all been happy with that. They all enjoyed Zadar's safe and lucrative patronage and they did what he said.

"What are you *doing*?!" she shouted at them.

She brandished the trumpet. They faltered. A bronze trumpet was no match for an iron anything, but her reputation bought her a couple of breaths. She threw the trumpet at her attackers, spun round, gripped the top of the palisade and somersaulted over it.

Lowa tumbled down the wall and thudded hard into scree at the bottom of the ditch. She was winded, but it should have been much worse because there should have been spikes down there. She scrambled up the other side. Thank the Mother it was a single ditch. She was very near the top when—

"Stop or we'll shoot!" She stopped. She didn't need to turn to know that several slings were aimed at her back. Her red dress wouldn't be much protection.

Fuck it, she thought, *maybe they'll miss*. She dived over the top of the outer bank, slingstones fizzing past her heels. She tumbled and bounced down the steep grass scarp, not trying to stop. Every time her feet made contact with the rushing ground she sprang more into the fall. It was the quickest way down the six hundred or so paces of hillside. The slope evened out, one of the tumbles landed her on her feet, and she pelted away across the long grass at a full sprint. She hurdled a low fence. She dared a glance back. *Shit*. They were already pouring down the hill towards her. Some were carrying torches.

A path led into the woods. Lowa followed it, running full tilt into the evening warmth of the trees. She didn't know the land. The woods were dark. She could trip or fall into a mire at any moment. Her only advantage over her pursuers was that she had nothing to lose. She saw a faint light ahead and ran for it, passing through a clearing and scattering a sounder of wild boar from their starlit grazing. Two boar ran ahead of her, groinking, then peeled off along tracks she couldn't see. But her night vision was improving. She could make out the way very slightly now. She slowed from a sprint to a fast run.

The path split; Lowa chose left. She held her breath for a moment as she ran. There was no sound but the pounding of her own feet. The path split again. She chose left again. Wrong choice. That way ended in another small clearing, maybe ten paces across, surrounded by thick brambles. There was a dark regular shape in the centre – a forest altar. *She could hide behind it*. No, they'd find her. She spun and ran back towards the fork. Torches were bobbing towards her through the trees.

Reaching the fork, she wrenched the shawl with the badger-or-dog design from her waist and hurled it back up the left track before running up the right one, hoping it wasn't a dead end as well.

It was.

She smelled the river before she saw it. The path ended at a low, short jetty. The river was way too broad to leap and she couldn't swim. She listened. Something scurried nearby, an owl hooted, and, not nearly as far away as she would have liked, her pursuers called to each other.

"Here's her shawl! It was round her waist earlier." That was Dionysia Palus, formerly Deirdre Marsh. Trust her to notice what another woman was wearing. "It could be a decoy. Let's split!"

She didn't have long. The brambles were impenetrable in both directions along the bank. To her right, upstream, the river stretched into the distance. An eagle owl flew lazily along the centre of the channel. To her left the river ran around a wooded corner. The only route was back along the path towards Danu knew how many former friends intent on murdering her. She had a knife. They'd have slings and swords.

She dashed out onto the jetty. *How hard could swimming be?* She'd seen children do it and children were idiots.

She crouched to throw herself as far into the water as she could and spotted the coracle. The tiny circular leather and wood boat was tied under the end of the jetty. She lowered herself gingerly but quickly onto the bench that bisected it. The crazily small craft – surely meant for a child – rocked alarmingly and sank until it was two fingers' breadth clear of the surface, but it didn't capsize. She cut the flax painter with Atlas's knife and pushed off downstream. There was a stout paddle under the bench. She rowed frantically. Calls came from the woods. More voices, getting closer. She heard thudding feet.

The boat moved out into the current but Lowa's paddling was just spinning it around. The curve in the river that would take her out of sight was a long way off. She could hear their panting now. They'd be on the jetty any moment. They wouldn't miss her on the starlit water. In a few seconds slingstones would smash her skull. She slowed her rowing to firmer, more purposeful strokes, one side then the other. That was the way. The strange little boat picked up speed.

It was too late. She heard feet thud onto wood. She crouched into a ball.

"A river." She recognised the voice. It was Carden's brother and Dionysia's husband, Weylin Nancarrow, the man who'd killed Cordelia.

"Well spotted, genius." That was Deidre/Dionysia.

"She's swum across or she's hiding back in the woods," said a voice she didn't recognise.

"I'm surrounded by geniuses." Deidre again.

"She can't swim. She told me." That was Weylin. They'd

talked about swimming not long ago. *Fenn's teeth! Never admit your weaknesses.*

"Wait a minute," said Dionysia. "There would have been a boat here. Look, there's a cut rope. What's that!?"

"What?" said Weylin.

"There, downstream. It's . . . I . . . I can't see it now."

"Couldn't ever see it, more like. She's hiding back in the woods."

"Then why is the rope cut?"

Their voices were quieter. Lowa risked looking up. The jetty and her pursuers were out of sight. She sat up and quietly paddled on. In the darkness ahead she saw Aithne's eyes pleading for help that she hadn't given. She saw Cordelia chop her way out of the mêlée only to be hacked down herself. She wondered if it was Maura or Realin's hand that she'd seen fly up into the air. A shudder of anger, sorrow and disbelief lurched though her. She dropped her oar and doubled over with grief.

No! She sat back up. *Crying could come later.* She would find out why Zadar had killed them, and tried to kill her, and she would have her revenge. First though she'd go back to Barton and get her bow and arrows. They wouldn't expect that.

She paddled on. The silvered black water was still, save for the gentle splash of her paddle. The silent woods watched her pass.

Chapter 9

"Weylin, Dionysia! My favourite couple of the Fifty! Welcome!"

They were the only couple in the Fifty, so it was a stupid thing to say. Felix's Roman accent made his cheeriness seem all the more false. Weylin did not like Romans, especially Roman druids as creepy and powerful as Felix.

King Zadar's chief druid and second in command stood from his chair on the raised dais with a grin on his smooth face and his short arms raised in greeting. He wore his usual sleeveless blue leather jerkin and purple glass necklace. The necklace's glass beads were each inlaid with a whorl of white, and it was said to be worth more than its weight in gold. Weylin wasn't convinced. Glass was much easier to smash than gold, so how could it be worth more?

Zadar wasn't there, which was a relief. Even though he didn't like Felix, Weylin much preferred the idea of explaining Lowa's escape to him. Felix might be a cruel and unbending druid, uninterested in anyone's welfare but the king's and his own, and capable of conjuring up a formori that would bite your head off, but firstly he wasn't Zadar, whose audiences had a much higher mortality rate, and secondly he was the height of a child and looked ridiculous. His light brown hair was thick but receding, his fringe a good ten fingers' breadth from his eyebrows, like a furry hood pulled halfway back over an egg. He wore his sleeveless jerkin in an attempt to look like a Briton, but his haughty, unmistakably Roman face and flabby arms made him look like a bard dressed up for a role.

Weylin was in fact dressed very similarly, and his hair had receded almost as much even though he was still in his late teens, but this didn't faze him. He shaved his remaining hair back to a straight line across his skull so it looked like his hairline was a choice. What remained hung down his back in a thick, matted, manly tangle. The arms sticking out of *his* jerkin were thick with muscle and already badly scarred, *and* he was a good two heads taller than Felix. Some said he had a big nose, but he knew it was a strong nose. The difference between him and Felix was that *he* looked good. And he *was* British.

Felix sat back down between Zadar's two bodyguards. *Why does such a powerful druid need bodyguards?* wondered Weylin. To the Roman's right, small wooden and iron shield in one massive hand and short curved wooden-handled blade in the other, was the giant German Tadman Dantadman. He looked like he'd taken a much smaller man's head but kept his own face, so he was all chin, nose and deep-set eyes protruding from a comically small skull. A blond moustache the size of a small broom head and a tussle of blond hair tied into a topknot added to the effect. As always, he was wearing a heavy fur jacket. Unsurprisingly, given the heat, his pale face was shining with sweat. Weylin shook his head. *Take your jacket off, you idiot!* he thought.

To Felix's left was Chamanca the Iberian, the much smaller but more dangerous of Zadar's guards. Tadman could stand and smite effectively enough, but Chamanca whirled through the foe's ranks like a greased weasel, leaving a trail of confused and mortally wounded enemies. She looked at Weylin now as if counting the ways she could kill him. He looked back. Her hair was like dried black grass, a soft frame around her hard eyes, shining gold-brown cheeks and lower-lip-heavy pissed-off pout. She wore epaulettes, elbow protectors, gauntlets, greaves, leather shorts and a double-cupped iron chestpiece inlaid with bronze swirls. Weylin looked from her

metalled breasts to her muscled stomach, over her tight shorts
which gathered into her crotch like an invitation, to her
thighs glowing smoothly in the candlelight. He looked back
up her body to her face. She was still looking into his eyes.
He gulped. She grinned, revealing teeth filed into sharp
points.

Weylin managed to look away. If Dionysia noticed him
gawping for any longer, there'd be trouble.

"These," said Felix, "are Elliax and Vasin Goldan." Felix
gestured to a bench where a man and woman sat, both
dressed in Roman-style purple togas which suited them about
as well as a hat suited a dog. Vasin's white arms were circled
by too many bronze armlets. Some of them looked painfully
tight, with mauve flesh bulging on either side.

"They're from Barton. Elliax is a fellow druid."

Elliax greeted Weylin and Dionysia with a rodent grin,
eyes flashing like a startled horse's. Vasin appraised Weylin
and Dionysia fatly, seemed to find them unworthy of her
attention and returned her gaze to the middle distance.

"So," said Felix. "Where is Lowa Flynn?"

Weylin looked at Dionysia. His wife narrowed her annoying
green eyes at him. It seemed that he was to do the talking.

"She got away."

Felix's little eyes bulged and his lips retreated into a humour-
free sneer. "Did she? You're telling me that she escaped from
a fort full of soldiers? From skilful highly rewarded soldiers
such as you, who were all *ordered* to kill her?"

Weylin breathed in, then explained what had happened.
Dionysia filled in the details that he missed. He was pretty
sure he couldn't be blamed for her escape, and anyway he'd
brought down the Bullbrow girl where others had failed.

"So. She either swam the river or took a boat from the
jetty." Felix looked around as if seeking an answer.

"There is a boat at that jetty!" Elliax Goldan piped up
from the bench. "Just a coracle but . . ." He noticed that all

the Maidun people were looking at him in surprise. "Oh. Sorry. I shouldn't have spoken unbidden . . ."

"Elliax, Elliax. A *druid* can always speak." Felix smiled at him like a wolf smiling at a lamb with a broken leg, then back to Weylin. "She's not a swimmer, so it's plain she escaped in the coracle. If I'm not mistaken, that river flows past Barton village. It's the same river we met by this morning. Geography, you see. The secret to success, Weylin and Dionysia, is knowing the land better than your foe. Geography makes history. And, of course, you have to know your enemy better than he or she knows him- or herself. So, knowing Lowa and knowing Barton, where would she go first?" Felix looked around like a teacher druid at a group of seven-year-olds.

"As far as she could?" piped Dionysia keenly.

Felix shook his head. "Good thing you're a fighter, not a thinker."

Weylin was pretty sure he could feel the heat from his wife's blush. *Ha!* he thought.

Felix continued: "Lowa won't stop until she has her revenge. She'll need her bow for that. So the first thing she did, knowing that she was being chased by dullards, was to get her bow from her hut."

"Shall we . . . ?" Dionysia asked, making as if to leave.

"No. She'll be long gone. Shame you didn't think to go straight there. No matter. We can't expect soldiers to *think*. But can anyone tell me where she will go next? I could relieve someone of their innards to look, but I don't need to. Intelligence tells me. Can anyone else say the same?"

"She'll run? To Gaul perhaps? I think she's from Gaul?" Dionysia looked about as if hoping for confirmation.

"No, no, don't think like a coward. Think like *Lowa*. And she's from Germany, but that's irrelevant."

Dionysia reddened. "She'll try to attack us here? Tonight?"

"Oh dear. Weylin?"

Weylin cocked his head and turned his palms up.

"Bladonfort," said Vasin Goldan from the bench. Everyone looked surprised that she had spoken, apart from Elliax, who looked terrified.

"What?" said Felix.

"She'll need information if she's on a vendetta. If I were her, I'd go to Bladonfort for that. If you want anything useful around here you have to go to Bladonfort."

Felix sat back, lower lip pushing up and eyes widening. "Yes, you're right. Of *course* she'll go to Bladonfort. She'll be desperate to know why her women were killed. One minute she was Zadar's pet, then next she was running for her life. Her desire to know *why* she fell from favour and why her women were executed will be even greater than her desire to avenge them. She knows that Maidun soldiers will be in Bladonfort tomorrow, drinking, buying weapons and armour, selling spoils, and she thinks that they'll know why the order was given."

"Why *did* Zadar order her killed?" asked Dionysia.

"It was necessary. Now it's more necessary. Which is why you're going take more people than you think you could possibly need, go to Bladonfort tomorrow, find her and kill her. You may go."

They turned.

"Actually," said Felix, like a man changing his order in a tavern, "bring her back alive. I've some new torture ideas that compassion has so far prevented me from experimenting with on everyday prisoners."

Weylin nodded. He and Dionysia walked out into the cool night air.

"That wasn't so bad?" said Weylin.

"You are such a prick," said Dionysia.

In the big hut Felix's bright little eyes bored into the couple from Barton. Elliax looked at his wife. She was picking around the edges of a scab on her hand.

Finally, when Elliax was thinking that he might have to scream to break the tension, Felix spoke: "Elliax. You've been collecting tribute for Zadar for a decade."

"Yes." It sounded like there was some sort of reward coming.

"And you started stealing from him right at the beginning. You've become increasingly brazen."

Elliax felt like someone had rammed a hook up his arse and pulled his guts out. "I haven't—" he peeped.

"Last year there were one hundred and twenty-two births in Barton, so you should have sent twelve slaves to Maidun, one for every ten born. How many did you send?"

How could he know? Elliax felt faint.

"But there was sickness."

"Don't bother trying to wriggle out of it. Of the two hundred and forty lambs born on Barton's lands you should have sent forty to Maidun. You sent fourteen. Shall I go on? Shall we talk about crops, textiles, iron working or flint mining?"

Elliax put his head in his hands, then slowly looked up. "Where's Zadar? Zadar won't have—"

"Zadar knows what I have told him and has asked me to punish you."

"What are you talking about!" Vasin made to stand up.

Elliax put a hand on her leg and shook his head.

"You . . . idiot," she said.

"Indeed, Vasin," said Felix. "But don't worry. I've got a fascinating and useful punishment for your husband, and you're going to help. A lot."

"Who do you think you are! I've never heard—" Vasin made to stand again, but Chamanca darted across, pushed the much larger woman back down with a stiff arm, straddled her wide lap and pressed pointed fingernails into her fleshy throat.

"Get off!" shouted Vasin, swinging a fist. Chamanca

caught her wrist and twisted her arm back to her side. She pressed her nails harder into the woman's podgy neck, then opened her filed-tooth mouth and leaned slowly towards the other side of her throat. Vasin's eyes bulged.

"All right, all right," Vasin deflated.

"Thank you, Chamanca. No need to hurt her," said Felix. "Now there's an experiment I've been meaning to try for a while. You are the perfect candidates for it. It's a good one. We are going feed you, Vasin, to Elliax. Bit by bit. Another druid will treat your wounds, and you are going to be very surprised to see just how much weight you can lose without dying."

Vasin made a choking sound.

"I know, doesn't it sound *interesting*? There is a greater purpose to this experiment, however, than entertainment, which will become clear. Meanwhile, you are what you eat, so we will watch as Elliax becomes his wife. It will be fascinating."

Felix held up his small hands in triumph and looked around the room nodding, encouraging the others to show their appreciation.

Chapter 10

Ulpius' pox-ruined face narrowed and the tip of his tongue crept out between his lips like a cautious little pink slug. He took aim. He swung, his hair tossed in a glorious arc framing his head and . . . *Whack!* The hand dropped away and the chunky bronze bracelet fell into the long riverside grass.

There were plenty of excellent pickings here on the edge of the field, without getting too close to Zadar's camp. Ogre thought the Maidun army had moved out, but it was better to be safe than tortured to death for bodyrobbing. There was nobody left from Barton to join in the scavenging and they'd scared off a few punters from neighbouring settlements, so they were getting rich second dibs plundering the bodies. First dibs had gone to the battle winners, but there was always still plenty to find afterwards, when you could search without the worry of a spear in the back.

Red-faced and round-cheeked with exertion, her usually neat long hair tangled into a scraggly clump on top of her head, the girl Spring was trying to drag the spoils cart over some obstruction — probably the range of molehills that Ulpius had noticed but not warned her about. The cart was for big finds like ringmail, swords and helmets. Smaller spoils — the more valuable glass and gold kind — went into the men's own bags. Ulpius had enjoyed watching Ogre tell Spring she was on cart duty. He'd said it was because she was too delicate to pull rings from death-swollen fingers and heave bodies about, but the real reason was so she wouldn't get a proper share of the booty, because she was small and annoying. But somehow the look on Spring's face when she'd been told, in particular the toss of her hair while wrinkling her nose and glancing in Ulpius' direction, had left *him* feeling stupid.

But now look at her, kicking molehills apart to clear the cart's path. She was all knees and elbows that girl, weak as . . . well, weak as a nine-year-old child. It was a superbly shoddy cart to boot, with bent axles and mismatched wheels. It looked like it had been assembled in the dark by a drunken carpenter, then rammed repeatedly into a wall.

Spring was getting left further behind, not just because of the cart, and not because she was doing anything useful like searching bodies, but because the wrong-headed little minx kept stopping to stare at everyday objects like herons and trees. She was always gazing intently at things that she'd seen before, like some kind of dimwit. Ulpius snorted out an involuntary giggle. If she carried on like this, it would only be a matter of heartbeats before she was out of the other men's sight.

A short while later Ogre and the others disappeared behind a copse and Ulpius saw that his moment had come. Ogre would know that he'd killed her, no matter what he said, but he wouldn't mind too much as long as Ulpius had the respect to do it out of his sight. Quietly, Ulpius drew the same little paring knife he'd used to kill Sulpicia all those years before, and headed back towards his tiny antagonist. As he passed the riverside reed bed, a glint caught his eye. Was that perhaps a richly clad dead Warrior lying half-hidden in the muck? It was a nice day and he was feeling generous. Spring could live a few moments more. He headed into the reeds.

The big, bearded ringmail-clad Warrior was dead or out cold. He had a heavy warhammer in one hand. *Jupiter's bollocks*, thought Ulpius. Here was a vicious-looking one.

Not a fellow you'd like to meet on the battlefield. *Better make sure.* He gripped the man's hammer arm in one hand and swung his knife at his neck.

The man's head moved as fast as a snake's, and the knife shattered on his helmet. Something blurred in Ulpius' peripheral vision and crashed into his head. He tasted iron in his mouth. He reached up, then pulled his hand away. He was holding a clump of his beautiful hair, far too big a clump, sticky with too much blood, attached to what looked like a large part of his head. Blood ran into his eyes. He blinked miserably and saw through a red blur the man he'd thought was a corpse stand and swing something at him.

That'll be the hammer, thought Ulpius as his world slowed down. If only he had stayed in—

Thunk.

Chapter 11

Dug woke.

Oh, his head hurt. His everything hurt. That was mud in his mouth. He must have got drunk and fallen asleep outside again. But the last thing he remembered was facing two chariots, about to die. They must have hit him on the head and left him for dead. Seemed unlikely, but here he was. Good thing they didn't have dogs. They'd have smelled him out and bitten his face off. He'd seen it happen. Nasty way to go.

He was lying in the reeds, cushioned on the muddy earth. He was comfortable and not too cold, although his head felt like it was being crushed in an apple press. He watched a small red spider crawl along a broken reed. He thought about the story of Cran Madoc, the northern king. Cran Madoc's army had been defeated and he'd fled, friendless. He'd sat in a cave and watched a spider build a web, then destroyed the web with the tip of his spear. Then the spider had rebuilt the web and Cran Madoc had broken it again. And on and on, until Cran Madoc realised that no matter how many times he destroyed the web, the spider would always rebuild. So perseverance was the moral of the tale. Cran Madoc took heart, rebuilt his army and retook his kingdom. Dug had always thought the story was a crock of badger shite. Surely the real moral was that no matter what you build, some vicious bugger will always destroy it?

He lay still, in no hurry to sit up and make his head feel worse. He wondered if he was dead. Plenty of people died with their eyes open. Maybe the dead could see? He'd never heard them deny it. He'd never seen the dead blink though.

He blinked. Alive then.

He remembered his dream and wished he *were* dead, looking out through sightless eyes from a southern funeral bed. Up north they gave the dead to the sea. In the south, miles from any sea, they left the dead on funeral beds so animals could strip them to bones. Then they used the bones for all sorts. He'd seen babies with rattles made from ancestors' teeth, and thigh bones of dead husbands used to stir the stew. A wee bit tasteless, he thought. Better to put the dead in the sea, he reckoned. He drifted back to sleep.

"Wake up!" Something poked him in the bottom. He spun round. Nothing but thousands of seals swimming through the land towards a hillfort . . . "Wake up!" The seals struggled up into the air like a flock of overweight birds, quacking like ducks. They whirled in a circle, zoomed up to him, stopped quacking and all shouted, "Wake up, you big fool!" His vision rushed away, came back and . . .

There was a woman sitting on him, plunging a knife towards his neck. Her other hand was holding his hammer arm. Actually it wasn't a woman, judging by the stubble and Bel's apple. It was a man in a wig. That would explain the strength of the grip but not the reason for it. Nor the strong smell of piss.

Whatever. Time seemed to have slowed, and the knife was still coming at him. He had plenty of time to move his head. As he felt the knife shatter on his helmet, he pulled his own long knife from its sheath with his free left hand and flailed it. He felt reasonable connection and the man lifted off him and staggered back.

He leaped up. His attacker was scalped and looked beaten. Better make sure though. He swung his hammer and connected. The man went down. Dug looked around. Oh,

Mother, was it bright! And, druid-fucking badger shit, his head! A burst of lights and nausea doubled him over. He coughed repeatedly and disgustingly. Had he had anything in his stomach he would have been sick.

In one direction was a river. Morning mist curled up lazily into bright early sunlight from its slow-churning water. In the other direction was a field littered with hundreds, perhaps thousands, of corpses. Arrows stuck out of the ground like new growth after a fire, and slingstones lay about in piles like wind-blown hail. Many of the bodies had legs sliced off at the knee or thereabouts, the standard running-away-from-a-chariot-with-bladed-wheels injury. Most of the leg-chopped were face down, heads towards the bridge, where they'd tried to drag themselves before bleeding to death or being finished off by one of the many options that had been available yesterday. Already there was a heavy buzz of flies. Crows and the odd raven hopped and strutted between the bodies. A vixen, muzzle red, looked up from her feast of entrails.

Well, at least it's sunny, Dug said to himself.

He looked about for a route away that wouldn't take him past the victorious army's camp, which was bound to be at Barton. Over to the right, on one side of a stand of trees, was a little girl with a rickety cart. Strange-looking girl, thought Dug. She was sizing him up nonchalantly, as if wondering what he might do next but expecting to be disappointed. With her messy hair and indifferent stare she looked like a scrag from the forest, where they lived like animals – hunting, fighting, shagging and giving scant thought to their appearance, hygiene or anything beyond where the next meal was coming from.

He shook his head to clear it and bring himself back into the present, and looked over to the left. There things were more problematic. Four angry men, presumably accomplices of the wig-wearing body robber whose skull he'd crushed, were advancing on him in a line, knives drawn. They were filthy, clad in tattered leathers. Three, in rough-spun woollen hoods, looked young, wiry and strong. The older one – hoodless, hairless and it seemed earless – looked like he knew what to do in a fight.

Dug, on the other hand, looked like a heavily armed ringmail-clad Warrior, even if he didn't feel much like one. His head! He could hardly see with the pain.

He opened his arms, bloody warhammer in one hand, bloody knife in the other, and roared, "Come on! Come and get it, you soft shites! Arrrrggghhhh!"

One of the hooded men turned and fled immediately at an efficient jogging pace. The other three looked at Dug, then at each other. Dug hefted his hammer and took a step towards them. The robbers turned and ran.

Nice, thought Dug, smiling to himself. Then one of the younger men stopped to pluck a sling from a corpse. He found a stone and slung it at Dug.

Dug dropped into the reeds as the stone swished by. He rummaged in his pocket, pulled out his own sling and fitted a stone in the leather. Through the reeds he could see the would-be assassin creeping towards him, sling ready. Dug took a few crouched paces through the reeds, leaped up and flung his slingstone into the centre of the man's forehead. The attacker's eyes widened in cross-eyed surprise and he fell. The other body robbers stared at him slack-jawed. It had been a lucky shot. Dug hardly ever hit anything with his sling. But they didn't know that. Fighting was one half bravado and one half luck.

"Fuck off or I'll kill you all with one stone!" He twirled the weighted sling in circles. Surely they'd know he'd never hit them at that range and that if all three of them rushed him he wouldn't have a chance?? But they ran away. Dug slung the stone at them. To his surprise, it whumped into the hairless robber's back. He staggered, then carried on all the faster.

He watched them go then crouched over his first attacker to see if he had anything useful on him. You could find good stuff, looting bodies. It never felt quite right, but if you'd killed them yourself then surely it was acceptable? And if someone else had killed them but not robbed them, then that was pretty much OK too, Dug always told himself. Some kings punished bodyrobbing with a cruel death, but they weren't watching. If you commit a crime and nobody sees you, then surely it can't be a crime?

There was a good leather bag across the man's chest. Dug dropped his hammer and wrestled it from the corpse's shoulders. He pulled up the toggle and opened the draw-twine. Inside, packed in wool, was a heavily gilded, well polished mirror. He held it up. It was a while since he'd seen himself. Brown eyes looked back at him from a straggle-bearded face caked with dried mud and blood. His otter-brown hair splayed wildly from under his helmet, with the odd silver strand running through it like spiders' web in dry autumnal scrub. His eyebrows seemed to have gone insane and sent long runner hairs out to probe the air around. His face was more lined than he'd thought, the bags under his eyes baggier and darker and his nose more lumpen from its innumerable break-ages. His beard had more even grey strands than his fringe.

He stared at himself. That's what he looked like. That's what other people saw when they looked at him. Weird. He'd been chosen as "Danu's most handsome" in a fair as a young man. Not much chance of that happening again, even if he did trim his eyebrows.

Then he remembered the girl with the cart, no doubt a member of the body-robbing team. He whipped round. It didn't do well to forget any of your enemy. The girl hadn't moved. She was still over by the trees, looking at him with disarming indifference.

He picked up his hammer and walked over, untying the leather chin strap and taking his helmet off on the way.

There was a big new dent in it, pocked with stone dust. That explained it then. He must have taken a big slingstone to the head while waiting for the chariots to attack collapsed into the reeds, and the chariots had seen someone else to go after.

As he approached, the girl's attitude turned from relaxed insolence to pert defiance. She was an elfin child beneath that pile of dirty blonde-brown hair. She had blue eyes, a wide mouth, an overbite that made her somewhat duck-like, and a nose like a ball fungus, but she was pretty all the same. He'd already decided what to do with her. Time was he would have left her, but in these bad days, far too often, he'd seen people killed by children they'd underestimated. Her cart was half full of battlefield spoil so she was definitely part of the gang that had tried to kill him. That settled it. If he walked away, especially in the state he was in, she might follow him and stab a knife up into his groin. He'd seen plenty of men killed by knife thrusts from apparently harmless foes, and it seemed like a particularly crap way to go. Plus, if he left her, Zadar's army would find her, and who knew what they'd do with a pretty little girl, especially one who'd been bodyrobbing.

The only option was to kill her. He'd be doing her a favour. He raised his hammer.

Chapter 12

Ragnall Sheeplord and Drustan Dantanner ducked under bright leaves as their horses splashed into the ford. The little packpony dug her hooves into riverside shingle, but Ragnall jagged her leading rein and she followed reluctantly through the fast, cold water.

The packpony was elderly and angry. Ragnall was young and superb. He was third son of Kris and Sabrina Sheeplord, king and queen of the Boddingham tribe. He had never been hungry, sick or insecure. By the age of ten he had the thrusting dimpled chin, spade-shaped jaw, bright iron-grey eyes, thick dark wavy hair, muscled limbs and long triangular torso of a legendary prince. By twelve he could outwit his eldest brother. By fourteen he could better all the boys – and most of the men – in wrestling, sword fighting, horsemanship and all the other sports in which magnificent young men excelled.

Despite his position, looks, abilities and youth, Ragnall was self-deprecating, empathetic and helpful. When his father was feeling his age, the young Ragnall would swoop in to ease whatever burden was troubling him. If ever you couldn't find him, chances were he'd be at the river helping with laundry or running errands for the tribe's infirm. All the teenage girls, many of the women and some number of the men desired him, but his eyes and polite fantasies had never strayed from Anwen Smith. While the other teens were zooming around, making moony eyes at each other and fucking like foxes, Ragnall and Anwen had walked about sensibly, earnestly discussing life's challenges. They didn't judge others, but he and his true love had decided to wait for marriage before becoming fully physically intimate.

He was so wonderful that most people hated him, despite wanting to sleep with him. The other children saw his good behaviour as a deliberate reproach to their own. Other parents saw his very existence as a slight on their parenting skills. So, when he was sixteen, his mother and father sent him to the centre of druidic life on the Island of Angels, some two hundred and fifty miles to the north-west, to train as a druid along with other young men and women from all over the druidic world – from the dusty plains of Iberia to the endless German forests and everywhere in between. It was for the best, they told each other. He probably wouldn't be a full-time druid when he grew up – although there were worse things, given the privileges that could come with the position – but the training would be useful for the high-achieving life that Ragnall was bound to have.

Ragnall loved the Island of Angels. Its groves of sacred oaks, wooden worship rooms and longhouses for sleeping, eating and learning sprouted all over the rocky, often rain-swept sanctuary. The halls and groves were linked by an intriguingly misleading network of passages, seemingly built over hundreds of years purely for him and his friends to explore.

The lessons were interesting, if disappointing. Back at Boddingham children thought that you went to the Island of Angels to learn how to bring bodies back from the dead, control others, see the future, bend elements to one's will and so on. To learn magic, in other words. However, it turned out that druids' magic wasn't magic at all. It was all about knowing which herbs treated what ailments and how to prepare them, learning which gods looked after what, memo-rising history, poems, songs and stories by rote and discussing the meaning of life. The closest they got to magic was sacrificing animals to the gods and reading their entrails to divine the future, but Ragnall, despite his unshakeable belief that there was magic in the world, was sceptical about these lessons. Only the predictions of the class wags – "I see Ragnall getting wet" before pouring water over him, for example – ever seemed to come true.

There were constant rumours that the older druids *did* perform what the pupils called "proper magic". Boys and girls were always claiming they'd seen wraiths floating out of the higher druids' windows or sages starting fires by pointing at bushes, or walking at night accompanied by their doubles from the Otherworld, but Ragnall saw only one wraith in all the time he was there, and that really could have been fog.

That didn't mean there wasn't plenty to see and do on the island. Despite the numbers of creatures killed in the class-room, the seashore was thick with animals, especially seals. A head druid four hundred years earlier, enchanted by seals' wide-eyed, undemanding amiability, had decreed that the rotund animals were children of Leeban, the goddess of the sea, and must not be harmed. Now they coated the island's shores like lazy bees on a hive. In summer there was a constant background of seal barks, coughs, clicks and honks, and pupils and teachers would play in the sea with the seal pups like Ragnall had played with puppies at home.

His friends were even better than the seals. Finally there were other boys and girls nearly as bright as him, and he could have proper conversations. He'd never realised that he was unpopular back in Boddingham, and he didn't recognise his popularity on the Island of Angels, but it felt more like home than his home ever had. He had, however, been deeply affected by the news that Zadar had taken Boddingham, saddened despite subsequent reports that his father had agreed to pay the warlord a tithe with not a drop of blood lost. A few of the elder boys mocked Ragnall, calling his father a coward. He'd wanted to rush home, but word from his father told him to stay put, and counsel from the druids eased his mind.

So, most of the time, Ragnall put his worries aside, got on with school life and remained true to Anwen despite almost daily invitations not to. Anwen came to see him on the island once, during his final autumn there. They'd walked the beaches, marvelling at Danu's creatures, discussing the other gods' roles and planning for the future. She'd told him how the size and power of Zadar's army had left his father with no choice, and almost all of Boddingham had agreed with the decision to capitulate and pay the tithe. Giving up a tenth of everything was no bother. People worked a little harder and had as much to eat and drink as before.

On her last afternoon, his manly hair blowing in the salt-tanged beach breeze, seals looking on and puffins, gulls, gannets and skuas spiralling overhead, Ragnall asked Anwen to marry him. She said yes, and they agreed to become husband and wife soon after he returned to Boddingham. That had been more than half a year before. He was aching to see her on a romantic level and, more and more, on a physical one. So the journey home – twelve days on horse-back – had been too long. Luckily, Ragnall had Drustan Dantanner for company.

Drustan was, Ragnall reckoned, the school's wisest teacher and the epitome of all that a druid should be. Unlike most druids, Drustan seemed genuine. He claimed no mythical powers of healing and didn't seem to be angling every utterance to make himself look more excellent and mystical. He seemed genuinely kind. The theory of human sacrifice had replaced practical demonstrations at the school centuries before, but it was Drustan who had insisted that teaching even theoretical human sacrifice was no longer necessary. What's more, Drustan had never put a clammy hand on Ragnall's thigh as so many of the other teachers were wont to do. And he *looked* like a druid from the stories of Ragnall's childhood. A few of the teachers used shells or iron razors to shave. Some were bald, some were women. Drustan was a good sixty years old but still sprightly, with a long white beard, an arc of curly white hair framing a shiny domed head and eyes bright with inquisitive intelligence. In his habitual long, undecorated and undyed woollen robe, he looked the part.

So when Drustan had suggested that he travel to his own home in the south-west via Boddingham and accompany him, Ragnall had accepted happily.

On the final morning of their trek, they clambered up the ford's flag-laid slope and on past a sheepdog sunning itself on a low embankment around a small farm. Smoke from the farm hut's fire curled up into the still morning air. The dog looked up at the two men expectantly. Ragnall smiled at it. Was there anything more pleasant than a well maintained ford, a charming farm and a happy hound?

"Good morning, dog!" Ragnall said, tossing the animal a bite of sausage that he'd saved from breakfast for that very purpose. The dog leaped from its perch, gulped the sausage, looped around Ragnall's horse's legs then rubbed its back on the road in absurdly grateful abasement. Ragnall laughed his warm laugh.

The men rode on in companionable silence. The air was soft, bright and warm. Ragnall was sure he'd never been happier. Finally he was on his way back to Anwen and his parents.

Up from the farm, a hare sat erect in the middle of the track. It watched them approach until they were ten paces away, then shot off faster than a slingstone northwards, across a field of cattle who remained unmoved by its speedy passage.

"A good omen?" asked Ragnall.

Drustan smiled, stroked his beard as he often did before

speaking, then said, "There are druids who'd say that it was a bad omen. You're returning to your family and your true love, so seeing an animal that's often in a pair on its own could mean that disaster looms." Drustan put on a booming, portentous voice – "You too are destined to run alone!" – and laughed to himself. "But there are others who'd say that it's a good omen. The herd of cattle represents those to whom you are returning. They are going to accept your appearance as calmly as the cows accepted the hare's."

"And what would you say?"

"That we saw a hare running across a field of cattle. It means nothing other than that the hare has learned to be wary of people but knows cattle won't harm it, and the cattle have learned that running hares and riding men are not dangerous. Probably. Druids like to make up reasons for the way animals behave and teach them as facts, but we don't really know why beasts do what they do. I believe the only relevance that the hare and cows have to you is that they prove your eyes work. However, I could be wrong. Perhaps Danu did send the hare as an oblique, indecipherable clue to your future, but it seems like a lot of effort for no point. Plus I have always thought that it is unlucky to be too superstitious."

Ragnall's laugh was like bubbling honey. "It would be good, surely, to have some idea if Anwen and I are destined to be happy? How can I know if I will love her for ever?"

Drustan rode on with his eyes closed. The sun shone on the bald dome of his head, lighting up his ring of woolly white hair.

"When people ask for advice," he said eventually, "they are usually looking for corroboration. You saw no omen in the hare and you knew that I wouldn't either. You asked me what I thought, even though you knew already. Why? Because hearing someone state what we ourselves believe pleases us, especially when we know that others disagree.

That's why like-minded people tend to group together, even though it would be more constructive to mingle with those of differing opinions." The old man slowed his horse as they came to a hill, then continued: "This is a little different, but also common when people think they're asking for advice. You seek praise. You want me to say that you're a great man and that Anwen, or any woman, would love you for ever."

Ragnall bobbed his head. "That would do."

Drustan smiled. "But I'm going to give you some real advice. When you see Anwen later, look at her face. Look into her eyes. Then use your imagination. Change her face in your mind into that of an old, old woman, wrinkled as a walnut, but keep her eyes the same. You'll be seeing Anwen in fifty years' time. If your stomach still lurches with joy to look into her eyes, even though her soft-cheeked youth has evaporated to leave an aged husk; if your breath catches with delight to know that she loves you, even though in your mind her once-firm skin hangs under her chin and her shining hair has become brittle and colourless, then it's possible that you will love her for the rest of your life."

"I'll try it. But maybe not when we're in bed!" Ragnall laughed heartily.

The old man chuckled. The horses plodded on through the warm morning, across open farmland and into shady woods.

"And how will I know that she truly loves me, and not my wealth and position?"

"Ah, that's much easier. Do you have the pick of your father's flock?"

"I should hope so, after all these years away."

Drustan wafted an inquisitive bumble bee away from his beard and returned his hand to the reins.

"Slaughter the third-best sheep. Make sure Anwen knows you are doing it for her. Have the best shawl made from its wool and the best boots from its skin. Give it all to her. Ask her which part of the animal she likes best to eat and have it cooked by Boddingham's best cook. Ten days later, slaughter the second-best sheep and do something similar with its skin – perhaps gloves and a hat this time. Nine days later announce your plan to have the best sheep killed for her."

"I can't kill all of my father's sheep."

"You need kill only two. When you say you are going to kill the third sheep, if she loves you, she will beg you not to. 'Please,' she will say, 'stop wasting your wealth on me. It's my turn to treat you.' She will offer to make you a stew of mushrooms or a linen shirt – something that is an effort to her and no cost to you. If she does that, she loves you."

"If she doesn't?"

"Do not kill the third sheep, break the engagement and find a woman who loves you and not your wealth."

"Hmmm."

"If she really loves you she will stop you even before the second sheep."

"What if she lets me kill the third sheep, but my desire to bed her is so strong that I keep her anyway?"

"That, my dear Ragnall, would mean that you are a young man who, like all young men, ignores the wisdom of his elders and will spend the rest of his days regretting it. Old age may look impossibly far away, but looking back it will seem but the blink of an eye since you married a woman with an ugly soul because she once had a beautiful body. And you will hate her and you will curse yourself for marrying her."

"Right."

"I know you are not paying me any heed, Ragnall. I can warn you over and over, but it will make no difference because you are a young man with beauty, strength and the firm belief that you know better than anyone who has ever trod Britain's green fields before you. In reality you have the judgement of a sex-starved billy goat with a head injury.

When you are old and wise, you will see what a fool you are now, and you will see life's cruellest joke."

The horses' hooves clopped on the stone road.

"Which is?"

"By the time you realise what a wonderful gift youth is, you no longer have it."

"You're wrong, Drustan. I'm already fully aware of how wonderful life is. I know myself."

Drustan coughed out a short laugh. "You don't. Men will know the ways of all the beasts and the gods before they know themselves. The only way men or women can know themselves is if there's almost nothing to know. If that was the case, however, they wouldn't have the nous to know even that."

"I thought *you* knew everything, Drustan?"

The old man smiled. "The wisest man or woman is but a child poking a stick into a rock pool next to a boundless ocean below an unending range of mountains. Which is why, Ragnall, it would do well for those druids who think they can explain everything to take their heads out of their own arses."

"I don't remember learning that on the Island of Angels."

"I would not be welcome there if I taught it, but it is something that everybody who aspires to be more than a sheep or a dog should know."

"Hold," Drustan said several miles later. He dismounted, walked ahead and bent down. The woodland track had narrowed so they'd been riding in single file with the druid leading. Ragnall couldn't see what had made him stop.

"Sword to the gut, I would say," Drustan said.

"What?" Ragnall slipped off his horse and ran forward. A dead man lay across the path. The woods felt suddenly colder. The birdsong had stopped. This was not part of his imagined homecoming.

Drustan lifted the dead man's shirt. There was a black wound. Dried blood was crusted down his stomach, trousers and leather shoes.

"I would say he has walked between five and ten miles after being stabbed with a sword," said the druid.

"Which means he could have come from Boddingham."

"It is a possibility. Do you recognise him?"

Ragnall leaned over the man's face.

"No. I don't think he's from Boddingham. More likely he's been attacked by bandits right here and your calculations are out by between five and ten miles."

Drustan raised an eyebrow. "Here, help me."

The two men heaved the body a little way into the trees. Drustan called on the beasts and birds to eat the flesh and return it to Danu. He asked that the man might be given a longer life in the Otherworld. As he stood and listened, Ragnall became increasingly worried. What if the man *was* from Boddingham? If his home had been attacked, then his father, his mother, Anwen . . .

"Let's go," said Ragnall as soon as Drustan had finished. They left a marker on the path so that if the murdered man's kin came looking for him at Boddingham they could tell them where to find his body.

Six miles later the road left the woods. Woodsmoke, thick and white, was billowing up into the clean blue air from Boddingham Hill. Ragnall kicked his horse into a gallop.

Chapter 13

"I like your ringmail. Did you make it yourself?"
"No."
"Is it heavy?"
"Yes."
"Was it expensive?"
"It would have been if I'd paid coin or bartered for it."
"What did you pay for it?"
"The blood price."
"The *blood* price?"
"I took it from a man I killed. Well, I think I killed him. Actually someone else probably killed him. But I killed the man who killed him. I think. Battles get confusing. I didn't pay coin for it or exchange anything is the point."
"Oh, I see."
Spring skipped ahead for a while, her pigtails bouncing. It was going to be a hot day, but it was still cool in the woods. A soft breeze shivered through a grove of aspen. The girl picked up a stick and slowed down until she was back at Dug's side, swinging her stick and looking up at the big northerner.
"Why was there a battle yesterday?"
"Because adults, as you'll come to understand when you are one, are fools."
"Oh, I already know that. Ulpius was a total fool."
"Who's Ulpius?"
"The man who put poo and pee in his hair, who you killed with your hammer."

"Oh yes."

"But why was there a battle yesterday at Barton?"

"You can look at it on two levels." Dug looked down and raised his eyebrows at Spring to see if she understood what he meant. She nodded.

"In the big picture it's because the Romans are coming. Go to any marketplace and you'll find a druid shouting about it. The Romans are very dangerous people who have conquered—"

"I know who the Romans are! Ulpius was Roman."

"Oh, OK. So the Romans are coming, and everyone's scared and they're behaving like even bigger idiots than normal. We could unite and defeat them but instead we're doing the opposite. It's like we're fowl farmers who know that a fox is coming. Instead of repairing our coops, we're running around like fools, killing each other's ducks and piling them up ready for the fox. In fact we're even shipping ducks to the fox before he gets here. All in the hope that he'll leave our own ducks alone when he comes. Which he won't."

Spring nodded wisely.

Dug continued: "At the heart of it all are three tribes. Really they're groups of lots of tribes, but everyone uses the dominant tribe's name to cover the lot."

"Got it!"

"In the south west are the Dumnonians. They're serious bastards from what I've heard, fierce as weasels and proud as cockerels. To the north and east of here the Murkans under King Grummog are more or less in charge. I worked for them for a while and they're nasty buggers too. Down here in the south you have Zadar, king of Maidun Castle. They say – although it's hard to know if they're right – that even though he has the smallest army of the three, he's the worst of the lot. They also say that Maidun Castle is the biggest and strongest of all the hillforts. It has three massive walls all the way round, a giant palisade and a labyrinth – a maze – for a gate. People get lost just trying to walk into the place. Zadar's army lives in this fort. Well, probably next to it. I haven't been there, but armies generally live outside hillforts unless they're being attacked."

"I know!"

Dug paused to clear a large branch that had fallen across the track in case a cart came along later.

"OK. So. We saw just how good Zadar's army was yesterday when a handful of them beat a much bigger host, probably without so much as broken nail." He thought back to the horse archers, the six who'd attacked first. He'd been thinking about them quite a bit, particularly their leader, the blonde one.

He felt Spring's warm little hand take his. He pulled away gently but she tightened her grip. Her hand felt tiny, cool and precious in his coarse paw.

They walked on. The going was soft, dry and shady under overarching trees.

It had been a very odd day already and they were only a couple of hours into it. Waking in the reeds, being attacked by that bizarre-looking man, and now walking with this child who he really should have killed back on the battlefield.

"Don't do that, please," she'd said politely. That had stayed his hand, and she'd run over to the man he'd killed with the hammer, rummaged through his pockets, produced an antler comb, tidied her hair, tied it in two pigtails and run back over. "There," she'd said. "I can look smart and we can be friends." And he'd gone with it. He hadn't killed her. He still wasn't sure why. He quarter-suspected that she was not a child at all, but a mind-bending imp, slipped over from the Otherworld when he'd been so close to it. She was definitely an odd little thing and something weird had definitely happened to the speed of time when he'd woken up. It shouldn't have been so easy to dodge that knife strike and to scalp the man who attacked him.

"So," he continued, "Zadar's doing what he wants, and

piling up more riches than any king before him by taxing half of southern Britain and selling the rest as slaves to the Romans."

"Why don't people stop Zadar?"

"They can't."

"Bet they could. Oh look! A squirrel!"

A red squirrel was watching them from the branch of an oak tree, a nut in its paws. Dug reached for his sling. The squirrel squeaked and ran to safety.

"Why don't *you* stop Zadar?" Spring asked.

"Me? What can I do?"

"Have you tried anything?"

"Not as such."

Spring didn't talk for a while, humming quietly as she walked. Her head twitched round at every rustle or tweet, trying to spot what made it as if she'd never seen a woodland animal before.

Dug strode along, mulling over his hypocrisy. Everyone else was selfish and blinkered, but he was off to join Zadar's army, which was arguably even more selfish and worse than blinkered because he knew what he was doing. But he hadn't started it. Why shouldn't he make the most of a bad situation that he didn't cause?

They walked into a grassy clearing. Bees buzzed about wildflowers, loud in the stillness.

"That cloud looks like a boar." Spring pointed to the sky.

"So it does," said Dug, "and that one's a gull's head."

"Yes! With a fish in its beak!" He felt Spring squeeze his hand. "I thought it was just me that looked at clouds like that."

"Aye well, I thought it was just me too. I used to do it the whole time with my girls."

Spring nodded as if she knew exactly what he meant.

"That one's a whale jumping," said Dug.

"What's a whale?"

"A big fish."

"Bigger than a pike?"

"Dear oh dear. Bigger than a thousand pikes. Have you never been to the sea?"

"I have. But only to the edge, never out in a boat."

"You should try it. The clouds are even better when you're at sea."

"Can you tell me the story of the war against the halfmen, please?" she asked a little while later as he lifted her across the gap in a broken bridge. Sunlight speared through the trees and dragonflies hummed along the babbling stream.

"Aye, well, that's a good one. My ma used to tell me that one, and I used to tell it to my girls. Many years ago, before the war of the gods and the time of ice, Britain and the rest of the world were one big land and you could have walked from here to Rome without getting your feet wet . . ."

Chapter 14

"You're a bad husband. Do you want to know why?"
Weylin didn't bother answering. She'd tell him
anyway. He looked over his shoulder. The six other riders
– also members of the Fifty who Felix had ordered to capture
Lowa – were far enough back and talking among themselves.
They probably couldn't hear Dionysia even if her voice was
like knitting needles in his ears. He sighed and looked at the
face he'd come to hate. Green eyes that were once seductive
now radiated sour misery. Once-kissable lips were ruckled
like a dried limpet. Freckles that he'd once traced with an
adoring finger were now a blight across flushed, angry cheeks.

"You never support me. You didn't support me in front of
Felix last night. You didn't take a Roman name like you said
you would. Worst of all, you didn't look out for me in the
battle!"

"A kingfisher!" Weylin pointed at the brightly coloured
bird watching them from a fence post. They were riding
along the riverside path to Bladonfort, so he'd been looking
out for kingfishers. "They're usually more shy than that. It
might be injur—"

Dionysia grabbed his arm and pulled him back towards
her. "Stop looking at the fucking wildlife and get back to
the subject. You. Were. Not. Looking out for me!"

The kingfisher darted into cover. Weylin shook his head.
His thick mane, lumpen from that morning's application of
beeswax, swayed heavily. The sun glinted off his freshly
shaved scalp. Not often you saw a kingfisher.

"All right. In which battle do you think I wasn't looking out for you?"

"At Barton."

"That wasn't a battle. Nobody was killed."

"*Thousands* were killed!"

"I mean on our side. None of ours even got injured."

"That's still a battle." Dionysia sounded unsure. Weylin loved the rare occasions when he wrong-footed her.

"Actually I did hear about one guy afterwards," he said. "A guy in the light chariots got stabbed by the woman he was raping about an hour after the battle. He'll live. She won't. He punched her face in. He had to finish off into her corpse . . ." Weylin chuckled.

"You are such a fucking animal. You think it was totally fine to rape her and kill her when she resisted? And then . . . a dead body? Do men have no shame?"

"I dunno. What does it matter? We won the battle; he can do what he wants. But he should be ashamed that he let her stab him, and she was stupid not to kill him. And what do you mind? I've never seen you try to stop the raping. And it's not like I join in." *Not when you're around anyway.* "But that's not the point. Point is, it wasn't a proper battle, so I didn't need to keep an eye on you. But, as it happens, because I am such a good husband, I *was* watching you. And what I saw was you, as always, showing off to Atlas and Carden."

"That's bullshit."

Weylin's horse skittered as a frog hopped off the road and into the grass. He rubbed its neck soothingly.

"I heard you shout, 'Atlas, Carden, watch this!' then ride, big arse in the air, at a group of peasants who you chopped down from behind. You almost fell off trying to copy Atlas's torso-in-half thing on a girl who couldn't have been more than twelve."

"I do not have a big arse!"

"Don't you?"

"It's smaller than Lowa's."

"Really?" Weylin rolled his eyes in disbelief, knowing how much that would annoy her.

"You turd. You're no looker with your . . . stupid, stupid hair . . . and that wasn't showing off to Atlas and Carden, it's my fucking *training*. I'm at a level now that you won't ever reach. I could have asked you to watch, but frankly I'm not interested in any criticism about my swordplay from anyone who isn't at least as good as Atlas."

"I'm a Warrior."

"We're all Warriors! It's not hard to kill ten people when you're in this army, although there are those who think that cutting down ten children shouldn't count."

"I have earned my Warrior medal again and—"

"Possibly, *dear*. But there are different levels of Warrior. And since I'm quite a few above you, there's no point asking you to assess my swordplay. That's all I'm saying."

"Cromm Cruach, paranoid *and* arrogant."

They rode on in uncomfortable silence, Dionysia gazing blankly at the road ahead, Weylin looking for kingfishers.

"You don't fancy me any more," she said after a while. "I saw the way you looked at Chamanca. Only you could fancy a woman with teeth like a dog's. But she'd never go for you, you know, not with that stupid hair and the brains to match. What does your hair look like? What was it Carden said? It was brilliant. 'Like a squirrel fucking a turnip!' That was it! I'd forgotten that! Just brilliant."

Dionysia bent over her horse's neck, almost choking with fake laughter. Weylin thought about opening up the back of her head with his sword. He looked back. Nah. The others were too close.

They rode on to Bladonfort.

Chapter 15

An hour later Dug and Spring came to the hideout described to him a moon before by a short-term travelling companion. He hadn't thought he'd need it, but it was always good to have an escape plan.

It was an enclosure maybe ten paces across, ringed with a ditch and low bank, tucked into woods skirting a grassy flood plain. Probably it had been a small fortified farm, but many generations ago it had been abandoned or sacked, looted for building materials and overrun by trees and bushes. Now it was part of the woods and far enough from the river that people walking the banks wouldn't know it was there. Dug was glad to see the vegetation was untrodden. Nobody had been here for a while. It should suit his purpose.

A battle, Dug thought, was like a boulder lobbed into a pond. The initial splosh of killing and uproar created waves and then ripples of violence all around for days. A petty thief might become a murderous highwayman. A women who'd been happy to be unhappy at home for years might suddenly butcher her husband, children, dogs and a couple of the neighbours before throwing herself off a cliff. That sort of thing. So Spring would be better off hiding here for a couple of days until the region had calmed. Dug wasn't concerned about himself. There were so many easy targets around that someone his size and ugliness needn't worry too much.

Spring sat on the bank and made a daisy chain while Dug stripped bark from a silver birch with his flint knife, folded it into a watertight box and pinned the corners with split twigs wound in bark twine. He walked over to the river, checking all the way that there was nobody about, and filled his new container. He drank it down, refilled it, drained it and refilled it again. A grey heron watched from the opposite bank. Dug felt for his sling. He'd left it with Spring. The heron, seeming to read Dug's mind – or actually reading it for all he knew – took off and flew lazily upriver.

He sloshed out quite a lot of water crossing the hummocky meadow, but there was enough left for the child. He handed the box to her, then rummaged in his bag and fished out a nub of dirty bread.

"Now be a good girl and stay here while I go into town."

"Why don't *you* be a good girl and stay here while *I* go into town?"

Dug sighed. "Because Bladonfort will be awash with Zadar's troops full of vicory, and nothing makes men into bigger twats – fools – than being in a gang of other fools with whom they've just won a battle. It's no place for a girl."

Not the safest place for anyone, he thought, but the sooner he joined Zadar's army the better. He'd been fantasising recently about garrison work. Being on the losing side the day before had bolstered his desire for a life of violence-free indolence. Assuming he could get into the garrison of Maidun Castle itself – and he saw no reason why he shouldn't, being a Warrior who was going to lie about a leg injury that would make him less useful in the mobile army – it would be a life of peaceful days, piles of food, gallons of booze, lots of sleep, a modicum of whoring and, who knew, maybe even a love affair with a comely milkmaid? He felt Brinna's disapproving glare from beyond her watery grave and dismissed it. She'd always be his true love, but she couldn't expect him to mourn for ever.

"Stay under the trees," he continued. "If you need more water, wait until dark. I'll be back tomorrow."

"When tomorrow?"

"Um . . . in the morning. Or maybe the afternoon."

"Will you get some hen's eggs? Or duck's?" Spring produced a bronze coin from her smock's pocket. "That should be enough."

Dug took the coin and frowned at it. He didn't like this southern "money" thing. Exchanging small discs of metal for food and services was plain weird. It wasn't that it was a bad idea. Metal discs were less cumbersome than the iron ingots or salt cakes that he'd had to get used to on his way south and definitely easier to handle than the buckets of seal blubber, skins and kludge − a cheese made from seal milk − that had served the same purpose when he was a child. They were a bugger to carry to market to exchange for meat and wheat. He could remember it all as if it were yesterday − the clouds of biting midges, the sore arms, the sweaty chafing and the stink. The kludge would always slop out onto him and he'd smell of fishy cheese for days.

So seal products, iron ingots and salt weren't as portable as metal discs, but they were useful things in themselves. Coins weren't. They were made from stuff that you dug out of the ground, so they were just pretentious pebbles. So how was it that you could swap them for useful things? They were unnatural and they were Roman. They were just a taste of the boring, sensible but deeply *wrong* Roman life that the druids said was coming.

He looked at Spring's coin. There was a crude picture of a horse on it, or perhaps it was a dog.

"Is that a dog?"

"It's a horse, silly! That's Zadar on the other side."

Dug turned the coin. A little bronze face with a gaping mouth looked back at him. "He looks like he's giving a blow—"

"Yes?"

"—by blow account of something."

"It's a bad picture. You can get at least a dozen eggs for a horse coin. Try to get more. Say that you got twenty in Forkton. You can share them with me, four for you and eight for me. You can have more if you get more than a dozen. I'll find garlic, mushrooms and an onion, and I'll get some cheese from somewhere."

"No, you won't. You're to stay within these banks, apart from getting water, which you do only at night. Got it?"

"Sure!" Spring smiled.

"OK, OK. I'll see you tomorrow." He patted the girl on the head and strode towards the low earthwork.

"Dug?"

He turned.

"Can I have Ulpius' mirror?"

"What?"

"The mirror you took from the man you killed with your hammer this morning."

"Ah that, yes. Well, no. Well you can, but I want to take it into Bladonfort to see how much it's worth. I'll give it to you after that."

"OK!" Spring skipped in a happy circle. "Thanks, Dug!"

Before he knew what was happening, she'd darted forward and was hugging him, face pressed against his stomach.

Dug disentangled her arms, said goodbye, climbed the bank and headed off downriver. He could feel her watching him from the trees. With any luck the after-battle rage would have dissipated by the two days he reckoned it would take for her to be certain that he wasn't coming back. He was glad he hadn't killed her. The world was a better place, he thought, with her in it. That was why he had to leave her. He liked her. The idea of taking her with him and protecting her did appeal, but he knew he'd end up getting her killed. Better for her, and him, that they went their own ways.

He walked downstream along the river, following an increasingly well worn path. It was early still but already

getting hot. He stopped to pull off his ringmail shirt. A fiery
wave of body odour made his eyes water. He toyed with the
idea of a swim, but he was starving. Good thing he'd got
half his Barton pay up front. He'd have a feast in Bladonfort.

He thought about crisp-edged mutton or perhaps a fatty
duck. His mouth filled with saliva and he swallowed. Maybe
duck, then mutton. And he had the girl's coin as well. That
would cover a few drinks. He felt a twinge of guilt. No, screw
her. He hadn't killed her when he should have done. She should
be grateful for that. Helping others got you killed. Britain was
no place for sentimentality. Not his fault. He had things to do.
She'd hate it where he was going. She'd be all right.

He walked on, a tune in his head and his step jaunty.

He felt slightly bad about taking the mirror, but it was
his. He'd killed the guy. She'd just asked for it. You couldn't
go about giving people everything they asked for. Danu
would agree.

It looked like the valley had once been pasture on both
sides of the river, with oak trees for shade. Now there were
stumps and wild grass untrimmed by grazing. The bones of
a cow jutting from the grass confirmed his theory, and told
him that the land had been pillaged more for pleasure than
necessity. Only the wanton would leave good marrow behind.

After a mile he stopped to look at a burned-out fortified
farm on the far side of the river. Its once substantial defences
– a ring ditch and a palisade – hadn't been substantial
enough. The thatch on the main house had been burned
away but its charred timber skeleton was still in place. Must
have been raining heavily when they set fire to it, or the
timbers would have gone too, thought Dug. The stilted grain
storage huts were smashed open, long picked clean by birds.
Grass had grown wild around the banks where peacefully
munching animals would once have kept it trim. Stone
outbuildings had been semi-demolished, most likely by
opportunistic neighbours after building materials once the

attackers had left. The walls that separated the small rectangular fields around the farm were mostly collapsed. Dog eat dog, thought Dug, then other dogs eat the remains of the half-eaten dog.

He pictured massed assailants breaking down the palisade in a rainstorm while a terrified family fought back, desperately sending their children into the woods with the household valuables, knowing the attackers would have thought of that and would be guarding the escape route, but having no alternative. Now the family would be dead or enslaved.

Things really were in a mess and Zadar's army was the only safe place. Which had to be wrong, since it was Zadar's army that had caused the mess. But you can't change the course of the river, as Brinna had always said, so just jump in and let the flow take you where it will.

Dug thought about Brinna and the farm where he'd once lived, and then pushed the thought away. Never get attached to anyone. No friends, no lovers. Simpler that way. Brinna, Kelsie and Terry were in his past now. As was the strange little battlefield looter that he hadn't killed. Spring.

He was about to walk on when a young deer emerged from the ruins of the farmhouse. It stood in the long, sunlit grass and stared at him. Dug considered taking it down with a slingstone. He could swim the river to get the carcass – or even walk back to it; there must be a bridge fairly soon – and sell it in town. But he didn't. The deer watched him walk away along the river, his mail shirt slung over one broad shoulder, hammer swinging from his hand.

On the road from the east to Bladonfort two oxen ambled along, drawing a cart. Dug finished stashing his helmet and ringmail a few paces into the trees. They'd be an encumbrance in town and, by his reckoning, he had to come back this way to get to Maidun. He kept his hammer though. You never knew.

He jogged up behind the cart. *Never stand when you can sit.* It was old and heavy with four solid wooden wheels rather than the lighter but much more expensive spoked variety. The oxen's harnesses were decorated with carved bone and polished bronze, however, more typical of a wealthy person's tack.

"Going to town?"

The carter hadn't seen Dug coming. He jerked in surprise, startling his oxen to a stop. He turned, eyes wide in a long, pink, cleanly shaven face below a mushroom of curly blond hair. His eyes narrowed, and he peered at Dug like an inquisitive but partially sighted sheep.

"I'd love a lift into town if you're going that way?"

"Yes, all right. Jump up," he said eventually. He had a surprisingly refined accent. Dug clambered aboard and settled on the driving bench next to him.

"Ya!" The carter flicked the reins, the oxen strained and the heavy cart creaked forward.

"Business in town?" Dug asked.

"It's market day. My workers left a long time ago, so now I drive into town myself with what we managed to hide from Zadar's collectors."

"Things that bad?"

"Not from around here?"

"I've come from the north."

"You should go back. My father knew Zadar, so our land hasn't been totally ruined – yet. But I made the mistake once of treating a passing group of Zadar's soldiers with less deference than they thought they deserved, so we lost all our livestock and almost all our workers. Hence you find me driving a three-quarters-empty cart to market when two years ago you would have found me falconing on my estate while my workers drove three full carts to town. Bit of a comedown. Still, there are people who have it much worse than me. As you'll see."

They drove on in silence until they reached a hill. The falconer-turned-carter asked Dug to jump down for a while. The cart was meant for four oxen and the two beasts were struggling. Dug leaned two-handed against the back of the cart so that it looked like he was pushing as the oxen plodded uphill. As they climbed he felt an increasing niggle that someone was watching him — that he was being followed. He spun round. Nothing there but an empty road. He climbed back up at the crest.

"This used to be pastureland, full of sheep," said the carter.

The farmland sloping down towards Bladonfort was churned, dried earth. Instead of sheep, there were people. A few walked around listlessly, but most sat around on the ground among the crappiest tents Dug had ever seen. Babies cried. Children stared glumly. The stench of bodies, excrement and disease was gag-inducing. A few skinny men approached to beg for food. They were dressed in scraps of wool and leather, sluggish with hunger. The carter ignored them.

"We'd be mobbed if I helped any of them, and besides I've barely enough to keep my family alive."

"Who are they?"

"They're people who have no place in Zadar's new Britain. He's taken their homes, their herds, their crops; enslaved their relatives . . . If you're on Zadar's side, things are OK. I sort of am, so things are sort of OK. If you're not on his side . . ." The carter gestured at a woman holding a baby. The mother looked up. Bright blue eyes stared accusingly from her grime-smeared face.

"It's not Zadar who gives me the willies," continued the carter, "as much as his druid, Felix. I've always been wary of druids. I get one in from the village sometimes when an animal is sick, and she seems to know her stuff, but I don't like talking to her. It's like she's looking into my head. And she's a well-meaning druid who uses the gods' magic to heal. The stories I've heard about Felix — from plenty of reliable sources, mind you — would make your hair curl. I saw him once. Ill-looking fellow. They say he's the child of the worm god Cromm Cruach and a wolf. I can well believe it."

They passed piles of rubble and the splintered shards of ruined buildings. These had been smelters, tanners, wheel makers and other artisans, the carter explained. A roadside pub which had been lovely in summer was now just shattered spars and two dogs fighting over a rag.

"All the businesses have moved inside the walls," said the carter, nodding towards Bladonfort's approaching palisade. "Stay out here and, well, you can see what's happened."

"What's that queue for?" Dug nodded at a long shuffling line leading to two tents which stood out tall and neat among the desolate camp, like white mushrooms growing from a cowpat.

"Slavery," said the carter, eyes never leaving the road. "Zadar's men. The people here would rather be well fed slaves than starving free men. Every day they queue. The strong ones are accepted. The weaker ones are sent away."

"To get weaker."

"Not necessarily. You can sell even a malnourished child for a couple of days' food. Rome won't buy an ill child, but some druids will read anyone's entrails. Sell your child for food early, before you're too sick yourself, and you might get your strength up enough for the slavers to take you."

"That's bad."

"Yup."

"Can't do anything about it though."

"Nope."

They reached the town. The carter nodded to a gate-keeper, who shouted a command for a drawbridge to be lowered across the river, which had been narrowed between banks of cut stone. The heavy wooden bridge creaked down on thick ropes and thudded into place. The cart trundled across.

"Badger's bumholes," said Dug, looking around. The contrast was striking. Bladonfort's eastern market, which he'd heard was the biggest and best in the world, was thriving. Men and women in colourful clothes strode around purposefully. Children and dogs dodged between their legs. A couple of druids were wailing their usual rants about the coming Romans. Vendors shouted their wares from stalls piled with all manner of goods. Music from at least three different bands filled the air, and was that a bear's roar he heard? Somehow the town wall kept out the stench of the destitute. Here it smelled of freshly baked bread and roasting meat, albeit mixed with the underlying ming of decaying food you always got in markets on hot days.

"I'm going this way," said the carter, nodding to the road that ran along the town wall.

"Oh aye. Thanks for the lift then and good luck!"

"Good luck with what?" The carter shook his head, not looking at Dug.

"Dunno. Life, I suppose." Dug jumped down and walked into the crowd.

It was indeed a very large market, and if there was a bigger one in the world he didn't know where. He wandered past stalls selling embroidered woollen clothes, rivet-decorated bronze bowls, jewellery of shale, iron, bronze and tin, wooden spinning whorls, bone bobbins, ornaments and tools carved from antler and bone, clay crucibles and other metal-working equipment, iron weapons and armour, and a vast array of pottery, from plain fire-baked everyday pots to highly decorated kiln-fired vases. Further on, stalls creaked under huge piles of vegetables. A row of pigs' heads eyed him calmly from a butcher's stall.

It was slow work pushing through crowds of shoppers, but Dug was in no rush, and the multitudes of well-off customers meant that the stallholders didn't hassle him. He couldn't abide the aggressively pleading patter of salesmen.

The difference between the beggars outside and these well fed people in their new leather, wool and linen outfits made him philosophical. Nothing but a wall, an accident of birth and the whims of a few powerful people separated this opulent happy throng from the misery outside. How come everyone agreed that this was OK? They didn't, but everyone with the power to change things was on the lucky side. And who was he to complain? He had a pocket full of coins. He could have given some of them, one of them even, to the downtrodden people outside. But he hadn't. He wanted to drink, eat and sleep in a soft bed, so he needed his coins. If he'd had more coins, it wouldn't have changed anything. He'd have just wanted better food and a bigger bed.

Dug darted a glance over his shoulder. It felt like he was being followed again, but there was nobody there but market-goers, a few of whom eyed him suspiciously. The feeling that he was being followed probably came from feeling guilty about taking the girl's coin. A laughing throng drew him to a dancing bear. It wasn't really dancing. It was staggering between two men with sharp sticks and two huge snarling dogs straining on chains. It looked ill and confused. Its fur was patchy, its movements erratic, its arse hair caked in a mat of its own excrement. The animal's eyes caught Dug's. It was the same look as the woman with the baby had given him. Around it all was laughter. Free, natural, unforced, pure laughter, directed at this unfortunate animal. A woman next to him in a flouncy white cloth cap bent over, hooting and beating her knee with mirth. How could they laugh? There was nothing funny here. Dug hated them for their mindlessness. *See something that's meant to be funny, laugh loud and laugh long.* They were more like trained animals than the bear was. He might have envied their simplicity, but he wasn't in the mood. They were cattle, stupid cattle, following the herd, questioning nothing, doing what they were meant to do. Perhaps worst of all, they were all doing better than him by pretty much anyone's measure.

That's enough depressing shit. Time for a drink. There were several inns around the lower market, but he'd heard of a better place with rooms up in town, where the people might not be any less offensive but they would be quieter. He was too old for the shouting of rowdy youths and bards blaring trumpets so loud you couldn't hear a word anyone said. He left the bear tormentors and the market, and headed up through tightly packed wooden buildings.

The houses were jammed in side by side like irregular teeth, leaning over the narrow lane until they almost touched. A stinking ditch ran down the centre of the road. How do people get their shit together enough to organise something as massive and complicated as a town, Dug wondered, when most people are the sort of dimwits who laugh at a tortured bear?

He walked up the hill. This time when he spun round, he was almost sure he saw someone ducking out of sight into an alleyway.

Chapter 16

Lowa Flynn strode into Bladonfort from the west and marched up the town's broadest street, her iron-heeled boots clacking on paving stones. She had a bundle of reeds strapped to her back, towering above her to half her height again. Combined with her dirty red party dress and riding boots, the reeds were almost laughably conspicuous, but it was more subtle than carrying her bow and arrows in plain sight. Anyway, it was her wild hair and glaring, sleep-deprived, grieving, revenge-bent eyes that cleared the good people of Bladonfort out of her way.

The prevailing wind was south-westerly, so, as in most towns, the richer people lived in the west, upwind on most days from the stink of industry and the poor. Modern stone houses with heavy wooden doors flanked the street. These large solid buildings – some of which had large solid guards standing outside – had been built since Lowa's last visit two years before. They were merchants' houses, belonging to men and women who sold crops, metals, animals and slaves at higher prices than they bought them for.

Lowa ducked into an alleyway between two buildings. On the right, the side of the house gave way to a wall. She peered over it. There was a yard with a couple of chairs, a cot and an open doorway leading into the house. The howling of a baby and fraught soothing attempts of a mother came from upstairs. Lowa slipped over the wall and into the house.

Ten minutes later she strode into the upper market square with her red dress exchanged for a black linen shirt, hair combed into a ponytail and her pockets heavy with coins. The long bundle of reeds suited the look even less, but there was nothing she could do about that.

In this, the more exclusive of Bladonfort's two markets, men in helmets guarded stalls selling furs, wine, meat, brooches and other hammered bronze ornaments, fine weapons, lathe-turned wooden plates, shale bowls and more. A stall selling gold and glass jewellery had three beefy minders. On the far side of the market a soothsaying druid yelped about "storm-waves of Romans" as a guard bundled him away. In the centre was a post with three hands nailed to it. The hands had presumably belonged to thieves.

"A handy warning," she would have said to Aithne. A rush of grief almost brought a tear to her eye. She shook her head and set off through the market.

Not quite outnumbering the marketplace guards were a few customers, none in any apparent hurry to buy anything. The women wore fine linens pinned with big brooches, hair artfully arranged in ringlets and decorated with duck and other birds' feathers. Lowa recognised sea-eagle tail plumage trailing from one woman's tresses. The men were in short summer togas, with close-cropped hair. This was no surprise: some of Zadar's army and a lot of the wealthier people in towns smaller than Bladonfort had taken to dressing like Romans. Lowa felt no call to do the same. Aithne had tried to explain fashion to her. She understood what it was, but not why.

Past the carefully dressed shoppers, at the far end of the market square, was a large tavern with a clear area in front for performers and outdoor drinkers. Since she'd last been there, two wooden storeys had been added to the tavern's ground floor. They teetered out alarmingly over the performers' area.

Three men and a woman that Lowa recognised from

Maidun's light cavalry were sitting at one of the ten or so tables outside the pub. She could have slashed open her bundle and put an arrow through three of them before they'd realised what was happening, then questioned the fourth, but lowly troops like these were unlikely to know why her girls and her sister had been killed. She ducked behind a milliner's stall. The milliner was busy flattering an elderly customer.

"What d'you want?" Lowa jumped. One of the market guards had come up behind her and she'd been so angry at seeing Zadar's troops that she hadn't noticed.

"Just browsing."

"Oh."

Lowa gave the man a coin.

"Is there another way into the tavern?"

The man looked at the coin. "Yeah. Round the back, by the stables."

The guard turned away. Lowa grabbed a green woollen cap from the stall and stuffed it under her shirt, hoping it was worth more than the coin she'd given the guard. She followed the smell of horses to the back of the tavern. A lane, muddy despite the recent dry weather, separated a large stable block from the inn. Along the back wall to the right of the tavern's back door was a low wooden gutter sloping into a tub. Beery men's piss, thought Lowa, collected for tanning leather. She was glad she wasn't a townie.

A portly guard emerged from the stable. "What are you doing back here?"

As she opened her mouth to answer, a horse-faced girl in leather trousers and wool shirt came out of the tavern door, carrying two buckets of water. The guard turned to watch the girl's swaying bottom as she walked into the stable. Lowa darted into the tavern, through a dark corridor and into the main room.

There was a strong smell of body odour and stale beer

despite the fresh straw on the floor. Two narrow windows with shutters thrown wide and an open door let in enough light and a little air. A melange of chairs and tables, all made by the looks of it by different people from different woods, spoke of regular breakages. This was the smartest tavern in town, but despite its veneer the rapidly growing Bladonfort was lawless – or at least its laws did little to stop drunken fights. In bigger towns she'd visited to the east there was a curfew at night, and only the richest citizens – merchants, gang bosses, some mercenaries and druids – were allowed to walk the streets. As far as she knew, they didn't have a curfew in Bladonfort yet.

To her right, facing the door, was a long wooden counter with a woman who looked like a half-starved troll scowling from behind it. Whoever ran this boozer clearly didn't hold with the comely-barmaid-attracts-custom theory.

Lowa bought a bronze-handled leather mug of ale that smelled of fart from the hatchet-faced barwoman, she settled in a dark corner that covered both entrances, lowered her new cap and waited.

People trickled into and out of the tavern, but none of Zadar's men and women other than those she'd seen outside. After an hour or so a big lunk wandered in and argued with the barwoman. Lowa must have lifted her head just a little too far, because the man seemed to recognise her. He smiled at her, not the mean smile of someone about to shop her, more the smile of a brain-damaged dog hoping against previous evidence to be given a scrap of food. There was something about him though, behind the brainless smile. Something dangerous, perhaps. She decided to keep an eye on him.

He looked at her chest with a clumsy attempt at nonchalance and sat at a nearby table, angling his chair towards her as if she were entertainment. Every now and then he glanced at her over his mug. After a very short time he got up and went to the bar again, walking with a strangely twisting swagger, as if sitting down for a short time had aggravated an old injury. He had another argument with the barmaid and returned to his table with a second beer and a bowl of food. He continued to sneak looks at her when he thought she wasn't looking.

Lowa watched him eat. He looked strong, if a little portly, and she liked his face. A bit lumpy, a bit weather-beaten, but he had kind eyes and a gentle way about him, somewhat belied by the well used warhammer and long knife hanging from his waist. And he at least had the decency to pretend he wasn't leering at her.

It was a while since Lowa had seen kind eyes. She decided that he wasn't one of Zadar's but just a man who found her attractive. Men who fancied her would usually just swagger up and pretty much plonk their penises on the table. This fellow's shyness was unusual. Three years ago maybe she would have thought it was pathetic. Now she found it more endearing than the cock-on-wood approach.

As the big shy man was getting up to buy his third drink, Dionysia Palus, or Deidre Marsh as Lowa preferred to call her, and Weylin Nancarrow walked in. Both were dressed in town garb – him in linen shirt and trousers, her in a linen dress. She was tall, but he was much taller. He always walked – indoors and outdoors – with a slight stoop, as if he'd learned his lesson after banging his head too many times. Deidre's shiny straight black hair was held in a centre parting with a white band, and she had her usual "I'm sooo fucking bored" scowl on the incongruously chubby white face that topped her slender frame. Weylin's head was newly shaved at the front, the usual tangle of long dark hair sprouting from the back of his scalp.

He'd killed Cordelia last night, but had still got up this morning and worried about his hairstyle. A wave of hatred and grief almost made her attack them in a screaming rage. Instead she pulled her hat further forward.

Dionysia walked to the bar and stood next to the lunk, but Weylin came towards Lowa, head forward as if he were being led by his large nose. She tensed, but he went straight past her, out to the piss trough at the back.

The lunk returned to his table with another beer, glancing at Lowa on the way. She waited, ears thrumming, hands shaking, until Deidre ordered drinks then, while her quarry was distracted by the price of the drinks, she slipped out of her seat and walked silently over to the bar.

"Hello, Deirdre."

Deirdre stiffened as Lowa pushed her knife into her back.

"It's Dionysia."

"Whatever you're pretending to be called," Lowa whispered in Dionysia's ear, "I know exactly where your liver is. And if I stabbed just a little harder than this—"

Lowa pushed the knife until she felt the tip pop though skin. Dionysia gasped.

"—then I'd puncture your liver and you'd die. Slowly, in pain. So I suggest you walk over to the table in the corner with me."

"Weylin will be back in—"

She pushed the knife deeper. "Just a bit further in, Dionysia. Just a tiny bit."

Lowa guided Dionysia to her table, pushed her into the corner and sat next to her, knife in her back.

"Why did Zadar kill my women?"

Dionysia flicked her hair and fixed Lowa with a low-lidded stare. That she still managed to look patronising with a knife poking into her reminded Lowa what a total bitch she was, and impressed her a little.

"My sweet, do you really think Zadar tells me all his plans? Any of his plans?"

"What are people saying?"

"Oh darling, we have better things to—"

Lowa twitched the blade.

"All right, if it really turns you on that much to know, the death of your women and your escape is the talk of the army. The upper *stratum* anyway." She emphasised the Latin word.

Lowa twisted the knife. Dionysia gasped, at least partially, it seemed, in pleasure. Lowa felt blood run onto her fingers. Dionysia licked her lips like a whore canvassing for work. *What a freak*, thought Lowa.

"Nobody knows, or at least nobody's saying, but *consensus* is that your women were overheard plotting against Zadar. I know that your idiot sister Aithne whinged to Atlas about Zadar's methods."

Dionysia turned, even though that twisted the knife deeper. She looked straight at Lowa.

"But don't worry; you won't mind for long. Your soul will be looking for a new body in the Otherworld soon. Very soon."

Lowa raised her eyebrows questioningly.

"Zadar knew you'd be in Bladonfort. He sent some of us here to find you. Oh, and by the way, before we left we all had a game of football. I'm not sure who won. I only played for a few kicks myself, but everybody agreed that Aithne's big head made by far the best ba—"

Lowa grabbed Dionysia by the chin and smashed her head into the stone wall. As Dionysia lifted her hands to wrench her face free, Lowa pulled the knife out of her back and plunged it upwards, through linen dress, through skin and fat, under her ribcage, into her heart.

Dionysia gasped and her eyes widened.

"Your. Name. Is. Deidre." Lowa twisted the knife with each word.

Weylin came back in on the last twist. Lowa didn't see him until it was too late. As she made to get up, Weylin pressed the point of his sword into her neck, pinning her. She glared at him, furious with herself for forgetting his imminent return and for killing her hostage.

"Don't move," he said, eyes darting to his dead wife as she slipped under the table with a sigh. He didn't seem overly surprised or bothered. "Arthur! Tristan! Any of Zadar's! To me!" he shouted.

A couple of seconds' silence, then the four soldiers that Lowa had seen out front came charging in. Weylin stood looking at her, pleased with himself, while two more Maidun soldiers piled into the pub. She was facing seven in all, armed with a swords or knives. A couple wore mail shirts. She was sitting and unarmoured. Her knife was stuck in Dionysia. Her longbow was out of reach, sheathed in reeds. Her attackers were too close for the bow anyway. One against one, with the one where she was, would have been long odds. One against seven . . . What could she do? Her mind raced and came up with nothing. She gritted her teeth.

"What's up, boss?" said one. "Oh, Mother! It's Lowa Flynn! Result! What's the reward again?"

"Go find some rope one of you. Or better, chain," said Weylin, not taking his eyes or his sword off Lowa. "The rest of you stay here, stay alert. She's a tricky bitch, this one. Arthur, keep an eye out in case she's with anyone. Everyone else, eyes on Lowa. You get the rope, Tristan."

As Tristan left there was a gap in the press and Lowa caught the eye of the big stranger sitting across the room. She widened her own eyes, imploring for help. He held her gaze for a moment, then looked down at his beer, shaking his head.

Chapter 17

"What?"

"You'll find most things are more expensive in Bladonfort than where you're from, sir."

Her voice was sharp, but she lingered on the word at the end of each phrase. Dug was impressed at how she'd managed to make her drawn-out "sir" sound about as deferential and welcoming as a gob of spit dribbled onto a stranger from a window.

She stared at him with hard little eyes. Her tight mouth was like a dog's arsehole in a face made from the bark of an ancient, diseased tree. He wondered when she'd last smiled.

"A coin the same as this one got me ten beers at Boddingham."

"Prices go up, love."

The "love" sounded as affectionate as a shit-smeared dagger in the guts.

"Why?"

"I don't know. They just do, sir."

"But why?" Dug looked at the barmaid. She looked back. He sighed. "One beer please."

She poured his drink from a spigot hammered into a wooden keg. Dug glanced at the woman in the corner. She looked up at the same moment and he instantly recognised the leader of Zadar's troop of archers that had made total arses of Barton's forces the day before.

Her eyes were the blue of glacier ice. Her skin was smooth and spotless, as if carved from the whitest heartwood. Her lips were red as yew berries, the upper one lifted at the middle and corners like the recurve bow with which she'd slaughtered dozens of Barton's denizens. Her hair was clean, nearly white blonde, swept back into a high ponytail. Even sitting, she seemed to zing with energy, as if she might suddenly leap up and cartwheel out of the door, yet he couldn't remember seeing a calmer beauty. Not since Brinna of course . . .

He noticed the bundle of reeds propped against the wall next to her. So she'd popped into town on a roofing job? That seemed unlikely.

Dug smiled his most dashing, sophisticated, I'd-be-fun-to-talk-to-and-amazing-in-the-sack smile. Not a flicker of emotion crossed the young woman's face. She looked away. He darted a subtle look to her chest. Her breasts were on the small side, but well shaped. Big tits, he'd found, had their attractions, but once a woman was past twenty or so, he decided that large jugs always disappointed in the raw.

He'd planned to sit outside with his beer, since it was a warm day. But, now he thought about it, he'd spent far too much time outside of late. He decided to take the chair facing the bar at the table by the door. It happened to give him a clear view of the beautiful archer.

"How you doing, all right?"

Dug jumped. It was a young prostitute with big blue eyes, a round nose and lips like a fledgling's beak. Her prematurely silver hair rather complimented her lightly tanned skin, but it was her figure, Dug guessed, that kept her in business. It looked like her white flax shirt and leather shorts had been sewn on and then shrunk. Firm, tanned flesh burst from leg holes, arm holes and particularly the broad neck hole. Dug guessed she was in her late teens. He glanced at the beauty in the corner. She was watching them. Or perhaps looking past them, at the door.

"No thanks, hen. I'm waiting for a friend," he said.

"All right," said the girl and headed off. She'd looked relieved, like someone visiting a disagreeable relative's hut out of duty and finding they weren't there. That rankled. Surely if you *had* to shag someone, he wasn't that bad? He remembered his earlier look in Ulpius' mirror. He had looked a lot older than he'd thought he did. He decided to sell the mirror. Just a bite to eat first.

He finished his beer and headed to the bar with a world-weary but capable swagger that he thought might impress the archer.

"Another of those, please." He dropped his mug lightly onto the bar. And a large piece of mutton with fresh bread."

"We don't do mutton."

"What do you have?"

"Stew."

"With bread?"

"Yes."

"What kind of stew?"

"The kind you eat."

"Has it got meat in it?"

"Yes."

"What kind of meat?"

"The kind you—"

"Eat. Yeah, OK. I get it. What made you want to be a barmaid? Was it your desire to serve or your love of people?"

"Do you want the stew?"

Dug looked for a flicker of humanity in her eyes. *Nope, not a spark.* "Do you know," he said, "I've always thought that people are about as happy as they decide to be."

"What?"

"Nothing. I would like some stew, please. And another beer."

The stew was gristle all the way. He took it back to the bar, half-finished despite his hunger, and got another beer. Beer was basically vegetable soup, he reasoned, so enough of it should slake his hunger. He thought he caught the archer looking at him again on the way back, which cheered him a little.

As he reached for his beer he noticed blood on his hand. He'd managed to get a huge splinter between his thumb and index finger while leaning on the bar. He was so focused on digging it out that he didn't notice anything awry until a man shouted, "Arthur! Tristan! Any of Zadar's! To me!"

A big Warrior, bald but for a black mess of waxed hair falling from the back of his head, had the beauty pinned against the wall with a sword. *What stupid hair*, thought Dug. Why did the young these days go to so much effort to make themselves look like such tits?

Soldiers stampeded into the pub, knocking Dug's table on their way to surround Lowa and her captor. One of them then left, leaving a gap in the throng for a moment.

She was looking straight at him. Her eyes widened just a little, asking for help. It wasn't a panicked plea, more an "If you've got a moment, I was wondering if you wouldn't mind . . . ?" She was cool this one.

And he would have loved to have helped her. He really would. Unfortunately, helping damsels in distress was the sort of thing that got you killed, especially when the damsel was surrounded by half a dozen competent-looking Warriors.

Badgers' hairy bollocks, he thought, looking back to his beer and shaking his head.

Chapter 18

"Wait!" shouted Drustan. Ragnall didn't hear him. The fort's outlying village was deserted but for mutilated dead. People and sheep and parts of people and sheep lay about. Flies buzzed, animals scurried over bodies and birds flapped and hopped among the corpses. A raven flew by with a bloody strip of flesh hanging from its beak.

What the Mother had happened? Driving his heels into his mount, Ragnall sped forward, praying to Her that he'd find the hillfort's gates barred, defenders alive inside.

The path up to the fort was littered with more bodies. He had to slow so that his horse could pick a path between carcasses. Mostly the blood was dried black-brown, but in some places it still pooled red, shining in the sun. One of the bodies was moving. Ragnall jerked his reins and leaped off. It was Mungo Strawhair, a horse breeder who'd taught Ragnall to ride. He was propped up against a corpse. His face was red and black with blood.

"Mungo! What happened? Where are my parents? What happened?"

Black blood bubbled from Mungo's mouth. He seemed to recognise Ragnall. He smiled.

"What happened?!"

The muscles in Mungo's neck slackened and his head fell to the side. Ragnall shook him but got no response. He dropped his dead riding instructor and ran on up the steep track. A cart lay on its side, dead oxen next to it, sliced open as if by an axe.

The hillfort's gates were closed, but next to them, where the chalk-carved ditches were shallowest – the fort's weakest point, which his father had always said must be fixed one day – the palisade was smashed, and the chalk scarred with hundreds of hoof prints.

Ragnall clambered over the wrecked palisade.

The village inside the fort, his childhood home, was gone. Not one hut was left standing. As a toddler he'd run from the bigger children through the narrow gaps between the stilts of the rectangular grain stores. The stores were all smashed to the ground now, stilts poking into the air like mooring posts in a lake of rubble. Some of the larger huts were still smoking. Flames licked around the remains of the longhouse.

Ragnall walked along the fort's main street, the road he'd walked every day for most of his life. He stepped over corpses of dogs and people. There was Rumo the falconer lying awkwardly across a quern stone, an arrow in his chest. His kestrel was lying dead next to him, also spitted by an arrow. *Arrows*. Not many armies used arrows.

Ten paces further in, Navlin Breadmaker, the fat cheerful baker who'd always given Ragnall scraps of cake, was sitting propped against a fence. She looked uninjured, eyes and mouth wide open. Her chest heaved as if she was struggling for breath. He ran over and shook her shoulders. A small rat squeezed out of her mouth and leaped onto his arm. He jumped up, roaring and flailing, sending the rat flying. Navlin fell forward. Her back was one gaping wound, crawling with several little rats and one big one.

A family, thought Ragnall.

He fell to his knees, where he was sick through his mouth and nose until there was nothing left, but his stomach wouldn't stop convulsing and he carried on heaving and coughing. Finally he finished retching, got to his feet shakily and walked further into the fort, into his father's fort, into the fort where surely somewhere he'd find his family and his true love hiding, all unhurt and glad to see him.

But here was his eldest brother. The face that had mocked him so many times was frozen in a purple scream. The hands that had ruffled his hair so often then later been thrown up in mock despair as he'd lost another game to his little brother now clutched at the arrow in his stomach. The higher arrow, the one through his heart, had clearly been a mercy shot, like you might give a fatally injured dog.

Ragnall walked on, his head screaming like a million horses driven off a cliff into a stormy sea.

His second-eldest brother was further into the fort, next to the smouldering remains of the longhouse. There were a lot of bodies here, the scene of a final stand perhaps. His brother was cloven in two diagonally, from neck to hip. It looked as if he hadn't died straight away. His head was propped on a corpse, looking wide-eyed at his own separated legs.

Ragnall searched the fort. He found more people that he knew, so many childhood friends. All dead. Killed in so many ways. Whoever had done this – Zadar's army, for sure – had enjoyed themselves. But others were missing. He found no trace of his father, mother or Anwen. His search ended back at his eldest brother, knocked down by a gut shot, killed by a heart shot. He sat next to him.

Drustan walked up a short while later, white hair bedraggled, eyes narrow in his uncharacteristically dirty face.

"I've tied the horses outside."

"Right."

"I'm sorry."

"Yup."

"I thought I'd leave you while I said the rites for the dead outside the fort."

"Good idea."

"Anwen?"

"No sign. Nor of my father and mother. Zadar's taken them. He's taken a lot of people of slave age by the look of things – there are no dead children, and fewer corpses of young people than there should be. The old and the brave he killed. Anwen will earn a good slave price. My father and mother . . . I'd guess they're hostages, but there's nothing to pay a ransom with, no one to gain political leverage over. We'll follow Zadar's army and take them back."

"We may . . . A different course may be . . ."

Ragnall looked at Drustan.

"All right," said the older man. "Help me give the rites. Then we'll get out of here. Then we'll talk."

It was almost dark when they left Boddingham along the Ridge Road. They rode all night under the stars.

Dawn was rising over a wood of scrubby trees when they came across a hedgehog sitting in the middle of the road, looking at Ragnall. It scooted to the side, looked at him again, then disappeared into an old flint mine, now just a steep-sided hollow in the chalk.

Ragnall dismounted.

"Ragnall?" said Drustan.

"Wait." He walked to the edge of the pit and looked into it.

At the bottom of the slope were three bodies held together by a triple slave collar – three iron hoops connected by two pace-long iron rods. Even in the semi-darkness he could tell they were dead. Even after five years the figure at the front looked familiar. Even before Ragnall had dismounted, climbed down the bank and turned her over, he knew he'd found his mother.

Chapter 19

"Got the rope."

"Where's Tristan? Who are you?"

"I'm Dug. Here's your rope." Lowa saw that it was the shy glancer. Was he going to help her? Odds were he was just another chancer trying to ingratiate himself with Zadar.

"Here, Arthur, take over here." Weylin kept the sword pressed into her neck as Arthur, a fit-looking fellow with tousled hair and a chin like a fist, took the hilt from him. Lowa knew Arthur. He was one of the Fifty. Not a friend as such, but someone she'd chatted with amiably enough. He was a charming man. She was pretty sure Aithne had shagged him. Possibly Maura too. *Why were they doing this?*

"Got her, boss," said Arthur.

"Right." Weylin turned, walked over and thrust his face at Dug's. "I said, where is Tristan?"

"Have you been eating onions?" Dug turned his head away.

Behind them the rest of the pub had cleared, apart from the barmaid. She was leaning on the counter, watching impassively.

"What?"

"Aye, nothing, but can you take a step back? I'm on your side. You're Zadar's troops, right?"

Weylin moved back a little. "Right."

"I'm a Warrior looking to join the Maidun army. I was sitting over there and I heard you ask for rope. So I got some. I don't have a clue where your man Tristan has gone. Thought maybe if I helped you, you'd help me join."

"Do I look like a recruitment officer?" Weylin turned to one side and then the other as if to bask in the appreciative laughter of his companions. None came.

Dug looked Weylin up and down, then leaned to look round at his ponytail. "I'm not quite sure *what* you look like."

A couple of the soldiers snorted.

"What!" Weylin reached for his sword. His fingers scrabbled at air. He remembered he'd handed his sword to Arthur and turned the scrabbling into scratching his hip.

"Hey, I'm just joking." Dug smiled. "Calm yourself. I just thought I'd get you a rope, and maybe you could tell me how to join up and perhaps put in a good word. So here's your rope."

Dug held up a thin pile of light brown hairy lime-bark rope. "I'll tie her up. I used to be a sailor. I've a knot she'll never escape."

Lowa looked at Dug. He didn't have the salt-, wind- and sun-cracked face of a sailor, nor the springy, bow-kneed walk that came from years of moving about on deck. He was no sailor. Did the lie mean he was going to help her? Possibly. More likely he did want to join the Maidun army and was simply a liar.

She silently pleaded with the big Warrior to help. If he didn't, she was caught and she'd die. That was bad enough on its own – knowing Zadar and Felix, it was unlikely to be quick – but what she really couldn't stomach was the idea of dying without avenging Aithne, Realin, Cordelia, Seanna and Maura. *Make him help me, please*, she begged the gods that she didn't believe in.

"Is that rope thick enough?" Weylin asked suspiciously.

Dug looked surprised. "Oh aye. I've used thinner rope to tow a clinker-built schooner from a lee shore in a complete hooly."

"Um . . . all right," said Weylin. "Tie her up."

Weylin shifted his large frame aside so Dug could get through. "Clear a space everyone. You, Flynn, stand up. Arthur, don't let the pressure off."

Lowa stood slowly, the sword jabbing uncomfortably into her trachea. It was a typical medium-length iron blade, made for slashing and hacking, not stabbing, so it had sharp edges but a dull tip. Pushed into her neck it was unpleasant but by no means incapacitating. It pained her that these men called themselves Warriors but didn't realise that. *If the lunk is on my side,* she thought, edging round the table, *this is going to be my best chance.*

She tightened her neck muscles and pushed, driving the sword and Arthur's arm back. He countered by thrusting the blade into her, as she'd expected. She dodged to the right, bringing her left hand up to grab the sword by the hilt. With all the power of her bow-drawing arm, she thrust her right hand, fingers pointed, into Arthur's windpipe. He went down with a strangled "Glurk!" and the sword was hers.

Not too soon. Already an overhead sword swing was coming at her from the nearest soldier. She parried, but she had Arthur's sword in an awkward, wrist-bent grip with the blade pointing back over her left shoulder. The blow smashed the sword onto her head, knocking her into a crouch. She rammed her fist up into her attacker's balls. He doubled up. She whammed the heavy sword hilt into his face. His nose crunched. She pulled him over, then, anticipating another swing, leaped over him in a diving roll. She came up onto her feet, facing the body of the tavern, sword in both hands, ready.

Dug was tossing his hammer from hand to hand in the middle of the room, facing Weylin, who had acquired a heavy iron sword. Smashed furniture and the three other Maidun Warriors lay around them. Two were out cold or dead. One was groaning and rolling, his head in his hands.

What the Bel? She reckoned she'd dispatched her two pretty quickly, but it looked like Dug had taken out three of Maidun's finest while she'd been busy.

Lowa raised her own sword and took a step towards them. She didn't fancy her rescuer's chances again Weylin, who was a good deal taller, and maybe twenty years younger. Dug was probably about the same weight, but Weylin was all muscle.

Weylin drew his sword back, but it was just a feint to entice Dug to move in, which the idiot did, looking at Weylin's sword. Lowa shook her head as Weylin's left fist swung, unseen, towards Dug's head.

Without taking his eyes off the sword, Dug flicked his hammer one-handed to meet Weylin's wrist. Weylin yelped. Dug darted in, grabbed Weylin's sword arm and spun the larger man like a father might spin a daughter in a Beltane dance. It ended with Weylin kneeling in front of Dug, his ponytail in one of Dug's hands and the pointed hammer shaft pressing into the small of his back.

Dug looked up at Lowa. "We'd better go."

Lowa leaped a body and slashed open her bundle of reeds. Her bow and quiver came tumbling out. She tossed the sword aside, grabbed the bow as it fell and slung her quiver onto her back.

"I'd wondered what that was," said Dug. "What should I do with this one?" He nodded down at Weylin.

"Kill him."

"That's a bit too . . . Well, he's done nothing to me."

"He killed my friend. But fine, I'll do it." Lowa reached into her quiver.

"Oh no, don't waste an arrow. If he killed your friend . . ."

Dug pulled back on the ponytail. Weylin strained to escape. Dug let go. As Weylin fell forward, Dug whipped his hammer round to clunk into the side of his shaved skull. Weylin went down.

"Right, let's go."

"You! Northerner!" The barmaid's voice sliced the air. She was still leaning on her counter.

"Yes?" Dug turned back.

"That was good."

Dug's eyes widened questioningly.

"Your fighting. I appreciate things like that. I see enough, and that was the best I ever saw. Next time you're here, the beers are on me, and I'll give you the stew that we eat, not the shit we give the customers. In fact, why not stick around now? I could talk to the boss about guard work?"

Dug looked lost for words.

"Come on!" said Lowa, walking out of the door.

Chapter 20

"That way!" Dug squinted in the sudden brightness and pointed across the market. Lowa nodded and set off at a jog. Dug followed. He hoped it was the best way. He'd come from the other direction and never been to the town before, so it was something of a guess.

As they passed the post with its nailed hands a shout came from behind: "Stop the blonde woman and the man! Zadar will reward you! With . . . big rewards!" It was Weylin, lurching out of the pub, one arm dangling, one hand holding his head.

"Sorry," Dug said. "He must have a thick skull."

"Never mind. Run!"

They never got started.

A dozen market guards barred their way, armed with knives, swords, cudgels and slings. Dug turned, but half a dozen more guards had closed in behind them.

"Badgers' scrotums!" He must remember, if he got out of this, to give himself a massive kick up the backside for breaking his rule about helping people. It was never, ever worth it.

He readied his hammer. Lowa plucked an arrow from her quiver, nocked it and half-drew.

The guards took a tentative step towards them. They were a handy-looking lot. A couple wore Warrior ringmail, which made sense. Dug had done some market guarding himself. It paid well.

"What's the reward?" Dug shouted to Weylin, keeping an eye on the guards. "Is it worth dying for?"

As he said "for", Lowa loosed an arrow. It went through the upper arm of the nearest guard, ten paces away. Before his dropped knife had hit the ground, Lowa had another arrow nocked and the bowstring drawn.

"I don't want to kill any of you," said Lowa, "but we are going to leave. If you try to stop us, the next shot will be through someone's head. So drop your weapons and move to the edge of the square. We're going to walk out of here and you'll live to see the sunset."

Dug looked at her. She was a cool one.

"Catch them, or Zadar *will* kill you and your families!" shouted Weylin.

That, it seemed, was more of an incentive. The guards charged.

One of their attacker's heads exploded with the promised face shot. *Badgers' helmets, what a bow*, thought Dug. Then they were too close. In half a heartbeat Lowa had jammed her bow lengthways into the ground to bend it, flicked the string off the end and gripped it in two hands. It was thick enough to make a decent fighting staff. Dug readied his hammer.

The five guards stopped in a line, three paces away, weapons raised.

Dug hoped Lowa knew that they needed to attack together. He took a step forward and she mirrored it. Good. Dug felt battle excitement bubble in his blood. Two on five suddenly seemed like reasonable odds.

"Come on, you horrible wee fuckers!" he grinned.

"Drop your weapons!" came a shout from behind.

Dug glanced over his shoulder. *Badgers' arses.* Quite an oversight. He'd forgotten the dozen or so other guards. Amazing how stupid battle made him. Half of them had blades and mêlée weapons, half of them slings, loaded and whirring round. There was no chance. He lowered his hammer a little.

Weylin walked over from the inn, swinging Dug's lime-bark rope in one hand. Despite his injury, a white-toothed grin cracked his face. He had them and he knew it.

"We're caught," whispered Dug.

"We are not," Lowa said, jaw clenched.

"OK. We're about to be caught. We have to surrender."

"No."

"There are twenty of them and two of us. We fight and we're definitely dead, or at least injured. We submit unharmed, we can escape later."

Lowa looked around. Dug could feel the rage boiling in her. She was about to make a move.

"It's not a choice," he whispered. "Surrender is our only hope."

She took a step, jabbing towards the guards with her bow. Dug heard the whirl of leather slings preparing to loose behind him. He raised his hammer in two hands, slipped the shaft over Lowa's shoulders and trapped her arms.

She stamped hard once, then again. He danced his feet out of the way.

"Stop!" he hissed in her ear. "You'll need me. I'll be more use without broken feet. Trust me."

She was stiff in his arms, humming with frustrated energy. She smelled fantastic and felt even better, but he tried to think about something else. He didn't want to weaken his image as a noble hero by nudging a boner into her back.

"We will get out of this," he whispered.

"We'd better," she said, "or I'm going to find you in the Otherworld, and I'm going to get you by the balls and—"

"Disarm yourselves!" shouted Weylin.

Dug heard Lowa's bow clatter to the ground. He let her go and put his hammer down.

"Well thank you, northerner!" said Weylin. "You wanted

to join Zadar's army? Looks like you're going to get your chance – as a practice dummy!"

Weylin looked about for laughter, but there was none.

"What do you mean?" said Dug.

Weylin's smile faltered. "I said you'll get your chance to join the Maidun army as a practice dummy!"

"Sorry, I can't see what you're driving at." Dug's smile grew as Weylin's dissolved into anger. His fist swung back. Dug saw the blow coming. He tensed his stomach muscles and shifted his gut sideways. The punch was ineffective.

"Oooooofffff!" he said, falling onto his side. He lay there breathing like an ill horse.

"Please, no m-more," he stuttered. Bravado was all well and good, but when caught he'd worked out it was less painful if you came across as pathetic as possible.

"There'll be more when I say so!" Weylin took a running kick at Dug, who rolled so that it glanced off his back. That seemed to satisfy the tall young man. "Lowa, on your knees!" He shouted. Lowa knelt. "Right you lot." Weylin addressed the guards. "Anybody good with knots?"

"I am," said Dug.

Weylin punched him in the face. Dug rolled his head with it, but this one did smart a bit.

"Anyone else?" Weylin asked, shaking his bruised fingers.

The guards discussed how best to tie up the captives. In the end one of them made a large noose with the rope. Weylin made Dug and Lowa stand back to back with their hands crossed on their chests. Dug held a big breath and tensed his arm and chest muscles as Weylin looped the noose over and wound the rope around them.

He was nearly finished when there was a shout from the other end of the square: "Weylin! Got the chain!" A Maidun Warrior was lumbering up from the road to the north-east gate, weighed down by a length of chain.

"Drop that, Tristan. Go and find a cart."

"A cart? Where from?"

"Find one! I don't care — There! That one!"

Well, that's odd, thought Dug as a cart came into the square driven by a girl who looked an awful lot like Spring.

Chapter 21

"**Y**ou can *borrow* the cart but only if I can drive it."

"I'm taking it. Get down now, or I'll—"

"You'll what? You'll hit a girl? Maybe you'll kill me? Is that the kind of man you are?"

Weylin rubbed his temples. Lowa smiled. This had been going on for a while now. It didn't take much to confound Weylin, but Lowa was enjoying the girl's pluck. She reminded her of herself at that age. There was something else familiar about the girl that she couldn't quite reach in the recesses of her mind.

"Weylin," said Dug, "how about you drive with your man Tristan up front, and let the girl sit in the back with us? That way she can take her cart back when you're done borrowing it."

"I'm *taking* the cart. Not borrowing it."

"Oh come on," said Dug. "You can't take a girl's cart. Her Dad will—"

"We took a whole tribe yesterday! Of course I can take a fucking—"

"Language!" said the girl. Weylin looked at her, mouth open. She smiled at him. "Now of course you can use my cart. I'm very glad to help with whatever's needed to get these horrid ugly criminals out of this lovely town. But I can't lose the cart and the oxen! My father is *such* good friends with Zadar that he'll probably get Zadar himself to punish me. Please can I come too? I promise I won't do anything wrong. I'll sit up front with you so you can keep an eye on me?"

"He's a friend of Zadar's, your dad?" Weylin asked, taking a step back.

"I say friend. They're actually cousins. But they act more like friends – you know, drinking beer and making plans and things. My dad has his own little army, so they talk about fighting a lot. It's really boring. They go on and on about different ways to torture people who annoy them or take things from them."

"OK, OK. All right."

"Weylin," said Tristan, "what if she's in league with them?"

"Good point. Are you trying to help them?"

"Why would I try to help them? He looks like a bear that needs a wash and she's got a criminal's face."

"Maybe you're in with the northerner?"

"Yeah, that's right," said Dug. "Every ageing northern Warrior has a wee southern girl for a partner."

Several of the market guards laughed.

"All right! Fine! You can come in the cart, little girl, and you can have it back afterwards, but you ride up front with me. Tristan, you guard these two. Now get them onto the cart." Weylin eyed Lowa's bow covetously. "Throw their weapons in too, but out of their reach."

"Maybe you should have tied us up after we'd got into the cart?" Lowa said. They were trundling out of the market, the girl driving. Weylin sat next to her, his broken wrist in a sling. The cart was a simple thing consisting of wooden planks nailed together into a platform surrounded by a rectangle of thick boards half a pace high. She and Dug were sitting on its bare boards, facing away from each other with their torsos tied together. It had taken almost all the market guards a long, expletive-filled time to lift them in.

"Keep talking," said Weylin, leaning back to look at them.

"You'll quieten down soon enough once Zadar has you. Keep a close eye, Tristan."

Tristan was in the back with them, holding Lowa's long knife. Her bow and Dug's knife and hammer were out of reach at the front. Behind them walked a press-ganged squad of market guards. They weren't happy to be there and the merchants hadn't been happy to let them go, but Weylin had promised them payment to guard the captives and threatened their masters with Zadar's wrath if they didn't.

Lowa had tensed all her muscles and breathed in when they were bound, so there was a good bit of give when she breathed out and relaxed, but not enough for her to wriggle free before Tristan would be able to stop her. She was about to ask Dug if there was any give on his side when the carter girl piped up, "By Bel and Danu and Toutatis' brother! Is that a gold necklace lying on the road there?"

"Where?" Weylin leaned forward like a curious pigeon.

"Oooh, it's just gone out of sight. We're going to run it over. It's on your side. If you lean . . ."

Weylin leaned out. "I can't see it."

"You'd better grab it or those guards will get it. If I hold your belt?" The girl gripped Weylin's belt. He leaned farther. The girl let go of his belt and shoved, at the same time whipping the reins with her other hand and shouting, "Yah!"

The cart lurched forward and Weylin fell out, barking with rage.

"You little . . ." Tristan jumped up from his perch in the back. The girl whipped the reins again, two-handed now, and the oxen jerked into a lolloping gallop. Tristan toppled.

"Go!" said Dug. Lowa felt him shrink as he breathed out and pulled his arms in. The ropes around her loosened massively and she slid out. Tristan was crawling up the bouncing cart to get at the girl, long knife in his teeth. Lowa leaped onto his back, grabbed the hilt of the knife and pulled. Tristan had been clever or was lucky enough to have put the knife in his mouth blade forwards, so he escaped without serious mutilation, but it was easy for Lowa to manoeuvre him to the back of the cart and kick him out.

Weylin was already up and running behind them with the guards. "Slings!" He shouted. Lowa dropped into the cart.

Dug was lying on his side, still struggling to free himself from the rope. "Watch out for slingstones, Spring!" he shouted.

"So you *do* know her?" said Lowa above the rattle of the careering cart.

"Aye. Like I said, every northern Warrior has a wee—" A stone whizzed through Dug's hair and he ducked lower.

Lowa peered over the back of the cart. The guards were ten paces away and keeping up. Slingstones flew. She ducked as they cracked into the backboard and zipped overhead.

"Where did you get the cart from?" shouted Dug.

"Where did you get the tart from?" Spring replied.

Lowa smiled. "Can we go any faster?"

"No. But there's a stable not far from the gate where we can steal some horses," answered the girl.

"Yes . . ." Lowa looked over the edge again. They were no farther from the running guards. She crawled up the cart, grabbed her bow and strung it. She peeked again, but the slingers were ready. She felt the wind of a passing stone on her cheek as she ducked. So she couldn't shoot the guards . . .

"Problem!" shouted Spring from the front. "Drawbridge is up!"

Lowa and Dug crawled speedily to the front. Bladonfort's residents were diving right and left to avoid the speeding oxen. Beyond them the drawbridge was indeed up, its counterweights hanging from ropes. Lowa looked at her quiver. There were two half-moon-headed rigging-cutter arrows in it, the ones she'd thought she'd never get a chance to use.

"Dug, I can cut the ropes, but the slingers . . ."

"I'll see what I can do." Dug gripped one side of the cart and shook. It didn't budge. He crawled across and tried the other. There was some give. "Arrgghhhh!" he shouted, pulling at the heavy plank.

"We're getting close!" Spring yelled. "What should I do?"

"Keep driving at the gate. Come on Dug!" Lowa shouted.

"We're nearly there!" Spring's voice was an octave higher.

"Drive at it! Don't slow down!" Lowa notched a half-moon.

Dug stood in a stoop and worked at the plank. Two sling-stones bounced off his back with painful-sounding *whumps*. The blows seemed to make him stronger. He wrenched the side of the cart free of its nails, spun and stood, holding it as a shield.

Lowa leaped up in its lee.

The counterweight was falling from the first severed rope as she loosed another arrow. It sliced the second rope, which whizzed through its pulley as the drawbridge fell open and banged down onto the stone quay. A heartbeat later the cart thundered across the River Bladon.

"Wait!" shouted Dug, leaping off the back with his hammer and makeshift shield.

Spring dragged the oxen to a halt.

"What are you doing?" Lowa shouted.

The guards, just the other side of the gate, saw their chance and sped up, yelling. Lowa could see Weylin a few paces behind them. "Take them alive!" he shouted.

Dug swung his hammer about his head, then down and round into the side of the bridge. There was a loud crack. The bridge shifted maybe a finger's breadth. The first guard was on the bridge, sword raised. Dug swung his hammer into the bridge again. There was a splintering, wrenching, crashing scream as drawbridge and guard fell into the river.

Dug sprinted and leaped back into the cart just as the first slingshots from the guards in the gateway hit the backboard.

Chapter 22

He was on the beach near the broch at night with Brinna. The light from the boat was like a white sunrise. They couldn't see who or what was aboard.

"What do they want?" said Brinna, clutching his arm.

"I don't know." Dug tried to wave the boat away. "We don't want you!" he shouted. "Go away!"

The light on the boat went out and the sun came up, and it was Lowa, standing in the place of a figurehead at the prow of a great sailing ship. The vast white sail was full, but the boat was still in the water, ten paces from the beach. Out of sight somewhere, all the horns of Maidun's army were blaring their cacophony.

"You want me to go?" Lowa said, pulling aside her brown dress to expose a firm white breast.

"No!" Dug looked at Brinna. Brinna stared back at him, ears smoking with hatred. "No, come here. We don't mind, do we, Brinna?"

Brinna opened her mouth to disagree, but instead she disappeared and became Lowa. She took his hand. The boat had gone and they were outside the broch. "Let's go inside," she said.

"Daddeee!" called both his little girls. They were standing on the sand dunes, wind whipping their red hair about their heads and the marram grass around their bare legs. Dug worried that the sharp edges of the grass would cut them.

"Forget them," said Lowa. "Come with me."

The wind rose and caught in his girls' dresses, lifting them and carrying them away.

It took Dug a moment to realise where he was. He was wrapped in a woollen blanket on the leaf-covered floor of the woodland enclosure where he'd tried to abandon Spring. They'd come back to it from the Bladonfort road leading two horses they'd stolen from the stable outside Bladonfort through the woods, diverting via his stashed mail shirt and helmet and waiting at one point as Spring stole blankets and food from a forester's house.

It had been dark by the time they'd arrived. They hadn't risked a fire in case anyone was looking for them, and it had been warm anyway. They'd supped on honey bread and apples stolen from the forester and Dug had gone to sleep quickly, Spring on one side, Lowa on the other.

Now the air was cold and wet but wonderfully clean-tasting after the dust and dung of the town. He rolled over. He could see Lowa's hair in the false dawn light, shining like polished iron. She was facing away from him, close enough that he could smell her scent of dried earth, musk and flowers. He closed his eyes.

"Do you want eggs? I found some duck eggs. After you didn't get eggs with my coin. Where is my coin?" It was full light now, and Spring was poking him with a stick. He looked about. There was no sign of Lowa. Someone had lit a fire. "She's washing. Do you want eggs? I have mushrooms too. And nettles. She picked some berries and fruit so we can have those too. And she gave me some salt. I'll put that in the eggs."

Lowa returned and nodded good morning. They sat on logs and passed the pan, taking turns to scoop out crisp egg and mushrooms with their fingers. Chewing, swallowing and

the whistles and squeaks of woodland birds were the only
sounds. When the omelette was gone, Spring filled the pan
with cherries, hazelnuts, blackberries and gooseberries, and
passed it around. The sweet food mixed well with the salty
egg remains, at least to Dug's ravenous palate.

His absorption with breakfast wasn't so total that it stopped
him from glancing at Lowa. After a night sleeping rough she
looked fresh and beautiful as a princess in a bard's story.
His interest was purely aesthetic, he told himself. There was
no way she'd be interested in him – she must have been a
good fifteen years younger. But there was no denying that
she was the first woman in a long time he'd been so immediately and powerfully attracted to. The first, in fact, since
he'd met Brinna at the ceilidh all those years before.

"That was good, child, thank you," said Lowa when the
omelette was gone. She had an accent that Dug couldn't
place.

"My name's Spring."

Lowa stood up. "I have to go." She wasn't a great deal
taller than Spring, Dug noticed.

"You don't," said Dug.

"See ya!" said Spring, snatching up the pan and heading
for the river.

"You don't have to go."

"I do. There are things I need to do."

"What?"

"I need to kill Zadar." Lowa picked up her bow and looked
about for her arrows.

"Right. What are you going to do for the rest of the day?"
She slung the quiver across her back. "Goodbye."

"Wait."

"What?"

"I'll help."

Lowa looked at him for a long moment then said, "No."
She turned again to go.

"What's your plan?"

She didn't reply. She was at the top of the bank now.

"You won't get anywhere, running at him with murder on your mind."

Lowa disappeared over the bank. Dug raised his voice.

"You'll be killed and Zadar will live happily ever after. You would have been killed yesterday if I hadn't been there!" No reply. He shouted, "And we'd both be dead if a little girl hadn't rescued us!"

All was quiet. She'd gone.

Ah well, thought Dug. *Probably for the best.* He looked for things to tidy around the camp, but it looked like Spring had done it all.

"OK. I'll admit that you may have been some help yesterday." Lowa was standing at the top of the bank, hand on hip. Dug smiled. The sun shone whitely in her hair. "But we would have escaped without the girl. We freed ourselves from those ropes."

"Aye, but we were well guarded. Without Spring it would have been near impossible."

"Maybe . . ."

"Let's face it. You're not much use on your own."

Lowa smothered a smile. "So what do you suggest?"

Dug shrugged. "That we make a plan."

"Why 'we'? Why do you want to help me?"

"I don't know why I want to help you. I just might as well. I had planned to join Zadar's army, but I've shat all over that path so now I haven't got much else to do."

"And I need you because . . . ?"

"I've been a busy mercenary nearly twenty years and a Warrior for over fifteen."

"So?"

"I'm still alive."

"That is a point." Lowa nodded.

Chapter 23

Weylin sat on the embankment, watching Zadar's court. The evening was lovely, but Weylin wasn't. His head was wound in an off-white woollen bandage and his arm was in a sling. His temples were tight with knots of pain. He felt sick. His wrist was pumping waves of hurt up his arm from where the oaf had whacked it with his hammer. Lowa Flynn had killed his wife earlier that day, badly hurt his brother and a good friend the night before and, worst of all, humiliated him. A wave of hatred almost made him vomit. *Why do bad things always happen to me?* he thought.

To cheer himself up he'd got pissed, obviously, then come to watch Zadar's court. The Maidun force that had crushed Boddingham and Barton was camped for the night in a broad, lush valley halfway between Barton and Maidun, by a bridge over the River Otterhold in the territory of the bee-worshipping Honey tribe. In common with most tribes, the Honey's gods normally dispensed justice through the druids. So, until recently, druids had been judge, jury and sometimes executioner. However, Zadar favoured a version of the Roman system, which separated law and magic, putting justice in the hands of magistrates. In Zadar's version, Zadar replaced the magistrates.

On that summer's evening Zadar was holding Honey assizes. Above him a few scraps of white cloud were drifting slowly across the blue sky. He was sitting on a throne – actually the village's biggest chair – in a fenced pasture. On benches either side of him were the usual crowd – Felix the druid, Chamanca and Tadman, the king's young mistress Keelin Orton, and others favoured by Zadar, including Savage Banba, a Warrior who Weylin had his eye on. Now that he was free of Deidre, there'd be more chance to do something about that.

His injured brother Carden and Carden's friend Atlas were absent, no doubt convalescing somewhere. Keelin was another who bore the scars of Lowa's escape. Her chin was swollen with purple-black bruising, and she had an expression like a hunting dog who'd swallowed one of the Honey tribe's bees. Weylin still would have given all the tin in Dumnonia for ten minutes alone with her. He looked away. It wasn't good to be caught staring at Zadar's mistress. So instead he looked at his king.

Zadar was wearing a close-fitting iron helmet, undecorated apart from a central iron crest the thickness of a finger. Lank blond hair spilled out along the rim, hanging down in front of his shoulders to the top of his plate iron breastplate, which was unadorned but for a necklace of boar's tusks. His fleshy lips were set in their usual thoughtful, piscine pout above a cleft chin coloured by days-old stubble. His large, hawkish nose seemed to be constantly sniffing out others' weaknesses.

The Honey tribe were gathered at the far end of the corral, surrounded by Maidun troops who were as much guards as spectators. As Weylin settled himself on the bank, two women peeled from the Honey tribe's ranks, approached Zadar and stood in full glare of his gaze. A man with an unkempt beard in a black peasant's smock and round yellow woollen hat – a local druid, Weylin reckoned, in a shit attempt at a bee-themed outfit – shuffled forward and placed a baby's basket on the turf.

"King Zadar!" cried the man. Everyone quietened. "Both these women claim this baby."

"What?" said Felix, face crumpling in disbelief. "How could that happen? Which one of you pushed it out?"

Chuckles pulsed from the Maidun troops. Both women started to talk at the same time.

"He's mine!"

"You bitch, I can't believe you were my friend!"

"You were never my friend, clearly! How could you claim him? He doesn't have your big ugly nose for a start, and another thing—"

"Quiet!" shouted Felix.

"Can anyone other than these women explain the situation?" Zadar asked. He sounded bored, but, even bored, his voice was like an iron sword drawn across a granite quern stone. Weylin shuddered despite the couple of skinfuls of medicinal mead that he'd knocked back.

"They came down the river in a skiff," said the yellow-hatted druid. "We never seem 'em before. They had a baby with 'em. She said it was 'ers." He pointed at one of the women, then the other. "And so did she."

"Hers died. This one's mine!" The women began accusing one another again.

"Silence!" shouted Felix again. Zadar leaned forward, chin in hand, and studied them. The crowd waited.

"The women will share the child," he said. "Tadman." The big bodyguard nodded. "Cut the baby in half."

Tadman strode forward, hefting his short-handled iron blade.

"Noooo!" screamed the shorter and older of the two women, dashing at Tadman. He met her with a backhanded slap. She fell. The other woman stood, arms folded, a small smile pulling up one corner of her mouth. The baby wailed.

"The one who attacked Tadman is the mother," said Zadar, wearily raising his voice above the baby's crying. "The smug one is the liar."

The rightful mother fell to her knees, moaning thanks. The other woman's smile dissolved. The Honey murmured approval of Zadar's wisdom. Tadman turned to walk back to his post.

"Tadman. You haven't finished." The German stopped. The crowd hushed. The baby's crying was the only sound. Zadar continued: "I told you to cut a baby in half. Why can I still hear a whole baby?"

The crowd gasped. The baby's mother collapsed. Weylin smiled. Tadman returned to the wicker basket and picked the squalling child up by its feet. He slid the blade between its legs. There was silence all around the field. Tadman looked at Zadar. Zadar nodded.

When it was done, Zadar said, "Give the rightful mother a piglet. She will learn to look after her young and I will see that piglet alive and happy on my next visit."

He turned to look at the false mother. A rare, barely noticeable smile crept onto his face.

"You, druid," The Honey's druid stared at him. "Fetch liars'-tongue scissors, a fire dog and a pot of cooking oil. You and you – " Zadar pointed at two of the Honey tribe " – help him. Someone else lay a fire." The woman made to bolt, but Chamanca was on her like an eagle on a crow. She tripped her, leaped on her back, gathered and gripped her arms, leaned forward and sank her teeth into her neck.

"Calm, Chamanca!" said Felix. "We don't want to hurt her yet."

Weylin smiled. This was what he'd come to see. Nothing like other people's troubles to make you forget your own.

Judging over, the Maidun troops dispersed, those of the Honey tribe still capable of walking carried those who couldn't away, and it was Weylin's turn to see Zadar.

He stood in the pasture in front of his king, bandaged head throbbing. The summer evening sky had turned the tenderest blue, melding to orange at the western horizon. Delicate insects floated up from the grass. Bees buzzed. Weylin could feel Felix's gaze worming through his mind.

"You let Lowa Flynn escape," said Zadar. It wasn't a question.

It wasn't my fault! But Weylin knew better than to disagree. "Yes," he managed.

"Her flight was aided?"

"By a band of men. Ten of them. Their leader said his
name was Dug."

"He introduced himself?"

"Yes. No. That's what his men called him. Tough buggers
they were. Northern. Murkan, I think. They killed everybody
else before we knew we were being attacked. Only my reflexes
saved me. I managed to do for four of them before they
knocked me out." He pointed at his injured head.

Felix leaned over to Zadar and spoke quietly in his ear.

"You were outwitted by a child. A girl," said Zadar.

How could he know?

"There was a girl." Weylin felt himself reddening under
the amused stares of Zadar's entourage. "But that was luck,
and it was mostly this northerner—"

"'This northerner'. Single. Not a group?"

Weylin looked into Zadar's emotionless eyes. They looked
like the eyes of a fish that had lain too long on the fishmon-
ger's slab. He glanced at Felix. Felix smiled back, terrifyingly,
then whispered something else to Zadar. *He knows what
happened.* The idea that Felix had been somehow watching
him made Weylin's bowels churn. What else did he know?
It was time to tell the truth.

"There was one northerner. He bested us through trickery,
with the child's help. They escaped on horseback."

"How old was the child?" Zadar asked.

Weylin's eyes darted to Felix. "Eight?"

Savage Banba barked a laugh. Tadman snorted. Even
Keelin's bruised mouth pulled into a pained smile.

"Tell me everything you can remember about both of these
rescuers. Leave nothing out."

Weylin told them all that came to mind. Zadar probed
further.

"So. Lowa has escaped you twice," Zadar said finally.

That was totally unfair. It wasn't his fault that the troops he took to Bladonfort had been so useless. And when Lowa had escaped from Barton, he and Dionysia had been two of many pursuers. Carden and Atlas were more to blame. They'd had her in their clutches and let her go.

"I am aware that others are to blame as well as you. I'm going to give you another chance, Weylin."

It was better than he'd hoped for. Felix looked disappointed.

"Pick twenty good Warriors and horses. Travel light and fast. I shall send shouts to all the tribes. They'll give you supplies and information. If they refuse, take what you need. Go back to Bladonfort and find their trail. Bring Lowa Flynn to me alive, uninjured. Bring me the child, unharmed. Torture the man Dug in front of every tribe you pass on your return. Make them watch. Explain that this is the penalty for defying me. I'd prefer him alive, but don't hold back. If he dies – " Zadar shrugged " – so be it. But make sure many people see him suffer. A lot. That will be all."

Weylin walked away through the warm, calm night into the camp. The shout went up behind him and echoed along the valley and over the hills: "To all! Capture Lowa Flynn and companions! Help Weylin Nancarrow!" The call would be relayed between the farms, hamlets and villages under Zadar's influence. By the end of the night there would be a network of people stretching a hundred miles in every direction ready to help him.

The shout's echoes died away as he walked through a camp that smelled of woodsmoke and horses. Zadar's rule that everyone must shit and piss well downstream of wherever they camped had caused much initial bitching, but nobody objected now that the camps didn't smell of a thousand people's crap. Plus it was brilliant riding through villages further down the river the following day and seeing their mills, dykes and fishing nets caked in turd.

Chapter 24

"So. What happened with Zadar?"

Lowa narrowed her eyes at Dug. What were his motives? Why had he risked his life for her and why did he want to help her now?

She abhorred vanity, but the most likely explanation was that he wanted to shag her. No, more than that – that he'd actually fallen for her. Not long ago a drunken Aithne had told Lowa that she wasn't overly attractive in any normal way, but she was the type that some men would always become besotted with. What Aithne had actually said was, "Not everyone gets you. Most guys would do you if they were drunk and you made it easy, but they'd just as happily shag me. However, there's something about you that some guys see and *really* go for, so there'll always be a number of men who'd be grateful to crawl two miles over jagged flint to sniff the cock of the last man who fucked you."

Aithne was right, perhaps not literally, but men did seem to fall heavily for her every now and then. It was a shame she never felt the same way. Usually she pitied her suitors, and pity was about as big a turn-on as incontinence.

Maybe Dug was different. He was old, but he was good-looking, and beneath a slightly bumbling exterior he was competent and relatively bright. And modest – she liked that. Even more, she liked that he hadn't tried to jump on her the night before. She couldn't see herself falling for him, but he was right, she could do with some help from him

and the weird little girl. Even if it was just guarding her
while she slept or being decoys while she escaped.

And if he did try it on . . . well, that would depend on
what sort of mood she was in when he made his move and
whether she'd been drinking.

"OK," she said. "I'll tell you."

Dug wobbled his bottom on the log like a duck settling
down on a clutch of eggs, making himself several degrees
less attractive. Spring, back from washing the breakfast gear
in the river, sat next to him and looked at her expectantly.
Well, Lowa thought, we've got hours before it'll be safe to
get back on the road, so I might as well begin at the beginning.

"My first memory is when our village was sacked and I
saw my mother, father, two older brothers and a younger
sister killed, along with uncles, aunts, cousins, my friends,
their families. All apart from me and my older sister Aithne.
We'd been gathering berries near the village . . ."

It took Lowa a long time to tell her story, accompanied by
the chirruping chatter of wrens and tits hopping about the
encircling foliage. She'd never done this before – she rarely
talked about herself – but she was surprised how easy and
enjoyable it was to tell everything to these strangers. She
wanted to get it out. She found herself impatient to carry
on when Dug spent too long off in the woods on his mid-
morning dump.

The rest of the time he listened attentively, asking questions every now and then. Spring whittled sticks. At one
point she left with her sling, came back with a moorhen and
cooked up a stew for lunch.

Lowa told them about her childhood of running and
fighting, how her band of archers had come together by
accident, how she'd come to work for Zadar, and how her
band had risen to the pinnacle of Zadar's favour before he

killed all those she loved and tried to kill her. She found herself telling Dug that the attack on Barton had been her idea. Zadar had intended to march straight past. Barton was a good fiefdom that paid its taxes on time. She'd persuaded him that they needed a strong northern base and that the slave price for the battle's survivors would cover a good few years of tax receipt. So it was her fault all those people at Barton had died, although, in her defence, she'd suggested blocking the bridge and capturing everyone, not slaughtering them.

Then, for no reason she could fathom, Zadar had had her women killed and tried to murder her too. So now she wanted revenge on Zadar. She didn't, she said, need or deserve any help.

Spring nodded. "We shouldn't help her, Dug. She's not a good person and she wouldn't help you." The girl had an intense look that naggingly reminded Lowa of somebody, but she couldn't think who. She kept almost getting it, but then the image dissolved like the tantalising memories of a dream.

"You're right. And I haven't asked for your help. But the people Zadar killed – my sister, the other four – were good people, and they deserve to be avenged, but . . . yes, there is no reason you should help me. This is my battle and I—"

"Shhhh!" Spring held a finger to her lips. She cocked her head. "Dogs. Over there. Coming nearer." She pointed in the direction they'd come from the night before.

Dug began to say something, but Lowa held up her hand for silence. Lowa had never met anyone with better hearing than herself, but it was a good thirty heartbeats before she could make out the barking of dogs. She looked at Spring. The girl smiled and nodded like a mother encouraging a toddler who's completed a simple puzzle.

Thirty more heartbeats, and Lowa was certain the dogs were coming in their direction. *Shit*. She'd thought she was clean away, but Zadar wasn't going to give up that easily. *What had she done?*

"Pack up. Quickly," she said.

Lowa gathered her bow and the meagre kit that Spring had pilfered from the forester, then helped Spring load the horses while Dug pulled on his mail shirt and helmet.

"Right," said Dug in his strange northern accent, already heading up one of the low banks. "We'll lead the horses up through the woods. There's a stream—"

"No," interrupted Lowa.

"No?"

"No. They're after me and they'll have my scent. You two take the horses and ride at speed along the river valley. You'll be faster in the open. I'll draw them up into the woods. When you hit the Bladonfort road, head west, away from Bladonfort. I'll meet you on the road."

"But they'll see us out in the open."

"Not if you're quick, and even if they do see you and for some reason they come after you instead of me, horses will outrun dogs."

"You're on foot!"

"I'll lose them in the trees. Get going. We don't have time for a debate. Just go."

Dug looked like he was going to say something else, but then climbed onto the larger horse. Spring, scowling, mounted the other, in front of their baggage.

"Yah!" Spring kicked the horse up the bank and out of the clearing. Dug bounced awkwardly after her.

Bow in hand and quiver on her back, Lowa Flynn set off up into the trees.

Chapter 25

Drustan and Ragnall carried the latter's father's tortured body from the battlefield at Barton on a stretcher made from spears and dead men's clothes. Ragnall was the same person he'd been two mornings ago, but so much was different. How could he be alive and unchanged when they were all dead?

Zadar's army had been easy enough to track. They'd followed the trail of looted farms and dead or terror-struck peasants. At night Ragnall hadn't slept. Terrible images — Navlin and the rats, his brothers, the angle of his mother's broken neck in the slave collar — tumbled in his mind. He'd thought he might go mad, but instead he went numb. So when they found his father among the corpses at Barton, dead with a bolt through each shoulder, attached to a cart next to some other luckless fellow, it wasn't a surprise.

Pupil and teacher carried the body to the woods and into a clearing, as they'd done with his mother. Ragnall felt sick with guilt that they'd left his brothers where they'd fallen, and everybody else at Boddingham for that matter. Drustan had told him that, given the circumstances, the gods would make allowances, and all the deserving would still drift happily to the Otherworld. They had given the rites, and that was enough.

He'd always accepted that when people died they went to the Otherworld, where they occupied new, strong bodies and lived lives of heroism, love and joy. Some druids could talk to the dead. Other people could see or hear the dead sometimes at liminal places – where the sea met the land, at the edges of woods, where fog became clear air. But they also said that the gods rewarded the good. His family had been good. Boddingham as a whole had been good. It was hard to see brutal early death as much of a reward.

Agonies and questions crawled over each other as Drustan chanted the rites for his father, Kris Sheeplord. Ragnall was the only Sheeplord left now. Probably. His brothers had had children, but it looked like Zadar had taken them, and when – if – they grew up, they were too young now to remember who they'd been. All he had left was Anwen.

He would find her. He would take her back from Zadar.

They left the stinking bodies on the battlefield and rode to the town of Bladonfort. Ragnall became like one of the dead himself. He stopped thinking. He did what Drustan told him to. They went to one of the cheaper inns by the lower market. It reeked of stale beer, bad food and vomit in the low-ceilinged common room, but the two men slumped down next to each other. Drustan signalled for beer. The old man was exhausted by the journey, Ragnall was still numbed.

It was shortly before sunset and the inn was busy with merchants, children of merchants, market stallholders and a small but noisy knot of soldiers. Nobody paid much heed to the two dusty men in the corner, incongruously quiet among all the liveliness.

Ragnall was halfway through his second beer before Drustan broke their silence. "We should head for Dumnonia."

Ragnall didn't look up. Dumnonia was Britain's southwestern limb. Maidun was directly south, a good distance from Dumnonia.

"Perhaps. After we've been to Maidun."

"Ragnall. What will happen if you walk into Maidun and demand Anwen?"

"If Zadar wants me to fight for—"

"Keep your voice down!" Drustan nodded at three

leather-clad soldiers at the bar. They were looking at Ragnall. He had been talking quite loudly. One was a large man whose luxuriant moustache was wet with beer. The other two were small and dark – brothers, even twins. Each had a small mace hanging from his belt. Drustan raised his mug and smiled at them. They glared back, about as friendly as a posse that's just caught up with a child killer. Drustan took Ragnall by the sleeve.

"I know it's difficult, but you've got to think about this more. There are so many obstacles on the direct path to Zadar, each of which is insurmountable. You've heard, for example, about Maidun Castle's gate?"

"What of it?" Ragnall finished his beer and signalled for another. The barman, a tall skinny man with a thin, disease-pocked face, picked an empty mug off the bar, wiped its rim with his apron and filled it from a barrel. He plonked the mug on the bar, looked at Ragnall, pointed at the beer with a long hairy finger, then headed over to where others were clamouring for drinks. Ragnall went to get his beer. The iron-ringed leather mug had a leak. He'd have to drink quickly.

The sat in silence again. Ragnall was thinking about Maidun's gates. It was the most secure hillfort in the land, they said. Its outer chalk wall was near-vertical and fifty paces high. The inner one was a hundred paces high, with a palisade all the way around. The only way in was through a mile-long labyrinth barred by three gates.

"You will not pass even the first gate," said Drustan as if reading his mind. "They will kill you for sport when you ask to see Zadar. They may decide that your demands to see their king are arrogant, and do worse."

"I'm not arrogant."

"No. But you look it."

It was true. Ragnall had heard it enough times before.

"But that's not the point."

"What is the point?"

"Victory comes from attacking when it is time to attack, and retreating when it is time to retreat."

They sat in silence until Ragnall said, "I can't do anything but retreat."

"You cannot attack alone."

"But who else——?"

"Come with me to my people in Dumnonia. Zadar holds no sway there."

"As far as we know."

"I've heard they're gathering an army. The best shot you've got at revenge is as part of a Dumnonian force. And a brain like yours will be useful to them."

"But Anwen?"

"Anwen's gone. Either she'll be kept in Maidun, where we can't reach her, or she'll be on a slave ship to Rome before we can get to the coast."

"We've got to find her."

Drustan's beard wobbled as he shook his head. "No. You're not thinking clearly. You think you'll be able to spirit her out of Maidun or perhaps follow her across the sea, rescue her and bring her home."

Ragnall had indeed been thinking along those lines. He said nothing.

"You will not. This is not a legend and you are not Lugh and you do not have a magic spear. Legends rarely dwell on practicalities, but these alone will beat you. What will you eat? Where will you get a boat? You will be killed and you might get her killed too. Chances are she will be sent as a slave to Rome. I have been there. I have travelled throughout the empire. Life under the Roman yoke is not nearly bad as they say. Away from the frontiers, in long-established territories, most Romans are decent. She will probably be taken in by a kindly family and have a good life. She may win her freedom or, more likely, have it bought for her by a man. If we do not find her when the Dumnonians take Maidun, then we can talk about tracking her to Rome."

Ragnall slumped a little. "If they take Maidun."

"Force is not the only way to breach walls. You have a great mind, Ragnall. Use it to help break Maidun, to defeat Zadar. Begin by coming to Dumnonia with me. Attacking with anger is like scooping molten iron out of a furnace with your bare hands instead of using tools to make a sword."

Ragnall thought about his brothers, his father, his mother. He saw those bolts through his father's shoulders. He must have died in miserable agony, knowing he was dying.

"No!" Ragnall stood up. "I will kill Zadar and I will do it today!" His chair crashed back against the wall and the table tottered. Beer slopped from Drustan's almost untouched mug as the druid grabbed it.

"You'll kill Zadar, will you?" It was one of the soldiers from the bar. He had a sharp nasal voice. His two friends looked on.

Ragnall walked slowly around the table. Drustan raised an arm to stop him, but Ragnall pushed it out of the way. He raised his handsomely cleft chin and looked down at the soldier along his well shaped nose. The soldier looked up with weasel eyes in a narrow, peasant face. Ragnall was a good head taller. He'd start his attack on Zadar by teaching this little –

Ragnall's balls exploded in pain. His breath left him in a feminine squeal as he went forward, hands gripping his groin in an effort to press out the agony. He saw a blur and his face was snapped sideways.

"Ragnall? Ragnall?" His head was bursting and his genitals were in a tightening vice. He could hardly think. Slowly the blinding blanket of pain became jolts of agony and he could see. He was curled on the sticky floor of the inn. Drustan was kneeling in front of him, a hand on his shoulder, looking into his eyes.

"What's your name?" he asked.

"What?"

"Tell me your name."

"Ragnall."

"And mine?"

"You're Damona the Sky Cow."

Drustan smiled. "Good. Have some of this." He handed Ragnall a beer.

"What happened?"

"You were a fool. You discovered the difference between boxing with a boy and fighting a soldier. It would have been worse but I paid him to stop."

"That little man?"

"Shhhh!" Drustan nodded back at the bar. The three soldiers leered at them happily and raised their mugs.

"The little one did this to me?" Ragnall said quietly. "He's half my size."

"Younger than you too. You may win in the boxing ring, but you were not made for rough fighting."

"Did his friends help?"

"No." Drustan wiped blood from the corner of Ragnall's mouth. "You are not ready to take on Zadar's army yet."

Ragnall put his head in his hands. "You could be right."

"It is interesting that a scare is always more effective than advice. We owe that little fellow more than coins."

"What?"

Drustan gripped the younger man's shoulder. "Never mind. But remember, when you set out for revenge—"

Ragnall interrupted. "Always prepare two funeral beds, one for you, one for your enemy. What I'd like to do to Zadar and the Maidun army though . . . we'd need a lot more than two."

Chapter 26

"She lied."

"What?" The earth was firm under the long grass of the meadow and the horses were trotting jauntily. Spring was rising and falling in rhythm with her little horse as if beast and rider were one. Dug felt like a jester riding for comic effect. No matter how he moved, he always found the counter rhythm to the animal's and whacked his arse against the horse's backbone with every bounce.

"That woman you're in love with. She lied."

"I am not in love with her."

"Are you going to marry her?" Spring treated Dug to a big mocking grin.

"How old are you?"

"Sixteen!"

Dug looked sideways at the girl. Her brown-blonde hair was billowing out behind her, self-satisfied little overbite smile and round nose pointed into the wind. She really was an odd little thing. He'd asked her how she'd come to be driving a cart in Bladonfort, and she'd ducked the question in such a way that he'd felt stupid for asking. She was brighter and more able than any child he'd met before, but there was no way she was sixteen.

"You're ten. If that."

"A formori cursed me to look young for ever."

"You've never seen a formori. They're all across the sea in Eroo."

"I've seen loads. They're a hundred paces tall and green

and covered in hair, and one cursed me to look young for ever because I'm too beautiful to ever grow old and ugly. There were two of them. The other one was blue. It didn't speak. It juggled sheep and farted like thunder."

"What do you mean she lied?"

"She said the dogs would follow her. They won't. Ogre had dogs. Five of them. If they're chasing riders, they track the horses' smell. Horses are much smellier than people. So a good way of escaping dogs is to change horses. But we only have these two."

"Who or what is Ogre?"

"My old boss. Boss of the man with the stupid hair who you killed too. He's bald. He looks like an angry egg. Ogre isn't his real name."

"The one with no ears?"

"Him. He has dogs and they follow horses. Not people. So that woman you're in love with lied."

As if to confirm her point, a deep-throated bark echoed along the valley. Dug turned. Three big dogs were bounding towards them through the long grass.

He couldn't believe she'd betrayed them. She must have been mistaken and she may have been wrong about who the dogs would follow, but surely she was right about horses being faster.

"See?" Spring smiled.

"Come on!" He whacked Spring's horse on the rump as she kicked its flanks. It sped ahead. Dug looked back again. There were four dogs now, already appreciably closer. They were British hunting dogs, tongues flopping in great black faces, dangling cords of thick saliva glinting, ears bouncing. They were not as tall as the great wolfhounds from Eroo, but much heavier. Like something between a bull and a bear, built of thick, springy muscle, with a hinged array of daggers for a mouth.

Behind the dogs three people burst out of the trees at a

sprint. It was the earless Ogre and the two other men from Spring's gang he'd seen off the day before. Now there was a coincidence. Were they following Lowa or chasing him for revenge?

He didn't have time to dwell on it. He heel-kicked his horse and it lurched. Somehow he gripped its mane and stayed on. The ground rushed underneath. They plunged into a dry stream bed and his tail bone hit his mount's back with a spine-jarring thump, then out again and the ascent sent him pitching alarmingly to the left. He hauled himself upright as the horse galloped on. He had never travelled so fast. Tears streamed from his eyes, snot bubbled from his nose and spread across his cheeks. The speed was extraordinary and his seat far from secure. He was deeply unhappy. Ahead, Spring was waving an arm over her head and . . . *singing*.

> Gosh, what a dong,
> Oh my, what a schlong,
> Thick as your leg and three paces long!

That spurred his confidence. If she wasn't scared then neither was he. He wiped his cheek with a sleeve. Grip with your thighs. He'd heard that somewhere. He tried it. The horse seemed to realise that he was getting his shit together and moved more smoothly. He leaned forward and patted it. *Aye, this was OK*.

The three men were dots in the distance now, but the dogs were closer. Maybe two hundred paces back, gaining every time he turned. *Badgers' tits!* he thought. These dogs clearly didn't know that they were meant to be slower than horses. Long distance, he consoled himself while shifting a thigh to free pinched skin. Dogs can't do long distance. Horses can.

A minute later the dogs were closer. It's easy to escape animals if there are two of you, he thought. You just need to be faster than the other bugger. He'd met a man once, a Gaul, who claimed he'd escaped a pack of wolves by tripping his companion and fleeing while the wolves ate him. He wasn't going to do that to Spring, but strangely he did seem to be catching up with her. Not just catching up. Overtaking her. Easily.

"My horse!" she wailed as he passed. Her eyes were bright with panic. He reined in. Spring caught up, but her horse looked done for. Every time its front right leg touched the ground it snorted with pain and half collapsed.

"I don't know what to dooo!" Her face was red and wet with tears. Her horse stopped. Dug dragged on his reins, slid off and ran to Spring, pulling his horse behind him. The lead dog was a hundred paces away. He grabbed the girl by the waist and swung her onto the uninjured mount.

"Noooo! Leave me and you go!" She grabbed at Dug, but he swatted her arm away and slapped the horse's rump so that it galloped off along the meadow. Spring turned, desperate-faced.

The dogs barked triumphantly, very close now.

The injured horse, reins still in Dug's hands, bucked in terror.

"I need my hammer, you stupid animal!" It was slotted through the leather straps that held the pack. He got a hand to its shaft but the horse reared again. As it came down, he punched it in the muzzle. It looked at him with hurt surprise.

He nodded an apology and struggled to wrench the hammer free from its bindings. His back was to the dogs. The barks were so loud now that they'd surely hit him any moment. Finally his hammer came loose.

He spun and stood ready, knees bent, bouncing from foot to foot, left hand up by the hammer's head, right gripped down at the shaft's end. The nearest dog was twenty paces away. It was big as the dancing bear from Bladonfort and coming at him – Dug realised with annoyance – faster than a galloping horse. Lowa had lied to save herself. He was an old fool.

The dog's eyes locked on to Dug's. It barked like a creature from the Otherworld and sped up.

He squatted lower, gritted his teeth and twisted to the left, ready to spring and backhand the hammer into the dog's head. His plan was to swing back left for the next dog, then repeat the manoeuvre for the other two. It sounded good in theory, but he'd never fought dogs. He'd seen what they could do on the battlefield though. Throats. That was their thing. The quick, efficient and devastating tearing of throats.

The dog leaped. Roaring fangs flew towards him.

The dog turned on its side in mid-air as an arrow thumped into its flank. It flew past him and thudded squealing to the ground.

Lowa stood at the edge of the trees, already loosing another arrow. An instant later the second dog was smashed to the ground, ploughing a furrow in the long grass. The power of that bow! The dogs were punched from their paths like they'd been hit by flying tree trunks. He'd never seen anything like it. No more than three heartbeats after the second dog had gone down, the third was somersaulting with a squeal. Now came the fourth. It was slower, a good thirty paces back from the others. Dug relaxed, smiling smugly at the dog about to die.

Nothing happened. The dog was still coming. It was the slowest because it was the biggest. By far. Come on, Lowa! Dug looked over at her.

She waved at him. He nodded towards the dog. She smiled and shook her head.

Badgers' fucking bollocks! Dug readied himself for the dog. It bounced its last few steps almost lazily and leaped for his face. He stepped to the right and swung the hammer. His weapon crunched bone. The dog was dead before it hit the ground. *That wasn't so hard*, he thought, almost collapsing with relief.

Two of the dogs weren't moving. One was yipping like a puppy and trying to scrabble to its feet, biting at the arrow sticking out of its shoulder. Dug walked over, said, "Sorry, dog" and caved its skull in.

"Shame, really," said Lowa, sauntering over from the trees. Dug remembered the human pursuers. He spun. The meadow was empty.

"They ran when the second dog went down," said Lowa. "They're probably watching us now. No point following them into the trees; they could ambush us too easily."

"Yeah. And thanks. Nice shooting."

"Not really." Lowa squatted to twist her arrow out of a dog's flank. "I can hit a running squirrel at twice that distance every time."

Dug made a *Well, aren't you clever?* face at the back of her head and said, "How did you get here so quickly?"

"While you were trotting, I was sprinting. I would have taken the dogs earlier, and the men, but there were brambles and other obstacles so I couldn't get out of the woods quickly enough."

"And the fourth dog?"

Lowa looked up and smiled. "I wanted to know if you could best a dog."

Dug fought his rising blush. "I could have bested all four of them."

"Sure!" Her dazzling smile seemed to leach the strength from his very bones. By Toutatis, she was attractive.

They both looked round at the sound of approaching hooves.

"You killed the dogs!" Spring reined back. For someone who'd been crying minutes before she looked very composed.

"That was your old gang," said Dug.

"Yes. And those are Ogre's dogs. The big one's called Titan.

The other three are Half-Titan, Anvil and Nipper. Do you keep your name in the Otherworld? Nipper was a girl. The other three were brothers. There was another one – Juniper. I wonder where she is?"

"Your old gang?" Lowa raised an eyebrow at Spring.

"Sort of." Spring looked away.

"Zadar must have contracted them." The arrow Lowa was pulling from the first dog's shoulder came out headless. She grimaced unhappily, and reached to her belt for her knife.

"Yes, he must have done." Spring dismounted and headed for the injured horse, which had limped down to the river for a drink.

Dug turned to Lowa, who'd plunged a hand into the dead dog and was reaching about for her arrowhead. "So you were . . ."

He was interrupted by a triumphant bark from the river.

It was the fifth dog. It must have come unseen along the other side of the river. It was charging at Spring, just paces away now. Spring's horse bolted limpingly, but the girl stood, frozen in terror.

Dug was far too far away. Lowa pulled her hand from the dead dog and dived for her bow, but it was too late.

The dog leaped and Spring disappeared beneath it.

Chapter 27

A few miles outside Maidun Castle, Elliax the Barton druid was walking beside his wife. They were joined by a light double slave collar – two iron hoops connected by a wooden rod. He was shorter than her, so he bore most of the pole's weight and it chafed his neck. Vasin could have stooped to relieve his burden, but she was walking tall with all the haughtiness that had grown over their years of marriage. If anything, she was striding faster than she usually did, rather than slowing down to allow for his shorter legs.

She hadn't spoken to him all day, and he did feel a twinge of guilt when he looked at the bandage that covered the wound where Felix had cut a small chunk from her arm. So he'd eaten it. So what? He didn't have a choice. She had plenty of fat to spare and they had to show willing now that they were among Zadar's upper echelons. Besides, he'd been hungry.

He was startled from his musings by a pained squeak from somewhere near Felix, who was riding next to them. The head druid's dark scowl slowly turned into a broad smile as he looked at something furry that struggled in his hands. Once it was still, he chucked it into the roadside ditch, cursing unhappily. He kicked his horse into a trot and rode away towards the front of the line. Elliax saw that the furry thing was a rat. It looked like it had had the life squeezed out of it. What the Fenn had that all been about? Nothing good, that was for sure. He shivered.

Chapter 28

Ragnall woke and wished that he hadn't. He thought he must have been poisoned and beaten with hammers. As the memories of the fight and the beer the night before pushed their brutish way through his mind like blunt knives through filth-sodden wool, he realised that he wasn't far wrong.

Drustan brought him water, then sat on the end of the bed and, as Ragnall drifted in and out of ill sleep, told him the story of the great flood.

"Many many years before even your grandfather's grand-father's grandfather was conceived, the gods went to war for a thousand years. Toutatis, god of weather, took to warring with particular enthusiasm and neglected to change the seasons. Kornonos, god of animals, was another keen war maker. He forgot to control the beasts. So the whole world froze in a winter that lasted a thousand years, the beasts became monsters and walked the land, and the magic that came from the gods was lost.

"Herds of hairy dragons with horns longer than a man gored or crushed anyone in their path. Great white bears, long-fanged cats and packs of enormous wolves hunted people. It was a bad time to be a human. Hunting parties were themselves hunted and eaten by beasts. Anyone leaving a village to forage on their own had little chance of returning. Soon animals began to attack the villages, smashing through walls, snatching babies from cots as the people fled.

"Thousands upon thousands were sacrificed to the gods in an effort to halt the scourge. Mothers sacrificed sons, daughters sacrificed fathers. All to no avail. The gods were busy with their war and had no time for the bleating of humans.

"Finally a wise old woman called Sara travelled from tribe to tribe, calling on them to unify, to flee the cold and the beasts. Desperate and dying, the tribes listened to her, and she led thousands south to lower land, where the frost was less severe. Under Sara's direction they built a wall, miles around, too high and too strong for even the largest beasts to breach. In a coming-together of tribes never seen before or since, they founded the city of Tans Tali.

"Sara showed the people how seeds produced plants, so they stopped foraging and fed on crops grown within the walls. She showed them how to rear herds of cattle and sheep, so there was no need for hunting. Outside the walls the animals howled and roared in the snow. Inside the walls all were safe and well.

"Sara said that the gods had forgotten humans, so humans had to look after each other. We don't need their magic, she told them. The people saw that she'd saved them from the cold and the beasts, and began to worship her instead of the gods. Tans Tali became a place of peace. Every life was sacred. There was no fighting and no murder. Animals were well looked after. When they were killed for food, it was done as swiftly and kindly as possible. No creature nor humans was sacrificed.

"Thousands of thousands flocked to Tans Tali. All who entered saw the town's inhabitants growing fat and old. Compared to life outside the walls it was a paradise, and almost all new arrivals quickly grasped Sara's ideals of peace.

"Some didn't like it. They said that Tans Tali was against the gods, and stubbornly stayed on the higher land, fighting the animals and the cold, making sacrifices that the gods didn't see and trying to use magic that the gods no longer gave to them. Their numbers dwindled as many were killed, or seduced by the comfort of Tans Tali. But some survived.

"Tans Tali grew. Walls were added to walls. Soon the city was a hundred miles around and still growing. All lived in harmony and all the tribes became one tribe. Before Sara died at the age of six hundred, she arranged for her successor to be chosen by the casting of lots. Every man, woman and child in the city had one lot to cast for the leader they favoured. This became their way after every king or queen died, so only the great and good were ever chosen to lead. Tans Tali flowered.

"Great houses became palaces. The farms became towers, with mobile mirrors reflecting the sun to feed the grass and crops inside. The palaces became places of learning, where men and women would write and read long scrolls. These written words had one main theme. They said that there were no gods and that man was the supreme being. Freed from worshipping the gods, the arrogance of men and women knew no bounds.

"People have to worship, however, so they worshipped each other. The strongest, fastest at games and most beautiful were made into human gods. The masses aped their ways, copying their dress and behaviour. They could not offer animals or human sacrifices as Sara had forbidden it, so instead they gave their time and belongings to these imitation gods.

"After two thousand years Danu and Bel were triumphant. The other gods bowed to them, then returned to their duties.

"Toutatis saw that Tans Tali had conquered the weather and was enraged. Kornonos saw that Tans Tali had subjugated the animals and was consumed with anger. Makka, god of war, saw that fighting had ceased in Tans Tali and was choked with fury.

"All the gods saw how men and women had forgotten them and turned to worshipping themselves. Warring, hunting, foraging, sacrificing – this was the way of things. Most of the gods did not like to see anything changed, particularly when it wasn't their idea. Some argued that they should adapt to the new ways. After all, had not the gods forgotten the people first?

"Toutatis, Makka and Kornonos were having none of this. Tans Tali was low-lying, now spreading hundreds of miles along a river in a broad valley. North of the city were sheets of ice two miles high, stretching for thousands of miles. Toutatis set about melting the ice with sunlight, lightning and hot rain.

"Danu saw their plot. She called the three gods to her, listened to their arguments and saw that they were right. Humans needed to be punished. But in her kindness she sent a signal to warn mankind of the coming doom. She mixed the sun and the rain to create a rainbow. Every day for a hundred days she made a rainbow above the markets, palaces and farms of Tans Tali.

"Almost everybody ignored Danu's sign. The gods had not been worshipped for hundreds of years in Tans Tali. The very concept of divine beings had become risible, food for intellectuals' mockery. But the few outlanders left in the wilds had kept the gods. They saw the rainbows and knew what they meant. Many fled to higher ground. A few went to Tans Tali to warn the populace. Most of them were laughed out of town. Some, however, with charisma and the power of their oratory, persuaded people from Tans Tali to leave with them, and small groups headed back to the wilds.

"While Danu had been making rainbows, Toutatis had made a broad deep sea far to the north of Tans Tali, held on its southern shore by the two-mile-high dam of ice.

"At dawn on Samain, at the end of summer a year from the end of the war of the gods, Toutatis destroyed the wall of ice with bolts of lightning. The sea flooded over Tans Tali, obliterating it and all who lived in it. More people than all those who live in the whole world today were crushed and drowned in an hour. The sea made by the flood is still there, separating Britain from the rest of the world and filling the ocean to the west. Everywhere else – in the lands of the black men, the yellow men, the red men – the sea level rose by a hundred paces. Countless other cities and tribes were obliterated.

"The tribes who'd escaped the destruction saw what had happened and swore never to forsake the gods again. They returned to the old ways of hunting and foraging and the gods were pleased. All writing – the pernicious symbols by which mankind had argued itself away from belief – was banned. To keep belief in the gods strong, it was decreed that all learning must be passed from mouth to mouth, from generation to generation, so for as long as people exist, the gods will be remembered. Despite this, the unforgiving gods now deemed humans unworthy of their magic. To this day, only a few men and women are able to access the gods' powers.

"The message of the gods remains today alongside their revenge. We must remain hard, we must war, we must hunt, we must forage and we must never write. We must accept that adversity is the way of the gods. When we lose those we love, we must remember that they are in the Otherworld. They are not lost and we will see them again. But there is no point in looking for them in this world."

Ragnall stayed curled up, facing away from Drustan. His face was sore and his balls throbbed. He'd heard the story of the flood a thousand times, but he knew what Drustan was trying to tell him.

But there was Anwen. He had to find her. If anything, the beating from the little man had been a blessing. He'd seriously thought he was just going to walk right on up to Maidun Castle, defeat a champion or two perhaps, and stroll away hand in hand with Anwen. Now he'd taken on one small man and received the beating of his life, the idea was less appealing. As a bonus, he'd also discovered that not all bullies were cowards.

"Drustan." Ragnall's voice was harsh. He coughed.

"Have some more water." Drustan handed him a skin and he gulped it down.

"You're right. I'll come to Dumnonia with you."

"Good. It is the only way."

It's the only way at the moment, thought Ragnall. Yes, he'd set off with Drustan and maybe even go as far as Dumnonia, but he wouldn't stop searching for opportunities to get back to Anwen and have his revenge on Zadar.

Chapter 29

"It died?" Dug scooped some dog spit off Spring's shoulder and turned her round, checking for injuries. She seemed unharmed. The dog that had attacked her lay on the grass. It was dead, but its eyes still looked alive, blazing with hatred.

"Its heart must have stopped," said Lowa.

"Bit weird," said Dug. "And look at its eyes. I'd say it was under a glamour – controlled by a druid."

Lowa looked at him pityingly. "And is the druid watching us from its dead eyes?"

"Maybe?" Dug reddened.

"It's not that weird. The heart pushes your blood around. If that stops you can't move and you die. I've seen Felix prove it. Your heart pushes the blood faster when you exert yourself, and it's more likely to break when it's going faster. The surprise of a breaking heart is enough to give any creature a strange look on its face. There's no glamour here."

"But just as it was leaping . . . ?" Dug looked at Spring, who was walking towards her horse, making soothing noises.

"If it's going to happen, it's got to happen some time. Why not just as it was leaping?"

"You don't think she stopped it with," Dug whispered, nodding at Spring, "*magic*?"

Lowa looked at him. *Oh dear*, she thought. "No. I don't. I've seen enough failed healings and false prophecies to know that magic is a story for children. Nothing more."

"But druids—"

"Are full of shit. One of their best tricks is persuading people that coincidences mean something. They don't. An eagle attacks a crow as an army lines up for battle and they all go 'Oooooh' and it's some big omen. But it isn't. It's just something that happens, happening."

"Aye, I suppose so." He looked a long way from convinced.

"OK, so what were the chances of us meeting? Of all the people in the world who have ever lived and ever will live, how odd was it that we were both in that tavern at the same time? Certainly no weirder than an elderly dog with a weak heart happening to die after a long run."

Dug looked up at the sky, then shook his head. "Nope, don't see what that's got to do with it. We were just in the pub. It's hardly the same as a dog dying when it's about to kill a wee girl."

Lowa sighed. "Come on. Let's get out of here before Ogre can report back."

Part Two

Kanawan

Chapter 1

They found a caltrop in the hoof of Spring's horse. With the three-spiked iron device dug from her footpad, the horse seemed happy enough walking with Lowa and Spring on board, but Lowa stole a third horse from the first homestead they came to. "Can't have too many horses," she said.

An hour further north, she asked Spring to steal food from another settlement.

"We'll leave a trail," Dug said while they waited for the little thief.

"We will." Lowa nodded.

As the day darkened, she led them off the road. They dropped down a steep wooded bank and doubled back southwards, single file along a dark streambed. After a few miles they clambered out of the widening watercourse onto a road that headed west, away from Zadar's territory.

The crescent moon and starlit road wound around hills, forded streams and a couple of rivers, and plunged through forests of broad-leafed trees. They skirted three sleeping villages. The round huts with their conical roofs, blue in the moonlight, could have been haystacks for all the life they showed. The only large animals they saw were a family of beavers, who lolloped ahead of them along the road for a short time before disappearing into the woods.

The night was old by the time they heard the shouts of Zadar's messaging system. Dug didn't catch the exact words, but "Lowa" was definitely one of them.

"We'll be safe where we're going," she said as the echo died.

"But they'll hear the shout. Whatever it was."

"'To all. Capture Lowa Flynn and companions. Help Weylin Nancarrow,'" muttered Spring.

"It doesn't matter if they do hear it," said Lowa. "We'll be safe. We've nearly reached a village called Kanawan. It's run by a friend of mine. We can lie low with him until Zadar stops searching for us and relaxes his guard."

The idea of lying low with Lowa appealed to Dug. Relaxation, he'd always thought, was most enjoyable when it was forced upon you so it didn't feel like indolence; like the time he'd broken a leg and couldn't do anything apart from lie in the sun, drink cider, eat and watch the world go by. But he didn't like the sound of this friend much.

Some while later the eastern sky began to pink behind them. Colour suffused the hills, meadows and trees so softly and sweetly that Dug almost had to blink back a tear at the beauty of it all. So quietly that he could hardly hear it at first, Spring began to sing.

> A formori is a fearsome beast,
> With purple fur and rows of teeth.
> Don't you ever hit it with a sword,
> Cos it'll rip off your prick
> And chew on your balls.

Dug assessed his two new companions. Lowa rode in front, head up, more like a hero setting out on a quest and still within view of his tribe than a woman who'd been riding all day and night. Next to him Spring lolled into sleep then jerked awake with a snort. A strange child and a beautiful, skilfully vicious young woman. By all the badgers' arses in Britain, what was he doing? Three days before he'd been on his way to sign up with Zadar's army for a lifetime of remunerated sloth. Now he was a fugitive fleeing Zadar's army out of choice, and he'd managed to adopt a child by mistake.

Yet helping Lowa seemed the decent thing to do, and it had been a while since he'd done the decent thing. Brinna would approve. He wasn't helping her because she was achingly attractive. It was nothing to do with the way that she made him feel like the king of the world every time she spoke to him. And the girl? He liked her. When he'd left her, it was because he couldn't bear being responsible for her. Now, it wasn't just that she was perfectly capable of looking after herself. There was something special about her. The gods clearly loved her no matter what Lowa said about coincidence. He felt honoured that she seemed to have chosen him to hang around with.

He looked from one to the other. He'd travelled with innumerable companions over the years – great Warriors, hilarious bards, fascinating men and women – but he could never remember being as happy as he was with these two. It's odd, he thought, where life leads you.

Pale dawn lightened into blue morning sky. The road crested a hill to reveal a thriving agricultural valley. Clusters of round huts, triangular grain stores and other buildings lay either side of a grey river. A patchwork of fields was outlined by a network of stone walls and wooden fences. Some fields were given to corn, flax or oats, others were pastures containing pigs, sheep, cattle and horses. On the far side of the valley the road climbed to a small hillfort. There was no sign of life on the fort, so it looked like everyone was down in the village, not expecting any trouble.

Chapter 2

Weylin didn't like him. He had no ears but seemed to be able to hear. That was freaky. If you block your ears you can't hear, so how can you hear if you don't have any? He'd have to ask Felix. The druid was sure to have chopped someone's ears off at some point to see what happened. Deaf or not, the squat, tough-looking man had an attack-first-and-don't-ask-questions-ever air about him. There were plenty of aggressive twats like that in the Maidun army. Weylin had found that one, it was best not to upset them, and two, they tended to upset easily.

He'd been asking in Bladonfort for information on Lowa Flynn. Annoyingly, the story of the day before had got about and he was getting more questions than answers. Who was she? Where had she learned to use a bow like that? Who'd made the bow? Who was the strong man who'd smashed the bridge? Had he heard about the child who'd outwitted Zadar's best? The last question was asked by people, he was pretty sure, who knew that it was he who the child had outwitted. Their mockery made him yearn to torture information out of them, but he believed that they didn't know anything more than he did about Lowa, and he didn't have the time for pointless torture. He had the inclination for it though. He resolved to return, find everyone who'd disrespected him that morning and make them regret it.

Down in the lower market Savage Banba had brought the man Ogre to him. She'd been the first person he'd picked to make up his twenty-strong pursuit group, more because he wanted to sleep with her than for her fighting skills. She hadn't seemed particularly impressed. In fact to get her to come at all, he'd needed to tell her that he was working directly for Zadar and to talk to him if she had a problem. No matter. He'd show her.

He stood close to Ogre, almost shouting over the din of the bustling market.

"You're sure it was Lowa Flynn?"

"Smallish, blonde hair, shoots a bow like Kornonos?"

"That's her."

"Travelling with a man and a child."

"Possibly."

"She killed my dogs. I want compensation."

Weylin stared at the man with loathing. Ogre looked back, small eyed, thin lips turned down at the corners in an inverse smile. *Compensation.* How he hated people who blamed every- thing on everybody else, who couldn't accept that accidents happened. He'd lost his fucking *wife* yesterday. He didn't need compensation. Revenge, yes. Gold or some other kind of unre- lated reparation, no. He stifled an urge to headbutt the man.

"You can get your 'compensation' from Flynn when we find her. Tell me all you know about where she was heading."

"Nah." Ogre put his hands on his hips. The corner of his lips rose into a smile, but there was no mirth in it, only derision and challenge.

"No?"

"Happens I'd like to catch up with her myself. Like you said, I need to collect my compensation for the dogs. I'll tell you where she went when we get there."

"What?"

"I'll come with you on your hunt. I can help you because I know which way she went." Ogre enunciated each word as if talking to a simpleton. Behind him his two henchmen grinned toothlessly. Their leader was teasing the Warrior, and they were loving it.

Weylin's head hurt. He'd managed to turn another conversation into a battle and, yet again, he was losing. How did other people manage to talk to each other so easily? *Fuck it* he thought. He'd take the earless thug and his two skinny men with him. He didn't want to overstate Lowa's skills – he could have definitely taken her in a fair fight – but having twenty-three people under his command would be better than twenty, and anyway the chances of a fair fight were very slim. He'd kill these three when he found her, or maybe Lowa and that fucker Dug would do the job for him.

"All right. But you're going to do what I say, and we take Flynn unharmed. Got it? I report directly to Zadar. You do not want to fuck with me."

Ogre looked him up and down. "You're right. I wouldn't think that anyone would want a fuck with you." Everyone laughed apart from Weylin. "But seriously," Ogre continued, "you can trust me, my friend."

When Weylin and his brother were children – he must have been about six years old and Carden ten – they'd swum in the sea. They'd gone to the coast with another family. Their mother, Elann the blacksmith, had as usual been too busy to come. "Swim between my legs!" Carden had said. Weylin did everything Carden told him to, so he'd taken a breath and dived down. Carden had closed his legs and trapped him. He'd thought it was a joke at first, but then Carden hadn't let him go. He remembered as if it were yesterday the moment when he'd realised Carden was trying to kill him. When his struggles had weakened, Carden had opened his legs and pulled him to the surface. "Learn a lesson, Weylin," Carden had said as Weylin gasped in sweet air. "Never trust anyone."

And he never had.

"Why do you want Flynn?" he asked Ogre.

"Like I already said twice. Compensation for the dogs."

Weylin looked down at the stout criminal, then looked

around. About ten of his own troops had gathered behind him while they were talking.

"Tell me what you want out of this—" Weylin leaned down and spoke directly into Ogre's puckered earlump "—or I'll cut you down here."

Ogre stepped back, palms spread in supplication but still smiling smugly.

"All right. I want the girl who's with them. She's my daughter. I'd let her go – cocky little bitch she is, more trouble than she's worth – but the wife wants her back."

So he wanted the girl that Zadar wanted. That was decided then. He'd definitely have to kill Ogre when he'd served his purpose.

"All right, my friend, I will trust you." He put a hand on Ogre's shoulder. "Lead the way."

Chapter 3

Drustan bought them places on a guarded caravan heading south-west to Dumnonia. They joined around twenty merchants and ten guards. The latter were swivel-eyed men and women, armed and armoured as if they were expecting the war with the gods to restart at any moment.

Despite the good roads, with several wagonloads of wares that had to be unloaded and displayed wherever anyone might have a coin or two, progress was halting through the strangely mixed landscape of southern Britain. In the first few places they passed, Drustan told Ragnall that little had changed since his last time on this road a decade before. Children and dogs ran out of prosperous villages and towns to greet the convoy, and the merchants laid out their wares for well dressed healthy-looking inhabitants. In other places Zadar's destructive tentacles were obvious. In the afternoon they passed several shattered, deserted farmsteads and then a village where they were stared at by moon-eyed peasants only a few missed meals from starvation. The wagons rolled straight on through these shabbier places while the merchants carried on conversations and looked at the road ahead.

"So go the whims of Zadar," said one of the merchants called Simshill when a particularly grim village's last broken hovel was safely behind them. Simshill was an even-featured woman about thirty years old, with tight leather trousers. She had the sleekest black horse and the most alluring come-get-me eyes that Ragnall had ever seen.

He'd heard of this new class of tradespeople. There had

always been itinerant merchants, but they tended to be eccentric lone operators, trundling about the country with a wagon-load of goods for barter. They were travellers foremost, keen to see the world or escape a particular part of it. The exchange of goods was a means to that end. Ragnall had heard that nowadays merchants were less travellers and more horders, as obsessed with the accumulation of gold as dragons. Melancholy after his string of tragedies as well as prejudiced against these coin grubbers, Ragnall didn't seek their conversation, but it was unavoidable. He was surprised to find that, for the most part, they were decent men and women whose motives seemed to be a mixture of enjoying themselves and improving the lot of their families. There was one unpleasantly opinionated man who thought he knew best and spoke over everyone else, but that was heartening because, as Drustan pointed out, every group needs its twat, and if you're in a group of people and there isn't a twat, then it's you.

He'd heard plenty of tales of far-off places on the Island of Angels, but the tales the merchants told were different because they were from an adult world and because most of them were about Zadar. On their first night at an inn the merchants outdid each other with tales of Maidun army atrocities. Some of them were truly horrific. Ragnall's resolve to bring the tyrant down was stiffened. To Ragnall's surprise, Simshill's glances and smiles were having something of a stiffening effect on him too. For the first time ever he was tempted to be unfaithful to Anwen, just days after finding his brothers and parents dead.

"Ah yes," said Drustan when Ragnall told him about his unbidden lust. "Grief is not as simple as we would like. Before we experience it, we imagine it will be as sluice gates that drop, shutting off all flows of joy and turning us into woe-weighted living dead. In fact, after grief bludgeons its way into their lives, everyone apart from the most self-indulgent posturers who don't need to work every day to provide food – kings, druids and bards, for example – find themselves carrying on very much as before. The mundane acts of existence temper grief more than kind words or fine philosophy.

"So, despite ourselves, very shortly after bereavement we laugh, enjoy food and yes, develop carnal fantasies. The latter is particularly common. I suspect it's because emotions have been stripped raw, allowing previously suppressed, baser instincts to surface. If I had a sheep for every grieving girl who had offered herself to me after I said words for her dead father . . . I would have four sheep. Perhaps four and a half."

The old man was right, he was sure, but Ragnall was determined to be neither happy nor horny. He was an iron-jawed hero out for revenge, with no time for frivolous humour or giddy fantasising. But his thoughts kept returning to Simshill.

"Of course that is one way in which we will be better off once the Romans get here."

Drustan was still talking.

Ragnall perked up. "The Romans?"

"Yes. In Rome and in their empire, woman have a subservient role to men. They are treated in a similar fashion to our horses or dogs."

"What?"

"Women's lives are better under Roman rule. They don't have to fight in armies. They don't have to train as smiths or jewellers. They don't have to face the same challenges as our women do."

"Don't have to?"

"Well, are prohibited from."

"They don't fight?"

"There are women neither in the Roman legions nor among the auxiliaries taken from the people they conquer."

"So men do all the work?"

"Men do the mentally taxing and dangerous work. Women do other tasks. They work the fields and dig for minerals, but men oversee building, govern every settlement, run all martial matters and so on."

"Wow."

"Yes. It is a better system."

"I'm not sure . . ."

"And of course men marry, but in Rome it's laughable that a man should be faithful to one woman. They can sleep with any woman they find attractive – friend's wives and daughters, slave girls, and prostitutes of course. Under Roman rule you could enjoy three days of lust with Simshill, and nobody would think that it diminished your love for Anwen. Anwen included."

"That's outrageous," said Ragnall. But he did see some benefits in the Roman approach.

On the third day, when they'd travelled only about fifteen miles in total, they arrived in an idyllic-looking village. Ragnall particularly liked the ancient bench that encircled an even more ancient oak tree in the centre of the green. The merchants set out their wares around it. He sat on the bench for a while, watching the villagers file past the trestle tables of goods. As the morning passed, he found himself taking a look at his travelling companions' merchandise for the first time.

He'd expected lucky charms, hair-growth potions, statues of gods, woollen scarfs and so on. In fact, it was mostly second-hand, everyday belongings. There were weapons, farming equipment, an ivory comb with several teeth missing, a three-legged wooden dog with nails for eyes, several rusty daggers, a great blade on a pole and other mixed oddments.

He wandered away and found Drustan lying on a grassy bank by their horses, studying the blue sky. His white hair and beard were bright in the sun. Ragnall shooed away the horsefly that was circling his old teacher's head and sat down on the grass.

"Have you seen the merchants' wares?"

Drustan started up onto one elbow and blew air out between his teeth. He looked troubled. "You are wondering where the merchants find their goods."

"What?" Ragnall looked at Drustan. Drustan looked back. "Where do they get them?"

"The merchant's wares come from battlefields and sacked villages," Drustan said in exactly the same tone he'd used earlier that morning to explain why only an idiot would build a windmill when a watermill was possible.

"They're bodyrobbers!"

"And?" Drustan was frustratingly calm. "It makes sense. The dead do not need these things."

Ragnall balled his fists and ground his teeth and spoke slowly. "They are making profit from the dead. That cannot be right."

"When a tree falls it is eaten by the forest."

Ragnall stared at Drustan and saw his eyes flicker away. He turned.

"Hi, Ragnall. Drustan." It was Simshill, heading back to her stall of murdered people's belongings.

"You know I can't travel with these merchants any further?" Ragnall said when she was out of earshot.

"Yes. There are other routes."

Ragnall turned to pack, then stopped and turned back. "You knew I wouldn't want to travel with them when I found out what they were selling, didn't you?"

"Yes."

"But you were happy to let me travel with them?"

"The situation has changed only because you know. Think of a woman who is unfaithful to her husband in the first year of marriage. Their son is another man's. The husband does not know. Ten years later he finds out. That is when the situation changes, not before."

"Oh for Danu's sake."

"Come on. We will go."

Chapter 4

They dismounted at the edge of the village and Lowa led them to a hut. It was the standard circular wattle and daub construction, but a strikingly large and tidy example. A low stone wall surrounded the straight-sided hut and a well kept space that was part agricultural workshop, part flower garden. A bare-chested young man was doing press-ups outside the hut's porch, apparently oblivious to their arrival.

"Eighty-six, eighty-seven, eighty-eight!" he counted as he pumped up and down. His arm muscles shifted like stoats racing through a haggis skin. *I don't like you*, thought Dug. He glanced at Lowa. She was eyeing the young man appreciatively, in much the same way, Dug realised with a sinking stomach, as he'd eyed her when she'd come back from washing in the river the previous day.

"Bet he just started when he saw us coming," he whispered to Spring. "He'd be sweating if he'd really done that many."

Spring was staring open-mouthed at the man and didn't seem to hear him. *Not her as well? thought Dug. Surely she's too young?*

Lowa pushed open the low gate into the garden. "Farrell."

The man leaped up and swept blond shoulder-length hair from his eyes. He was medium height, about Lowa's age. His square jaw was beardless. Welcoming blue eyes shone from a tanned, effeminate but handsome face that radiated relaxed confidence and decency. He wore clean woollen trousers and leather boots. His lean, hard, lightly tanned torso was unscarred by battle. He wore a jewelled gold bracelet on each wrist. Dug found himself clasping his one remaining plain bronze bracelet as if to cover it up.

"Lowa!" The young man strode over and embraced her manfully for far too long, before looking up at Dug and Spring. "And who are these?" he asked, his ruling-class accent tinged with the laughter of happy welcome. Lowa told him their names and said: "This is Farrell Finda, King of Kanawan."

"Come come!" boomed Farrell. "You must have been travelling for hours. Enid!"

A girl about Spring's age with straight eyebrows, a high forehead and a freckly nose walked out of the hut, wiping her hands on a white apron. "Dad?"

"Put the horses out please darling, for Lowa, Spring and Dud. This is my daughter Enid."

Spring giggled.

"That's Dug," said Dug.

"Sorry, old man! Come in, come in and meet Ula! We've enough food for all. You must sit and rest and tell us what brings you to our humble village." Farrell swept a woollen coat from a hook on the wall and pulled it on. It was the reddest coat Dug had ever seen. Farrell fastened it with five bone toggles carved, if Dug wasn't mistaken, into the shape of mice.

He looked down at his own tatty, brown, unadorned outfit, then followed Farrell into his big round hut. Inside it was clean and neat. There were tartan rugs draped over furniture and furs on the floor. A section of the conical roof had been folded back, so all was bright and airy. Shelves were lined with swirl-decorated pots, long-necked jugs and a few of the smaller, patterned Roman wine amphoras. Along one wall was a display of long-handled, short-toothed, antler-carved wool-weaving combs, decorated with circles and lines. Arranged teeth up, they looked to Dug like a row of dandy dogs' paws. Up north, the kind of time devoted to producing such fancy goods was channelled into making better weapons.

The home was large enough for the sleeping quarters to be two separate little rooms, shielded from the main chamber by heavy leather curtains. A pot bubbled gloopily over the central hearth. A large oval shield leaned against one wall. Its polished bronze boss was surrounded by an elaborate design of what was meant to be two dragons with their tails in each other's mouths but looked more to Dug like canni-balistic tadpoles. He curled his lip at it. That lovely piece of kit had never deflected a spear blow, and, with that soft bronze boss, wouldn't last long if it tried.

But it did look good. The whole hut did. Expensive and unnecessary decoration aside, the hut was exactly the sort of place Dug would have loved to have lived in. In fact, replace the poncey decorations with functional kit, swap the cow leather for sealskin, change the mud and wood walls for stone, and it wasn't that different from the broch he and Brinna had so lovingly and enthusiastically done up when he'd been a little younger than Farrell, before it had all gone wrong.

A woman emerged from one of the sleeping chambers.

"This is my wife, Ula," said Farrell, chest swelling as he pointed at her. "I'll leave you here for a while. You're in good hands!" He ducked out of the hut.

Ula was a svelte young woman with black hair falling sleekly over her shoulders onto incongruously large breasts. She had questioning eyebrows, large blue eyes, a sharp chin and plump, almost bruised-looking pink lips with a mischie-vous curl of smile. Her only adornment was a heavy blue-glass bracelet – no gold – but the way she held herself suggested that she had a hoard of riches packed away and didn't feel the need to show it. *Old money*, thought Dug. Her woollen dress was simple but well made, lighter than Dug had seen wool spun before, with braid edging and a woollen belt that accentuated her narrow waist.

She pulled rug-draped chairs closer to the hearth. "Please, do sit," she said.

They sat and Ula doled out a hot porridge of oats, nuts, seeds and honey. The ladle was polished bronze, and the bowls lathe-turned, of a quality that Dug had only ever seen used for display. The porridge would have been good at any time. After their sleepless night on the road, it was sigh-inducingly delicious. The three of them guzzled in happy silence as Ula looked on, pleased at their enjoyment. As they were finishing, Farrell returned. He leaned against the porch's frame, smiling. "Now, tell me what's going on."

Lowa told him that she'd had a disagreement with Zadar and needed a few days away for him to cool down before she resolved matters.

"And how do these two fit in?" Farrell asked, open palms pointing at Spring and Dug.

Lowa looked at them as if thinking what to say. "They—"

"What are you going to do about Zadar's shout?" interrupted Dug.

"Shout?"

"You know."

Farrell's lips tightened into a grimace for an instant, but his smile of universal kindliness quickly covered it. "Yes, the shouter on duty heard Zadar's message last night. But he didn't pass it on and we will not act on it."

Dug stood. He was a head taller than Farrell. "If you knew about the shout from just a few hours before, you can't have been surprised to see Lowa. But you acted like you were, and you didn't mention the shout, which, if you were friends, you'd think you would. So there's something odd going on. What is it?"

"I . . ." Farrell looked at Lowa.

"And," continued Dug, "where did you go just now? Were

you sending someone far enough away so we wouldn't hear him shout to Zadar?"

Farrell shook his head. "Dug, old man, I'm grateful that you're so protective of Lowa. You obviously care a great deal for her. But I do too. That's why I didn't mention the shout." Farrell's face shifted from smiling to sincere as if a lever had been pulled. "Look, I'll be entirely honest with you, since you're clearly too sharp for me not to be. I decided not to tell you that we'd heard the shout to put you at ease."

"And why would you want us at ease?"

"Because . . . because I want you at ease! I want you to have a good time here. I loved Lowa like a sister when I knew her back then. And in other ways."

He winked, and Dug resisted an urge to kill him. He glanced at Ula, but she was busy with their dishes.

Farrell continued: "Zadar I hardly know. Yes, we are part of his web of shouts. We receive . . . benefits that would make us mad not to be. And it might be useful one day if, say, we get invaded – and that is going to happen, by the way." He nodded grimly, then shook his head. "But, I would never, never betray Lowa. Just now, while you ate breakfast – my breakfast, by the way, which I gave up for you – I was arranging lookouts on the roads into Kanawan. So now we've got our own little web of shouters who'll tell us if anyone comes looking for Lowa. I was also sorting out some huts for you to stay in."

Dug shifted uncomfortably.

"I'm proud of my village, Dug. I want you all to relax and enjoy it without constantly looking over your shoulders. That's why I didn't tell you about the shout. I want you to feel safe, happy and chilled." Farrell walked over to Dug and put his hand on his shoulder. "My friend – and a friend of Lowa is a friend of mine – you are safe here."

Dug looked over at Lowa, expecting her to be annoyed with him for attacking her friend, but she smiled reassuringly. "I trust him, Dug. But Farrell, this row I've had with Zadar, it may be a bit more serious than I said. What will you do if Zadar's troops do come?"

"They won't come in numbers. Zadar respects my boundary ditches, just like the Dumnonians do. We're a buffer between them. That may change if either side decides to attack the other – and that is a real worry – but right now they're evenly matched and I don't think either will risk a war. So you're safe here. They may well send a rider or two to look for you, but there are plenty of places to hide and my people can be trusted."

Lowa stood. "We're safe here, Dug. Farrell and I have been through a lot. He owes me his life at least twice over."

"I'd say it was the other way round. Remember Cadbury?" Farrell jabbed Lowa in the ribs and she laughed.

"I had that guy. You got in the way and nearly got us both killed!" Lowa jabbed him back.

"I knew a man called Farrell once. A bear ate him. Pulled his arms off first," said Spring.

"You're a funny one, aren't you?" said Farrell, ruffling her hair. Spring looked as if she might bite him. Farrell laughed but pulled his hand back swiftly. "Now, you've been up all night. Let's show you somewhere to put your heads down. Would you like to share a hut or have one each?"

"I'll have my own," said Lowa.

"So will I!" announced Spring.

"No, you won't," said Dug. "The girl and I will share." Spring scowled.

"Marvellous. Now come on, let's get you to bed. We'll have you woken in time for lunch."

By now the villagers were up and busy with rural industry. They walked past thatched huts, weaving sheds, dyeing pools and stone grain stores. Blacksmiths, carpenters and potters working outside in the already-warm morning nodded greetings. Farrell introduced all the villagers by name, but Dug didn't take any of them in. He was too tired and there were too many.

He did notice how well off everyone looked. Every villager, young and old, was dressed in new-looking cottons and linens. Even the ironsmith's leather apron looked well made and was almost free of burns. Many of the men had shaved faces. Their hair was neat and clean. In every other settlement this size he'd visited people tended to have one or two sets of clothes that they wore all year. Even in summer most people – most people being field-working peasants – would be clad in patched and re-stitched rough woollen frock-smocks. Only the queen, king, chief or whatever their ruler was called and their families would be well dressed and tidy. Here everybody was.

Dug ran a hand through his own bush of beard and discovered a twig with a leaf attached. Elm, if he wasn't mistaken. He tossed it onto the roadside. He pushed his fingers through his knotted, greasy hair and found quite a lot of spider's web.

Ahead of him Spring was busy scrambling her hair with both hands into a bigger mess than it already was. She clenched her fists and walked with her knees bowed outwards and shoulders rolling like a teen trying to look tough.

Farrell introduced them to everyone as Poppy, Rose and Grampus.

"Those are the names I'll give you while you're here, by the way," Farrell said quietly, "You're mother, daughter and grandfather. Your farm was sacked by bandits and you're on the way to relatives in Dumnonia and a new life. I know Lowa – Poppy – from years back. Which is true of course. The closer to the truth, the better the lie."

"Can't I be Poppy?" asked Spring.

"No, you're Rose, I'm afraid, my sweet." Farrell reached to ruffle Spring's hair again and she ducked aside.

"Why?"

"Because I mentioned Rose after Poppy, and when we list names here, we do it in order of importance."

Farrell walked them through a courtyard of cart garages and closed-up winter stables. The carts were the finest quality – light but strong, with spoked wheels.

"Whose carts are these?" Dug asked.

"Shared by the village. We share most things. Just up here is our communal cookhouse where everyone eats. Why use wood for a hundred cookfires in summer when the huts don't need to be heated and one will do? We eat in shifts." Farrell looked up at the sun. "Should be the girls about now."

"Everyone apart from you and your family eat here, you mean?" Dug said.

"I'm chief, old man. I'd love to muck in with everyone, but one has to keep a distance. Eating together builds bonds, but not the sort of bonds that a chief needs. Sometimes a chief has to take decisions that don't benefit everyone. Cosy up to one group, and you're going to get those decisions wrong. I really would like it if the people could see me as just another one of them with similar tastes and needs, because that's what I am, but they'd lose respect and it wouldn't work."

"And then you'd have to eat what they eat."

"I do eat the same food as them. Have a look. You'll see they're tucking into exactly what you just had." Farrell smiled kindly, or perhaps pityingly, at Dug. Dug felt heat flow into his ears.

On the other side of the stables was a longhouse with two long tables outside. Around thirty girls were sitting on benches at the tables, eating porridge with nuts, seeds and honey. Four elder women sat at the ends of the tables. The women looked to be around Dug's age, the girls were all maybe three or four years older than Spring. They looked up at the newcomers' arrival and smiled a greeting.

"These are the girls from our school and their teachers. Hi, girls! Hi, teachers!" said Farrell.

"Hi!" "Hello!" "Good morning!" the girls said back. Dug spotted a particularly good-looking one with golden hair and white teeth. Then he noticed that the girl next to her was a beauty too, as was the girl next to her . . . They were young enough that he told himself to think of them as pretty, rather than attractive. He looked along another rank of seated girls, thinking yes, they are all pretty, maybe it's true what they say and people do become better looking as you head south. Then his eyes met a teacher's. She raised an eyebrow. Dug looked away, ears reddening again.

"These are my guests, Poppy, Rose and Grampus," said Farrell. "They'll be staying for a few days. Be nice to them!"

"We will!" "Sure thing!" "See you around, Poppy, Rose and Grampus!" said the girls.

They walked on, along a street that climbed gently towards the hillfort. Largeish huts lined one side. Each had a little porch angled south-east to catch the rising sun. Several had roof flaps flung open. They were all encircled by drainage channels which fed into a flagstone-lined ditch in the centre of the road. This, thought Dug, is not a village. It's a rich little town.

"The girls are all here for our summer school," said Farrell. "We have girls in every summer now. We teach them how to run a village, and how to speak correctly, act correctly, that sort of thing."

"Speak and act . . . correctly?" asked Lowa.

"Yeah, I know. I'm sorry. It's a Roman idea. It's only for a few weeks in the summer."

"Girls only?"

"Yeah."

"So they can serve men better?"

"Sorry, Lowa. Like I said, it's a Roman idea. People like Roman things and the coin is useful – we built this street with it." He waved a hand at the neat little homes. "They're all chiefs' and kings' daughters who are going to have a life of ease. If they spend a while with us learning how to cook and sew, what's the trouble?"

"They don't learn that at home?"

"Here are your huts!"

They'd turned right onto a track that ran along the valley side. Set back on the left, on flat plots cut into the hill's slope, were two huts with the same south-east-facing porches and drainage channels running out to the road, although they couldn't see where the channels began because each hut was ringed with a bed of flowers. They looked and smelled nicer than any huts Dug had seen before.

"We keep these for guests. You'll find fuel, nettles for tea, nuts, berries, dried meat, a couple of jugs of water – everything you need."

"We'll take this one!" Spring cried, running into the hut on the left. Lowa shrugged and headed for the hut on the right.

Dug turned and looked at Farrell. Kanawan's young chief was looking over the valley, hands on hips and hair blowing in the wind.

Dug stifled an instinct to push him down the slope. Instead he stood next to him. "What's that?" he asked, pointing across the valley. From up here they could see across Kanawan and the river to a large wooden structure in a field. It consisted of an enclosed corridor running into a circular building with high walls, the shape of thick-edged pan with a wide handle. Wooden stairs were built out from the side nearest them, finishing in a platform flush with the top of the wall. Inside the structure's circular body, open to the sky, steps tiered down towards a wall encircling a bare earth centre.

"It's an auction circus. Another idea from Rome. We've been the centre of livestock sales for miles around since we built it – another good source of coin. Each animal is driven along that tunnel into the centre. That's seating you can see around the edge. About four hundred people can all sit comfortably, view the animals and make bids on them."

"Oh right?"

"Yeah. Things are good."

"But wouldn't it be better to have a way out as well as a way in? You could get the animals through more efficiently."

Farrell reached a hand round Dug's shoulder, like a father overlooking a scene with a taller son.

"You know, old man, you might just have something there. You are a clever fellow. Perhaps you'd like to stick around for a while? Share some ideas? But now why don't you get some shut-eye, and we'll see you later?"

"Aye. And thanks for all of this. Sorry if I've been a bit off. There was a battle, then we didn't sleep last night . . ."

"You're very welcome. And I totally understand. I don't think she needs it, but I'm glad you're being protective of Lowa. Any friend of Lowa's . . . Just let me know if there's anything else you need."

"There is one thing."

"Yes?"

Dug lowered his voice. "Where can I go to take a crap?"

Chapter 5

An hour later they were riding through the woods side by side, Ragnall leading the angry little packhorse on a long rein. He was vexed that his mind kept returning to Simshill. He'd stop himself, think about Anwen or the death of his family, but then his thoughts would drift off only to lap ashore invariably on Simshill's leather-clad bottom. Part of him wanted to return to her despite what she was selling and, worse, despite Anwen. He tried to think about something else, and a realisation struck him like a slap to the face.

"Drustan, how did we pay for the inn at Bladonfort? And to join the convoy?"

"With coins."

"What coins?"

"Coins taken from corpses at Boddingham. Quite a lot came from your brothers' and your parents' huts."

"How could you—"

"Think, Ragnall. Who was hurt or inconvenienced when I took these coins? How can they help in finishing Zadar's reign? It is good that your morals are strong, but letting them flail in each and every direction is not helpful. Imagining offence on behalf of others is the pastime of morons. Save your energy for real wrongs."

"But the rightful owners of the coins are dead!"

"And so cannot own anything or be angry that their possessions are taken."

"Or speak out when people wrong them."

"Exactly."

The packhorse stopped to munch on track-side grass and Ragnall was jerked to a halt. Drustan rode on ahead. Ragnall gave his horse the reins so that he might eat too. He wanted a little time away from Drustan's sense.

Chapter 6

Dug lay awake, breathing in fresh, warm air from the open door. He felt good. He'd slept for a while, but now in the middle of the day it was too hot. Not that that was stopping Spring, who was snoring like an asthmatic piglet in her bed on the other side of the hut.

He lay there thinking about Lowa. He'd had relationships and liaisons, but he hadn't been in love with anyone since Brinna. But then again he hadn't met anyone like Lowa. Maybe if he'd been ten or even five years younger he would have fallen stupidly in love with her and made a fool of himself. But now he was pragmatic. Or boring, perhaps. Whatever it was, it made life easier. Meeting Farrell had stiffened his resolve not to make any sort of play for her. The man was a smug wanker for sure, but he was also the sort of man that Lowa should and would be with – good-looking, successful and, most of all, young. That was the way of the world. Young, strong women got it on with strong young men while tired old men looked on with envy. The fact that old men desired young women – and old women desired young men, he supposed – was just another example of the gods' twisted sense of humour. The only way a man his age could pull a wonder like Lowa was by amassing piles of riches. However, it was becoming increasingly obvious that he was never going to amass much more than scars and memories.

His musing was interrupted by a girl's voice from outside, inviting Lowa to lunch at Farrell's hut. It was Enid, Farrell's daughter, he guessed. He was surprised by a pang of jealousy when he heard Lowa agree to go without asking whether he and Spring were asked too. He was cheered when Enid knocked on their hut door, then bumped back down when she told him that he and Spring would be more than welcome to lunch at the communal cookhouse. Never mind, he told himself. He might not be spending time with Lowa today, but at least he wouldn't have to put up with Farrell.

They left Lowa combing her hair and headed off down the hill. Spring had dreamed that Dug could fly and was telling him all about it without, as far as Dug could work out, breathing. She broke off mid-word when they arrived at the cookhouse to find two long tables of Kanawan faces looking up at them.

They halted and stared as if they'd found their path blocked by a badger brandishing an axe. Dug was not socially confident, and neither, it seemed to his surprise, was Spring. Luckily the villagers were effusively welcoming, and they soon relaxed.

Dug sat with Spring on one side and a large, curly-haired young man called Channa on the other. Some girls from the school, who'd eaten earlier, served roast pork with mashed apple, bread and a sharp paste made from crushed mustard seeds, which overtook the morning's porridge as the best thing Dug had ever eaten. Mutton was by far the more common meat, and Dug was happy with that, but it was a long time since he'd eaten pig, and he'd forgotten how much better it was. Spring stayed mercifully quiet while Channa told Dug about Kanawan's crops and industry, especially his speciality, the retting of flax.

After lunch the schoolgirls were free from lessons and serving duties. A few came over to ask Spring to join their games. She was reluctant, but Dug helped to persuade her so he could carry on talking to the interesting and friendly young farmer. Besides, he thought, it would be good for her to mix with people her own age, or at least nearer it. He wondered if she was playing with other girls for the first time, and realised with a mild jolt that he didn't actually know anything about the girl's background. Spring went off unhappily, but shortly afterwards galloped back past the tables clopping two wooden bowls together and whinnying like a frightened horse, pursued by five barking girls.

Dug spent the rest of the afternoon with Channa on a tour of Kanawan. He was struck by several of the innovations, including the retting field. He'd seen people soak flax or hemp in ponds and streams to separate the fibre from the stem. That had the downside of making the water smelly and undrinkable. Here they laid their flax out in a field and the dew did the work, without making a tenth of the smell or ruining a pond. Dug didn't like change as a rule, particular Roman-inspired change, but the chubby young retter was so honestly enthusiastic, and Kanawan so undeniably prosperous, that he found himself coming round. Here, he thought, was a good society. He decided to forget garrison work at Maidun and get back to farming. Maybe even learn some carpentry. What was he thinking, wanting to be a mercenary with Zadar? Perhaps he could stay here and farm, and leave Lowa to her crazy revenge mission? He could get back to the life of creating things that he'd had with Brinna, and away from the Warrior's life of destruction.

He'd have to put up with Farrell of course, but he could stand that. He'd just do the standard human thing and put on a friendly face while undermining him behind his back.

Late that afternoon, great black thunderclouds rolled across the blue sky from the south-west. A chill breeze whipped up whirls of leaves and blossoms, and the world darkened. Dug said a quick goodbye to Channa and marched back to their huts. He arrived just as the first fat drops of rain began to fall. He looked into Lowa's hut. She was still at Farrell's lunch. In his, Spring was curled in a ball on her bed, thumb in mouth and snoring again. He thought about waking her so that she'd sleep that night, but then remembered how much his own girls had slept and left her.

He sat on the floor of the porch and watched as the raindrops came harder and faster. Soon it was total downpour. It was the sort of rain you saw only every few years, like a giant had scooped up all the sea and was tipping it onto the hills and valleys. The drainage channels running from the huts became rivers, and the central one in the road a mini torrent, but, Dug noticed with a satisfied nod, they seemed to be holding up nicely. This really was a well put-together little town.

At the height of the downpour Lowa came running through the rain. She stopped when she spotted Dug and stood, panting and smiling, wet hair clinging to her head and neck, white hemp shirt plastered to her, transparent.

"Hello!" she laughed.

"Hello there." He raised a hand in greeting, trying to keep his eyes focused on her face.

"It'sh raining!" she said, looking up at the sky. *Clearly a good lunch*, thought Dug with a pang of envy.

"Oh aye? I hadn't noticed."

"Well, move over then."

He leaned to one side and she ducked past him into his hut. He turned. She was already peeling off her wet riding trousers. He looked back to the storm. A minute later Lowa squeezed onto the ground next to him, wrapped in a wool blanket. It was narrow enough that her arm pressed against his arm and her thigh against his thigh. The weather was coming from behind the porch so they were dry, but half a pace away rain thundered into dancing earth. Lowa leaned her head on Dug's shoulder. They sat in silence, watching as the heavy rain became heavier hail, shifting in swishing curtains across the valley. Very quickly the ground had a covering of little ice balls, bouncing as more pellets fell.

They watched as the hail became fresh rain, still without saying anything. Dug could feel Lowa breathing. He could smell her wet hair. Rills of rainwater washed the hailstones into miniature hills and valleys. The raindrops became smaller and fewer, the sky brightened and then it wasn't raining any more. The silence seemed almost loud after the heavy beat of rain. Within moments sunlight was lancing down and steam rising from the dazzling gold road. On the far side of the valley the sky was still the black of wet slate and rain was lashing the fields, but the trees were brightest sunlit green.

The rainbow was so faint at first that Dug wasn't sure if it was there, then suddenly it very much was, preposterously bright and gigantic, forming an arch over the path they'd taken from Bladonfort. Dug turned to say something to Lowa, but she turned at the same time, grabbed the back of his head and kissed him.

Chapter 7

It felt like they were moving faster than the merchants'
convoy, but given their circuitous route, ducking under
branches, following valleys, winding along meandering
rivers and skirting swamps, they almost certainly weren't.
They stopped in a few villages remote enough to be
untouched by Zadar's barbarism and, it seemed to Ragnall,
remote enough to be deeply weird. At one collection of huts
clustered under a circle of great trees at the bottom of a
meadowed valley they found, once they'd penetrated the
dialect, that the inhabitants couldn't, or wouldn't, count
higher than four. Any number above four was "many".
Ragnall struggled to buy eight apples.

As they rode away, Ragnall marvelled at their stupidity.
Drustan replied that numbers were good only for showing
off and warfare and that they'd all be better off without
them.

"What if you needed to know in advance how many visitors from another tribe to cater for?" Ragnall asked.

After a long pause Drustan said, "See if you can work
that out for yourself."

Got him! thought Ragnall.

Chapter 8

Somebody had once tried to persuade Weylin that it hardly ever rained.

"Just think," they'd said. "You train outside for, what, at least two hours every day? How often does it rain?"

"Hardly ever," he'd had to admit.

"And people say we live in a rainy land! But it *hardly ever* rains," the smug arsehole had concluded. Well it was raining now, like a bastard. If the rain denier had been on hand, Weylin would have drowned him in a puddle. The only upside was that they seemed to be heading in the right direction. Several peasants had seen three riders, and two roadside farmers had had things stolen, including a horse, which would corroborate Ogre's story that their quarry had had only two horses between three.

However, right track or not, the downpour was so deeply unpleasant that he called the halt for camp a few hours early. Riding along with water trickling through his head bandage, down his back, round his armpits, down his arse crack and around his groin was nasty enough, but when the wet leather began to chafe his inner thighs raw, it was time to stop. They pitched their supposedly waterproof leather bivouacs. Weylin picked the best spot, a fallen tree trunk where a previous traveller had made a good lean-to with branches, sticks and leaves. But still it was wet. Combined with his bivouac, the lean-to kept him dry from above, but the very air was sodden. He sat spread-legged and shivered. His *bones* were wet.

By Bel, he was going to take this out on Lowa when he caught up with her. Such a shame he couldn't kill her. He prayed to Toutatis that the lunk who'd helped her escape was still with her. Thinking about strange tortures he'd visit on the northern bastard finally lulled him into peaceful sleep.

It had stopped raining by morning, thank Toutatis, but the rain had obliterated the tracks that had already been difficult enough to follow on the busy road. The only course was to continue north, but it didn't feel right. At first everyone they asked had a story about the man, woman and child who'd passed, but for the last few hours the people in the roadside settlements swore they hadn't seen any travellers fitting their descriptions for days. Morale was low. Two of his men had caught colds in the sodden night and were sneezing at him.

At first the beautiful freshness of the land framed by rising tendrils of mist as the summer sun boiled the rain out of the ground had buoyed him a little. Steadily though, as they rode further and further without a sniff of Lowa, Weylin became increasingly depressed. He'd just resolved to take his misery out on the next person they came across when the shout came faintly in the distance, then ringing clear from a nearby hamlet.

"Have Lowa. Village of Kanawan. Do not repeat this message near Kanawan."

Weylin pulled his horse round, raised his sword over his head and bellowed like a hero from a story, "We ride for Kanawan!"

He might have continued looking like a hero had he galloped off in the direction of Kanawan, dirt flying from his mount's hooves and surcoat flapping in the wind. Instead he almost fell off – riding with one arm in a sling was not easy when you let go of the reins with your good hand – then sat still on his horse, head jerking in random directions like a dog that's heard a fly somewhere. The nub of the problem was that he didn't know where Kanawan was or even what general direction it was in. He'd never heard of it.

Felix, for all his crowing about the importance of geography, was never keen to share his knowledge. He had some plans of the land etched on vellum, but he kept them to himself. "Never let the right hand know what the left is doing," Weylin had heard him say. Which was a bit fucking annoying when the right hand was holding a map and you were the lost left hand.

None of his company nor Ogre and his men had heard of Kanawan either.

The final person he asked was Savage Banba. She smiled at him, her distractingly white teeth shining from a tanned, square face beneath asymmetrically bobbed black hair. "I have no idea where Kanawan is," she said with a short, barking laugh.

"What's funny?" he asked.

"Nothing." She looked down as if deciding whether to say something, then looked up again. "Although it *is* somewhat amusing that our search tactics have involved riding into the middle of nowhere, rather than staying warm and dry in Bladonfort. So that now that we do know where Lowa is, we have no way of knowing where that where is. But if we'd stayed in Bladonfort, we could have eaten well last night, slept in dry beds, got the shout this morning, asked a merchant where Kanawan is and been on our way there already. Rather than standing here like drunk children who've finished the beer they stole and don't know what to do next."

Ogre and a few others sniggered. Weylin reddened under his dirty bandage. He had to regain the upper hand somehow.

"We should have stayed in Bladonfort, you're saying, because someone in Bladonfort will know where Kanawan is?"

"I imagine that every merchant there knows where it is."

"Good. Go and ask them. We'll wait here." Weylin pointed at a nearby farmhouse. A worried-looking farmer was standing on his doorstep, watching them. They'd give him reason for that worried look in a moment, thought Weylin with a smile.

"But that'll take—"

"The rest of the day and all night. Yes. Be back here by dawn with directions to Bladonfort, or I will whip you until you're dead."

"You can't—"

"Yes I can, *Savage* Banba. Zadar's orders. He wants Lowa. I have to do everything I can to get her. Anybody who stands in the way of that will soon find themselves standing in a whole heap of shit."

"But my mount isn't fresh."

"Your problem. See you later."

Weylin dismounted and led his horse to the farmhouse. He heard Savage Banba gallop away, but he didn't turn because he knew that not turning would look better. He felt the admiring gazes of his troop on his back.

Chapter 9

The broch is the stone fort's gatehouse. The lower half of the broch tower is carved from the cliff's rock, the upper half built from skilfully shaped, immovable blocks of stone. The only way into the fort is up wooden stairs to an iron-barred door ten paces up the broch wall. The wooden stairs can be raised on pulleys.

High, smooth walls sweep back from the broch in the shape of a pulled longbow, until they meet the towering, sleek, black cliff. On the very stormiest days, with the wind blowing across the longest possible fetch, spray from waves *might* come over the walls. As far as attackers are concerned, however, the fort is impregnable. With the stairs pulled up, anybody trying to climb to the door or scale the walls gets a rock on their head or a faceful of boiling oil.

Behind the walls, sheltered from wind and the salt spray, warmed by the sun in the day and by heat radiating from the south-facing cliff at night, are plots of vegetables and wheat. And fenced enclosures of livestock. And, why not, a flower garden. She'd probably like that. In fact, there's a stream running out of a cave in the cliff that babbles prettily through the flower garden before plunging into a sinkhole just before the wall. Their helpful children do the laundry and wash the pans in the stream. The cave is long and dry, despite the stream running along its base. In it is a storehouse with enough provisions – smoked and salted fish, seal and pork in barrels – to last fifty years of siege.

Around the corner from the broch the cliff sweeps inland

above a wide estuary where salmon nets trap fish every tide. Their elder sons and daughters collect the fish every day and take it back to the cave, which, deep down, has an ice chamber where fish and game can be frozen. The children sleep in the cave, in comfortable rooms built of oak and lined with fur. On good days they play outside. When the weather's bad they explore the caves and make up stories.

He and she live in the broch, nearby but separate from the cave. The tower is well lit, warm and comfortable, with an indoor shitter that drops directly down to the subterranean stream, so it never smells bad, even in winter. The top floor is a circular bedchamber with a giant bed. A wooden chest overflows with covers of stitched-together baby seal furs, so they're snug on the coldest winter nights. In summer they leave the shutters open on the two big windows looking out over the sea. Sometimes they sit and watch the sunsets and the stars. Sometimes the sunsets and the stars watch them.

Another window looks back over the garden. There's a pulley at that window which lifts a bucket of clean water from the stream. They can spend whole days eating smoked salmon, drinking cool water and making love in the broch, while the kids look after each other and tend the crops, the animals and the nets.

Lowa sighed in her sleep. Dug put an arm around her and she wriggled closer. The soft hairs on her shoulder brushed his nose. She smelled of heady joy. Her firm body was prime with vitality. She radiated the heat that she'd absorbed during her day in the sun. He'd never lain with a girl who'd done that before. Soon though her hair was irritating his face and a film of sweat had slicked into existence where his flesh touched hers. He pushed her away and she slept on. In the fantasy broch he was building in an attempt to get to sleep, the sea breeze would keep the sweat away, and her hair, washed daily in seal fat, ash and seaweed soap, would never irritate his nose.

Chapter 10

Some time after dawn, Weylin was returning from the stream when Savage Banba pulled up in front of the farmhouse. He watched her dismount, stand for a moment as if lost, then collapse onto her back. She lay there, chest rising and falling while her horse stood breathing hard, its nostrils finger breadths from the ground. Banba raised her head, struggled to her feet and stumbled toward the farmhouse, leaving her horse where it was.

"Banba!"

She turned, surprise and fear on her exhausted face. Weylin smiled.

"I'm sorry . . ." she panted. "I went as quickly . . . I know where Kanawan . . . is. We can be there . . . soon." She tried to square up and catch her breath. "I'm sorry I wasn't back by dawn . . . It was . . . too far."

Weylin smiled. This was brilliant. "I know I said I would, but I'm not going to whip you to death, Banba. Not if you see me right." He nodded towards a nearby grain shed and grinned. "We shouldn't be disturbed in there."

Chapter 11

"**P**ssst! Wake up!" said the voice.

Lowa was already awake, adrenaline fizzing though her limbs. The attempt to approach the hut stealthily had woken her as surely as an avalanche of bronze cowbells down an iron mountain might have woken others.

"Is that you, Spring?" said Dug, thick-voiced. He sat up, wafting a mushroomy musk. Lowa stayed down. The footsteps were heavier than Spring's. The girl probably wouldn't be back for a day or two anyway, judging by the intensity of the sulk she'd thrown on waking the previous morning to find Lowa in Dug's bed.

Lowa slipped her hand under the straw mattress and pulled out her knife. She held it ready to flick into the intruder's chest. Assassins didn't wake you first as a rule, but neither had she ever been woken just after dawn for a welcome reason.

"It's Channa!" whispered a voice at the door, more loudly than most people spoke. "The retting guy," he added a little louder.

Dug put a hand on Lowa's arm. "It's OK. All right, Channa. Come in."

Channa ducked through the porch. He squatted next to the bed and knocked Lowa's leather water cup over. As he apologised, she drew the wool blanket around her and leaned over Dug's bulk. She squeezed his shoulder. He reached a hand back and clasped her thigh.

"There's something you need to know about Kanawan,"

Channa said. Even in the semi-darkness she could see his wide eyes, like two full moons under his storm cloud of black curls.

"Let me get up. I'll get some tea going." Dug made to sit up further, but Channa put a hand on his arm.

"No, no, please. I don't have much time. Listen." Channa looked round as if somebody might have followed him into the hut. He smelled of wet hemp. Lowa kept the knife ready. The young man seemed soggily ineffectual, but you never knew.

"Have you seen that building on the other side of the river?"

"Aye, the auction ring?"

"It's not for auctioning farm animals. Well, actually they do do that there sometimes, but that's not what it was built for. It's for slaves. It's for whores. It's for . . . murder! Farrell's got a monster!"

"Slow down, slow down. A monster?" said Dug. Lowa lay back. *Yup*, she thought, she should have realised. Farrell's village was too good to be true. The young Farrell she'd known was a fun kid but also a wicked shit who'd never put up with Kanawan's rustic dreariness unless there was something twisted going on.

"A demon, an imp, a formori, a troll? I don't know." Channa's voice was getting louder. Lowa shushed him and he continued more quietly. "Some Otherworld beast. Farrell keeps it in a cage. He makes people fight it. He calls it the Monster. It looks like a deformed, hairy child with little legs, but long arms. It's got the strength of twenty men. It tears people apart while we all watch. A lot of people cheer. I cheer."

"A demon?" said Dug.

Channa began to cry. "Yes! I thought you'd be able to *help*. Someone's got to stop him. It's got to be stopped!"

Dug continued asking about the "Monster" but Channa

kept crying and repeating himself. Lowa slipped out of bed and dressed quickly. She couldn't listen to people who thought that saying the same thing in different words passed for explanation. She took Channa gently by both hands, calmed him and made him sit on the hearth stone in the centre of the hut, where he hunched, shaking and rocking.

Now he was under the roof hole, Lowa could see more clearly his pallid, doughy, chinless face blooming with moles like mould on a soft cheese. His black hair sat on his head like a badly made, unravelling woollen hat, ready to be plucked away by premature baldness. Not a looker, this one. She made soothing noises as he bubbled snot and looked at his feet, then gripped the lapel of his frock-smock and slapped him.

He blinked wounded surprise at her.

"Stop crying. Now. And forget about the Monster. Tell me about the slaves, then the whores."

Channa gibbered, tears bulged anew, and Lowa drew her hand back, this time clenched in a fist. The fat farmer looked at her knuckles. He wiped his nose on his shoulder then his wrist, took several short but deep breaths, then told them all about Kanawan.

He told them that Farrell Finda was Zadar's general in the area. He told them about the Wounders, Farrell's bodyguard, ten bullies in black leather armour who were the terror of the region. Channa himself had only settled here a few years before, and didn't know how it had all started, but people whispered that Zadar had Farrell's son held hostage. The local chiefs and kings, Channa continued, were all in thrall to Kanawan and dared not rise against Farrell because they were terrified of the Wounders, of Zadar's retribution and, worst of all, of going into the ring with Farrell's Monster. At this point he crumbled a little and Lowa had to raise her hand again.

Channa recovered. The local chiefs sent Farrell slaves, he

explained, lots of slaves – their own people, captured enemies and travellers. Most of them Farrell sent on to Zadar, but some he kept to fight in his arena, against each other, against dogs, wolves and, worst of all, against the Monster.

Well that makes sense, thought Lowa. So many slaves came to Maidun Castle from the west that some sort of regional hub was likely. Not just slaves . . . Lowa guessed what was coming next. Farrell's school.

"But that's not the worst of it!" Channa cried. "You've got to do something. Those girls, those sweet girls. They think they're learning to be princesses, but he's preparing them for Zadar. He does it every year. All the villages and towns nearby send their most attractive girls. They daren't not."

"What? Zadar can't need them all?" Dug yawned, pulling the cover around himself as if preparing for a couple more hours' sleep.

"He doesn't take them all," said Lowa, hoicking her thumb at Dug in a get-out-of-bed gesture. He sat up. "He only keeps the ones he likes best. Some are sold to Rome. Others he gives to his inner circle. A few will join the army. The rest go to Maidun's whorepits."

The whorepits were another thing that Aithne had complained about and Lowa had told her to put up with. She really should have listened to Aithne and killed Zadar when she'd had the chance. Countless times she could have impaled him with an arrow from a couple of hundred paces, leaped on a horse and been away. But no. She'd blanked out the evil and lived the good, selfish life. And now all her girls were dead and killing Zadar was almost certainly going to mean her own life too. She was weakened by shame momentarily, then dismissed it. No regrets. Only amends.

"OK," she said. "We have to go, now. If Farrell's so tight with Zadar, then he must mean to give me up. You, Dug, he'll want to trot out in his gladiator arena."

"His what?" asked Channa.

"Place where people get killed for the crowd's amusement. Comes from Rome. Where you've been cheering as your friends get ripped up by the Monster."

Channa began to cry again. At least he's repentant, thought Lowa. He was doing something to stop the evil, which is more than she'd done until she'd been forced into action. She put a hand on his shoulder. "Go on," she said in the gentlest tone she could manage. "Go home. We can't do anything now; there aren't enough of us. But we'll be back, in greater numbers."

"I'll find Spring," said Dug, rolling off the bed and pulling on his trousers.

"No. There's no time. Channa can tell her where we've gone."

"But what if Farrell finds her first?"

"Zadar's death is more important than one girl."

"I'm going to find her." Dug reached for his ringmail shirt.

"No. We can sort a meeting place with Cha—"

"Now, where could I be? In the woods playing with formoris? In the river swimming with the swans?" It was Spring. She'd been under the covers on her bed on the other side of the hut all the time.

Lowa stared at her. How had she come in unnoticed? Nobody had ever managed to creep into a hut where she was sleeping. Lowa woke up when birds flew over. There was simply no earthly way Spring could have got in.

"How did you . . . ?" Spring glared at her and Lowa sighed. *What a fuck-up*, she was surprised to find herself thinking. She actually felt guilty about upsetting Dug's odd little tag-along. No time for that now though, they had to get moving. "Channa, what are you still doing here? Go home, now. You two, pack. We're leaving in a matter of heartbeats."

"The horses?" asked Spring, already gathering up her things.

"The trick with escape is to get the fuck on with it. We'll get more horses. Pack."

"Language!" said Spring.

"You've got to stop Farrell!" Channa wailed.

"Fuck. Off. Home!" Lowa was tempted to hit him again. "We're going to kill Zadar," she said slowly, carefully and loudly, as if speaking to a halfwit. "Then we'll come back for Farrell."

"But the girls!"

There was a scrape of metal on metal from the front of the hut. It sounded like a bolt being slid into place. *Fuck*, thought Lowa. Channa's blubbing had riled her and she'd been talking so loudly that she hadn't heard whoever—

A laugh boomed from outside the hut. Farrell.

"'Going to kill Zadar!' Brilliant! Off to kill Zadar with your mighty army – a scrawny girl and a washed-up nobody." Farrell began to clap. Others joined in. About ten people, Lowa reckoned.

While Channa and Dug gawped at each other, Lowa dived for the back of the hut and speared her knife through the wattle and daub. She shook the blade from side to side, gouging out clay, dung, straw and twigs. The uprights seemed surprisingly tough. She slashed upwards and easily sliced the horizontal hazel twigs that made the wattle, then attacked the uprights again. The knife wasn't cutting into them even a little, nor shifting them at all. The hut's frame must be made from fire-hardened wood, she realised, or . . . She slashed left to right and up, opening a narrow gap.

"No need to come out!" Farrell shouted. "You're in a very neat little trap. I'm sure Dug will appreciate it. I've always found that older men are impressed by good engineering."

Farrell blathered on, but Lowa blocked him out and focused. Wall packing cleared, she scraped the blade against one of the uprights. It was iron! For the love of Danu, who the fuck builds huts out of iron? She couldn't budge the bars a hair's breadth. There was no way she could make the hole between them big enough for her, let alone Dug. There was a tap on her shoulder. It was Spring.

Lowa helped the child squeeze through and watched as she crawled into the bushes behind the hut. Farrell's bombastic goads covered any noise Spring made, and his Wounders hadn't circled the hut. She was glad to see that her captors were inept, and that Spring had got away, but she and Dug were still Farrell's captives, and it wasn't like the girl was going to be any help..

The Wounders began to strip the wattle and daub from the hut's iron frame. Soon Lowa could see that they were men and women in uniform black leather armour. Each had a short mace hanging from one hip and a blade scabbarded on the other. With their faces twisted into what were meant to be menacing snarls, they looked like finalists in a gurning competition, but she could see uncertainty in their eyes. They'd probably never faced a Warrior before, let alone two. The moment her chance came . . . One of them leaned through the bars to grab Dug's bag. Lowa could have grabbed her and killed her, but she didn't want to antagonise them while they were in a cage, and her bow was in her own hut. Zadar would want her unharmed, or at least alive, but chances were he'd made no such stipulation about Dug. Piss them off too much and they'd spear him through the bars.

"Nice little troupe you've got, Farrell. Do they dance? Actually, no, sorry, they look a bit dim for dancing. Can they grunt in unison?"

Her former friend ignored her. As she watched the Wounders strip the walls, she thought how she'd spent a totally enjoyable few hours drinking and reminiscing with him just two days before and never picked up a hint of his coming treachery. Just like she'd seen Zadar act like the kindest uncle before forcing someone to suffocate his own brother for his entertainment. It wasn't a failing in her ability to judge people, she thought, as one Wounder kicked at some stubborn wattle and she resisted the urge to grab his foot and break his leg. You can't foresee treachery in the world's real shits because for them it's not treachery. If it benefits them, then it's just how things are – what should be done. Why would they look guilty when they genuinely don't give the tiniest of craps for anybody but themselves?

Soon they could see Farrell strutting up and down outside with his thumbs hooked over the lapels of a leather jerkin. He wore a tarted-up version of the Wounders' uniform with silver detailing, very different from his previous rustic garb. The dawn light highlighted his long blond hair with golden flashes. The way he was shaking his mane at each turn, it looked like he knew it. How had she ever thought of him as a friend?

"Genius, don't you think?" he said once he knew they could see him. "Not guest huts. Cages! Made of iron instead of wood. And you walked right in."

"Aye. Well done. You're very clever," said Dug.

Farrell ignored him. "Thanks, by the way, Lowa, for bunking up with Grampus. The huts take a while to re-assemble so it was thoughtful of you to crowd into the one. But, by Bel, he'd old enough be your grandfather's older boyfriend! I'd have given you a sympathy fuck if I'd known you were that desperate. Too late now."

"He's only old enough to be my father, you preening prick. And fuck you with your tiny cock? I remember not noticing it at all the last time." If Lowa could goad him into fighting her, then they were away.

"What, this tiny cock?" Farrell pulled down his trousers and waggled his penis at the hut. It was actually quite long and fat, if strangely tapered.

"It looks like a diseased carrot," Lowa said, curling her lip. "And you don't know what do to with it. Other than put it into your own kids. Enid does have the look of a girl whose daddy takes hugs too far."

Farrell laughed. "I'm not going to fight you, Lowa. Zadar wants you, so, much as I'd love to, I can't wipe that smug smile from your face on the arena floor. You never were nearly as good as you thought you were. But don't worry, you won't have to wait long. We got the message just now. A fellow called Weylin Nancarrow will be here to pick you up in a few hours. Channa and your elderly friend here, on the other hand, are this morning's entertainment. It's been a while since we saw the Monster tear someone to pieces."

"I'll kill your wee monster for you," said Dug.

"No. You won't. You'll watch as he rips your limbs off, then, if you're lucky, you'll pass out before he eats your face." Farrell smiled.

"It's true!" Channa sobbed, burying his face in his fat white hands.

The Wounder who'd taken Dug's bag handed Ulpius' mirror to Farrell, who stared at his own reflection for a few long seconds.

"Well, well. This is lovely! Roman, if I'm not mistaken. Not British, anyway – far too well made! Tell me you were carrying if for Lowa, old man? It's too depressing to think you use this to look at your own decaying face."

"So you're Zadar's puppy now?" said Lowa.

Farrell looked up from the mirror. "No, I'm his top dog. You're the puppy. At least you were. Now you're more like his piglet, ready to be spitted and roasted alive. Worse, probably. That Zadar! Makes the Monster look like a fairy godmother." Farrell strode off down the hill chuckling, leaving his men stripping the hut.

Channa was still sitting on the hearth stone, crying. Dug was on the bed. Lowa went to sit next to him.

"I've been in worse scrapes," he said. "We'll be all right."

Lowa took his hands and looked into his brown eyes. He

was a good man. That wasn't going to help him much against the Monster though.

She had an idea what it might be. A couple of years before, Felix had brought back an animal from a voyage to Rome. A homunculus, he'd called it. It was like a hairy, twisted, impossibly strong child. It was meant as an amusement for Zadar, but it had gone mad and killed a couple of girls from the harem before Carden Nancarrow had knocked it out.

Nobody had seen the homunculus after that. Some had wondered where it had gone. It looked like Lowa had found out.

Chapter 12

"I cannot believe those fools in the last village were terrified of the sky falling on their heads. And that tower they'd built to hold it up? Wow." It was early evening. Ragnall and Drustan were sitting on a log next to the remnants of some previous travellers' campfire on the edge of pastureland between the track and a river.

Drustan coughed several times with a fierce, wet rattle. He'd been coughing like that all day. Ragnall didn't like the sound of it. The druid swallowed phlegm, then spoke slowly and quietly: "They are not fools. They are humans. Humans like the idea of a preventable doom. It makes them feel important. Usually the gods fulfil that need. People say that the gods will crush us if we don't live our lives in a certain way. It gives them purpose. However, those villagers have persuaded themselves that there are no gods, so they've invented a replacement – the idea that the sky is falling down, and that they can prevent it by building towers and so on. That has become their purpose."

"Do the gods exist?"

Drustan gave Ragnall a look that made him feel uncomfortable. "I have been meaning to talk to you about this." He coughed again. "I do not know if there are gods in the forms that we believe in on this island – Bel, Danu, Toutatis. The Romans have gods; the Greeks have gods; the Iberians, the Helvetians, they all have gods, and they are all different. Some believe that there is one all-powerful god. What is more likely – that we are right and everybody else is wrong about creation, existence and supernatural forces, or that different people *create* different gods?"

"So religion is . . . senseless? Madness?"

"No. It can be dangerous, almost laughably so when people attack others who have slightly different versions of the same stories, but humans will always find excuses to fight and kill. Religion is not as important in that process as the atheist philosophers like to claim." Drustan shuddered as he coughed. He sounded like a dying bear gargling honey.

"You don't sound well."

"I'm not. This is the longest I have spent riding and sleeping outside for a long while. The rain did not help. I have developed a sickness. But I shall be fine by morning, I am sure."

Ragnall nodded. The old man coughed a little more and seemed to recover.

"Where were we?"

"You were telling me that pretty much everyone I've ever met is wrong and you're right, and that there are no mysterious forces in the world."

"No no no. No mysterious forces? Oh, quite the opposite. Do you really think that something as complex as you – with your loves, quirks and proclivities – came from nothing? No, that really is an arrogant notion. Of course there are gods or there is a god – we just don't know his, her, their, its . . . form. But we don't need to know. Whatever name or names we use, some of us can draw on the power of the gods." Drustan paused and looked at Ragnall. "I'm one of those people. I think you are too."

It wasn't a very good jest, but Drustan was ill. Ragnall smiled. The old man looked back levelly.

"Um . . . ?" A small laugh burst from Ragnall's nose.

"I think that you're one of the few who can draw on the power of the gods. A true druid."

"Yes, I'm a druid I passed the—"

"No. There are thousands of druids who can slit open birds and make non-specific predictions that seem to come true. There are many who do good work as healers, philosophers and dispensers of justice. There are many more who pretend they can cure, and others who console and judge for their own benefit."

Drustan shifted uncomfortably on the log. Ragnall offered a steadying hand, but Drustan waved him away.

"Here is a story. A man walks into a tavern. A druid begins talking to him at the bar, looks at the pattern in the dregs of his beer and tells the man that he has two days to live. The man stabs the druid for his impertinence. Two days later the man is executed for killing the druid."

"So the gods—"

"So the gods nothing. That story, which may or may not be true, shows that calling on magic can make it seem like it exists. But beyond coincidence, beyond trickery, there *is* real magic. However, there are very few druids left that can use it, perhaps fewer than ten. I am one. I think that you are another."

Ragnall stared at Drustan open-mouthed, then laughed. He stopped when he saw Drustan wasn't laughing along.

Drustan pointed at the long-dead fire. It was blackened logs and sticks rather than just a pile of ash, clearly extinguished by rainfall or a bucket of water. "Split that into four piles please, with a good pace between each."

Ragnall did as he was bid then sat down.

"Now watch."

Drustan looked at the pile of charred wood nearest him, closed his eyes, screwed up his face and bunched his fists. His face went red, then he began to shake and his face turned purple. Ragnall was about to say something to stop him – he did not look well – when he caught movement in the corner of his eye. A wisp of grey smoke was rising from the pile of embers nearest Drustan. There was a soft pop and small flames began to lick along the edge of a log.

"By all the gods . . ."

"Or by just one of them. I was drawing on Danu. Or at least I think I was."

"Is this anything to do with ley lines?"

Drustan laugh-coughed. "No, no. Those are made-up nonsense."

"Not lines of power, making up a network of—"

"There are places of power, I think, and you can draw lines between them, but that doesn't make the lines powerful."

"Well . . ."

"Two horses in a field. Is the space between them a horse line?"

"No."

"No. Several horses. Does that give you a network of horse lines?"

"No."

"No. Now watch this."

Drustan coughed, then reached into his bag and raised his arm, dangling an earthworm between thumb and forefinger. He brought his palms together, the worm in between them. He twisted his right hand, mashing the worm, and pointed at the pile of burned wood furthest from him.

Woof! It burst into bright flame.

Nearby, birds took off in a clamour of leaves and a fox screamed.

Ragnall looked at the merrily burning little fire, then at Drustan.

"Are you all right?" Drustan looked terrible. His hair was pasted to his head with sweat, and his face shone orangely in the firelight.

"Yes. Now. You try. See if you can will a pile to take light."

Ragnall stared at a pile of wood. *Light!* he thought at it, then felt stupid.

"Concentrate!" coughed Drustan. "Call on Bel."

Ragnall screwed up his face, clenched his fists, tensed

every muscle he could find and said, "Bel, please light the fire."

"Not out loud."

Ragnall pleaded in his mind for Bel to light the fire. Suddenly it felt as if *something* was pushing into his head through his ears. It wriggled through his brain, down his neck into his chest. He kept on at Bel to light the fire. He pointed his fingers at the charred wood. He felt the strange presence pass into his shoulders, along his arms, into his hands and out.

He opened his eyes. The fire remained unlit. He knelt down next to it and blew. Nothing.

"I felt—"

"It will not come immediately. But try again. This time take this worm and kill it." Drustan reached into his bag and produced another worm. "The death of a creature opens the magic path much wider. I do not know why. Nobody does as far as I am aware. But it does seem that the higher the animal, the wider the path. So kill a sparrow, and you can start a bigger fire or perhaps extinguish one, which, you might be surprised to hear, is harder. Kill a man and you can do more." Drustan dangled the worm at him.

"You've been collecting worms?"

"Yes."

Ragnall took the worm. He squeezed it between his palms like Drustan had. He tensed, closed his eyes and called on Bel, willing the fire to light. He crushed the worm, still thinking about the fire lighting and begging for help. He felt nothing. He tensed more, crushed the worm more – perhaps he hadn't killed it yet, he thought – and willed the fire to light. He felt nothing. He kept trying for twenty or so more heartbeats but still felt nothing. He sighed and opened his eyes.

Three of the fires were burning now, including the one he'd been trying to light. He looked at Drustan.

"I've never seen anyone get it so quickly," said the old man wearily.

"I didn't feel anything."

"Obviously not. It lit very soon after you closed your eyes." Drustan leaned forward, bringing his hands to his face.

"It's a trick. It must be. Are you all right?"

"It's no trick. And no, I'm not—" Drustan toppled back off the log.

Ragnall leaped up and ran over. He gripped Drustan's robe and shook him, but the old man was out cold.

Chapter 13

The Wounders finished stripping the hut of its twigs, mud and dung, leaving just the iron cage. They goaded Dug, Channa and Lowa with spears and chained them to the bars, then opened up the metal grille that had blocked the door and came in to remove the furniture. They swept out the rushes then used spades to scrape away the packed earth, revealing that the hut floor was also made of iron bars.

Channa was glum with odd bouts of crying. Lowa was angry and beautiful.

"So, the Monster," Dug asked Lowa, "have you got any idea what it might be?"

"It's evil!" cried Channa. "It'll rip us to pieces, then eat us."

"I suspect," said Lowa, "that it's something Felix brought back from Rome. Everyone said it was the cursed offspring of a mother and son, but Felix told me it was an animal from Africa. So it's no more a monster than a bear is, but fighting bears isn't a lot of fun. This creature is smaller, but it may be stronger, and ripping limbs off did seem to be its thing. It won't be hard to beat if you have your hammer though. If you don't—"

"You ain't going to be armed," said a tall, laughing Wounder, "especially not once the Monster tears your arms off! You'll be *unarmed* then! Get it? *Unarmed!*" The Wounders guffawed.

"Jay, how can you do this to me?" Channa groaned.

The tall man shrugged. "Nothing personal, mate. If I had

my way, you'd be back doing whatever it is you do to those plants. Beyond me, I tell you, what it is you do. But we got a good thing going here, ain't we? There's only one person to blame here, mate. You."

"But who's going to look after Kelly?"

"You should have thought of that before." Jay picked up Dug's warhammer. "Nice piece of kit. I'll have this."

"Who's Kelly?" asked Dug.

"My pig."

"Oh."

The Wounders left with their spoils and returned with six oxen. They attached thick ropes to the hut, the top of a heavy oak cross and the oxen's yoke. The oxen heaved, the cross creaked upright and the end of the cage jerked into the air, showering earth. Underneath, the Wounders fitted an axle with thick wooden wheels and iron brakes. They repeated the whole process for the other end, turning the hut into an iron prison-cart. It was, Dug had to admit, quite clever.

They trundled down through town, six oxen ahead and a Wounder manning each wheel brake. Villagers followed, looking more interested and even concerned than triumphant, Dug noticed. He couldn't see any of the girls from the school anywhere. Could Spring have persuaded them to escape with her?

The oxen pulled them across the bridge to the arena. It seemed that everyone from the village was following or lining their path. The strangely subdued mood persisted, however. Rather than the decaying foodstuff missiles and jeering that a man might expect on his way to execution, Dug felt a stubborn resentment from the populace. He saw some of the larger villagers jostling some Wounders with an "Oh *sorry*, mate!" here and a "*Do* excuse me!" there.

So Farrell's rule was not so popular, thought Dug, and he felt a surge of hope. Then he saw other villagers, uncoerced, climbing the wooden stairs on the outside of the arena, carrying wine amphoras, bags of food and cushions. They may not like their ruler, but everybody loves a violent spectacle, thought Dug, his short-lived fantasy of a pre-show revolution leaking away.

Farrell swaggered up, flanked by Ula and Enid. The chief's wife and daughter didn't look overly festive either.

"Take the woman out. Leave the two sacks of shit," Farrell commanded.

Jay, the tall Wounder to whom Channa had appealed, detached Lowa from the cage but left her hands chained behind her back. "Out you come, sweets," he said.

Lowa didn't budge.

"Or my spear comes in." Jay waggled his spear.

She stood, hunched, arms behind her back.

"Don't worry. I'll get us out of this," said Dug, rattling his shackles. "The only problem is deciding which one of my many plans to use."

Lowa winked at him, then walked nimbly across the bars to the door.

Jay reached in to help her. She crouched as if about to jump down, but instead exploded into a leap, her feet flying up over her head in a forward somersault. Jay tried to dodge, but iron heels crunched into his chest, his ribs splintered into his lungs and he fell back with a high-pitched, sucking gasp.

Lowa thumped to the ground on her back, rocked onto her shoulders, brought her chain-bound wrists under her feet so her hands were in front of her, and sprang up.

Three Wounders moved in, spear points first.

"Don't kill her!" shouted Farrell. "But do hurt her!"

A narrow-waisted but heavy-arsed Wounder bounded forward, her spear aimed for Lowa's midriff. Lowa jumped and whirled round like a dancer, kicking the spearhead with the inside of her right foot and slamming the outside of her left boot into the Wounder's head with a sound like a mallet whacking a barrel. The Wounder fell.

But so did Lowa. As she rolled over to stand, a Wounder cracked the flat of his spearhead hard into her skull. She collapsed and lay still as two other Wounder spears pricked into her midriff.

Nearby, Jay struggled to suck in air and the other injured Wounder lay still, bright red blood pulsing through her short hair. Farrell strode up and kicked Lowa in the stomach. Air *oofed* out of her.

"Keep your spears on her," said Farrell, "and fetch some leg irons."

Lowa didn't resist as her legs were chained. It seemed like the blow from the spear had knocked all the aggression out of her. Farrell pulled her up and pushed her ahead of him to the arena. He said something to her at the bottom of the wooden stairs, then slung her over his shoulder and headed up, followed by Enid, Ula and more spectators.

Dug pulled at his shackles again, but they weren't going to give. He had nothing to do apart from watch Channa gibber, listen as the noise from the crowd inside the arena grew from a hubbub to cheers, and wish that he was armed and armoured.

After a while three Wounders approached.

"It's your turn!" said the largest, smiling like a cruel boy fetching his brother for punishment.

Dug sighed.

Chapter 14

"Right," said Ragnall, once Drustan was fully awake, propped up and sipping a cup of water. He'd decided while Drustan was unconscious that he'd take charge of the situation rather than relying on his teacher to make all the decisions as usual. This new spirit of resolve was a direct result of the previous night's "magic". He was embarrassed that he'd gone to sleep believing that he'd lit a fire by squashing a worm. How could he have thought that? More and more, he was wondering if he was as clever as he'd always believed.

He still couldn't work out how Drustan had done it, though. Or *why* he'd done it.

"Right," he said again, pacing. "We'll go back to that village where the sky's falling. They'll have a healing druid. He or she will cure you."

"No," whispered Drustan. "I know a better place . . . Mearhold. It is further, but . . . I know what is wrong with me."

"What is it?" Ragnall squatted next to the old man. He had to wait for a reply as Drustan's throat convulsed and he hoiked up goo from his lungs. He spat it weakly at the fire and missed. The gob of sputum was yellow, green and streaked with blood. Drustan looked at it and nodded weakly.

"Yes. I have a disease in my lungs."

"What should we do? A sacrifice? Got any more worms?"

"No, no . . . I need to . . . rest . . . Not here though . . . Weak and vulnerable . . . Friends in Mearhold . . ."

"I'll make a litter." Ragnall sprang to his feet.

"No . . . we cannot take horses to Mearhold . . . I will ride as far as I can . . . Just sleep first . . . then ride a bit . . . until we get there . . . or . . . I . . . die."

"*Die?*"

"Yes . . . Lung disease at my age . . . Probably die."

Drustan passed out again. His breathing rattled wetly but regularly. Ragnall squatted next to him and looked about. *What do I do now?* He'd already tidied everything away that wouldn't be needed before they left. He tried to make a tree burst into flame by looking at it. Nothing happened. Of course. And, Ragnall thought, here was final proof, if proof was needed, which it wasn't, that he'd been tricked. If Drustan really could command the gods' magic, why didn't he cure himself?

Chapter 15

Channa ran to the far side of the ring, wrapped his arms over his head and hunkered down in a craven ball against the wall. A Wounder leaned over the arena wall above him, hawked and dribbled spit onto his back.

Prodded by a spear, Dug had no choice but to follow Channa out of the corridor into the open circle. It was twenty paces across, with a packed-earth floor and smooth wooden walls about double his height. Above the wall it was all faces. All were looking at him. Sweat sprung from his armpits. The Wounders, Farrell himself and a few more were cheering and jeering, but most of the crowd were clapping unenthusiastically, looking uncomfortable and avoiding Dug's eyes. He walked into the centre of the arena, massaging his wrists where the shackles had rubbed. He felt outside himself, a bit drunk. He guessed it was the effect of having so many people looking at him.

There was Lowa, between Farrell and Ula. Dug gave her a little nod. She smiled wryly and waved as much as her manacled wrists allowed.

The door to the arena slammed shut. He heard a heavy bolt slide, then another.

The one way in and, more importantly, out, was blocked. So where was this Monster?

"Come on!" shouted Farrell, trying to waft some enthusiasm from the spectators by waving his arms. Lowa and, Dug noticed, both his wife and daughter looked at Farrell as if he was encouraging all the fathers to hit their children.

A few more people clapped, but it was still far from the frenzy that Dug had seen at similar events.

A crazed scream followed by alien hooting made Dug stiffen. He heard the bolts on the arena door slide back. It swung open. In came the Monster.

It waddled towards him on comically short legs, swinging incongruously long arms. It looked like a little, old, crazily hirsute man with a low hairline, swollen brow, wrinkled brown face, wispy grey beard and thin lips lining a wide mouth set in a round, yellow-pink muzzle. Its ears were huge and hairless, sprouting at right angles from its head like fan fungus from a tree stump.

Demon, animal or man, it picked at its lips with one hand and scratched its arse with the other, looking at him like a friendly dog.

Dug glanced up at Farrell. Was this a joke? The happy, hungry look on Farrell's face suggested that it wasn't. Lowa looked scared. That was nice but not heartening.

Channa wailed, "No!" and reburied his head in his hands. The Monster screamed at Channa, Dug, the crowd and then the sky. In its mouth were four yellow, human-like incisors flanked by long, pointed yellow canines like a bear's.

It came at him in a rolling jog. Dug raised his right hand, palm flat, as if to calm an aggressively drunk idiot. The Monster stopped, reached up and slowly curled the long black fingers of its left hand around Dug's right wrist. Monster and man looked at each other. Dug shook his wrist. The grip tightened to somewhere between uncomfortable and unbearable. Dug tried to jerk away.

"Let go, you wee—"

The Monster snarled and pulled. Hard. There was a loud sucking noise and Dug cried out as his upper arm bone dislocated from his shoulder. He tried to pull free, but any movement was agony. Still holding his wrist, the Monster walked away. Dug had no choice but to follow as it waddled around the ring. His shoulder was blazing with pain. He stopped, and pulled back a leg to kick the beast, but that stretched his shoulder too much and he couldn't bear it. He jogged a step to catch up.

Some of the crowd were cheering. Lowa was trying to stand but Farrell had an arm across her.

Channa stood and ran. The Monster sped up to a waddling jog after him.

Dug could do nothing but jog behind. He could *hear* his pain, blaring from his shoulder through his entire body. Every step made him want to scream, but even through his horror he was aware of the crowd – and Lowa – watching him, and he was keen not to look any more pathetic than he already did.

Finally Channa fell and the Monster stopped. Dug stood useless, wave after wave of hurt surging across his chest, searing through his legs, exploding in his balls even. Channa, apparently too terrified to stand or think, crawled to a wall and scrabbled at it uselessly. The Monster followed, pulling Dug. It reached Channa and raised its arm to whack him. Dug gritted his teeth and powered his left fist into the side of the Monster's head.

The next thing he saw was the swirling sky. Must have passed out, he thought. Now, where the badgers' tits— A whump drove the air from his chest, and there was the Monster, sitting on his stomach, pinning his arms to his sides with finger-like toes, beating its chest with its fists and screaming. Dug rocked, but he couldn't move. The beast hooted wildly and looked down at him.

It didn't look inquisitive any more. It looked properly fucking angry. It leaned forward, mouth gaping. Dug shook with all his strength, to no avail. The Monster bit into his chest, through cloth, skin, muscle and fat. Dug felt its teeth scrape ribs. The Monster pulled back. His blood dripped from its muzzle. It chewed his flesh messily. Morsels of his skin and fat fell back onto him. He tried to pull free. It was totally hopeless but he felt strangely calm, beyond pain, beyond horror.

The Monster swallowed, smiled at him with bloody lips and bent down for another bite.

Chapter 16

Lowa squirmed on the bench in impotent fury. With her feet and hands bound by heavy chains, Farrell could keep her pinned with an arm across her chest and enrage her even more by gently squeezing her left tit.

The locals watched but, she saw through her own frustration, they did not look happy. Only the Wounders and a few others were getting off on Dug's slow, gory death.

Down in the ring it looked like her new friendship – her new love? – was about to be cut short before it ever really began. Blood dripped from the Monster's fangs as it dipped its round head for a second bite of Dug's chest.

Channa was curled in a useless ball at the side of the arena. Dug flailed his legs, raised his head to try and butt the creature, but he couldn't shake the weight from his chest. He was being eaten alive and he knew it She could only watch. The rage boiled over and she screamed in anger.

Farrell squeezed her tit again. "Nice," he said. "Would you like me to call the Monster off?"

"I would." Surely he wasn't going to?

"OK. One condition."

In the ring Dug roared. The second bite wasn't as clean as the first. A ribbon of flesh the breadth of two fingers was still attached to his chest. The Monster yanked its head, lengthening the strip with every tug.

"What?" said Lowa. She could guess what it was.

"You stay here for five years as a retter, to replace Channa, who I'm not in the mood to save."

That was a surprise. "Fine."

"And you'll be a sex slave for the Wounders and anyone else I allow to use you."

There you go. "Also fine."

"Really?"

"Yes. Call off your beast."

The strip of flesh had torn free. It was quiet enough in the arena for them to hear the Monster slurp it up through rubbery lips.

"Call it off now. I'll do whatever you want," said Lowa.

A grin spread across Farrell's wide face and he chuckled warmly, as if remembering a wonderful childhood summer. "Do you know, Lowa, I actually would love to keep you here. The things I'd do with you . . . but Zadar wants you, and what Zadar wants . . ."

"I'll deal with Zadar. I could train an army, improve your hillfort. He wouldn't be able to touch us while we gathered—" She was interrupted by a cry from the crowd as the Monster dipped for another bite. "We could defeat him. I know how to do it. I know his ways. You could be king of all his lands, and more. The whole island. Call off the beast."

Farrell laughed again. "Oh Lowa, what a lovely idea. But no thanks. I'm not so greedy, and things are good as they are. And besides I already have lovely Ula." He squeezed his wife's thigh. She picked up his hand and returned it to him, shaking her head.

The Monster bent for a fourth bite.

Shit thought Lowa. It was nearly over. She dug her fingernails into her palm. If *she* couldn't do anything . . .

"Channa!" she shouted as the creature went in for another bite. Were those Dug's ribs she could see? "Show some fucking character! Help him!"

Farrell chuckled. "Not many men are brave when push comes to being shoved into the maw of a ravenous animal. The Monster hasn't eaten for three days, by the way. Your old friend is fat, but the Monster's hungry and he's going to reach something vital very soon."

"Channa!" shouted Ula, more like a captain bellowing at troops than the demure queen that Lowa had thought she was. "Help him!" Lowa and Farrell looked at her.

"Shut the fuck up!" Farrell tried to backhand his wife, but she caught his arm.

"Channa!" Lowa and Ula shouted together.

"Come on, Channa!" roared Ula, standing up.

"Shut up and sit down, you mad fucking bitch!" Farrell made a grab for Ula. She swung her arm back, her heavy glass bracelet crunched into Farrell's nose and he crumpled. The crowd was silent, ignoring the man being eaten alive in the ring to stare at their felled leader and his wife.

"We have had enough!" shouted Ula. "Dug is a good man. He has done nothing to us! Nothing! Do you all want to watch him die on the whim of a distant king who brings us nothing but horror and shame?" *And riches*, thought Lowa, but she stayed quiet. "I do not," Ula continued. "Come on, Channa! Help Dug! Come on, everyone. Encourage Channa! It is time for us to say no to Farrell and his horrible reign."

"Channa! Channa! Come on, Channa! Get up!" yelled several people in the crowd. The Wounders jabbed their spears at a few of them, but there were too many to control. More and more joined in, until almost everyone was shouting at Channa.

The Monster sat up straight and looked around at the noise. It hooted angrily.

Dug lay prone, bright red blood oozing from his chest and soaking into the packed earth.

"Channa! Channa! Channa!" Now almost all the crowd were on their feet. Lowa shouted along, willing, praying, pleading for the man to help Dug. The Wounders looked about themselves. They looked at Farrell. He was moaning and holding his broken nose. A few of the crowd made to rush the ring, but the Wounders threatened them with spears.

"Does anyone have a weapon?" Lowa shouted.

Two men wrestled a spear off a Wounder and hurled it into the ring.

Channa seemed to hear it land. He uncurled from his ball, wiped his face, walked over and picked it up.

The crowd went quiet. All eyes were fixed on Channa, apart from Lowa's. She was looking at Dug. He wasn't moving. She peered harder. It didn't look like he was breathing.

The Monster, who'd been watching Channa with interest, seemed to realise the danger. It clambered off Dug and walked towards the retter.

Dug lifted an arm. Lowa let out her breath in a rush.

Channa raised the weapon, cracked his neck from side to side, bounced from heel to heel and raised the spear as if to throw it.

"Don't throw it!" shouted Lowa. If he threw it and missed, the fight would be over.

The monster was two paces from Channa. Channa jabbed. The Monster batted the spear aside and howled.

Behind it Dug pushed himself into a sitting position, one-armed. Lowa gripped her chained fists and shook them with joy and hope.

Channa jabbed again, and the Monster circled on its little legs, keeping its distance. It understood the weapon's threat.

Dug struggled to his feet. The Monster looked round and saw him. Channa saw his moment. He lunged with the spear.

The Monster dodged the blow and leaped at Channa. It grabbed his spear hand, clamped its jaws onto his wrist and shook its head savagely from side to side. Channa's hand detached from his arm. He staggered back, blood squirting in pulses from his severed wrist, saliva and horror bubbling from his lips.

The crowd gasped.

Farrell, holding his bloody nose, chuckled.

The creature ran to the other side of the ring with its grim trophy held aloft. It howled, then threw Channa's hand back at him. The bloody missile went wide and thudded soggily into the arena wall. Channa slumped and hit the ground at the same time as his severed appendage.

Across the ring, Dug had managed to stand. His face was a mess of blood. His shirt was mostly gone. One shoulder drooped horribly. Blood ran down and through his linen trousers and dripped onto the arena floor.

He looked at the Monster. The Monster looked at him. The crowd − Wounders, Farrell and Lowa included − held its breath. Dug walked towards the creature. The creature walked towards him.

"Come on, Dug!" someone shouted.

"Quiet!" Dug held up his good arm. Hush returned to the ring.

Dug and the creature stopped and faced each other, two paces apart.

Dug sat down.

The creature screamed and rushed forward, arms held aloft.

Dug bowed his head and didn't move. The creature stopped and lowered its arms. It leaned forward, sniffed the top of Dug's head, then leaned back with a long inquisitive hoot. It raised both arms to strike, then slowly lowered them.

It walked away, turned and looked at Dug. Dug stayed seated, head down. It walked back. It bent over to look into Dug's eyes, but he lowered his head further. *Fingers into windpipe!* thought Lowa, but Dug didn't move. The creature seemed fascinated by the top of his head. It began to pick at Dug's scalp like a mother plucking dirt and leaves out of a child's hair. The crowd watched in silence. The creature stood back again and looked at Dug. The northerner slowly raised his left arm, finger pointed, and jabbed his injured right shoulder.

"Ow," he said.

The creature peered at Dug's shoulder. It leaned forward, pursing its pink lips, and kissed the bruised flesh. Cooing a gentle trill, it raised a hand to stroke his injured chest. It sounded to Lowa as if it was ooo-oooing an apology. She looked around. Everyone, villagers and Wounders alike, was rapt, staring silently as if the world's best bard was telling the world's best tale.

Dug raised his head, looked the Monster in the eyes and nodded, smiling. The Monster hooted like a bereaved owl. It sat. Dug reached out and stroked its head. The Monster started at his touch and the crowd gasped, but it immediately relaxed and slumped forward into Dug's lap like an exhibitionist boy throwing himself onto his bed after an exhausting day.

The Warrior looked up at the Kanawan people. "It's no monster," he said. "It's an animal that's been treated badly. By him." He pointed at Farrell, who glared back, still holding his bloody nose. Silent tears flowed down Ula's face.

"Farrell Finda is the monster here. And, just like he has with this poor creature, he's made you monsters. You've become murderers and slavers. Is that what you wanted?" Dug looked around, stroking the furry creature. "When you were children, did you think, When I grow up, I want to be the most repellent bastard that I can be? Did you think, I want my ancestors in the Otherworld to wish they'd never lived so that I hadn't? Do you want your children and their children to hang their heads in shame when your name is mentioned? In exchange for an easy life, you have become monsters. Even if you're not directly involved, you're supporting those who are, feeding and clothing them and making sure it can all happen, even though if you think about it for half a heartbeat you know it's wrong."

None of the crowd would meet Dug's eye. "It's not too late. You do not have to do what you're told any more. Farrell is only one man. These Wounder idiots, there are only ten of them. Maybe eight or nine now, after they messed with Lowa. And she was in chains, so they're not so tough. Tell them no. Tell them you've had enough."

There was silence apart from one man clapping, slowly. Farrell.

"Eloquent words, old man. But can you give these people the riches and stability that I do? Can you—" *Thwock!* Farrell fell back.

Lowa looked for the shooter. Spring stood on the arena wall, fitting another stone into her sling. Around her the schoolgirls clambered up onto the outer wall and filed along. All held loaded slings. The spectators stared at them goggle-eyed.

Spring looked down into the ring. Her face morphed from cockiness to horror.

"What have you done!" She ran down the arena steps, leaped the wall, thudded onto the earth and ran over to Dug. "What have you done to him?"

The Monster glared up at her, but she ignored it.

"Are you all right?" she asked.

"Never better," Dug replied quietly. He closed his eyes and fell back, head thudding onto the bloody earth floor.

Chapter 17

Drustan woke and coughed up yellow-green, blood-flecked mucus. He apologised, asked how long he'd been asleep, said he'd need another few hours and passed out again.

Shortly afterwards, Ragnall had tidied the camp again and mended the hole in one of their leather saddlebags. For lack of anything else to do, he decided to make a horse litter to carry Drustan, even though he'd been told not to. He couldn't just sit there looking at his mentor hoping for him to get better.

He wandered down to the riverbank. A couple of swans stood up, arses waggling like elderly washerwomen's. They gave Ragnall a *We're not scared of you, in fact you should be scared of us, but we were leaving anyway* look, launched themselves into the river and drifted off downstream. You didn't often see swans in populous southern Britain those days because people tended to eat them. Ragnall took the sighting as a good omen.

He walked upriver and soon found two straight young poplars. He cut down the trees and stripped them with the iron hatchet that had come all the way from the Island of Angels as part of their camping kit. "When you travel by horseback, you can travel heavy," he remembered Drustan saying when they set out what seemed like a lifetime ago. He chopped a pace's length off each of the poplar poles, then lashed the four spars together with leather strips to produce a rectangular frame with four shafts. The shape reminded him of the shark's egg cases – mermaid's purses, Anwen had called them – that littered the Island of Angels' beaches. Again, that conjured images of just a few days before, when he'd had a family and a fiancée. He almost slumped to the ground with grief for his parents and brothers, but stiffened himself and got back to work.

The adult poplars nearby provided plenty of sticks and twigs for weaving through the frame to create a bed. He dragged the litter back to their camp and found his teacher still asleep. He built up the fire to keep animals away, checked Drustan again, then headed off up the road to explore.

Chapter 18

"This is it, boss," said Savage Banba, riding next to Weylin on a fresh horse. The one she'd ridden to Bladonfort could no longer walk. Banba looked fine though. Very fine, despite her long ride and sleepless night. He was impressed. He'd also enjoyed their visit to the grain store that morning and it seemed that she had too.

He put his romantic musings aside as Kanawan appeared in the valley below them. It looked peaceful and innocent. He smiled.

He rode on, then called a halt when he saw a woman walking up the hill towards them, unhurriedly, hips swinging. Her blue dress stretched to compress her ample bust, clung to her eye-catching pelvis, then stopped coquettishly just above her knee. Leather sandal twine criss-crossed her shins, as if inviting Weylin to climb her legs with his lips and teeth, lifting that light skirt . . . He shook his head. Play could come later.

"You must be Zadar's men?" she said, flicking her dark hair and looking up coolly at the mounted troops.

"We are. You have Flynn?"

"I'm Ula, Queen of Kanawan. And you are?"

"Weylin Nancarrow, Warrior in Maidun's Fifty, representative of Zadar. Do you have Flynn? I will not ask again."

"Fifty? I heard that Lowa Flynn had made it more like forty?"

"It's always fifty. If someone leaves or dies, they immediately move someone up from the—"

Weylin heard a snigger behind him.

Makka! He needed to look tougher. He put a hand on his sword pommel. "But that's nothing to do with you. Do you have Flynn?"

"Perhaps I do. Perhaps I don't. What is the reward?"

Oh Bel. Weylin had no idea what the reward was, or even if there was one. There probably wasn't. A curse on Dionysia for dying. She'd have known how to handle this. He was no good at lying, not to strangers anyway.

"You will be in Zadar's favour, which is the greatest reward there is. Please just hand her over." He heard a stifled guffaw from Ogre and realised that he needed to be a good deal more uncompromising and hard-faced. "Or we'll ride into your village and kill people until you do."

Ula regarded him fearlessly. Weylin felt uncomfortable. "All right," she said eventually. "I'll give you Flynn. And her companions. But only three of you can ride down into the village to collect them. The rest wait here."

"We need food. We'll all ride down." Weylin was taking charge.

"I will not have my village full of soldiers that you cannot control, so no, you will not all ride down. But we will give you enough food for your return to Maidun. You can send three people. Two to guard the prisoners, one to carry the food."

Weylin looked back at his troop. They were grinning as if enjoying his indecision. They *were* enjoying his indecision, he realised, all together. They must have all been talking about him behind his back, and were now united in mockery. Bel knew it had happened enough times in the past for him to recognise it. They had the look of a group who'd been slagging someone off and were watching their character assessment proven. His ears became hot.

"Ten of us will come. The rest will wait here."

The woman looked awkward. "All right," she said eventually.

Yes! thought Weylin. *I win.*

He picked nine of them.

"I'm coming as well," said Ogre.

"No, you are not," Weylin commanded. Ogre shrugged and relented. *Double win*, thought Weylin.

Twenty paces away Lowa licked her thumb and smoothed a fletching feather on her half-drawn arrow, keeping her eyes fixed on the Maidun troop as they split into two. Weylin led one group down the hill to Kanawan. The remainder dropped their reins and let their horses have their heads to pull at the roadside grass.

She'd told Ula that Weylin would insist on sending more riders down into the village than she said he could, and that had happened, but she hadn't expected the squad to be so large. Even split into two, there were too many. And it was a shame that Weylin was one of those heading downhill. She'd wanted to kill him herself, to avenge Cordelia. She should have asked Ula to keep him alive, but you can't think of everything. It had been tricky enough organising the yokels into a decent ambush while making sure their druid didn't kill Dug with his care. You never knew with druids. Some seemed to work miracles, others could cripple a healthy person in minutes with their cures.

She looked along the old boundary ditch. Good. Nothing moving. Spring and the twenty older girls were all nicely tucked down, resisting the temptation to look up at the invaders. What they'd be like once the fighting started . . . Lowa had baulked at the idea of using the girls for the ambush, but after a day's training from Spring they were by far the best slingers in the village. Somehow the little girl knew things about sling work that most Warriors didn't, and she seemed to be preternaturally capable at communicating her skills.

They had a good position too. Along much of the edge of

the ditch between the girls and the riders were coppiced hazels. These were trees that had been repeatedly cut back, so they grew in fans of thick sticks rather than trunks. These sticks were woven together to create mobile fences and pens for livestock, but they also made an excellent defensive wall. The girls would be able to shoot through the gaps, and the horses should theoretically shy at the idea of charging through them. Still, twenty young girls and her against . . . She counted fourteen riders left on the hill, most of them Warriors.

She could hear their conversation. "Weylin is an idiot," seemed to be the central theme. There was her old friend Savage Banba. She hadn't seen her at the Barton party where her women had been killed, but it was a safe bet that she had been there. She recognised most of the others too. Banba was the most useful in a fight, as far as Lowa knew, so she'd go first.

A little behind, whispering together, were Ogre and his two henchmen. So it looked like they were working for Zadar after all. She'd entertained the idea that, since they were Spring's old gang, they'd actually been after the girl with their dogs. That they were here in Weylin's troop proved that Lowa had been their prey all along.

Weylin and the others were almost at the bottom of the hill. She waited. She looked along the line of girls to check them again. Spring looked very relaxed. Hang on a minute, thought Lowa, *she's asleep*. The Warrior archer looked about for a stone to bung at the child.

"They're in there. Go and get them."

He had seen the pan-shaped structure on his way down the hill. Ula was pointing along the passage that led into it. The entrance corridor was strongly constructed from heavy oak planks, with leather nailed to its pointed roof for water-proofing, and a hefty oak door reinforced with iron bands.

A nice job. This was a rich village. But if they all went in and the door was closed behind them, they'd be trapped.

He turned. Queen Ula was looking at him with an expression of loathing and disrespect. Behind her a clutch of slack-jawed villagers were staring at him as if he were a dancing polecat. They did not look dangerous. His nine had dismounted, tied up their horses and were all now looking at him, the hint of a smile on a few of their faces as if happily anticipating another fuck-up. He didn't want to walk into a trap, but he didn't want to look cowardly in front of these bastards, who already thought he was a fool. Bel, sometimes he hated life. What to do? Sweat ran down his back like cold grease.

"Why don't you send them out here to us?" Weylin asked.

"I'd love to," said Ula, "but they're more than we can handle. We managed to chain them to the wall in there, but it wasn't easy. They killed three of mine and I don't want to lose any more. Surely a Warrior like you should be able to handle them?" She nodded at his boar necklace. Weylin looked down at it and heard a cough of laughter from one of his men.

"Why is that door so thick?" he said quickly, hoping to catch her off guard.

"We use the ring for auctioning cattle. They'd kick through a weaker door."

That seemed reasonable. *Oh Fenn!* What would Dionysia do? He could feel his troops' disdainful eyes boring into his brain.

On the hill Lowa held her breath. It had looked like Weylin was about to go into the arena, but he'd stopped. Had he seen through their plan? Surely not. This was Weylin after all. But if he and his Warriors didn't go into that arena, a lot of people were going to die. *Shit.* She thought about running down, but she was needed up here. Even with her, the girls would be lucky to take out fourteen soldiers without losing at least a couple of their own. She'd promised Ula her plan was solid.

She hadn't expected so many.

Chapter 19

A plank lay across the roadside ditch, leading to a gap in the gorse hedge. Ragnall ducked through it. Straightening up on the other side, he found a group of standing stones encircled by a low bank. Tall beech trees leaned in overhead to create a cool, shady, high but cavernous leaf-walled chamber. The nine upright stones, about his height, were the centrepiece. Each stone was roughly conical, a pace and a half in diameter at the bottom, tapering to a domed top.

It was a stone henge. He'd been taught about them and seen a few. They were ancient places of worship where long-gone people had worshipped gods which had disappeared when their people had been defeated and enslaved, as was the way. If a tribe was conquered, it adopted the conquering tribe's gods because those had proved to be more powerful than their own defeated deities.

Stone henges and other standing stones had once been as common as today's forest shrines, but for centuries they'd been seen as nothing more than sources of building material and obstacles to be cleared so that crops might grow or sheep might graze more freely. Those left were in remote places, far from agriculture and building, so it was weird to find one here, in the well populated south-west, with all the stones still standing and well maintained. Clearings like this would become overgrown in no time, so somebody must have been tending to it.

He walked around the circle. Perhaps, thought Ragnall, there was a tribe nearby which saw it as a curiosity to be

preserved. Or maybe . . . Maybe they'd strayed into the
territory of an obscure tribe that still worshipped the old
gods. The clearing suddenly seemed cooler. He jerked round
at a sound. It was a squirrel.

A thought struck him. Maybe this was a magic place.
Maybe the ancients had commanded magic and these menhirs
acted as a focus. Maybe that in itself kept it from growing
over. Maybe the gods had meant him to find it . . .

There were several slugs around the base of one of the
stones. He picked one up and glanced about. Definitely
nobody around. He stared at a dry leaf, willing it to burst
into flame. Nothing. He squeezed the slug, still looking at
the leaf. He felt the slug pop. He carried on staring at the
leaf, commanding it to consume itself with fire, beseeching
Danu to give him the power to make it do so.

Nothing happened.

Chapter 20

"OK, we'll get them, but you go in ahead of us." A masterstroke, that last idea. It had come to him from nowhere. Weylin congratulated himself on his ingenuity. Or was that Dionysia looking after him from the Otherworld?

"All right." Ula agreed without a moment's thought. The Kanawan queen walked into the corridor. So it couldn't be a trap.

"Come on everyone!" Weylin followed. Lowa Flynn was so close. He felt a nascent erection pressing against his trousers.

The whole building was a very weird construction, just the sort of thing that remote tribes with too much time on their hands got up to. The corridor was about twenty paces long and noisy with the jingle of his Warriors' ringmail as they crowded in. He turned round to tell them to stop jostling, then turned back. There was a burst of light as Ula pushed open the door at the end of the corridor. Then she raised her hands – and flew up out of sight.

What the . . . ? The outer door slammed shut behind his troops and he heard bolts slide into place. *It was a fucking trap!* For Bel's sake, why did it always happen to him?

"Don't panic," he said, trying not to panic. "We're heavily armed, and there's one door still open. On the count of three, we rush it. One, two . . ." He paused and heard a loud whistle from outside. *What did that mean?* "Three!"

Lowa heard the whistle from the arena. She leaped back onto the bank of the ditch, drew, aimed at Savage Banba, and loosed.

Banba flew backwards off her horse as if she'd been tugged by a rope. The other riders looked about in panic. Lowa shot another. They spotted her. She shot another. The riders hesitated.

Lowa knew their dilemma. When ambushed by projectile weapons like bows or slings, cavalry could either flee or ride down their attackers. Unless you were already almost out of range, attack was usually the best defence. But that went against a person's and his or her horse's instincts, so it was a decision that only the most experienced made immediately. Even then, it could be difficult to get the horse to go along with it. She drew, aimed, loosed and another rider flew from his horse. That decided them.

"Attack!" shouted one. They pulled out weapons and heaved on reins. Lowa shot another before the charge started. Five down, nine to go. She shot the lead rider before they were fifteen paces away. The next went down before five.

"Now!" said Lowa.

Along the ditch the girls leaped up, swung slings and loosed stones at the riders. Lowa saw a couple fall, and shot one more herself before another was right on her and a sword was swinging at her face.

Chapter 21

Yet again the gods had shat all over Weylin. His soldiers lay dead around him. Sixty or so tribespeople peered down at him, javelins primed. Somehow the first three volleys of their wicked little spears had missed him. He closed his eyes and waited.

"Hold!" Queen Ula's voice. "You. Weylin."

Weylin opened his eyes. "Yes?"

"Why does Zadar want Lowa?"

"I don't know."

A few people jeered.

"If you tell me, I'll consider letting you live."

Oh crap, thought Weylin. It was obvious what had happened here. They'd caught Lowa, sent out the shout, then Lowa had used her twisty ways to persuade them that she'd been wronged. He could see why she might think that she'd been hard done by. (Ha! he thought. Screw you, Dionysia. I can think from another person's point of view.) But that didn't explain why they'd taken her side against Zadar. They must be mad.

But now, more importantly, what could he say that would persuade Queen Ula to let him live? He couldn't think of anything. Why did Zadar want Lowa dead anyway? He had no idea and couldn't begin to guess.

"I really don't know," he said.

"Oh well," said Ula, "then I'm afraid I have no choice . . ."

A thought appeared in Weylin's head as if Dionysia had shot it there with a sling from the Otherworld. "But I do know why *I* want her dead."

Ula looked at him for several heartbeats.

"Why?" she asked

"She murdered my wife." Weylin nodded. The lie was easy because it wasn't even a lie. Brilliant.

Ula sat back. Her eyebrows converged and lifted like two caterpillars squaring up for combat. Was this his chance?

"And she killed my brother and my best mate."

"Why?"

"Zadar . . . wanted to talk to her. That's it, nothing more. My brother and a guy called Atlas − lovely guys, family men, had ten kids between them − were sent to get her. She killed Atlas before they'd even seen her with that Bel-cursed bow. They never had a chance. She shot my brother in the back as he ran for cover. I don't know why she did it. I guess she'd done something to make her scared of Zadar. People said that she'd murdered others, and it's true that a lot of people she didn't like disappeared.

"Then we were riding along the next day, heading back to Maidun. An arrow came out of nowhere and killed my wife, and I saw Lowa riding away over a hill. So I don't know why Zadar wanted to talk to her in the first place, but I know why I want her dead."

"But Zadar killed her whole troop of archers? And her sister?"

"Who told you that?"

"She did."

"Far as I know, she didn't have a sister. She certainly didn't have a troop of archers."

Ula was looking worried. Maybe he was going to get away with this. Ula whispered to a man, who left the arena.

"Kill him!" someone shouted.

"No," said Ula. "Let's see what Lowa has to say first."

Ah yes, there was the flaw in his plan. And he'd been doing so well.

Chapter 22

Lowa sprang back out of the ditch, arrow nocked. The woman who'd swung at her was down. No riders remained seated. The girls were among them, launching larger short-range stones from a few paces, then moving in with knives.

"Lowaaaa!" came a distressed wail. She looked for its source. *Bel! How had that happened?* Spring was clasped to a rider's chest, looking over his shoulder as he galloped away. Lowa raised her bow and steadied for the shot.

The rider was the earless Ogre. If she shot, it would probably go through him and into Spring. She could reduce her pull so the arrow didn't penetrate all the way, but the shot would still have to be powerful enough to go through his mail. It was too chancy. A head shot would do it, but the way their heads were bouncing she'd as likely hit Spring. If she took the horse out, Spring might be killed in the fall. *Shit.*

She slung her bow across her shoulders, raced for the nearest horse and leaped onto it. By the time she'd gathered the reins and turned the animal, Ogre and Spring were over the ridge and out of sight.

When she crested the valley top, they were perhaps four hundred paces away. Ogre had stopped and dismounted to change onto one of the scattered horses. *He must know which are freshest,* thought Lowa. Spring, still clutched to his chest, was whirling fists and feet like an enraged wildcat. The selected horse bucked, Ogre had to leap to avoid its crashing hooves, and Spring broke free. She spotted Lowa and started towards her, but Ogre picked up a spear and flung it. Spring staggered for a few steps, looked down at the spearhead protruding from her chest, then toppled forward.

"No!" screamed Lowa.

Ogre ran to Spring, put a foot on her back and pulled the spear out. He scooped her up, slung her light, limp body over a shoulder, clambered onto the horse and sped off.

Rage boiled from Lowa's stomach. She dug her heels in and her mount sped up. He had a two-hundred-pace head start, but Lowa's mount had a lighter load. Two miles later she was a hundred and fifty paces behind. A mile after that the gap was a hundred paces. With fifty paces between them, her horse was panting more than she'd heard a horse pant before. Spring was lifeless over Ogre's shoulder. Blood ran down her back and dripped from her hair. Lowa could have shot Ogre without harming Spring from here a hundred times out of a hundred, even with the longbow being so cumbersome on horseback. Bringing down the horse would have been even easier. But shoot Ogre or the horse and it meant Spring hitting the ground hard, and she dared not risk further injury to the girl, in case she'd somehow survived a spear through the chest. It was a ridiculous hope, but Lowa was clinging to it.

Twenty paces. She could hear Ogre's horse panting. Spring's blood had run down its flank. Too much blood.

Ten paces.

"I'll be on you in moments!" Lowa shouted above the drumming of the hooves on the metalled road. "Stop now, give me the girl, and I'll let you live!"

Ogre ignored her. Five paces. She bent low in the saddle, squeezing her thighs to urge on her tired horse. The horse, perhaps sensing an end to its exertions, sped up. Without turning, Ogre reached back and stabbed a knife into his horse's rump. His mount screamed and bounded forward, but Lowa was still gaining.

Four paces. She could smell his rank odour. Three paces. Spring's body was bouncing on his shoulder. Two paces.

"I'm here!" she said. "This is your last chance!"

Still he ignored her.

She took an arrow from her quiver. She'd grab Spring and stab Ogre in the neck in the same movement. She reached out. Her fingers brushed through Spring's hair. The girl's eyes were glassy.

As if he sensed Lowa's momentary distraction, Ogre turned and threw his knife. Lowa gasped as the blade sank to the hilt in her horse's right eye. The animal's front legs buckled, its head hit the road and Lowa was catapulted. She landed hard on a shoulder, a pace behind the hooves of Ogre's horse. She rolled twice and was back on her feet to see Ogre twist round again, this time to wave goodbye.

Her bow had landed further along the road, undamaged, thank Danu. She unslung her quiver. A couple of shafts were broken, but it was the heads that mattered. She picked out three good arrows, stashed the quiver in an old badger hole a few paces from the road and covered it with a leafy branch. Not perfect, but hopefully she'd be back soon. She slashed a tree with her knife as a marker for her quiver in case somebody took the horse for meat. She picked up her bow and arrows and set off at a jog along the road after Ogre. She didn't know why, but she very much wanted to retrieve Spring's body.

Chapter 23

"Run me through it again." Queen Ula stood, hands on hips, looking down at Weylin. Six men and women in black leather stood around her, throwing spears ready.

There were javelins everywhere, many sticking out of dead bodies. He could have grabbed one and hurled it at Ula, but he'd probably miss, and her guards would kill him with their spears if he tried anyway. Brains, he thought. That's what I'm going to need to get out of this. I'm definitely fucked.

Surrounded by corpses, he told his tale again, hoping it was the same as the first time. He was just following orders. Lowa was a criminal who'd murdered his wife, brother and best friend. He'd been given the task of chasing her down and meant no harm to the good people of Kanawan. He'd been stunned when they slaughtered his troops, and very confused, particularly given how Zadar would respond.

To his surprise it looked like Ula might be believing him, or at least not totally rejecting his tale. She was biting her lip and looking around, presumably waiting for Lowa. She'd sent several people out of the arena and they'd all come back shaking their heads. If they couldn't find Lowa – or Dug or the girl for that matter – then . . . He decided to risk it.

"She's disappeared, hasn't she?" he said, trying to sound conciliatory rather than triumphant.

Ula looked uncertain.

"I don't know what she's told you, but that Lowa Flynn, she knows how to talk. Much better than me. I guess if I were her, looking for sanctuary with decent people, I'd say

Zadar had killed some of mine and I'd escaped. I think that's how she got that guy – Dug, is it? – to go along with her. He killed a couple of ours when she escaped before. That's why Zadar wants him too. No doubt he thought he was doing the right thing but, well, he's in trouble." Weylin sucked air through his teeth. "And you, Queen Ula, have a very similar problem. You've helped somebody who's wronged Zadar."

Ula wouldn't meet his eye. Weylin took this as a good sign. He looked about at his dead comrades and shook his head theatrically.

"You sent the shout, you see? Zadar knew we were coming here. And when we don't come back? It won't be so easy to trick the next soldiers he sends. And there'll be many, many more of them. Zadar'll probably come himself. You heard what happened to Cowton? I was there. I tried to hold our people back, but Cowton had wronged Zadar. So he killed *everyone*. Children, dogs, chickens – every living thing. And most of them not quickly. Some of the things I saw . . ." Weylin thought back to that day at Cowton and managed to muster a shudder, even though he'd been one of Zadar's most enthusiastic sadists.

"Find Lowa!" Ula ordered one of the troops in black out of the arena. At the same moment one of the women whom she'd sent out earlier appeared over the top of the arena wall. She tripped down the steps to Ula and whispered something.

"Fuck. Well, go after her," said Ula. She glanced at Weylin then raised her eyes to the sky as if looking for answers up there.

Weylin smiled. So Lowa had done a runner. He wondered why.

Lowa ran, tripping along lightly at her keep-going-for-ever pace. Her breath was even, her head bobbing gently and regularly. The road was through woods, shaded from the sun, which made things easier. Pipits and tits flew from tree to tree alongside her, chirruping aimlessly. She couldn't work out if it was the same few birds following her or loads of them lining her route.

She'd seen Ogre once, near the start when the road crossed a broad, open valley. She'd hidden by a tree until he was out of sight. He'd certainly be able to outrun her on a horse if he pushed it, but if he didn't know she was following she had a good chance of catching him. He didn't know that she'd been running long distances for pleasure since she was a girl so hopefully he'd decide that she couldn't still be after him.

She felt good, happy even. That was strange given the last few days and given that she was chasing a child's corpse, but that was what running did for her. It delivered a sweeter, cleaner euphoria than any alcohol or mushroom.

Why, she thought as she ran, had Ogre taken Spring? His gang must have been after Spring all along. Had she met Spring before? Something had nagged at her about the girl – a look, a mannerism, a way of speaking that she recognised perhaps. Maybe she'd just seen her somewhere? Lowa had travelled a lot with the army and seen a lot of people, so it was more than possible.

She ran on, clutching at and failing to grab any memories of Spring. What she didn't wonder for a moment was why she was running back in the direction of all her troubles to rescue a dead girl.

"I might be able to help you," said Weylin.

"How?" said Ula eventually.

"I could talk to Zadar. He listens to me."

"Go on," said Ula.

"Well, it depends."

"On what?"

"Where are the rest of my troop? The ones I left at the top of the hill."

Ula turned to the woman who'd returned with news of Lowa. They spoke quietly so he couldn't hear, but he saw the woman draw her finger across her throat.

Ula looked at him.

"Are they all dead?"

She shook her pretty face from side to side as if wondering what to tell him.

"Tell me the truth. If none of them got away, I might be able to help you."

The two women spoke again. Ula straightened. She narrowed her blue eyes, beat her fingers against the back of the bench in front of her, then said, "One got away. He took Spring. Lowa went after him. So she didn't just run off. Everyone's saying that Lowa's trying to rescue the girl. That's hardly the behaviour of a murderer saving herself."

Bel's balls, thought Weylin. By Kornonus he hated lying. Not because there was anything wrong with it, he just wasn't very good at it. Then it came to him. He ran a hand through the knot of hair on the back of his head and chuckled.

"Oh she's good. Covering up her flight like that . . . She's not coming back. She's used you and she's off. That's what she does. Now, if you let me go, I'll go to Maidun, talk to Zadar—"

"No." Ula looked like someone who'd made up their mind. *Shit*, thought Weylin. "Perhaps you're telling the truth about her, but—"

"I *am* telling the truth."

"Fine. Will your story still be true tomorrow?"

"Yes . . ."

"And the next day?"

"Yes, by Fenn, of course."

"Then you'll stay here until Lowa comes back. Then we can test your stories against one another's."

"You let me go now, and I'll stop Zadar from killing all of you."

"No. You'll wait."

"He'll kill every fucking one of you! And worse!"

"If Lowa comes back, and you're right, then we'll take her captive, and Zadar will be grateful. Surely that would be better for you too? Unless of course you're *not* telling the truth."

Fuck. This was why he hated lying.

"All right, all right, but she's not coming back."

"We'll see."

Chapter 24

Drustan woke in the early afternoon. He scorned Ragnall's litter, stood up and collapsed. Ragnall dashed forward and knelt next to him, holding his head as his body pulsed with racking coughs.

"Ah," Drustan said when he'd recovered. "Perhaps the litter is not such a bad idea. Since you've already made it." He coughed again.

Ragnall dragged the litter over to him.

"I am sorry," said Drustan.

"I'm sorry you're ill. I just want you to get better."

"Yes. Well. I have to be kept warm."

"But you're—"

"Sweating, yes. Still, need to be kept warm. I bought some barberry jam in Bladonfort. Find that and I will try to eat some."

"OK, I'll get—"

"Wait." Drustan coughed up sputum. It was more light grey than yellow now. "There is more. It is possible my mind might . . . slip. Important that I keep drinking boiled water and eating barberry jam. And warm. Use all the blankets on the litter, as many below as on top. And I will need boiled water to drink."

"Right." Ragnall stood and began to unstrap the packs that he'd just strapped to the sullen little packhorse. "And if," he said over his shoulder, "well if . . . Where are we going?"

"South-west. Place called Mearhold."

"Right."

"But you can't get there . . . Swamp . . . Head for Gutrin Tor. It is the highest place for miles around, with a square tower on the top. Ask for Maggot – Mearhold's druid. He'll help. For now barberry jam, water, rest . . . is what I need."

"OK. One more thing."

Ragnall paused. Drustan nodded weakly.

"Why don't you use magic? To cure yourself?"

The druid shook his head and muttered incoherently. Ragnall layered wool blankets on the litter and rolled Drustan onto it, piled more blankets on top, then secured him with hemp ropes. Shortly afterwards Ragnall led the three-horse procession up the road: the two mounts with the litter first, then the packhorse. He'd decided to walk next to the horses rather than ride to keep the pace calm and slow. As they passed the hole in the hedge that led to the henge, Ragnall found himself silently asking the ancient gods to restore Drustan to health.

Chapter 25

At sunset, Lowa was still running but she was immeasurably less chipper. To begin with she'd pumped her arms, arrows in one hand, bow in the other. Now the wooden weapons felt heavy as granite, and it felt like her hip bones were grating directly on her pelvis. Her underarms were chafing painfully and the insides of her leather boots were slick with what she hoped was sweat, could be blister fluid, but was probably blood.

Judging by where the sun had been when she left and her normal speed, she'd come around thirty miles, a good ten miles further than she'd run before and a good fifteen more, she'd decided, than was pleasant. She'd stopped briefly only to gulp water from streams and four other times, three times at villages and once to talk to a man driving an ox cart. People at two of the villages and the carter had seen Ogre. At the last village, about a mile back, a woman had said that an earless man riding with a pack slung over the back of his horse was half an hour ahead of her. None of the villages had had horses for her to borrow, or at least they'd said they hadn't, and she hadn't seen any. They had, however, given her food, for which she was grateful.

She wanted to stop, a lot. The girl means nothing to you, said a weaselly internal voice. Just think how nice it would be to stop, it said for the thousandth time. How about a lovely sit-down on the grass? You could rest a while, wander back to Kanawan and get on with avenging Aithne and the girls. This is not helping. *The girl is dead*. You're following nothing. That bundle on the horse isn't Spring, he dumped her body in the woods miles back. You're running for no reason. Just stop. *Rest.*

But another voice, a stronger voice, told her to keep going. She ran on, fording streams, speeding down hills and schlepping thigh-burningly up them.

It was dark when she finally slowed to a walk, cloud cover blocking the stars and moon. She told herself that Ogre would camp for the night to rest the horse, and she didn't want to overtake them. Her relief at stopping was short-lived. Spasms cramped through her legs. She leaned on a tree stump and pulled a foot up to her bottom to stretch her aching leg muscles, but it didn't help. She walked on, the pain in her thighs so intense that it made her giggle. She jogged for a few paces, but that was sore in a different way and she soon stopped. She had to walk. She didn't want to miss . . .

Something told her to stop and listen. She did, holding her breath. Nothing. But then . . .

A horse's whinny, faint, off the track and back a few paces. She stopped, closed her eyes and strained her ears. Nothing. She walked back in stealth gait – feet wide, hands splayed, palms facing down – the pain in her legs ignored. There wasn't much point trying to be stealthy though. It was so dark that she couldn't see where the road stopped and the woods began, let alone spot snappable twigs or other potential alarm raisers. For all she could see, she might have been approaching a precarious stack of bronze cymbals.

She held her breath. She heard only the swish of bats taking advantage of the cleared track to swoop for insects, the skittering of timorous beasts in the undergrowth and the far-off scream of a fox.

And then, there! Definitely a horse's gentle nicker. She walked slowly back along the track, cursing silently when she kicked a stone and it clicked lightly into another one. Yes, there it was. A flickering light a hundred paces away through the trees. She looked away, but the fire still flickered on her retina. It couldn't be them, could it? Surely Ogre wouldn't light a fire?

She crouched and closed her eyes for a hundred heartbeats to optimise her night vision. She opened them. *Better*. She crept along the road, trying to pierce the night with her eyes and find a path into the woods. She looked at the trackside, resisting the temptation to glance at the fire and ruin her night vision again.

She found the gap, a blacker circle in the black vegetation. In a perfect world she'd have waited there until dawn, or at least until the clouds cleared, rather than stumble blind towards a possible enemy camp. But that was the point, annoyingly. It was only a *possible* enemy camp. It might be any other traveller or forest dweller, and Ogre might be making good his escape, or even bedded down for the night just a few hundred paces further up the road. She had to check.

Slowly, as gingerly as a child with a tyrannical father coming home hours after curfew, she edged forward. The ground, sheltered under a roof of leaves, was still soft from the recent rain. Hands outstretched, she could feel foliage either side. It was a trappers' or foragers' path, she guessed, used just enough to keep it from growing over. She could smell horse and man. She moved on, slowly, slowly, breathing shallowly, bow searching the ground and air in front of her like a blind man's stick, testing for traps. If she was Ogre, she would have left a few surprises on the path for any pursuers.

The light from the fire crept into her peripheral vision.

She stepped on a twig. *Crack!* In the quiet night it sounded like rock split by frost.

"Who's there?" came a rough voice from the fire.

"Choppy-chup-chop!" squeaked Lowa, shaking a bush. Her badger impression was, she liked to think, good, but she crouched down anyway. Slowly, firmly, she pushed her three arrows into the mud, then bent her bow into the ground and slipped the leather string into the notch on the horn tip. She heard the soft steps of a worried horse, the soothing whispers of a man, then nothing. She looked up. The fire was perhaps twenty paces away, around a bend in the path.

She counted a hundred breaths, heard nothing more from the camp and decided that her badger ruse had worked.

She crept along the path until it turned towards the camp. Carefully, she poked her head around the corner. The brightness of the fire made her eyes water and she blinked away tears. The camp was in a small clearing. To the left was a small forest altar. It wasn't a hunters' track then, but the path to a little-visited shrine.

Sitting on the far side of the fire, staring into it, was earless Ogre. To the right of the fire was the horse, standing placidly and breathing deeply, perhaps asleep. There was no sign of Spring.

Chapter 26

Weylin leaned against the arena wall in the night, surrounded by his dead troops and javelins. He was cold, even in his leather and ringmail. His broken wrist stung, his head throbbed, he was as hungry as a stepchild in a famine and he was miserable. He'd failed Zadar again. Some people believed that the path to success was failing over and over with a smile on your face until you got it right. Zadar didn't. Most people failed the king of Maidun only once then spent the short remainder of their lives regretting it.

He looked up. Half the sky was bright with stars, but a line of clouds was gradually covering them like a slowly shutting roof hole. Soon it would be very dark. If it rained, he thought, he might very well use one of the javelins on himself. Or maybe two. He could put the points up his nose then slam the butts into the ground. But there was no need. He'd be all right. Death, he'd observed, was something that happened to other people.

Chapter 27

"Why the fire?"

Ogre jumped up. She was a few paces into the black woods, on the other side of the campfire. The bandit peered through the flames like a half-blind dog looking for its tormentors.

He bent to pick something up. "Ah ah," she said. "I've got an arrow on you. Make another move and it's in you. Now tell me, why the fire?"

"Bears." Ogre's voice was deep, from somewhere further north, but not as far north as Dug's strange accent, nor from across the sea like hers.

"Bears?"

"Bears."

"Why bears?"

Ogre stayed silent. He looked like he might burst with rage.

"Answer me, or you'll never speak again."

"I've seen what those nasty fuckers can do."

"But there are no bears around here."

"Wolves, then."

"I guess. But still . . . lighting a fire that can be seen from the road by anyone looking for the girl? Was that sensible?"

"What girl?"

"Spring. The girl you took from Kanawan."

"I've never been to Kanawan."

"I know who you are, Ogre. You used to be Spring's boss. You used to have five dogs. Very soon, if you don't tell me where the girl is, I'll send you the way of your hounds."

"I haven't got her. She ran off." He looked down to the left. "I stopped for water and she legged it."

"No, she didn't. You put a spear in her back. She won't be running anywhere for a while."

"All right." His head slumped. "You're right. I dumped her body miles back."

Chapter 28

Weylin walked up the broad ramp to Maidun Castle's upper area, the sacred part where Zadar lived. Few were allowed up there and Weylin had never been before. The world was awash with golden light because everyone was wearing golden clothes, and their cheering was like golden noise in his ears.

"*Weylin!*" they chanted. "Wey*lin!*" They were all there – Atlas, Lowa, Dionysia, Ula, Carden – all cheering, all cheering *him*. Zadar was waiting with arms outstretched. Felix, a genuine grin beaming from his streamlined face, was clapping and nodding admiringly.

Weylin turned to wave to the crowd. The lower expanse of Maidun was packed with thousands of cheering admirers, almost all of them attractive women. All around the great castle, stretching for miles, the farmland was filled with all the people in the world, all there to cheer Weylin. Babies were held aloft, women bared their breasts, men wept at his magnificence.

He turned to head up to Zadar, to join him as an equal. As he lifted his foot, he felt a great rumbling in his stomach, precursor to a huge fart. There was no holding it in, but nobody would hear it above the noise of the crowd.

Still smiling and waving, he strained, pushed, and *Oh fucking Bel!* His arse cheeks flapped like wet lips blowing a raspberry and a great glob of shit exploded from his arse.

He looked around the crowds, trying to keep the look of horror from his face. Nobody had noticed anything wrong.

He reached around and put his hand on the back of his bare leg. What? Why wasn't he wearing trousers? He pulled his hand up. Lumpy brown turd ran down his fingers, palm and wrist. How could there be so much of it?

"He's *shat* himself!" squealed Felix gleefully. Zadar looked disgusted and turned away. All the people in the world laughed at his shame, apart from one boy who ran up and grabbed his arm. "Pssst!" Weylin flailed at the child with his sword but missed.

"Pssst!" said the boy again.

"Pssst!"

Weylin woke and looked up. A head was silhouetted against the dark sky, looking down at him from the arena wall. Weylin remembered where he was and sighed with relief.

"Hello," he said.

"Shhhhh," said the head. "Listen. What you said about Zadar – can you stop him from retaliating?"

"From doing what?"

"Retaliating."

"I can hear you," Weylin whispered, "but I don't know what 'retaliating' means."

"From attacking us because we killed his soldiers?"

"I see. Yes, I can stop him."

"How?"

Weylin had worked this all out earlier. "Easy. I'll say we came to the village, and you handed Flynn and the others over. Like you should've done. Then, on our way back we were attacked by a raiding party from Dumnonia which outnumbered us three to one. Everyone was killed but me."

"Won't he come looking for the Dumnonians?"

"If he does, so what? He won't find them. You get everyone here to say that I headed off with Flynn and that they'd heard reports about a Dumnonian war band. Which, they've also heard, has gone back to Dumnonia."

"But he'll ask why we didn't send a shout about the bandits?"

"Look, I can't think of everything. Maybe you can send a shout when I'm gone? Let me out of here, and I'll do my best to persuade Zadar that there were bandits, and Kanawan did nothing wrong. Otherwise, mate, you're fucked. Even if you all leave he'll track you down and slaughter the lot of you. Let me go. I'm your only hope."

Chapter 29

"**Y**ou're lying. You've got her."

Ogre's eyes darted down to the left again, then back up, searching for Lowa in the darkness.

She walked out into the little clearing slowly, bow three-quarters drawn, eyes everywhere. She was almost certain he was alone, but "almost certain" hadn't kept her alive all these years. However, the camp looked clear.

The altar had a couple of small human skulls on it. Could be child sacrifices but more likely bones from children who had died elsewhere and been brought here by a freaky druid. Away from Maidun and Zadar's army, very few people killed children.

There *was* a bundle on the ground. Ogre had looked at it a couple of times now. She couldn't tell with a quick glimpse if it was Spring. It looked so small, and his glances may have been a ruse. She took a couple of sidesteps so that there was an oak tree directly behind the earless kidnapper.

"Where are you taking her?" she said.

"I wouldn't worry about that. Worry about where he's taking you!" Ogre pointed into the trees behind Lowa. She didn't fall for it, but Ogre seemed resolved on carrying out the second part of his distract-then-attack plan. He dropped into a crouch, then leaped at her, mace in hand.

She squatted and loosed. Her arrow punched through his left shoulder, flung him back and skewered him to the broad-trunked tree. The arrow had a slim bodkin but a thick shaft, designed for hampering the flight of large game, but it suited this purpose too.

He roared, then screamed as Lowa's second arrow ripped through his right wrist and into the trunk.

Lowa ran to the bundle. It was Spring, curled in a ball.

Lowa rolled her over. Even in the copper firelight she looked as pale as someone who'd bled to death from a spear wound. Lowa pressed two fingers onto the girl's neck, held them there for a good while, then shook her head. She stood up, nocked her final arrow and pointed it at Ogre's face.

"I asked where you were taking her."

"You've . . . you've fucked my arm! And my shoulder!"

"You'll live if I take the arrows out, which I'll do if you answer my questions. I'll know if you're lying. Lie, and the next shot is in your guts."

"You bitch. I'll make you mine in the Otherworld, and I'll beat you every—"

"Where were you taking her?" Lowa drew.

"All right! She wasn't dead a moment ago, I swear. I was just trying to throw you off when I said she was dead. It was fucking weird, I'll give you that. I wanted her alive, but my temper . . . She bit me. That's why I stuck a spear through her. Could have sworn I killed her. It should have killed her, but then we were riding along and she started talking and she was fine. She was sitting up and talking not long before you got here. Check again. She's probably asleep – sleeps like the dead, that one."

"I don't make mistakes. She is dead. Looks like sticking a spear through her then bouncing her around on a horse all day wasn't a good idea. Who'd have guessed?"

"I swear—"

"You swear nothing!" Lowa strode forward, pressed her knife into Ogre's neck and put her lips to his ear. "You're going to tell me where you were taking her, and why, and

I'm going to believe you, or I'm going to leave you here for the bears. Let's start with where you were taking her."

Ogre slumped, then stiffened with the pain. He gathered himself and said, "Don't suppose it matters now. I was taking her to Maidun Castle."

"Why?"

"Zadar wants her."

"Why?"

"A moon ago we got her drunk for a laugh. I was helping her be sick, away from the rest – I was good to that girl – and she told me something."

"What did she tell you?"

"She told me she was Zadar's daughter."

Chapter 30

"I'm sorry, that's really all I know. But you must know why he wanted the girl?"

Ula put a pint mug of wine on the table beside the bed next to the empty one that Dug had downed moments before. The morning light from the roof hole brought out the tinge of red in her dark hair. Even though she looked as if she hadn't slept, Dug thought she was so beautiful that she must be a goddess. But, then again, he usually thought that about women who looked after him when he was injured. And he'd drunk a pint of wine.

"Lowa'll get her," he said carefully. Any movement in his chest hurt, which made breathing a bit of a bugger.

"That's not all. I'm sorry, but we let Weylin go."

"Weylin?"

"Of course, you don't know what happened." Ula sat on the end of the bed. "Nobody was happy with Farrell's rule – the slavery, the girls – but they didn't know that everybody else felt the same. After your speech, people started shouting, then they got violent. A couple of Wounders were killed, and the Monster. Spring tried to protect it – she's a funny one, that girl – but she couldn't stop the whole tribe. Then I managed to restore order by . . ." All the mischief that had been in her smile that first morning in Kanawan was gone. "By killing Farrell. I killed my husband."

Dug's eyebrows flew up like seagulls caught in a gust. Ula looked at her hands.

"I stabbed him in the heart. It surprised everyone into

calming down. That saved the Wounders who were still alive. They aren't bad people. And it confirmed my right to lead the tribe. We need a strong leader."

"I'm sorry."

She smiled as tears appeared. "Don't be. You should be the opposite of sorry. I and all of Kanawan owe you a great debt. And besides—" she scratched the back of her head "—I've wanted to kill Farrell for years. I loved him when I married him, but very quickly I realised that he was a . . . what's a good way of putting it?"

"A wanker?" Dug suggested.

Ula breathed a deranged-sounding laugh. "I've hated him for years. I keep – I mean I kept – trying to like him. He'd do something kind or he'd look at me in a certain way or we'd have great sex or a really good laugh and I'd start thinking that he wasn't so bad after all. Then he'd do or say something so unthinking, arrogant or just rude that I'd realise that he was simply a very unpleasant man. It wasn't the big things. Yes, sending the girls to Zadar was awful, unforgivable, but it was the little things that got to me. Like when we saw you coming down the hill with Lowa and he whipped his top off to run outside and exercise."

"Aye."

"Yes. And that was only one of about fifty things he did just that day that made me think 'you are such a dick'. It's a horrible thing to think about your own husband . . . But I was telling you about Weylin. We knew, because of Farrell's shout, that Zadar's people would be here any moment and guessed that they'd search the village, so, with you in no condition to travel, Lowa came up with a plan to ambush and kill them. It worked, even though twenty soldiers arrived and we'd been expecting six at most. We killed them all apart from their leader – this man Weylin – and the fellow who escaped on horseback with Spring."

"Why did he take Spring?" Dug said slowly.

"I thought you'd know. I don't. Lowa's plan was to split them in two. We'd take out half of them down here, and she, Spring and the girls would deal with the others on the east road, up the hill."

"The girls?"

"The girls from the school. Spring taught them to . . . But that doesn't matter. The point is that one man survived and snatched Spring."

"Lowa will get her back."

"I'm sure she will." Ula sounded distracted. She looked up, blinking. The light twinkled in her tears.

"And Weylin got away?" Dug asked gently.

Ula rubbed her tears away and shook her head. "Two people were guarding him last night. He persuaded them that he could prevent Zadar from retaliating against Kanawan if they let him go. So they did. I understand why. Zadar has wiped out tribes for a lot less than we did. But I wish they'd asked me. Even if Weylin has any influence over Zadar, which I very much doubt having spoken to Weylin, why would he try to save a village that defeated and humiliated him?"

"He wouldn't."

Ula smiled sadly. "Yes. So we've freed a captive who will tell Zadar what happened here. But that's not the worst of it. Killing Farrell wasn't the worst thing I did yesterday." She closed her eyes and shook her head. "I also killed my son."

"Your son?" For a moment Dug thought of the Monster.

"He won't be dead yet, but Zadar has our son Primus as a hostage. Farrell insisted on the name, by the way. Zadar takes hostages from every tribe that he can. Farrell said living at Maidun was for Primus' education, to build his character, make him a better man and so on, but we both knew what it really was. Now the best thing Primus can hope for is a quick death. I've send riders after Weylin, of course, but he had such a head start . . ." Ula closed her eyes. Tears dripped onto her fine wool dress. "He's only four."

Ignoring the pain in his chest, Dug reached up and put a hand on her arm. "Zadar won't kill him."

"Why not?"

Dug took a long but shallow breath, then spoke slowly: "I was with a tribe a few years back, working my way, and I saw it from the other side. Their king, Weeza, murdered plenty in lots of nasty ways. Worse than Zadar probably, but smaller scale. He had a hostage, a wee girl called Willow, from a nearby tribe called the Cluddens. She was their king's only child. Despite him having Willow, the Cluddens attacked Weeza's people and killed a few of them. Weeza struck back with his usual enthusiasm. Treachery got us into the Cluddens' hillfort and we killed everyone in there. Everyone. I was getting paid and I was following orders. So I understand how easy it is. Anyway, the whole episode – from the Cluddens attacking to being wiped out – took about a moon. In all that time, Weeza didn't harm the wee Cluddens hostage. She's still alive, as far as I know. The last of the Cluddens."

Ula looked up, hope in her wet eyes. "Why didn't he kill her?"

"No point. A hostage's value lies in preventing something. As soon as that something happens, the hostage is worthless. Look at it from Zadar's point of view. You've killed some of his, so he'll come here to wipe you out – you know that?"

"Yes, we're packing up the village and leaving for Dumnonia today, or possibly Eroo."

"Aye, smart move. So, you've killed twenty of Zadar's. He'd hoped that having Primus would stop you from doing anything like that, but it didn't. It's happened. Why would he kill Primus now?"

"To teach others a lesson?"

"Aye, that is a point, but it won't happen because Primus is still useful to him. Zadar doesn't know the situation here. Maybe he'll come and you're holed up in the hillfort, so he can use Primus to pry you out. Maybe he'll keep him and then present him in a few years as the rightful king of Kanawan. But you're going to bugger off, so there's nothing Zadar can use Primus for."

"To bring us back from exile?

"No. He'd have to know where you'd gone to do that. Go through Dumnonia, and he won't. Primus is safe. And you never know. Zadar might fall soon, and then you'll be reunited."

"There's that . . ."

"And of course Zadar probably likes the child."

"Zadar?"

"Aye. People aren't good or bad. They're good *and* bad. That same guy – Weeza – nasty torturing type – loved animals. Made sure the farm animals were well looked after, didn't eat meat, got in a panic when his pet cat didn't come back in the evening . . . Point is, once you get to know a child, it's difficult to kill them."

Unless her son takes after his father, thought Dug, in which case Zadar would have brained the wee bugger a long time ago.

Ula put a hand on Dug's arm. "Thank you. You might be right. But I mustn't dwell on it. I'm the leader now and I have to save my people. I've got to get everyone packed up." She stood up. "You're too badly wounded to travel quickly."

"Aye. Leave me here. I'll be fine. It's my fault you had to attack Zadar's men and get yourselves into this mess."

"Don't be stupid. I discussed it with Lowa before Weylin arrived, and it's been decided. She's going to take you to a tribe not far away where Zadar has no sway. Their town is in a marsh and you can get to it only if they want you to. Their druid's a good healer who will help you recover quickly."

The thought of being taken somewhere by Lowa made him smile. "I've heard of the marsh tribe – Mearhold, isn't it?"

"That's it."

"Neutral tribe that the big boys and girls have agreed to leave alone. Why would they risk that for a fugitive from Zadar?"

"I know them. I go there often to get clothes. The island's secure and they're not the sort to be frightened by bullies. Besides, who's going to tell Zadar you're there?

"Ah, if you say so." Dug's chest was blazing with pain now. He reached for the pint of wine.

Chapter 31

It was late afternoon when Weylin heard the faint cries: "Help! Please!"

He dismounted quietly. There was a narrow path burrowing into the woods. He tied the reins to a branch, held his fingers to his lips and said, "Sssshhh!" to his horse. There was no need really. It was a good little horse and hadn't complained since he'd found in it the woods above Kanawan, even though he'd ridden all night. He'd stopped only a few times, for water mostly and when he'd hidden from Lowa, riding with a large bundle behind her and her bow in her hand. Thank Bel he'd been able to hide before she'd seen him. Unarmed, there was no way he was going to take her on.

"Help!" Another cry. Yes, he was on the right path. It turned a corner and opened into a shrine clearing that had been used as a camp. Over to the right, pinned to a tree by arrows through his wrist and shoulder, was Ogre. His shirt and trousers were dark with dried blood. His earless head was pale with blood loss.

Weylin chuckled.

"Weylin! Please. Water and . . . get these fucking arrows out."

"What happened to you?"

"Lowa."

"She left you like this?"

"Yeah."

"That's not nice. What did you ever do to her? She's trouble that one." Weylin sat on a log, rested his elbows on his knees, placed his chin on pointed fingers and looked up at Ogre thoughtfully.

"Water, please," begged the earless bandit.

"You know it's funny." Weylin shook his head. "I remember asking you for help back in Bladonfort. You tried to make me look stupid."

"Please."

"Then you laughed at me behind my back all the way to Kanawan. I saw you smirking with your friends. And my company."

"Weylin, I've got coins. Take my bracelets."

"Don't worry, I will. Oh, what's this?" Weylin picked up Ogre's small mace. It was a crude thing, just a lump of iron on the end of a stout stick. "I'd like to take those arrows out and help you down, but I think it was you who warned Kanawan that we were coming. You're the reason we didn't catch Lowa."

"You think that?"

"Yup."

"She stole my girl. She killed my dogs. Now she's killed my men and left me here pinned to a *fucking tree*." Ogre coughed. "And you reckon I warned her we were coming!"

"Yup."

"Then you really are as stupid as everyone said."

Weylin's mace blow smashed Ogre's knee.

The earless man screamed and convulsed. Weylin smiled to see fresh blood well from his shoulder and wrist wounds. He pulled the mace back and cracked it into the other knee.

"And now," he said to the whimpering Ogre, "I'm going to get nasty."

Before he died, Ogre admitted that he had betrayed Weylin and his troop to Kanawan and Lowa. He was a bit shaky on the details of how he'd done it, but the confession was good enough for Weylin.

Part Three
Mearhold

Chapter 1

"All right, you got it? Frog and watercress soup at lunch, as much as he'll take, more of that barberry jam whenever and as much water as he'll drink."

Maggot waved a finger at his nodding child assistant, then led Ragnall by the elbow out of the hut, leaving Drustan asleep under wool blankets on a cot lined with moss. The morning sky was a cover of bright white cloud split by the odd shifting smear of blue. Blusters of breeze carried a salt and mud tang from the marshes to the west. An arrowhead of pelicans flew north across the wind, so low that Ragnall could hear their wings creaking.

Maggot gripped Ragnall by both arms. "We'll leave Drustan to sleep. He might live." Mearhold's druid pointed his fingers at Ragnall's nose and waggled them. His surfeit of metal rings – at least three on each digit – clacked. He saw Ragnall looking at them and grabbed his fingers to his chest as if to protect his hoard. He leaned in until his face was nearly touching Ragnall's. He looked about, seemed to decide that nobody was eavesdropping, then whispered, "He might not."

Ragnall was used to weird-looking and weird-acting druids. In fact, with his plain dress and riddle-free reasoning, Drustan was about the most against-type druid he'd met. Maggot, who spoke, moved and dressed as if he'd lost his mind, was much more the norm.

He wore leather slippers and smart half-length tartan trousers gathered around his bony hips by a leather belt that looked like it had been chewed, swallowed and shat out by a goat. His fat-free, sinewy upper torso was unclothed, but, like everyone Ragnall had seen so far in Mearhold, he was adorned with jewellery and other accessories like a fir tree at winter solstice. About his neck was a band of tight yellow glass hoops, a bronze and shale necklace and two leather thongs, one dangling a disc of skull bone onto his bumpy chest, the other threaded through a triangle of flint. Jangling on his arms were bronze, copper, shale, wooden, iron and tin armbands above the elbow, and a clutch of varied brace-lets below. His long blond hair was swept back, but orange feathers dangled from a headband over his ears and cheeks.

He stared at Ragnall as if waiting for him to say something.

"What?" said Ragnall.

"Exactly! Exactly. You've never been here. I'll show you around. First, we'll look at people making cloth. Why not? That's what a lot of people do here. Keeps us afloat, they say. Me, I've always thought that it was all the logs piled below us that keep us afloat. But the gods are odd, man."

Maggot winked and walked off at a nippy pace. Ragnall followed more slowly, still wary on the island's clay paths, which felt like they might crack any moment and plunge him through into the marsh, or whatever was below them. "Semi-floating island" was how Drustan had described Mearhold in one of his lucid moments on their short but difficult journey.

They passed several large, pristine round huts with thatched roofs and a man wearing even more jewellery than Maggot who was introduced as the glass-bead maker. There weren't many other people about, but not far away a baby was bellowing, and earthily pungent smoke escaping from the huts' conical roofs showed that several of the inhabitants were busy with breakfast.

"A fire in every hut?" asked Ragnall. "In summer?"

"Peat burns." Maggot nodded away from the rising sun.

"Over there the land's made of peat. So yeah, people cook for themselves. And over there – " Maggot pointed to the edge of the island where a rectangular building looked like it was on fire " – is where we smoke food. Duck, goose, swan, beaver, frog, bittern, eel, trout, bass, mackerel, snake, snake eggs . . . you name it, we catch it and we smoke it. *Please* try the smoked limpets while you're here. They look like a little bit of person picked up off an old battlefield, but they are very fucking tasty. We also salt a lot of food, but the smoked stuff's better."

They passed some children playing dice and a woman working with molten bronze behind a windshield of latticed sticks and reeds, and arrived at the promised group of cloth makers. There were seven of them, men and women working with whorls and looms, singing,

> Oh there'll always be a bigger fish,
> To turn an eater into a dish!
> Oh there'll always be a smarter eel,
> To turn the eater into the meal!

They watched for a short while before Maggot said, in full earshot of the workers, "Boring, isn't it? And these cunts do it all day. Come on, let's go to Gutrin Tor."

Oblivious to the workers' scowls, the druid led Ragnall to the clay and wood wharf on the island's eastern edge where he and Drustan had arrived a few hours before. An array of longboats cut from oak trunks was tied to the low dock, clonging against each other in the current and breeze. Maggot ushered him into the prow of one of the smaller ones. After his sleepless night, Ragnall felt dreamily but brightly awake, with everything a little fuzzy at the edges. He clambered down into the narrow tippy boat.

Maggot unwound the mooring rope from a cleat and pushed off across a clear stretch of water towards a wide channel cut through the reeds. As he paddled, he called out the names of the wildfowl that darted between the reed clumps.

"Coot. Moorhen. Teal, that one. Male tufted duck over there. Look at him with his ponytail and his why-don't-you-all-fuck-off beak. He'd lose a fight with a dormouse, but he thinks he's Nanoc the Warrior's big brother. That all-black one, following behind, is a female tufted duck. Probably his mate. You can see how embarrassed she is."

"How can there be so many different kinds in one place?" Ragnall asked.

"Yeah, well, we're good to them. We keep the eagles, falcons, otters, kites and all that away with a bit of clever slinging. The swamp itself protects them from all your other would-be duck eaters: your foxes, your martens, polecats, wildcats, wolves, our cats."

"Why protect birds?"

Maggot laughed. "Like all things people do, it's selfish. We like to eat them and their eggs. We treat them well, we get more. Like a good king gets more from his people than a bad one. In the long run, anyway."

They floated along for a while, then Ragnall asked, "And the village is man-made?"

"More or less. It's loads of logs, packed with reeds, rubble and the like, then topped, in part, with clay. Clay's mixed with ash to stop it cracking when it dries, in case you're interested in the drying of clay." Ragnall turned his head and Maggot winked at him.

"But why here? Why on the edge of the world? And why make new land when there's plenty all around?"

"It's all about the festival. And who says it's the edge of the world? How d'you know it's not the middle?"

"The festival?" Ragnall shifted and the boat tipped alarmingly. He gripped the sides.

"Don't worry about a tip or two. They'll give you a scare, but they're more stable than they look, these boats. Although you can turn 'em over if you try hard enough." Maggot paddled a few strokes in silence.

"Right. The festival?"

"We have a big festival every year – music, dancing . . . People come from everywhere. You've missed it this year. It was about a moon ago. Not that you missed much. It's not what it used to be. Thirty summers ago, when I was a bit younger than you are now, it was beautiful. Hundreds of us would get totally off our tits on cider and mushrooms, the bards would play all night, and everybody was up for pretty much anything." Maggot sighed. "Now though, it's a victim of its own success, isn't it? Now it's all about families, food and merchants, more about people bartering and taking coin off each other than getting messed up and having a good time. Which is not the end of the world, because I quite like taking my kids to it now, and I'm not into staying up all night any more, but still . . ."

They rounded a corner, and the stepped triangular hill of Gutrin Tor rose ahead. Bands of differing greens decreased in size towards a grassy top tipped by a black tower.

"It's a shame because it had been like it was for hundreds of years," Maggot continued, paddling regularly. "And that's why Mearhold is here. Six, seven generations ago there were some people who loved the festival so much that they stayed. There weren't many of them, just four families, so they built an island rather than live on the land with the wolves and the bandits. Why not, I reckon, eh?"

"Yes, I can see—"

"And it's safe as the biggest hillfort cos we control the boats. Every night they all come back to Mearhold. There are plenty of other people living around the swamp, but we don't let 'em have boats. We catch 'em building one and we kill 'em. Seems harsh but, as everyone likes to say, we're protecting our children. Actually of course we're protecting ourselves. But that's fair enough, someone's got to. And because we're so serious about it, everyone knows not to build a fucking boat. So we never have to kill anyone – well hardly ever – so it all works. And it's nice for me to have a human sacrifice every now and then . . . Here we go. We're here."

There were plenty of boats moored at the base of Gutrin Tor but no people about.

"Yeah," said the druid. "All these boats'll be going home to the island tonight."

"Where are the people?"

"I don't know? Doing shit? Looking for things? Mending stuff? Whatever it is people do. I don't get involved. Keep your foot in the middle of the boat as you step out, mind. There, that's it!" said Maggot.

Ragnall climbed out onto the dry dock and took a few paces. The ground felt reassuringly solid after Mearhold Island's spongy floor.

Maggot waved his arms at the hill. "Gutrin Tor. An island in the swamp."

The wiry druid strode off along a path up the hill. Ragnall followed.

On the lower slopes they passed peas and beans growing in neat rows, then apple orchards—"for the cider," smiled Maggot. Further up were barley, oats and wheat. Nearer the top stood stands of coppiced hazel and grazing sheep.

Maggot stopped and peered at Ragnall. "Looks like it's been like this for ever, right? It hasn't though. This hill, my boy, is older than we can imagine. And it'll be here for longer than we can imagine. See this?" He picked a blade of grass. "The building of Mearhold, all that's happened to people there and all that will happen, that's less important to this hill than this blade of grass is to us. It's the earth that matters. People are specks of dust that land on it one moment and are blown away the next."

The druid headed up the hill again, loping at an astonishing pace.

Despite his youthful athleticism, Ragnall was soon puffed. He was glad when Maggot stopped and pointed north. "We didn't make this land. We didn't even make these terraces." He waved a hand at the steps in the hillside. "Who did? Dunno. Why? Dunno. Druids, bards, kings and others will tell you who built them and why with absolute fucking certainty. They'll swear they know. But they don't."

Maggot carried on up and disappeared over the final rise.

The square tower was bigger than it had looked from the marshes, maybe ten paces high, made from heavy blocks of dark, pocked stone. It looked ancient. There was a door guarded by a man and a woman wearing the laid-back garb and jewellery of the other Mearholders, but armed with swords and shields. Maggot was nowhere to be seen. Ragnall hesitated.

"Don't mind us – we're here to stop animals, not people," said the woman. "Maggot went up to the top. Asked us to ask you to follow."

"Thanks!" Ragnall nodded to each of them and ducked through the door.

Inside was a dark staircase. Ragnall guessed that the tower had been built with a double wall, with the staircase between the walls. He could see no way in to the centre, so possibly the middle of the building was hollow and unused. There were a couple of buildings like it on the Island of Angels.

He headed up and came out onto a wooden floor, maybe ten paces across, surrounded by stone walls a pace high. The floor was littered with human bones and bird droppings. Maggot was leaning on a wall, looking to the west. Ragnall tiptoed across to him, trying not to step on anyone's remains.

"And this . . ." said Maggot

"Is where you bring your dead? To be eaten by birds?"

"A shrewd man. We do bring our dead here. Apart from babies of course. We bury those for Bel. If they die, that is. I try and stop that happening. But they're not why we're here. Look around."

Gutrin Tor was the highest point for miles and the view was colossal. To the west was flat marsh all the way to the sea, other than a a few hummocks that made islands in the mire. To the south, east and north the marsh was edged with woodland, then low hills. He could just make out a hillfort he'd skirted with Drustan on his litter, twenty miles to the north-west.

It was a simplification, but it was reasonable to say that to the south-east and east all the land was under Zadar's iron control. To the south-west was Dumnonia. They were at a liminal point, an invisible flagpole in the sand. It all looked the same peaceful, welcoming green, but here, surely, if what everyone said was true, there would soon be a great clash between Dumnonia, the Murkans from the north and Zadar, probably backed by the might of Rome.

"I'm looking."

"Big change will come when the Romans come, but the land will stay the same."

"You're sure the Romans will come?"

"They're already here – in coins, clothes, wine, haircuts – and more than that. Attitudes, the way people think. That's changing. Everything will change. This tower, right, been here for ever?"

"Yes?"

"No not for ever. What seems for ever to us but just a click of the fingers compared to the whole of time. Take this tower apart, roll the stones down the hill and into the mud, and it will disappear and be forgotten in the way you've already forgotten about that blade of grass."

"But I remember the grass. Won't the story of the tower remain?"

"Nah. Think of the blade of grass like the *story* of the tower. Could you find that blade of grass now?"

"No."

"No. Without the tower to look at, people will forget the

stories. So this tower can be forgotten, even though it's been here for a hundred of our lifetimes and it's made of massive fucking stones. So how easily can we disappear, made of water and crumbing bone as we are?

"I guess—"

"Which brings us, young Ragnall, to why you're here."

"Drustan's ill – he needed somewhere safe."

"Sure. But why are you travelling with him?"

"We're going to Dumnonia."

"Ah. You see that long ridge?" Maggot pointed south-west. "Yes."

"That's where Dumnonia begins. So it's not far now. Why are you going there?"

Ragnall looked at Maggot. Some of his orange feathers were stuck to his face with sweat from the climb. For once his eyes were still, looking straight into Ragnall's.

"Zadar has my fiancée, Anwen."

"So why do you want to go over there?" Maggot nodded south-west. "Zadar's that way."

Ragnall told him what had happened. Standing on the tower, with the land all around, it came tumbling out, from growing up in Boddingham, via school on the Island of Angels to arriving at Mearhold with Drustan. Maggot was quiet throughout, looking out over the scene, watching the rising birds. Ragnall finished his story. They leaned on the wall, wordless, as above their heads the white cloud mass shifted, broke into corrugated ranks, then into huge, bright, individual clouds.

"So," Maggot said eventually. "Question stands. Why are you rescuing Anwen by heading away from her, towards Drustan's home, where he was headed anyway?"

"Drustan says it's the best way."

"Drustan says a lot."

"Drustan's reasons for me going to Dumnonia are sound. I can't face Zadar on my own and Dumnonia is building an army."

"Drustan's reasons."

"Which are now my reasons because they make sense."

"Yeah, yeah. Come on, let's go back to Mearhold." Maggot stood back from the wall. "But remember this. When someone tells you that helping *them* is in *your* best possible interests, do you really reckon it is?"

Chapter 2

As they waited for Ula to come back up from Mearhold, Lowa looked at Spring and tried to work out for the hundredth time what could explain her apparent reincarnation. She'd been dead – run through by a spear – at Kanawan, then not just alive but uninjured when Lowa found her and Ogre. Lowa had pretended otherwise to confuse the bandit into spilling his secrets, but she'd been confused enough herself. She'd *seen* the spear go through Spring. She'd seen the blood dripping down the side of Ogre's horse. She'd seen her dead eyes, for Fenn's sake!

Spring said the spear had gone under her armpit. Lowa wanted to believe her. Indeed, she had been far away and *could* have mistaken. She'd seen bards fake death blows by stabbing swords between arm and chest, and it could look convincing. But the blood on the horse, the sightless eyes, the clotted blood caking her clothes. How could Spring have faked all that? And why?

The whole thing had shaken her. Magic was nonsense. It had to be. The gods were a human creation to teach morals to children and to keep the moronic masses under the heel of their brighter rulers. She'd known that as long as she could remember. She'd always assumed that everyone else with a grain of intelligence understood it too but kept quiet because gods and magic worked very well to control kids and thicker adults, and because if people wanted some kind of reason for living and something to look forward to after death, why deny them?

But it had to be bullshit. She'd seen no evidence of any invisible, interfering beings. Quite the opposite, in fact. When she and Aithne had watched from the bushes as their mother was raped and killed, Lowa had decided that if there were gods, they weren't worth bothering with. She'd realised then that humans were just ridiculously self-important animals, grubbing along, shagging and dying, looking out for nobody but themselves, no better than pigs and no more deserving of any gods' interest.

Yet Spring had come back to life. And it had happened at a woodland shrine. Then there was the dog that died an instant before it was going to rip her throat out. And back in Bladonfort, Spring had somehow known that Weylin needed a cart. There was also her extraordinary ability with a sling and the unnatural way she'd taught the Kanawan girls so quickly and effectively. Was there a point at which co-incidence became less likely than a mystical explanation? Could Lowa have been wrong all this time?

Her atheism was hanging together by sinews.

Next to all this, the fact that Spring was Zadar's daughter was almost immaterial. Lowa had sort of known anyway, she told herself – she'd definitely recognised some mannerisms. Besides, what Ogre apparently hadn't known – or he would have attached less value to just one of them – was that Zadar had dozens of children. So finding one of Zadar's kids wasn't particularly amazing. Not nearly as amazing as a girl killing a dog without touching it, then coming back to life.

But no, she told herself. Whatever the evidence, there were rational explanations. The dog could have just died, the blood could have been the horse's – she'd seen Ogre stab it, hadn't she? And just because Spring was preternaturally good with a sling didn't mean the gods were involved. No, she should forget all this gods nonsense and concentrate on what was important – how she might use Spring to kill Zadar. On the way back to Kanawan after she'd rescued the girl from Ogre, Spring had said that she'd grown to hate her father because of what she'd seen him do, and that was why she'd run away. She'd asked Lowa not to tell Dug or anyone else that she was Zadar's daughter, and Lowa saw no reason not to keep her secret, for now anyway.

Since then, she had considered various ways of getting Spring to return home and stab or poison Zadar, but the girl was so weird – or maybe just so young, to be fair – that she couldn't trust her to carry a plan through. And, of course, she was his daughter, so might baulk when it actually came to patricide. Plus Lowa wanted to kill Zadar herself.

She shook her head. Enough pointless musing. They were on the cart on the road above Mearhold, looking towards the floating island and waiting for Ula. Spring was asking Dug why sticks floated and stones didn't.

"Don't hassle him, Spring," Lowa said.

"It's fi – ine," Dug said, his voice breaking halfway through the word. He'd found speaking painful for the whole journey. That hadn't stopped Spring trying to get him to talk for almost all of it. "I'm feeling pretty much fine," he finished quietly.

Lowa half-smiled but didn't look down. "So you'll be walking down the hill?"

Dug had seen plenty of man-made islands in lakes further north. Crannogs, as they called them up there, were round huts on stilts at the end of wooden jetties, perhaps ten paces out over a lake's calm waters. They were said to be good for defence, and certainly animals and unprepared marauders would have trouble attacking them, but a lobbed torch or two would ask questions that straw- and wood-built crannogs couldn't answer. Still, he'd stayed on a few and he liked them. They were good for fishing, and, providing you synchronised with any neighbours, you could collect drinking water easily and have an effort-free dunny.

But this was something else: a mega-crannog. Propped up in the cart, he could see Mearhold perched in the swamp like a great spider, paths like spindly legs stretching from its engorged body. There were maybe a hundred huts of varying size on the roughly triangular island, as well as outdoor work areas, storage sheds and a longhouse that probably housed the chief, a guy called King Vole, apparently. There was a grey network of tracks on the island itself, and a couple of paths led to the great marsh off to the west. Beyond the brown of the marsh, he was pretty sure he could see the brighter blue line of the sea at the horizon, but he might have been imagining that because he knew it was there and he wanted it to be there. He liked to be near the sea.

None of the tracks from the village stretched as far north as the hill they'd stopped on, nor could he see any leading to the stepped triangular hill that towered above the countryside to the east of the island.

"How do we get to it?" he asked, reaching for his large but nearly empty skin of mead.

"Here comes Ula!" Spring leaped up, rocking the cart and making Dug wince.

Queen Ula of the newly nomadic tribe of Kanawan rode up the hill from Mearhold on her shaggy horse. She was wrapped in a red and yellow tartan shawl that she hadn't been wearing when she left them. Her lips were pushed into the same small smile that had played there for most of the three-day journey from Kanawan. Spouse murder clearly suited her. Dug had seen it before: killing the one person who had been ruining their lives did tend to cheer people up.

"All arranged," said Ula. "Head down the hill and you'll find a boat waiting. In return for the cart and horses, you can stay at Mearhold for as long as it takes Dug to recover, and then on for up to four moons in total. They haven't asked that you do any work, but it would be nice if you helped out with hunting and so on. Sorry. I'm sure I don't need to tell you that. I'd suggest that you, Spring, try to get in with the weavers. They make the finest woollen cloth in the land here, so you could learn a useful trade from the best teachers."

"Get in with the weavers and learn a useful trade," Spring said slowly "That sounds fun. I will definitely do that."

Ula laughed. "They also hunt in boats, go slinging for birds on the marsh, and fish. You'll find beds of sand around here that contain thousands of the most perfect slingstones. I should think you'll find plenty of things to do that aren't weaving. But my advice stands."

"I might try some of those other things first. Probably the slinging first of all. But then, if you'd like me to, and there's time, I'll try to get in with the weavers and learn a useful trade. I will."

"Good girl."

"What have you told them about us?" asked Lowa.

"As we agreed, I told them the truth." said Ula. "I told them about Zadar's pursuit and what happened to Weylin's troop."

"What?" Dug nearly sat up again. "Why did you tell them all that? And they still—"

Lowa put a hand on Dug's shoulder "Sorry, you were asleep when we discussed it. I knew you'd agree though."

"Agree what?"

"That Mearhold and King Vole should know the risks of having us on their island."

Dug shook his head. "So they can shout to Zadar where we are? Because it might take them, what, as many as four heartbeats to work out that protecting strangers makes less sense than staying on side with the world's most powerful bastard?"

"I've spoken to Ula at length about King Vole. He won't give us away."

"He won't," Ula chipped in. "But do try to avoid any conversation with him."

"Why?" asked Dug.

"Because he's a . . . Well, you'll see. But he's also a decent man, fiercely proud of himself and his tribe. That makes him about as loyal and good an ally as you could have."

"Aye, OK, so he might hold back from telling Zadar. But what about everyone else in the village? It only takes one of them to send a shout and we're fucked." Dug darted a glance at Spring. She was watching some geese flying over and not listening. "An island may be a refuge, but it's also a trap."

Lowa shook her head. "It's not Kanawan. Sorry, Ula. Mearhold has no reason to betray us. In fact, it's the opposite. Mearhold thrives because it sits between Dumnonian and Maidun territory. The festival here is one of the things that keeps the two sides from attacking each other. Mearhold won't do anything to favour one over the other."

"Lowa, if Zadar sent that many people to Kanawan, he's not going to give up. He might send someone who can tell the difference between their arse and their head next time. With an army."

"He won't know where we are. He doesn't know about your injury, so he doesn't know that we have to lie—"

"Aye. My injury. You could get to safety. You could be across the sea tomorrow."

Lowa narrowed her eyes as if trying to focus on something in the distance.

"Sorry to interrupt your tiff," said Ula, "but I've got to push on now if I'm to catch the tribe by nightfall."

"Aye," said Dug

"Of course," said Lowa.

Ula looked to each of them in turn. "Lowa. Dug. Spring." She shook her head and smiled as tears shone from her eyes. "I owe you my life and the life of my tribe. You rescued us from ourselves. The Kanawan tribe will always be ready and willing should you need us. I'm sure our paths will cross again. May Danu and Bel and all the gods favour you and protect you until they do."

Queen Ula pulled her horse around and rode away to the north, iron horseshoes crunching on the metalled road.

"So," said Dug when she was out of earshot. "Do you really think Zadar will give up the chase?"

"I don't know. I don't know why he sent so many to Kanawan. I don't know why he killed my sister and my women in the first place. The thing is Dug, I am going to kill Zadar. I have a plan which may work. But . . . it involves you. With good care you'll recover in half a moon. If you're prepared to help, I'll wait. The plan isn't carved in stone yet, but it's likely to be difficult and possibly fatal."

"You sell it well."

"I don't want to lie to you."

Dug looked up at Lowa, standing over him on the cart. It was a good angle.

"I'll help you."

"What about me? Can I come?" Spring asked.

"You don't have to, Spring. But you could help a lot. Do you want to help?"

"Course. Now can we stop talking and get to this Mearhold place? I've never been in a boat."

Chapter 3

A boy carrying a hemp sack came into the hut behind the druid.

Dug had been asleep. After the cart it was bliss to stretch out on a decent bed. The summer heat had returned after the rain, but a cooling breeze wafted through the windows and door, carrying the muddy ming of the marsh mixed with a mild sniff of salt and the aroma of cut reeds.

His chest already felt easier, possibly because of the rest but more likely because of the cider. He'd never had the like. It tasted no more potent than watered-down apple juice, but moments after the first couple of gulps he'd felt the alcohol fumes swimming up into his head like a confused but persistent school of ethereal fish.

"All right," said Maggot. "This is going to seem weird and you're not going to like it, but it works. All right?"

"You've done it before?"

"Loads of times. Some people almost survived. Joking. It won't harm you. Now lie back and don't move."

Maggot unlaced Dug's leather jerkin, said, "Up on your elbows," and eased the sleeveless top off him. The druid leaned forward, lank blond hair draping his face. With fine iron scissors he snipped through the bands of wool that held Dug's chest bandage in place and peeled it down slowly.

Dug closed his eyes. He could feel strips of skin coming away with the cloth. He was booze-numbed enough that it didn't hurt overly, but it did feel disgusting. And the smell! It was like unwrapping a wheel of cheese and a hunk of beef that had been left bound together in the sun for a moon. He swallowed to avoid gagging.

"Not bad, not bad." Maggot seemed not to notice the stench. "You'll be walking in six days, all right in twelve, back to how you were in a moon."

"Good. Thanks."

"You're welcome." Maggot eased a woollen blanket under Dug's back, went to the other side of the bed and pulled until there were equal lengths of blanket hanging out either side. "And here's the fun bit. Sack, please."

The boy stepped forward, holding open the top of the sack. Maggot delved a hand into it. Dug almost laughed when he pulled out a fistful of wriggling maggots.

"Ah, hence the name."

"No, actually that's just a coincidence. I'm called Maggot because I have a small penis."

"Ah."

"And that was a joke. I'm actually hung like Kornonos."

"I see. What are the maggots for?"

"They eat dead and infected flesh, not the healthy bits. You're infected. That's why you stink. With these, the infection will be gone before you know it."

"And without them?"

"You'll be dead in three days."

"Hmm. So you're going to cure a big animal's bites by getting a bagful of wee animals to bite me?"

Maggot nodded happily. "Great, isn't it?"

Dug looked at the crazy-faced druid. To his surprise, he trusted him. He couldn't have said why. It was probably the cider. He nodded.

Maggot's smile widened. He pressed the handful of maggots into the largest of Dug's chest wounds, then grabbed another handful.

It was disgustingly ticklish. Dug had to battle the urge to yell, sit up and brush the horrible little fuckers away. But he closed his eyes and twiddled the bed sheet, trying to concentrate on how the woollen fibres felt between his fingers and how they rubbed against each other. Distraction, he'd found, was an effective pain relief.

When the bag was empty, Maggot placed a few layers of cloth of a type Dug didn't recognise over the writhing larvae, then bound the whole lot up in the woollen blanket.

As he tied the last few knots, Lowa walked into the hut.

Maggot stood aside and Lowa bent down. If she noticed the smell, she didn't show it. She kissed him gently on the lips.

Dug had had a hot mud bath once. Lowering himself into it, he'd groaned with pleasure and relief as warm comfort eased its way into every pore. Lowa's kiss felt a lot like that.

"How are you treating him?" she asked Maggot.

"Maggots."

"Good." Lowa seemed unsurprised. "Anything I can do?"

"Judging by that grin, a kiss like that every now and then should help. Otherwise, leave him to rest. I'll go now. Please let him sleep soon."

"Sure."

Maggot's jewellery jangled as he left the hut.

The sunlight through the opened door was bright in her hair. "Are you really OK?" she asked.

"Never better. Is Spring all right?"

"She went fishing with some people in a boat. She looked happy. They looked nervous."

"Good. You all right?"

"Course I am. I'd better go and let you sleep. You get well, OK?"

"Aye. I'll be up and at 'em before the day's out."

Lowa leaned over and kissed him again. Dug breathed in her musky scent and went to sleep.

Chapter 4

Lowa pushed the hut door closed, then leaped out of the way as a man carrying logs came careering towards her, so intent on watching his feet on the wobbly island floor that he didn't see her.

"Gods, sorry!" he stammered. "I . . ."

Neither spoke for a moment, but Lowa found herself smiling broadly, first at the man's honest horror at having nearly bumped into her, but more at how preposterously attractive he was. His strong dimpled chin was almost comically heroic, his neat hair casually ruffled as if today's wind had been created solely to produce the effect, and his eyes shone with vigour. Under his clean white flax shirt was the outline of a lean, muscular torso.

"I'm Lowa Flynn," she said. "I arrived this morning."

"Ragnall," said the young man, gripping the logs with one arm and reaching out a hand. "Ragnall Sheeplord." He had the confident region-free tones of a ruling family. Lowa took his hand.

"Are you a local?" she found herself asking, her usual dislike of small talk put aside for a moment.

On finding that they both accompanied recovering invalids, Ragnall suggested that they go for a walk up nearby Gutrin Tor. Lowa acquiesced. She couldn't see any massive problem in spending the day with a charming, good-looking young man.

They reached the summit tower. As they'd climbed the hill, her mood had soured again. She wanted to kill Zadar and she shouldn't have been arsing about on recreational country walks, but no matter how hard she tried, she could not come up with a plan.

Ragnall nodded hello to the guards and they headed up, leaned on the south wall and looked at the huge view. Lowa walked off and looked over all the other walls in turn. Yup, spectacular. She came back and leaned against the wall next to Ragnall. "Why are you and Drustan here?"

The tall young man looked down at her.

"Same as you and your man."

"I wouldn't call him my man."

"Oh, you're not . . . er . . . together?"

"You mean are we sleeping with each other?" Ragnall coloured. "No, I just assumed . . ."

"I don't belong to anyone. Neither does Dug."

"OK."

"So, how did you end up here?"

"We were on our way to Dumnonia when Drustan got a lung disease."

"Is that home?"

"No. It's complicated." His eyes were grey, shining with energy and youth.

"Tell me. I have nothing else to do today."

"All right," he said, nodding to the south-east. "The reason we're heading to Dumnonia lives over there somewhere in the world's most impenetrable hillfort"

Ragnall told Lowa a brief life history and what had happened, then about Maggot's opinion of Drustan's motives and his indecision over what to do next.

"What do you think?" he asked when he got to the end, fixing her with his intense stare. His curly hair shifted softly in the wind, other than where sweat from the climb had pasted tendrils to the sides of his strong face. He was, Lowa thought, a bright young man as well as a handsome one. The important word there was young. He was maybe six years younger than her, but the differences between their lives made it more like a hundred. With his parents newly dead, his mentor incapacitated and no other teachers around, he clearly needed someone to tell him what to do. If she ever managed to devise a plan, she'd be able to use him. How, she wondered, should she play it?

She knew first hand about his home's destruction. She'd led the charge and been first over the wall, shooting arrows into the peace-softened bodies of the ineffectual defenders. She'd killed a lot of people that day, possibly – probably – more than anyone else. Chances were she'd killed at least one of his brothers. From his description, she was pretty sure she knew who Anwen was. She'd been taken alive from Boddingham.

"I was in Zadar's army," she said.

Ragnall blanched. Lowa heard his teeth grind.

"Why didn't you . . . before I . . . ?"

"I wasn't part of the raid on Boddingham. I was in a small band of archers with my sister and some other women. My sister was the only family I had left, and the women were my only friends. We did more hunting and scouting than fighting, and we were away scouting when Zadar attacked Boddingham."

"But you were still part—"

"Exactly. Were. A few days after Boddingham, at a place called Barton, Zadar had my sister and my friends slaughtered. They tried to kill me but I escaped. Now I only have one desire – to kill Zadar."

"Barton?"

"Yes."

"My father . . . I found his body."

Lowa shook her head. "Yes. I don't know why Zadar had my women killed, and tried to have me killed, but it may have been because I spoke out about your father's treatment." She had in fact thought that Zadar's treatment of Kris

Sheeplord was distasteful, but she'd been a long way from caring enough to say anything.

The young man seemed appeased, however. "Do you know what they did with Anwen?" he asked, eyes full of puppyish misery. "Drustan said she'd already be halfway to Rome."

"I don't know. She might be. But it's as likely she's still at Maidun. Is she good-looking?"

"Beautiful, the most beautiful—"

"Then it's very likely she's at Maidun."

"Why? What will they be doing to her?" Ragnall gripped Lowa's shoulders and shook her. He stopped shaking when he saw the look on her face. He took his hands from her shoulders and reddened. Lowa paused to let him stew in his own awkwardness for a moment, then continued.

"If she's as beautiful as you say, chances are she'll be in Zadar's harem."

"Oh Danu . . ."

"It's the best place she could be. She'll be treated well there."

"But she'll have to—"

"He won't rape her." She didn't add that people were generally so grateful to escape slavery and be placed in Zadar's harem that they seldom needed coercion to sleep with their charismatic rescuer.

"OK. Thanks. Sorry for grabbing you."

"Don't worry about it."

"But . . . But why should I believe anything you say? You're with Zadar."

"*Was*. Was with Zadar. And I was never fully *with* him, and when he killed my sister and my friends I became a different person." Lowa gripped his arms much harder than he'd gripped her shoulders. It shocked Ragnall into silence. "Nothing matters to me, nothing at all, apart from killing Zadar. Help me with that, and I will help you find Anwen."

"But Drustan. . ."

She loosened her grip but kept hold of his muscled arms. They felt good. "Drustan will have you running to Dumnonia while Anwen suffers in Maidun. Now remind me, which epic tale tells the story of a hero reacting to the kidnap of his woman by running in the opposite direction?"

"You have a point."

"I do. Who knows what will happen? Yes, people are saying that Dumnonia will attack Zadar, but the Murkans might equally conquer Zadar and save Dumnonia the job. Or the Murkan tribes might unite with Maidun to attack Dumnonia. People say a lot and people are often wrong. Even if they're right, it won't happen this year because it's only a couple of moons until harvest. Maybe it won't happen next year or the year after. Maybe the Romans will get here first. Going to Dumnonia now is no way to get Anwen back. Come with me. Come to Maidun."

"I'll . . . think about it."

"Do that. You have some time. I want to wait until Dug is healthy enough. But while we're here, don't speak to me, or anyone, about me being in Zadar's army. That time is over, I swear." This, she thought, was not a lie: she really was a changed person, appalled at what she'd done for Zadar.

"All right." the man-boy nodded.

"So," said Ragnall as he climbed into the boat to paddle back to Mearhold, "you only met Dug a few days ago?"

Lowa smiled. "Maybe five days ago. I lose track."

Chapter 5

Dug's hut was one of three squatting in a semicircle on the southern edge of Mearhold's man-made island. From his door in the central hut Dug had a view across cleared, shallow, wildfowl-busy water. About a hundred paces away there was a fringe of reeds, then spindly but leafy birch and alder trees reaching out of the swamp like the hands of trapped, drowning men. The image made him shiver. But that's the injury talking, he thought, and its treatment. Having creatures crawling around in your chest and being hungover for Toutatis-knew-how-many mornings in a row is bound to dredge up melancholy thoughts. The trees probably looked lovely to most.

Beyond the trees, a good few miles beyond, low hills loomed. Off to the left was a long lozenge of a mound which presumably led to Gutrin Tor, but he couldn't see that far from his sickbed.

It was his third day of lying flat on his back being chewed by a chestful of worming horror. Much of the time he distracted himself. He watched the birdlife on the water — fowl swimming, swifts dipping, kingfishers plopping. Ducks landing was his favourite avian spectacle. They came down panic-faced with mad flapping wings, looking like they were going to land with all the grace of a horse thrown off a pier. But instead they slid onto the surface with a musical splash and sailed off as if they'd planned it that way all along, eyes forward and beaks haughty.

Often the splashes and quacks of the ducks lulled him to

sleep, but mostly he lay awake, thinking. Sometimes he mulled over memories of his wife and daughters, for the millionth time fantasising about what would have happened if he'd got home in time to meet the raiders who'd murdered them. Mostly, however, he fantasised about life with Lowa. He'd kill Zadar and they'd go north, maybe back to his old broch or, even better, to one of their own. He'd always get stuck however on *how* he was going to kill Zadar. To kill a king, you have to get close to him. How were they going to do that?

Maggot changed the maggots every morning and dropped by throughout the day. "If I don't take 'em away and put new ones in, they'll turn into flies and they'll fly you away, man, across the sea," he'd said that morning before telling Dug about the land of giant leaf-eating bears that lay on the other side of the ocean. "Two, maybe three moons in a boat, man, you'll be there. I might go myself if this Zadar ruins the peace any more."

Spring hadn't been around in the day at all, but Lowa had popped in a few times. Always with the young man Ragnall. Ragnall, he'd found, was polite and intelligent. He was interested in Dug and had interesting things to report about Mearhold. He was a decent, charming, well put-together young chap who was helping to keep Lowa from boredom. Dug didn't like him at all.

King Vole had visited the previous evening. He was prematurely balding with a haughty bearing, but, half shitfaced as he was on Maggot's medicinal cider, Dug hadn't paid him much attention. Reasonably enough anyway, the king had been more interested in Lowa than Dug. So it looked like Lowa was being courted by a king and a young lord, which wasn't ideal.

"Hello."

His reverie was broken by a visitor. He hadn't seen him before, but Dug knew who he was. In the evenings, while Lowa was out with Ragnall or sitting on her bed quietly

fletching arrow shafts, Spring had told him at great length
about everyone in the village. She'd said the wisest-looking
druid she'd ever seen was ill next door. With his long white
beard, wrinkled face and brightly inquisitive eyes, this had
to be the guy.

"Hi. You're Drustan the druid. I'm Dug. Good to see you
up. How are you feeling?"

"I am surprised and pleased to tell you that I am almost
fully recovered. Do you mind?" Drustan gestured towards a
three-legged wooden stool.

"Please do. Before you sit though, could you grab me that
cider off the side, please?"

"A pleasure." Drustan handed the cider to Dug and sat down.

"Aye, it's meant to be this evening's dose, but I've drunk
the afternoon ration already and I can still feel the wee
buggers. Anyway, you're looking well? Spring said you had
a lung sickness?"

"I did. But that Maggot is a talented healer."

"And a strange one?"

"Perhaps. Ragnall told me about your maggots. I have
heard the idea, but it is intriguing to see it put into practice.
You are very brave."

Dug laughed gently.

"What?" asked Drustan.

"Bravery is jumping into a storm sea to save your dog,
something like that. Tolerating treatment for illness or injury
isn't bravery. It's life."

"Yes, yes. I had never thought that through, but you are
right. What an interesting fellow you are. Perhaps you could
tell me what you are doing here, if it is not too troubling
for your chest?"

Dug liked the old man already. "The pain's almost gone.
It's my last day with maggots. But I am fairly drunk?"

Drustan chuckled. "The best stories are told after a drink
or two."

"Or six or seven?"

"Or indeed, six or seven. Perhaps you could tell me the story of how you met Lowa, and how you came to be on Mearhold? She is intriguing. I'd like to know all about her."

"I bet you would."

Drustan chuckled. "Not like that. One's skin is not the only thing that droops with age. It is her story, and yours – and Spring's – that I am interested in."

"OK, I'll tell you how we all ended up here." Dug closed his eyes. "It was a sunny day and I didn't think there was going to be a battle . . ."

Chapter 6

Weylin held his breath, light-headed with anticipation. After all those boring, boring miles, finally it was coming, it was coming . . . He crested the ridge. He kept his head lowered and screwed his eyes shut to tease himself. He waited, waited, then opened his eyes and boom! There it was. Maidun Castle burst from its brown surrounds like a giant molar tooth, bright white against the blue sky, a giant fist raised in defiance of people and gods. He felt joy bloom from his stomach and almost cheered. He'd pictured it so often, he'd dreamed about it every night, but every time he came back, the first sight of Maidun always struck him like a bucket of cold water to the face.

It was so awesome. Even from this distance, just seeing its triple chalk walls topped with a stout palisade would put a wobble in the stride of any attacker, no matter how great his courage or his army. Get up close, and all hope would flee like hares from a wolf. Oh, would hope flee! Get up close, and the most courageous strutting hero would feel his mighty balls shrivel into rotting hazelnuts and his bowels churn with slurry.

They said that people had started to flatten the top of Maidun hill and carve out walls from its flanks thousands of years before, before even the end of the Great Winter. Over hundreds of generations, thousands upon thousands of men, women and beasts had dug and cut and carried the chalk rock to create today's magnificent, impregnable fortress. Thinking about the time it must have taken, the amount of work that must have gone into it, hurled Weylin's mind into a spin.

It made all the other hillforts look like ambitious badgers' setts.

It was more than a thousand paces long and four hundred paces across. The outer wall was fifty paces high, with a tall palisade on top angled flush with the slope's vertiginous incline, so that if some gods-blessed fool managed to make it up the near-vertical chalk wall without being killed by slingstone, spear, boulder or arrow, he'd have nowhere to hide and nowhere to go. Maybe he'd be lucky then and get a boulder on his head. More likely he'd be doused in burning oil and fall screaming down the slope. He'd crash flapping into his comrades below, splashing them with oil, and they'd catch alight and fall too. Weylin rubbed his hands together with glee at the thought.

And that was just the outer wall. There were two more inside that. They were even more formidable. The inner one was a hundred paces high. All three had palisades, linked to each other and the fort's interior by wooden bridges which could be burned if the outer walls fell. The bridges made the defence of the fort a total doddle. A blast on the trumpets and everybody could be on the outer wall in moments. In between the walls were ditches so steep and deep that the sun seldom shone on the spikes spread along their depths. Weylin almost wished it was possible for an attacker to gain the palisade of the first wall, just to see the look on his face when he looked down into the ditch, then up at the second and third walls. Then there was the western gate, with its twisting, wooden-walled entry passage overlooked at every step by heavily armed sentries. An army attacking the gate would wish it had tried the walls.

But, and Weylin thought this was something of a shame, no attacker would ever get near the gates or walls because first they'd have to get through the army. Blighting Maidun's surrounds and sprawling towards him was a mess of a camp, containing – they said – more than twenty thousand soldiers, plus another ten thousand cooks, grooms, smiths, carpenters, wheelwrights, coopers and so on. On top of those directly employed by the army there were innumerable hangers-on – merchants, druids, bards, thieves, wives, husbands, children and a few ropey prostitutes operating in competition with the whorepits to the south of the castle. The camp stretched for miles, covering all the land that he could see north and west of the fort. Its buildings, roads and people blended into a dirty landscape, brown except for the odd green hummock of an untouchable ancient burial site.

A couple of times he'd heard Felix refer to everyone who lived outside Maidun's walls as plebs. He liked the word. Weylin wasn't a pleb. He was one of the Fifty. He was better than them. The pleb soldiers were farmers most of the time, just soldiers for a few moons in the summer. Weylin was always a Warrior. He suddenly remembered Dionysia. Was he sad to be returning home without her? He looked at the sky and thought. Nope, not a twinge of grief. The opposite, if anything. A hero like him was much better off striding solo through life, free to do whatever, and whoever, he wanted.

He kicked his horse and was soon passing through the smoke of countless pleb cookhouses and forges. The yelling of pleb babies, the hollers of pleb men, the bleats of pleb women, the blaring of pleb goats, shouts coming in from all about the country, the clang of forges, the bang of carpenters' hammers and a dozen other sounds all melded together into a buzzing camp clamour which made him smile.

He passed a few men, tough army grunts by the heavy iron swords slung on their shoulders. But not Warriors. They nodded manly greetings at him and he nodded generously back. They'd know he was one of the Fifty, a Warrior – in case they didn't, his boar medallion was out and dangling.

They might even know him by name, and that evening they'd show off to their friends that he'd acknowledged them. They'd say that he was on his way to *The Castle* – that's what the plebs called it. "We saw that Warrior Weylin Nancarrow on his way to *The Castle*. Good bloke that one, got time for the little people." That's what they'd say. Then they'd swap tales and rumours about what it must be like up there. Only the Warriors of the Fifty, the elite cavalry and charioteers, and a few more of Zadar's closest were allowed through Maidun Castle's gates. And all the cooks, cleaners, delivery people, guards and others like them of course.

Oh, it was good to be home. His journey back had been mildly soured by concerns about how Zadar would react to what had happened at Kanawan. But it hadn't been his fault, he knew that, and he shouldn't worry, but still . . . He'd sent a shout from the first village he'd come to after fleeing Kanawan, saying they'd been ambushed and all killed save him, and that he was on his way back. As far as he could see, the rational reaction to that would be to congratulate him for surviving and give him a couple of days' leave – much of which he would spend down at the whorepits. But Zadar wasn't always rational.

Looking at Maidun Castle though, all those concerns evaporated like water flicked onto red-hot iron. A big grin leaped onto his face, he gave his horse some heel.

He looked over to the left and saw the arena – ranks of wooden seats rising up the fort's outer wall, above the huge, enclosed display area.

"Ohhh!" He slapped his forehead.

"Are you all right?" said a passing pleb.

"Yes, thanks."

He wasn't all right though. He should have *known* that the construction in Kanawan was an arena. OK, so the Kanawan one was much smaller than this and wasn't built onto a hillside, but all the bigger settlements were building them and he should have known not to go in there. Spectators aside, nobody ever went into an arena for a good reason. He'd seen almost as many people killed in Maidun's as he'd seen dispatched on the battlefield.

Still shaking his head at his stupidity, he dismounted and handed his horse over to one of the grooms. He patted her farewell.

"Put her in a good field," he said, handing the groom a small bronze coin. "I'm not sure when I'll be needing her again." The boy bowed his head a few times, muttering obsequiously. Weylin smiled magnanimously at him, then walked on with a jaunty version of the rolling, unsteady gait of a man who has spent several days in the saddle. It was great to be back and nothing was going to shake his good mood. The first gate opened as he approached it. He nodded thanks to the guards. Someone had once told him to be nice to the little people as his fame increased. Sometimes he remembered. There was more to the advice, he couldn't help thinking, but he couldn't remember it.

He walked between the heavy plank walls built over steep earth banks, turning left and right through the labyrinthine entrance. The track was wide enough for carts, but the wooden walls on each side, well over even his head height, were oppressive. Slingers and spear-holding guards looked down at him, faces hostile even though they knew who he was. He knew better than to try to talk to them. He'd been on duty on these walls himself, before he was promoted to the Fifty. Look hard, talk to nobody, be ready always. Those were the rules. Breaking them meant pain.

Another gate swung open as he approached and he didn't break stride. A few more turns and he was on the bridge that spanned the ditch in front of the main gate. The hefty oak doors ahead remained stubbornly shut. A figure appeared on the palisade to the right of the gate, anonymous in a black leather hood and iron helmet.

"Weylin," said the figure. "You're expected. Go straight to the Eyrie."

The Eyrie! The western end, the upper part, the secret section, the elite zone! Weylin's efforts and sacrifices were finally being rewarded. Ever since he'd been allowed into Maidun, he'd ached to know what was up there, on the other side of the palisade that bisected the hillfort's enclosure. Everyone who went in, including Carden and Atlas, was strangely cagey about it. Weylin had always pretended that he didn't give a crap. If they wanted to have childish secrets, then they could. But really he was *dying* to see what was up there.

Weylin nodded coolly, as if every fibre wasn't singing with excitement. The gate swung open and he strutted through.

Maidun's defended entrance didn't end at the gate. On the other side of the oak doors was an open passage cut into the hilltop, leading through the body of the fort. It was three paces deep at the start, becoming smoothly shallower over a hundred paces and lined with flint nodules along almost all its length. As a final defence, it was pretty unnecessary. Nobody was ever going to get this far, but rulers liked to put captives to work, and some previous king or queen had decreed that this pointless passage be dug.

Weylin walked along happily and emerged at the business end of Maidun Castle's larger, lower section, near the deep pits and rectangular wooden sheds on stilts for storage of barley, oat, wheat and other crops. They'd been built by earlier less powerful rulers who faced the possibility of a long siege. These days only one in twenty of the sheds was needed to store more than enough food to feed the fort's occupants through any winter. Weylin had heard people say that they should store more in case the crops failed, but that sounded like lame-arse talk. If you ran out of anything and wanted more, you took it from somewhere else.

Past the storage area and towards the centre of the vast fortress's plateau interior, he approached the top Warriors' huts. They were stoutly made, their well tended conical thatch roofs each cased in a grid of supple but strong willow twigs as defence against the gales that could pummel the exposed hilltop. He looked around for friendly faces, but only a few people were about and nobody he knew well. No surprise. It was the middle of the morning, so Warriors would be off training, and apart from them the hillfort was sparsely populated. Neither animals nor children lived up here. The only industries were the forges and smelters of a handful of the best iron and bronze workers, people like Elann Nancarrow. He could hear the regular smash of Elann's unmistakable heavy hammer now, over the bangs of unseen sword and shield practice.

A couple of fellow Warriors who clearly didn't know about his odyssey nodded hello as if this were just a normal day. He passed Carden's hut and thought about popping in to see how his brother's foot was healing. But that could wait. He would see what Zadar wanted first. *That must be it!* he thought with a jolt. Zadar was going to give him Lowa's hut! He could see it now, up ahead on the left, surrounded by a garden of hardy plants and a small wooden fence. It was one of the best. He smiled. He'd been sharing a craphole hut half the size of hers with Dionysia, hard against the south wall. It was about time he got recognition and a hut to himself. Yeah, that would bring 'em in. Women liked a man with his own hut.

He strode on. Up ahead was the palisade that separated the Eyrie from the lower camp. The ramp up to it was over to the right. This was going to be his first trip up that ramp, but soon it would be an everyday journey. Maybe one day he'd live up there himself . . .

"What you smiling about, you wanker! How's it going? You all right, yeah?" called a cheery voice. It was Nel, loping along the path towards him. He was a recent addition to the elite chariots and Weylin had deigned to talk to him a couple of times. His jaw had been knocked askew in some battle, but he still wore a permanent grin. People mocked him because he spent so much time with his top off, lying on banks and browning his skin in the sun. Weylin didn't mind that – each to their own, he always thought – and he liked him.

"Can't stop and chat, Nel. Sorry. I'm heading up to the Eyrie."

The smile dissolved from Nel's face. He rocked from foot to foot. "Ah, shit. You just got back, right? Ain't seen Zadar yet? Shit."

"What do you mean, 'shit'?" Weylin's veneer of cheer cracked a little.

"Well, you was sent after Lowa, right?" Nel looked nervous. "'Ave you got 'er?"

"No, but—"

"And where's everyone you took with you?"

"They're dead. But we were ambushed. Nothing I could've done."

"Yeah, that's what your shout said. And after that, what, you went after Lowa again?"

"No. That would've been stupid. I was on my own and she had a whole bloody army. I escaped."

"Yeah. People've been saying you'd better come back with Lowa or not at all."

"What?" Weylin peered into Nel's eyes. Was this a joke? "Well, people are twats. I'm the hero here. I may have lost a battle, but that happens. A true leader knows not only when to retreat, but has the courage to do it. Zadar said that."

"Yeah, well, maybe Zadar'll see it like that. Better not keep him waiting though."

Weylin watched Nel stride away.

At the top of the ramp to the Eyrie the gates swung open and he walked in. He stopped and looked around. To his right, south, was the awesome drop over three palisaded walls down to the Winter River. This was the highest part of the hillfort. He could see the long dormitory-style double shed of the whorepits, surrounded by its own ditch and fence, then farmland dotted with farmers' huts, stretching to the sea. He'd been expecting a good view from here.

Looking around, however, the rest of the Eyrie was not what he'd been expecting. Not at all.

Chapter 7

"What do you think of Lowa?"

Ragnall and Spring were crouched with slings on the marsh among the cotton grass and heather, stalking partridge. Ragnall had a brace of birds lashed to his belt. Both had been brought down by Spring. She was an odd one: more accurate than any adult with a sling and a faultless stalker, yet full of childish questions.

"Why do you want to know?"

"Why don't you want to answer?" Her eyes flashed.

"What do *you* think of Lowa?"

"I asked first."

"We're meant to be hunting partridge. We need more than these two."

"There aren't any around at the moment. There'll be more along. Best thing we can do is stay right here. Meanwhile let's fill the time by . . . oh I don't know . . ." Spring put her finger on her lips. "I've got it! Why don't you tell me what you think of Lowa?"

Ragnall sighed. "She seems very sure of herself. But with good reason. I haven't seen her use that strange bow she was carrying when you arrived, but I bet she's good with it. She gives off an air of never having got anything wrong, and not expecting that she ever will. And she's funny, in a clever way. Witty. But I still haven't seen her laugh, not properly. She smiles, but it's like she's smiling despite her sadness."

"Do you think she's pretty?"

Ragnall laughed. "I wouldn't say pretty."

"What would you say?"

"She's . . . she's . . ." *She's beautiful*, he thought. He cocked an ear and put a finger to his lips. "What's that over there? Sounds like partridge to me!" He sneaked off around a marshy hummock in a crouch.

Chapter 8

Drustan and Dug sat on a bench, leaning against a hut under the shade of its protruding thatch roof. Lowa sat on an upturned wooden bucket in the sun, seemingly unworried by the unbearable glare. Dug was sweating like a fat and normally sedentary man who'd just run up a hill.

It was odd, thought Dug, that Lowa spent a great deal of time in the sun, yet, at most, her pale skin might blossom into a pinkish glow towards the end of the day, while everyone else in summer was as brown as beaver fur. It supported his new, when-drunk theory that she was at least part goddess. Although that theory had been somewhat undermined that morning, when she'd waited until Spring had left to go hunting, pulled back his covers, pumped at his cock like a milkmaid in a hurry for the two heartbeats it took for it to be ready, then leaped on him and satisfied herself while he was still half asleep.

"Do pay attention, Dug."

He shook his head. "Sorry! Mind wandered."

Lowa was explaining her plan to kill Zadar to the two older men. Nearby some children were splashing in the water. Most of the Mearholders were away working: clearing channels, hunting, tending to the farmland and so on. Lowa had been out hunting all night, so she had excused herself, and the two men were still deemed to be recovering and incapable of labour. They'd been asked to keep an eye on the children, but the children seemed able to keep eyes on themselves.

The day before, Maggot had declared Dug free of infection

and mucked out the last batch of maggots from his chest. Dug had celebrated his grub-free state with more of Maggot's fine cider. Too much more. Now his hangover smothered him like a stinking, wet blanket.

"You're right – it is a crap plan," he said when Lowa had finished.

"Thanks. Helpful."

"Well yes," said Drustan. "It is not totally crap, but, as I know that you know from your hesitancy in outlining it, it is only the beginning of a plan – a model, one might say, to work from."

"Aye," chipped in Dug. "I can't see how you get from just being in Maidun Castle to killing Zadar. And you missed the little bit on how I avoid being tortured to death when they realise straight away that I'm no bounty hunter."

"I know it's not there yet," said Lowa. "But that's why I'm talking to you. No matter how hard I try, I can't come up with a better plan. So I thought that maybe you two, with your vast experience and years of wisdom . . . but if you're not up to it then I have other things I could be getting on with."

"No, child." Drustan smiled. "Let us start from the beginning. Zadar is no coward, but he is cautious when it comes to his own safety and he knows what you can do with your bow, so he's unlikely to leave the hillfort while you're free and possibly nearby. So you have to get in. We can discount force since you have no army. So that leaves trickery or stealth. No doubt you know the story of the Trojan horse?"

"No," said Lowa.

"It should really be called the Greek horse." Drustan leaned forward onto his knees.

"I know a story about Greek whores?" Dug offered.

"No, horse. Although your story may be similar, if it involves Greeks fucking someone." Lowa and Dug looked shocked at the teacher's profanity. He winked at them. "A few hundred years ago the Greeks besieged the city of Troy for ten years. Troy had high, stone walls, which the Greeks could not breach. Finally, a bright fellow named Odysseus came up with a plan, and the Greeks built a huge, hollow horse out of wood. Some troops hid in it and the rest boarded their boats and sailed over the horizon. The Trojans woke up to see that the Greeks had gone and someone had left a huge wooden horse outside their gates."

"So they shot the horse with fire arrows and watched it burn?" asked Lowa.

"No. They opened the gates and pulled it into their city. Did I mention that it had wheels? It did."

"Then they set it on fire."

"No. They left it. That night—"

"What? These Trojans—"

"You must remember, Lowa, this was a simpler time, when—"

"People were stupid?"

"Simpler."

"A city full of people and nobody thought, *Hang on a minute*?"

"Let him tell the story, Lowa."

"Hmmm."

"Thank you Dug. The Trojans, so the story goes, assumed it was a gift from the gods. You are right though. That does seem incredibly naïve, but this is the history that has been passed to us and we would be foolish to fully believe any history. So. The concealed Greeks waited until nightfall, crept out of the horse and opened Troy's gates to let their army in."

"Zadar's not going to fall for that. *Weylin* wouldn't fall for that."

"It's not the worst idea," said Dug. "But you change it a bit. So you hide yourself in a hay cart or a food barrel. Something a bit more everyday than a giant fuck-off wooden horse."

"And hope that they wheel it up to the Eyrie and leave it outside Zadar's hut? Rather than unload it immediately and find mc in there?"

"The Eyrie?" Dug asked.

"Upper bit of Maidun Castle, where Zadar lives."

"You see." Drustan smiled. "The Trojan horse plan is the same scheme as your false captive idea, and so it falls down at the same point. You may be able to gain access to Maidun Castle, but how can you be sure of reaching Zadar unmolested?"

"Exactly."

"So trickery will not work. It must be stealth. You must sneak in!" Drustan clapped his hands and stood up. The old druid was getting excited by the talk of derring-do.

Lowa didn't look impressed. "Did I mention the three huge walls, palisades, hundreds of guards, spiked ditches . . ."

"Yes, yes. And you told us about the convoluted gate. Is there just the one way in?"

"There's an eastern gate, but it's blocked off and no easier to cross than the wall."

"So the eastern gate is inaccessible, and the western gateway is protected by a heavily guarded maze." Drustan sat down again.

"Yes."

"Then where is the lowest part of the wall?"

"There is no low part." Lowa looked frustrated.

"There is though a least high part?"

"The walls are lowest, compared to the surrounding land, on the north side of the western gate," Lowa admitted. "But they're still high. And impossible to climb without being seen by the guards."

"Forget the guards are there," said Drustan, craning forward. "Could you climb them?"

"I could. Yes, with climbing spikes."

"What colour are the walls?" asked Drustan.

"White – they're bare chalk rock."

"At night somebody dressed all in white would be difficult to spot, pressed against the white cliff of the wall?"

"Yes . . ."

"So you would need a white outfit. Now, what do they make here?"

Lowa's lips pursed. "That might work."

Dug looked at them both. If they were suggesting what he thought they were, it was an insane plan, but they both seemed to be serious. He shook his aching head.

Chapter 9

One of the guards caught him by the elbow. "Over there. To your left. Follow the fence along."

Weylin nodded and walked off along the palisade. To his right, in the centre of the Eyrie, was a circle of huts. A woman was weaving on a loom, another was playing a clay flute. Children were darting about, and he could hear the squeals of what sounded like a multitude of them at play. There weren't any men. It had to be Zadar's harem. Weylin had pictured the harem as beautiful women in giant luxurious huts, eating grapes and lounging naked on furs near waterfalls, ready for shagging at a moment's notice, not this child-heavy commune. He stood and stared at the working women and gambolling children. Nobody paid him any heed.

Ahead was another palisade, sprouting at right angles from the one that separated the Eyrie from the main body of the fort. A chalk path led to an open gate. Chamanca the Iberian stood on one side of the gate, bouncing from foot to foot like an excited child, clad, as always, in not very much. Tadman Dantadman, in his usual fur jerkin, stood immobile at the other gatepost, looking even larger than normal next to the diminutive Chamanca. His eyes swivelled to meet Weylin's, but he didn't move.

Chamanca splayed her hands extravagantly to indicate that he should go through. He couldn't help but steal a glance down at her toned thighs. Oh, they were lovely. He looked up. She'd seen him looking. She licked her lips. Weylin felt his cock raise its head and shuffle about for room. Chamanca, huh? He'd never considered he'd have a chance with her, but now he was on the ascendant . . .

He smiled as he passed through the gate and into an enclosed square. To his immediate right were three large, conical huts. Chained to a rail next to one of the huts was Elliax, the guy from Barton that Zadar had set to eating his own wife. Had he lost weight? Weylin wondered with an inner grin. The wife was nowhere to be seen.

To his left was the spiked wooden fence that hid the Eyrie from the rest of Maidun Castle. Up ahead, on a platform protruding from the base of Maidun's outer palisade, were Zadar and his crew, sitting beneath a high sunshade suspended with twine ropes from the palisade. It was the same set-up as Zadar used for his travelling court. There were three chairs in the centre: a large, carved throne padded with stuffed vellum for Zadar, and two smaller chairs, one for that terrifying greased turd Felix and one for hot young Keelin Orton. Chamanca and Tadman walked past him to take their places behind Zadar.

Stretching out from Zadar on two long benches were the usual onlookers, gathered as if awaiting a bard's show. Over to the left Weylin spotted his big brother Carden, sitting with the foot that Lowa had smashed propped up on a stool. Next to him, holding his hand, was a young woman in a plain V-necked woollen dress. Her dark hair was cut in the same style as Chamanca's, long and even, on the straighter side of wavy, with a fringe almost brushing her eyes. But where Chamanca was deeply tanned, exotic and usually as approachable as a stoat with its tail on fire, this girl was paler and homely-looking with eyes the innocent blue of a baby wildcat's.

Weylin had seen her before. She was one of the captives from Boddingham. The hottest captive. He remembered at the time mentioning to Carden that she was too good for the whorepits. His big brother had said nothing, only given him that look that made him feel like he'd shat himself. Typical Carden. You had to admire him. He'd had Lowa in his grip and let her go, but while Weylin had been having a crappy time charging around the country after her, Carden had been lounging back at home with his foot up, looked after by a fresh beauty. Weylin smiled, nodded hello and lifted a palm in greeting. Carden condescended to raise an eyebrow.

Atlas Agrippa was sitting along from Carden. His face was still bound from where Lowa had stabbed him with the deer bone, and his dark eyes smouldered with a look that might crumble granite. Weylin liked the large Africa. Now that Weylin was in the Fifty, the Kushite treated him like an equal. He was glad to see Atlas and his brother alive. When he'd made up the story that Lowa had killed them, he was worried that the gods might have really killed them to punish him for lying. You had to be careful with that sort of thing.

Next to Atlas were a few of the more favoured Warriors, male and female, and some young men and women who'd been chosen for Zadar's court for their looks.

Finally he turned to Zadar.

Zadar's big, blue, darkly quizzical eyes bored into him. The king was clean-shaven and clad in excellently crafted new leather armour. A thin black leather headband held his blond hair in a centre parting. He was an average-sized man, much smaller and less muscled than, for example, both Carden and Atlas, but he seemed to exude more power than the rest of the group put together. He leaned and said something quietly to Felix.

Felix nodded, listened, then looked up at Weylin. The onlookers seemed to hold their communal breath.

"Tell us," said Felix, a smirk spreading across his stream-lined face, "what you've been doing since we saw you last."

Weylin breathed in, ready to start his long, plausible tale. He'd worked it out while riding home. If featured him as the hero, and everybody else as workshy traitors whose laziness and avarice had spoiled his clever plans to capture Lowa. He looked at Felix. Felix smiled back, eyes twinkling. Oh, Cromm Cruach, he thought. Felix knew. He'd known last time and he knew this time. Sweat trickled from his armpits. Clouds of confusion rushed into his head, he wobbled on his feet and thought he might faint. They were all staring at him.

He looked at Carden. *Help me!* He tried to send the message to his brother by thinking at him as hard as he could. It didn't work. His brother looked at Felix then hung his head, shaking it sadly. He felt water bulge in his eyes, then the tickle of a traitorous tear trickling down his cheek. This was not how he had planned things.

"Tell us what happened," Zadar said, his eyes iron. "You have nothing to fear."

Weylin sniffed, then told his tale.

He started with Ogre in the market. He told them about the ambush at Kanawan and how he'd tricked them into letting him go. He explained how he'd hidden and watched Lowa ride past with a girl on her horse, but, being unarmed and her having her bow, been unable to do anything. He told them about the pinned Ogre, and how he'd confessed to betraying them to Kanawan.

Zadar asked questions about Kanawan, about Lowa, about Dug, about the girl and about Ogre's confession. Weylin answered as fully as he could.

"Have you anything else to add?" Zadar asked finally.

"No." Weylin had stopped sweating. He'd stopped worrying. He just felt sad.

"You weren't the man for the job."

"I wasn't."

"Your desires are greater than your means to fulfil them, although your desires are meagre."

Weylin didn't know what he meant. He just wanted it to be over. He nodded.

"And you failed me."

"I did."

"So you know what will happen." It wasn't a question.

He did know. He'd been lying to himself all the way home. He'd known all along what he was coming back to. He sighed. After everything, it was a relief. Finally he could stop trying. He looked at Carden. Carden looked back. Was there a hint of sorrow in those deep-set eyes? Weylin closed his own.

"Yes. I know," he said. He wasn't going to make love to Chamanca after all. Zadar wasn't going to give him Lowa's hut. His constant fantasising had been his way of ignoring dreadful reality. He was never going to sleep with a woman again. He didn't mind. Again it was a bit of a relief. Finally he'd be able to rest.

Eyes still on Weylin, Zadar beckoned Chamanca forward. "Make it quick," he said.

Felix rolled his eyes, disappointed.

Chamanca was small, not much more than half Weylin's height and less than half his weight. He watched her come. She was holding a small mace, a plain ball of iron attached by a chain to a fired wooden handle. It was a neat little weapon. One of his mother's, no doubt.

Weylin raised his fists, more out of habit than anything else. There was a flash of movement from Chamanca. Pain exploded in his right knee and he was pitching forward. Something smashed into his head. He heard a *gouff* noise, like the cry of a speared ox, and realised as he fell that it had come from him. The ground rushed at him, the world collapsed into his eyes and all went dark.

He was kneeling, head swirling. Faces swam, Zadar's in the centre, then Felix's, then Carden's. He wanted to fall onto the grass but something was holding him up. Arms snaked about his head, across his face. He lifted his hands and grasped them. They were bare, firm, comforting. He stroked them. They were smooth, strong, nice. Tight. They smelled of warm hay. He smiled, closed his eyes and leaned his head into their embrace. He felt an erection growing. My last stand, he thought.

"Am I dead?" he mumbled. It was difficult to open his mouth.

"Not yet. You will be soon."

"Oh. I don't feel too bad."

"That's good."

"Chamanca?"

She didn't answer him.

"Chamanca?" he said again. No reply. But he couldn't remember what he wanted to ask.

Chapter 10

"Where have you been?" Ragnall helped his mentor out of the boat and bent to tie the rope to the dock.

"I have been walking on Gutrin Tor. I am grateful to Maggot for his ministrations, but the wet air of the marshes hampers the clearing of the final sputum from my lungs. So I have been over on the Tor, coughing like a diseased donkey."

Ragnall stopped mid-knot and looked up, brow knitted. "How odd. I've just come back from there. Lowa and I were practising with swords and helping to rebuild an old sheep pen. 'Double-fencing,' she said." Ragnall laughed and Drustan chuckled politely. "We must have missed you somehow. But we shouldn' have done, with you making so much noise?"

"Not odd necessarily." Drustan pressed his fists into his back and stretched. "Sound does travel in strange ways. Sometimes you can hear a whisper from a mile away, and sometimes you cannot hear a shout from a matter of paces. The wind, the shape of the land, these will affect the spread of a sound. Whereabouts on Gutrin Tor were you?"

Ragnall pointed. "About halfway up on this side." We were clashing swords and using a hammer—"

"That would explain it." Drustan set off away from the dock. "Come! Let us go and see how the Warrior's marvellous recovery is progressing."

Chapter 11

Mal Fletcher sat up, but that didn't help either. It was like his guts were wound round an ever-tightening capstan pushed by strong and relentless sailors. He held his breath to kill the pain. It was those half-rotten turnips. Nita had said they'd be fine, and indeed *she* was still snoring happily despite his best efforts to wake her with his trumpeting farts. Zadar must have heard his massive parps up in the Castle, but Nita slept on. She hadn't eaten nearly as many as him of course. She'd watched him eat his, then given him half of hers! She'd poisoned him.

He had to sleep. There'd be much to do the next day, getting the carts finished. Or at least putting the wheels on, hopefully. Carts he had, plenty of beautiful carts – the best they'd made yet, Nita reckoned. The problem was that that Bel-cursed weasel Will the wheelwright hadn't delivered the wheels.

He'd ordered the wheels, oh yes, and Will had given him a delivery date. And he'd left it at that. He'd trusted the man. He'd assumed the wheels would arrive when Will had said they would, and planned around that. And that was the problem. He should have known. Again and again he'd trusted carpenters, farriers, wheelwrights and the like to do what they said they were going to do, and again and again he'd been let down. Every single time. Someone who seemed perfectly decent would say something like, "Don't worry. You'll have all the wheels by the full moon. They're nearly done; I've just got to get them to you. And it's not hard to

move wheels!" And Mal would trust them. After all, when
Mal said he was going to deliver something, he delivered
when he said he was going to. But every Makka-cursed time,
when he asked where his order was, it was all "Well I
would've had 'em to you, but what with the rain the other
day and my gammy leg and my aunt being ill . . ."

And now he wasn't going to be able to deliver his carts
on time, and Maidun's quartermaster would curse him, or
worse.

A new spasm gripped his insides. He sat up and massaged
his gut. That relieved the pain a little, but there was no
denying it any more. If he was going to sleep at all, he was
going to have to visit the crap huts. *Toutatis tread on all
turnips.*

He pushed open the tent flap and clambered out into
the night. The camp slept around him, including Nita.
Above, the full moon was brilliant. To the south Maidun
Castle shone unnaturally, like a ghost hill.

It was ten minutes' walk to the riverside latrines. That's
what had put him off getting out of bed until he was certain
he had no choice. Back in the day, he would have risked it
and squatted behind someone else's tent. But that's what
Moli had done. He'd been seen by someone watching from
the walls. They were always watching. He could see them
up there now, silhouetted against the starry sky. They'd seen
Moli shit and they'd seen what tent he'd gone back to. The
next day they'd put Moli in the arena.

Mal had gone to watch with hundreds of others. Tadman
had broken him, bone by bone. It had taken a good hour. Mal
didn't want to end up in the arena, so he set off for the river.

He walked past rows of shelters, men and women sleeping
outside, gently smoking blacksmiths' fires, stilled wood-
workers' lathes and motionless potters' wheels. The journey
seemed longer at night, without people to talk to and look
at.

He was nearly at the latrines when the shout came in.

"Lowa Flynn at Mearhold . . ."

He tripped over a tent rope. By the time he'd got back up, the shout was over and he'd missed the rest of it. Never mind, he thought. They were never anything to do with him anyway.

Chapter 12

Dug woke up hangover-free for the first time in a while and felt warmly at peace with the world. Lowa suggested that she accompany him on a recuperative walk on the dry land to the north and raised a saucy eyebrow at him. Spring, however, had been badgering him to go fishing with her for days.

The night before he'd felt well enough to get into bed with Lowa for the first time since Kanawan, but Lowa had pointed at Spring and shaken her head. Which was fair enough. There was something a bit grim about shagging in the same hut as a pre-pubescent girl. Although Bel knew he'd had sex with Brinna enough times with Kelsie and Terry sleeping nearby. But family was different.

So he very much wanted to go for a walk with Lowa, but Spring was bouncing on the island's springy surface chanting, "Please please please please please."

"Aye, OK. Sorry, Lowa, but I did say I would."

"It's not a problem," said Lowa. She spun round and walked away briskly, almost exactly as if it was, in fact, a problem.

Spring's tanned cheeks bloomed with pink joy. "We'll take a big boat for all the fish! We'll need nets, and a spear hook. I'll show you!" Dug looked after Lowa. By Danu her bottom looked fine in that light Mearhold dress. Spring cantered off to find things, chattering excitedly to herself.

It turned out to be a good day, albeit in a different way from how he'd hoped. They paddled slowly on the still waters and dropped lead-weighted nets across channel necks. Spring pointed out all the birds whose names she'd learned from Maggot, Ragnall and the fishermen while Dug had been "lazing about". Dug showed her how to hook trout from under mud banks with bare hands and flip them onto the bank. Spring said it was the best thing she'd ever done.

"It's called guddling," he told her.

"Guddling," she said, copying his northern accent. "Guddling. I like it."

"People will tell you it's a great skill – you have be patient, approach carefully from behind, win the trout's trust by tickling it, then gently grasp it—"

"But that's wrong! You just grab it! Couldn't be easier!"

"Aye."

They guddled enough young trout to feed a multitude, collected their nets, tossed back the smaller fish and whacked the bigger ones on their heads. Shadows were lengthening by the time Dug paddled home. Their catch was piled in the centre and Spring knelt high in the bow like a youthful figurehead, looking for interesting birds.

She turned and looked at Dug. He winked back.

"Can I call you dad?" she asked.

"No," he replied without thinking.

"OK." She went back to her duck watch.

It had been an instinctive response. Kelsie and Terry had called him dad. Nobody could or should replace them. But he felt bad.

"Dug sounds a bit like dad anyway?" he offered.

"Yes, it does. A bit." Spring didn't turn round.

The next morning, over a magnificent breakfast of smoked pork, bread and duck's eggs, Spring begged him to go fishing with her again. The day after that, Spring pleaded with him to go fowling with her on the marsh.

To his surprise, Dug enjoyed his days with the girl very

much. She was young, but she was at least his intellectual equal. He told her what he thought about the state of the land, the gods, life . . . She asked him questions which made him analyse his views more deeply and even change a few of them. He found himself believing some things more strongly, for example he was now more certain than ever that the Romans would not be a welcome addition to Britain.

By the fourth day out of bed, a dull ache in his shoulder and swiftly healing scabs on his chest were the sole physical reminders of his battle with the Monster. At breakfast in their hut he told Spring that he was going to go for that walk on the northern hills with Lowa. He'd seen her only briefly every evening before he'd fallen asleep and, since Spring was always in the hut, seeing Lowa was all he had done.

"Ah," said Lowa when he said he was hers for the day. "Thing is, I've been teaching Ragnall how to fight. He needs it desperately. I promised him archery today . . ."

"Oh. OK. Never mind then. I think Spring might be up for a day's fishing?"

"Yes! Yes! Hooray! Ow!" Spring sprang so happily from her bed that she hit her head on a shelf.

"Sorry, Dug, but I'd be letting him down, and I thought, since you were always with Spring these days—"

"Really, it's fine. It could not be finer."

"Maybe we'll go for that walk this evening?" she said with a smile that could have melted an iron ingot.

Happiness returned to Dug like water through an opened sluice gate. "Aye. That would be grand."

Chapter 13

Mal Fletcher yawned and scratched at his trimmed beard. "Sorry, are we keeping you up?" A grin split Will the wheelwright's turnip-shaped face. "Or did young Nita keep you *up*?"

Oh fuck off, Mal thought. "I didn't sleep well."

"I'll bet you didn't. 'Ave you seen Nita?" Will nudged his apprentice, a dim-faced boy who wore only a pair of woollen pants and a leather apron. His long, bare arms were strangely skinny for a manual worker. "No, I ain't seen her. Nice, is she?"

"Nice? Why do you think he keeps his beard and his hair trimmed like a chief from the east? You'd have to work hard to please a little bit like that. If I had her . . . What does a girl that young *feel* like, Mal?"

"Can we get back to my wheels? And besides, she's twenty-two. Not that young." Mal had a headache and his guts were far from settled. He looked at Will. Sometimes he wished for another war, because sometimes he missed killing people.

"Yeah. But you must be, what, fifty?" Will looked for a response and noticed the look in Mal's eyes. "All right, all right. Your wheels. Thing about your wheels . . . Danu's tits!" Will was looking over Mal's shoulder. Mal turned to see what it was.

Maybe a hundred riders were pounding up from the stables to Maidun's west, sitting tall on good mounts. Each was wearing simple dark clothes, but they were armed, most with broadswords strapped to their backs. The rearmost led a gaggle of packhorses, which had bundles of rectangular wooden boards to their flanks.

"That's Felix at the head," Mal muttered. "And Tadman and Chamanca behind him. And that's the Fifty behind them. Rest must be elite cavalry. "

"Danu's tits," said Will again. "They look the bollocks."

"Must be important for Felix to lead them. But why aren't they in armour?" Mal mused.

"Who's Felix?" asked the apprentice.

"You really are stupid, aren't you?" Will cuffed the boy across the back of his head. "He's only the druid who commands dark magic. He's only second in command after Zadar. He's only been that since he came from Rome *before you were born*. All your life you've lived here, and . . . I don't know. The young today. They have no idea what's going on around them. These things are *important*." Will cuffed the boy again.

"What are them boards for then?"

"That I do not know. Mal probably has a guess?"

"Temporary bridge maybe? No, you'd need supports too . . . I don't know. Big shields?"

"Yeah, weird. Tell you what though: I wouldn't like to be whatever's at the end of their journey."

"No," said Mal. "Me neither. Now. When am I going to get my wheels?"

Chapter 14

Ragnall and Lowa crossed the island. Ragnall was tired after the day's training, but Lowa seemed fresh as a hyperactive lamb. She jogged ahead, bow in one hand, quiver joggling on her back. As the path turned a corner, Ragnall watched her pale bare leg flash through the slash in her brown cotton dress with every other step.

He noticed that the lace on his sandal was undone. He bent to tie it. There was a brilliant green beetle on the clay path next to his foot.

He smiled. No, it would never work. Be interesting to try though . . .

He picked up the beetle and thought of his favourite love god. "Branwin, make Dug ugly to Lowa. Branwin, make Dug ugly to her." He looked around. Nobody was watching him. The next part was on even shakier moral ground. It's not as if it's going to work, he told himself, then mumbled, "Make Lowa love me, Branwin. Branwin, make Lowa love me." He crushed all life out of the beetle, then tossed the gooey little body aside and, feeling stupid, guilty and excited, ran after her.

"Got you!" he said, tagging Lowa's back as they arrived at their group of huts.

She turned, looked up at him and took a step closer. "You wouldn't have caught me if I'd wanted to get away." Her chest swelled. She kept his eyes fixed on his.

"I-I . . ." he stammered.

"Hello there!" It was Drustan, sitting on a chair outside his and Ragnall's hut.

"Oh hello!"

"Dug and Spring back yet?" Lowa asked.

"They did get back from fishing, but Spring has dragged him off onto the marshes. A rare white bird has been sighted. Spring is keen to kill it. He is a good man, your Dug."

"Yes. Yes, he is. See you later!" Lowa skipped into the hut she shared with Dug and Spring.

"See you," said Ragnall.

"How goes the training?" Drustan asked. "Can you shoot an acorn from a squirrel's head yet?"

"Not quite, but she's a good teacher. And she could shoot a flea off an acorn on a moving squirrel from a mile away. She's amazing."

Drustan smiled. Ragnall reddened.

"Amazing at archery. What have you been up to?"

"I have been talking to the sea fishermen. Here, sit down. After what they said, I have been pondering an important point which I would like to discuss with you."

Ragnall sat on the clay ground. He was keen to indulge the druid. Drustan may have recovered from his sickness, but he looked like he'd aged ten years and he'd been strangely quiet of late.

"The fishers returned a few hours ago after several days away with a prodigious quantity of fish and other strange animals from the sea. I would have enjoyed looking at them with you. They told me their methods, which are innovative and make good sense, but almost all of which come from Rome. A few years ago, they told me, there was a great debate about whether it was right to take these ideas from an alien culture or whether it was an insult to their ancestors. Once they discovered that the new methods tripled their haul, the argument was quietly forgotten. So I came back here, and I've been looking out over the water, pondering the idea that the nearer you are to a thing, the more difficult it is to behave correctly."

"What do you mean?" Ragnall asked.

Drustan paused for a long time, then drew breath. "Let us say that these Roman fishing methods are morally wrong."

"Morally wrong fishing methods?"

"A hypothetical example. Accept please, for the sake of my point, that it is a self-evident truth that the way that the Romans trap fish is as wrong as, say, murder."

"OK."

"So, in this situation, we could sit on the Island of Angels and condemn them: 'By Toutatis, those coves at Mearhold are using immoral Roman fishing methods. They are wrong to do that and they would be right to stop.' At the same time, however, in Mearhold they are saying, 'We are catching three times as many fish as before. We will salt them and smoke them and store them, and we will eat well this winter. We will exchange them for coin and other food so that our diets will be healthy, our fortifications secure and our children will grow up strong. These methods benefit us, so we will ignore the fact that others consider them to be "wrong". Their opinions are but air, not food for our table nor coin to buy things that we like.'"

"Right. So?"

"So. It is easy to be morally courageous at a distance but difficult when you are benefiting from the dubious course. Equally, it is difficult to do something that you know is right, but will have a detrimental effect on the people you know and love."

Ragnall could hear splashes of pouring water as Lowa washed in her hut's tub. "Yes. Yes, I see that. We studied this. It's the idea of the greater good. I like this one. The problem comes at where you draw your boundaries."

"Indeed. Carry on."

"Well, what comes first? Yourself, your family, your village, your tribe, your island – or all people? If your tribe is doing something to the detriment of all others – like Maidun is – then do you betray your tribe?"

"And the answer is?"

"In theory, yes, you betray your tribe. It's right because it's for the greater good. If Maidun could be brought down, that's for the greater good."

"And in practice?"

"If you and your wife were soldiers or workers in Zadar's army, if all your friends and family were too, if you were bringing your children into a warm, well fed life that depended on not betraying Maidun, then you wouldn't. It's hard to persuade somebody that something's wrong when their comfortable life depends on it. And, besides, it would take superhuman courage to betray one's family and friends."

The old man smiled sadly. "Indeed."

Chapter 15

"Now, I hear you've been dabbling in the noble sport of the archer?" King Vole pulled up a chair next to Ragnall's and Lowa's, placed his cider mug carefully on their table and sat down in the straight-backed pose that all good children know about. Ragnall and Lowa looked at each other. They'd been discussing Lowa's plans to break into Maidun Castle, sitting apart from the Mearholders in a way, Lowa would have thought, that showed they were having a private conversation and didn't want to be disturbed.

"Listen carefully, both of you," said King Vole. "I am going to give you a masterclass in archery." He leaned back and nodded magnanimously, as if to say, "Yes, you really are that lucky."

Lowa flashed a *what-the-Bel* look at Ragnall. King Vole didn't notice. He was holding his clay cider mug up to the firelight, admiring its craftsmanship. His face looked no older than Lowa's, but his only hair was a hand's breadth swathe slapped onto the back of his head like a cluster of black seaweed on a shiny boulder. A delicately pointed nose and chin poked from his clean-shaven, flabby face. He moved the mug to his nose and sniffed carefully, as if holding a fragile instrument over a volatile liquid.

"The best cider in the world." He took a sip. "From the finest clay." He sucked bubbles of air through the liquid, swallowed and sighed exaggeratedly. "Now. Archery."

"You're an expert?" asked Lowa.

"*The* expert. Listen and learn."

"Looking forward to it."

"We'll start with the basics. Few people see the benefit of a bow over a sling. Indeed a bow does have many drawbacks."

Ragnall laughed.

"What?" King Vole looked offended.

"Drawbacks? Bows?"

"Yes, that is what I said."

"I—"

"You'd be better off listening and not laughing. Now . . ."

Lowa stopped listening. She imagined how King Vole's expression might change with a knife driven through the top of his skull. But he wasn't that bad really. He'd lent Ragnall his sword readily enough for sword practice, even though it was as good a sword as Lowa had seen: light, edges nearly as sharp as a flint knife, the leather-wrapped handle free from frivolous adornments. So the king was generous. However, he liked to talk. When they'd borrowed the sword they'd had to listen to half an hour of largely inaccurate fencing theory.

King Vole droned on: "Some claim the whole body should be used to bend the bow, but they're wrong. A light touch is . . ."

King Coot, they called him behind his back, after the water-dwelling birds with black feathers and a white skullcap. Lowa had heard that name "Vole" came from his mother, Queen Vole, who'd ruled before him and been such a fan of voles and the qualities that she believed they possessed that she'd adopted the animals' name and sought to emulate them. Since she thought that voles were hard-working, tolerant and generous, that worked out well for the tribe, and she'd been a popular queen, even if nobody had taken to the bark, grass and insect Vole's diet that she'd tried to foist on them.

"Lowa!" King Vole was looking at her.

"Yup?"

"Try to keep up. Now. I was saying that I saw that stick you arrived with. Far too long and rough to be a useful bow. I suspect you made it yourself after hearing a story from a bard or perhaps seeing a band of archers."

Lowa looked around and caught Dug's eye. He was talking to Drustan, Maggot and a few Mearholders. She smiled as he drained a big mug of cider in a few gulps, despite King Vole telling him the night before that the *only* way to drink such fine cider was to sip it. Dug lowered his mug and winked, his eye twinkling in the firelight. Lowa felt a twinge of annoyance. She couldn't put her finger on why, but her growing affection for Dug had waned somewhat. In fact his constant good cheer and reasonableness was beginning to annoy her.

" . . . why a recurve bow will always," King Vole continued, "always be superior to straight bows like that crooked stick you've got. It's to do with—"

There was a scream from the eastern side of the island. Then another.

Lowa jumped onto her chair to get a clearer view. Dark figures holding swords, spears and unusually large shields were climbing from the water all along the eastern fringe of Mearhold. A few gathered into a group and headed towards them. More lined up into a shield wall.

She looked around. There were no weapons nearby other than the fire itself, a stack of logs and some chairs. Her bow would be much more useful.

"Come on." She ran for their huts, Ragnall following. Dug was already ahead. He was speedy for a large, recently injured man. He had ignored the longer route along the clay paths and was prancing across the island's reedy surface like a fat deer.

Arriving at the hut, she found Dug tying his bag of valuables to his belt. Spring was sitting up on her bed, a rug over her knees.

"What's going on?" The girl rubbed her eyes with her fists.

"You can swim, right?" Dug said. Lowa grabbed her quiver and slung it over a shoulder.

"Yes. Can you?"

"There's no time for sass, Spring. Zadar's here. Get out now. Get in the water. Swim to the reeds and stay there until I come to get you. If I don't, you're on your own."

Spring looked at Lowa. "He wants me to swim to the reeds."

"Do it. Hide among them and stay there. If it gets too cold, climb a tree."

"Climb a tree? I'm not a squirrel."

Lowa bent her bow on the floor and slipped the rawhide loop into place. "Now, Spring."

Spring shrugged and skipped out of the hut.

Bow strung, Lowa followed, Dug on her heels. They were joined by Ragnall, who'd collected King Vole's sword. Screams, shouts and the sound of iron striking iron came from the other side of Mearhold, interrupted by a splash as Spring jumped into the water.

Back at the central fire there were dead bodies all around. Some were attackers, most were Mearholders. Drustan was lying motionless. King Vole was standing over him, brandishing a carving knife and a heavy oak ladle at a swordsman. the king lashed out and stumbled. The attacker swung a killing blow at the king, but before it struck, he flew backwards, chest spitted on Lowa's arrow.

She drew and loosed twice more. Two more attackers were flung back like flicked woodlice. The advance guard was dealt with. Lowa caught King Vole's eye, waggled her bow at him and winked.

The rest of the invaders were advancing in a steady line across the island, large rectangular shields held at a tilt above their heads. She tried an arrow. It glanced off a shield. *Shit.*

Too many, and they knew what they were doing. She'd recognised the two that she'd already killed from the Fifty. If the rest of the Fifty were here, goodbye, Mearhold.

As she watched, a clutch of Mearholders dashed from between grain stores and attacked the line. Spears flashed out between shields like tongues from a row of lizards and the Mearholders fell. The invaders advanced. She gripped her bow in frustration. Drustan was sitting holding his head, Ragnall tending to him. Dug was heading towards the advancing enemy line, hammer in his hands.

"Dug!" she shouted.

The big man turned. "Aye?"

"Stop. Too many. We have to run."

"I was hoping someone was going to say that. Come on then."

"You and Ragnall take Drustan. Back to our huts, then into the water, find Spring and hide in the reeds. I'll cover with the bow. King Vole, go with them."

"I will not." the king turned to Ragnall. "My sword, please."

Ragnall looked at Lowa. She nodded. Ragnall handed over the sword.

"Find me in the Otherworld. I'll be a king again by the time you get there. That bow of yours might be useful in my Otherworld army, Lowa." King Vole raised his sword and ran towards the invaders. "For Mearhold!"

Dug nodded his respect to the king and tossed his hammer to Ragnall, who almost fell under the weight. He heaved Drustan over a shoulder and turned for the huts, then stopped and swung round again.

"Lowa, can you swim?"

"Get them to the reeds. I'll join you there."

He held her gaze.

"I can swim," she said.

"Aye, all right."

He jogged off, Drustan bouncing on his shoulder.

"I'll bring up the rear with you." Ragnall brandished the hammer, but only just.

There was a long scream and an angry yell, much closer.

"No. Go. Protect Drustan and Dug. I'll be right behind you."

Ragnall went. Lowa followed, walking backwards, turning one way then the other, arrow nocked, scanning for any more attackers who'd crept ahead of the main group. Screams of rage and pain and metallic clangs rang from the east of the island. She heard King Vole shout "For Mearhold!" again and saw him throw a burning log onto the wall of shields. A gap opened and he was through, sword swinging. The gap closed, the shield wall came on.

She was just about to turn and run when she felt a shift in the surface of the island behind her. She dropped into a crouch. A sword swished in an arc where her neck had been an instant before. She launched backwards into a spinning jump and powered the end of her stout bow into the face of the swordsman. He staggered away, blood streaming, jaw hanging by a hinge. Another was coming at her, sword raised. She nocked, drew and loosed. It was only a quarter draw, but the arrow sliced through his soft stomach and crunched into a vertebra. He gasped a short breath like a man waking from a nightmare, dropped his sword and fell.

A woman with a spear was on her before she could reach back to her quiver. Lowa parried with her bow. She recognised this one from the elite cavalry. Tillyanna. She'd been a farm girl near Maidun. One of Zadar's riders had noticed her speed and agility while she was playing with her friends and trained her to be a Warrior. Lowa had sparred with her a couple of times. She'd liked her.

Tillyanna jabbed with her spear again. Lowa batted it away with her bow, two-handed.

"Tillyanna, what's this about?"

"What's what about?"

"What do you think? Your hairstyle? This attack."

"I don't know. I never know. I just do what I'm told. Like you used to."

"These people have done nothing to Maidun."

"Right. And the hundreds of people you killed for Zadar were all guilty of horrible crimes?"

"Pfft. OK. Keep coming and I'll kill you. Before I do, do you know why Zadar killed Aithne and my archers?"

"I don't know. Nobody seems to. But everyone's pretty sure it was your fault." Tillyanna jabbed the spear again. Lowa flicked it away and whipped her bow tip onto Tillyanna's bicep. The young Warrior screwed her eyes up in pain.

"Why no armour?" said Lowa, stepping back.

"We swam across."

"But the weapons?"

"On wooden floats buoyed by inflated bladders."

"The shields . . ."

"Floats became shields. Felix's idea. He knew that your bow would be the only real danger here. Doesn't work so well up close though, does it?"

Tillyanna edged forward. Lowa took two steps back and found the hard clay of an island path under her feet. Tillyanna was still on the unstable straw and wood.

"I don't want to kill you, Tillyanna."

"That suits me." Tillyanna thrust, much faster than before. She'd been holding back. But so had Lowa. She swung the bow underarm, knocking the spear clear and throwing Tillyanna off balance. Lowa reached back to her quiver, grabbed an arrow, lunged forward and rammed it into Tillyanna's eye.

She eased the dead woman to the ground, pressed her bow against her forehead and pulled at the arrow. The bodkin tip was lodged in the inside of her skull and needed some wiggling.

She heard someone clapping behind her.

"Good. Very good," said a mocking, Iberian voice.

Chamanca.

Lowa twisted the shaft and felt something give inside Tillyanna's head. She pulled the arrow out in a gush of gore and whipped round. Chamanca caught her wrist and darted in with her head. Lowa turned and the headbutt whacked into her cheek. She wrenched at her trapped wrist, but Chamanca's grip was too strong. Chamanca grinned her spike-toothed grin and squeezed. Lowa fingers opened and the arrow dropped. She swung the bow. Chamanca's spare hand shot up in a blur and grabbed her other wrist. Lowa was caught. Chamanca pulled her head back to butt her again. Lowa twisted, but not far enough. The Iberian's forehead crunched into her face. Sparks burst behind her eyes. The next butt smashed into her nose and the world heaved in sickening circles. She felt her bow being twisted from her hand. She was spun around. Something crashed into her back and she fell. She lay, face forward on the reed floor, brain whirling. She choked cider-flavoured vomit into her mouth and swallowed it. This was not good. She had to ignore her spinning head and act quickly or it would be over.

She flipped around onto her back and swung her legs over her head in a retreating backward somersault. Her opponent read her. As she came up, Chamanca grabbed her by the hair and drove a knee into the side of her head. Lowa collapsed onto her back.

Dug stood on the soggy edge of the man-made island and lowered Drustan into the water, hands under his armpits.

The cold water shocked the old man into consciousness. "Stop. Pull me out."

"There's no time for arsing about."

"Pull me out. Now."

Dug did as he was bid. The old man sat. Ragnall gripped his shoulder.

"Drustan, we have to go now."

"You do. I don't."

"They'll kill you."

"They will not kill a druid."

"These are Zadar's troops. They'll kill anyone."

"Not a druid."

"Dug?" said Ragnall.

The sounds of battle were getting closer. There was no sign of Lowa. Ragnall was staring at him imploringly. "You're not meant to kill druids," agreed Dug, but he doubted that Zadar's lot cared much for *not meant to*.

"Go on." Drustan's voice was weak. "If I am submerged in that cold water my lung disease will recur and this time I will die. Moreover a decrepit old man will hamper your chances of escape. In summation, leave me here and I will probably be fine. Take me with you and I will definitely die and you probably will too. So go."

"Sounds like impeccable reasoning to me. Come on, Ragnall. And give me that hammer."

Ragnall looked at his tutor.

"Go, Ragnall. You know I am not lying. They will not kill me. I will catch up with you."

Ragnall nodded.

Drustan smiled weakly. "Take this purse. You will need it more than me."

Ragnall handed the hammer to Dug and took the purse from Drustan. "But what about Lowa?"

The two men looked back across the island. Still no sign of her.

"She can look after herself. Come on." Dug lowered himself in and waded off towards the darkness.

Ragnall looked down at his tutor.

"Go. I will be fine. As will Lowa."

The young man followed Dug into the water.

Lowa shook her head and propped herself up on shaky elbows. Chamanca stood over her, holding her longbow, one eyebrow raised in disdain. Her sleek black hair was scraped back into a ponytail and she was clad in leather shorts and chest armour that had troubled a cow for even less of its pelt than her usual skimpy garb. The fires glowed orangely off her tanned skin. She bent the bow easily, one-handed against the clay ground, to unstring it. She seemed to hum with energy and strength, ready for anything. Lowa felt exhausted and weak, with nothing to offer.

"Lowa. Little Lo-wa. I've looked forward to this since we met." Chamanca grinned and moved her hips from side to side in a supple, sultry dance. Lowa didn't know if she had the strength to even stand.

"Hello, Chamanca." Lowa managed a small smile. "Still dressing like a blind whore, I see."

Chamanca stroked a hand over her stomach and onto her chest. "If you looked this good, you'd dress like this too."

Lowa touched her nose and felt wetness. Chamanca watched her. Lowa's mind raced. The Iberian would be on her before she could do anything. Maybe if she could goad her into a rage . . .

"I've always thought it's like polishing a turd," she said, feeling about on the ground for something to throw, "when someone as ugly as you spends so much time worrying about—"

Chamanca flicked the end of the bow into Lowa's temple. Multicoloured lights danced and convulsed in her eyes.

"You're not going to sweet-talk your way out of this one. I've always been better than you, Lowa. Much better. Only your bow made you Zadar's favourite."

Chamanca strode around her, tapping Lowa's bow into her palm. Lowa groaned and leaned her head back as if fainting, then darted a hand at Chamanca's ankle. The bow came down on her knuckles and a bolt of agony shot up Lowa's arm. Chamanca laughed.

"A new feeling for you, I think, defeat?"

Lowa shrugged. "There's always a bigger fish."

"Yes, there is. Now close your eyes."

Lowa kept her eyes open. Chamanca unhitched her mace from her belt and dangled the small but heavy iron ball on the end of its chain as if taunting a child. Before Lowa saw what she was doing, there was a whoosh of air. Chamanca had swung the mace, missing her face by a finger's breadth. Lowa jerked her head back involuntarily, knowing it would have been too late if Chamanca had meant to hit her.

"Close your eyes and keep them closed, or it ends now."

Lowa closed her eyes. She felt the knitted reed ground shift as Chamanca walked around her. Something gripped her hair and pulled.

"Up, onto your knees. Keep your eyes shut."

Lowa did as she was told and climbed up into a kneel, half-pulled by her hair. The hand let go. Lowa kept her eyes shut, boiling with desperation and utterly out of ideas.

Chamanca was in front of her again. "Push your hands into the back of your belt. Good, that's it. Bit further. Good. Now keep them there. I see them move, you die. Got it?" Lowa nodded. "Good girl."

Lowa felt the end of her bow tickle her face.

"Now, keep your hands where they are and open your eyes."

Lowa blinked. Chamanca was three paces away, one knee on the ground, one pointing towards Lowa. She took the bow in both hands and pressed it across her thigh. "Remove the bow, and what do you have? Just a girl. A weak little girl."

Chamanca pushed the thick yew stave down onto her leg. The muscles in her chest, shoulders and arms swelled and stiffened.

The bow snapped. Rage exploded and Lowa sprang without thinking. Chamanca fell back. Lowa was above her, then the air was driven from her lungs as Chamanca's feet smashed into her chest and threw her up and over.

She thudded down with a choked gasp, flat on her back. By the time she breathed in, Chamanca was astride her, pinning her arms with strong legs. Lowa tried to pull free, but the Iberian's thighs were immovable. She bucked, then lifted a leg to hook a foot around Chamanca's neck. Chamanca leaned forward, crushing Lowa's breasts painfully, and easily avoided her thrashing limb.

"Your bow is gone. What are you?" she whispered, shifting downwards along Lowa's body, gripping her arms with her vice-like hands, trapping legs with legs, then lowering her face as if to kiss her. Lowa turned her head. Chamanca licked her neck and cheek with a long, slow lap, then pressed the tip of her tongue into her ear and rotated it slowly. Lowa shivered. Lips brushing her ear, the Iberian whispered, "You taste good, but you are nothing. With no bow, you are a little girl. Not even a girl. You are a shrimp. I am going to eat you like I eat a shrimp. I'm going to bite your head off first."

Lowa bucked and strained, but she was powerless. She wasn't scared of death, but she refused to be killed by this idiot. Especially after the tongue in her ear and that bullshit shrimp spiel.

She felt Chamanca's head move away from her ear. She tucked her chin into her chest, but a hand gripped her hair and pulled her head back, exposing her throat. She felt another long lick, then warm wet lips on her neck. She tensed, pulling sinews tight, trying to turn her neck into iron. She felt sharpness bite.

*   *   *

They were still a good way from the reeds when Spring shouted, "Dug! Is that you? I'm over here!"

"Shhhh!" said Dug.

"What?" Spring shouted.

They found her at the entrance to one of the channels through the reeds and stopped there, watching the island. It was a little too deep for Spring to stand, so Dug crouched in the water with the girl balanced on one knee and his hammer on the other. They could see people running along the paths out to the western marshes. Others were swimming from the island, but none in their direction. They couldn't see the line of attackers, but they could hear the screams that heralded its advance, and the sky was increasingly orange as more huts were set alight. There was no sign of Lowa.

"We should go and look for her," whispered Ragnall.

"Aye," said Dug. "You'd think that, but there's no point. She'll be fine. She'll always be fine. We go back and we'll die."

"We can't leave her!"

"We stay here. Every tribe's got a story about a man who jumps into a swollen river to rescue his dog, right?"

"I've heard that a few times, but—"

"What always happens?"

"The man drowns."

"Aye, always. And the dog?"

"The dog lives."

"Aye. Every time. We've got the same thing here."

"I suppose."

"So hold tight. Lowa will be here any moment."

"I'm not convinced," said Spring.

"Shush."

"And I'm going to tell Lowa that you called her a dog."

Lowa closed her eyes. She felt Chamanca's teeth pop through the skin on her neck. So this was it. Killed on a stupid floating island by fucking Chamanca of all people.

The bite released. The weight came off her chest as Chamanca stood, clutching at her neck.

"That's right. Over here, my love, bit this way. Up you get, Lowa!" It was Maggot, beams of firelight glancing off his jewellery. He was at one end of a two-pace-long iron pole. The leather noose at the other end was tight around Chamanca's neck. Lowa recognised it as a dog- or bear-training pole. Ideally, you needed two of them and two of you to fully control a raging animal, but Maggot seemed to be managing. The feral Iberian was ducking and twisting like a hooked shark, but Maggot followed her movements and kept her at pole's length as easily as a master dancer leading a novice.

"Let me go!" Her face bulged.

Maggot flicked his wrists and spun Chamanca off her feet to lie face down on the clay path, iron pole pressing into her neck. She bucked. "Carry on like that and you'll choke yourself. You can see stars, right? That means you're about to pass out." Maggot winked at Lowa. "You'd best go."

"In a moment." Lowa took an arrow from her quiver.

"You had better kill me." Chamanca twisted her head round. Her eyes were like a snake's, pulsing up at Lowa with cold hatred. "If you don't, I will find you and I will crush you." Her fingers grappled ineffectively at the leather noose.

"Fingers off, please." Maggot twisted the pole.

"I'll go one better than killing you." Lowa lowered herself onto the prone Chamanca and pressed the arrowhead into the small of her back. "I'll take your legs."

"Nah nah nah." Maggot took the pole one-handed for a moment and wagged a remonstrating finger at Lowa. His bracelets and rings clacked.

Lowa hesitated.

Chamanca writhed. "Do it," she said. "If you do not, I will find you and kill you."

Lowa touched her bloodied nose. She could see one half of her bow, splintered like broken bone. "All right then."

"No," said Maggot, "I'll hold her here while you get off the island." He gestured south with his head.

Lowa shook her own head. It hurt her neck. "No. I'll cripple her. Then you're coming with me. Otherwise she will kill you."

"Sorry, love, I don't do orders. Off you trot. I'll be fine."

Lowa ran, but slowed immediately to a jog, then a walk. She did not feel well. She leaned against a hut, then dropped into a crouch and vomited a spurt of acidic cider. She walked on, pretty sure she was heading in the right direction.

Yes, here was the hut she'd shared with Dug. Just a few more strides and—

"Hello, Lowa."

Oh for fuck's sake, she thought. There were two of them barring the way, armed with heavy iron swords. She recognised them. They were cavalrymen.

"You're coming with us."

"All right." She was too tired to fight them. Maybe she could try to escape later. If Chamanca didn't kill her . . . She turned back towards the middle of the island.

There was a *thomp* behind her. She turned. One swordsman was falling forward. The other was spinning, sword swinging in a wide arc. Dug dropped onto his back under the blow, swinging his hammer as he went down. The heavy iron head crunched into the Maidun man's knees. The cavalryman half fell, raised his sword and sliced it down. Dug reached out with both hands, caught the hilt and slammed it once, twice, three times into the cavalryman's face. The Maidun man toppled.

Dug stood.

"I thought you wouldn't need rescuing." Dug ran a hand through his wet hair to lift it off his face.

She smiled. "Will you get my new outfit from the hut, please?"

He walked towards her.

The world whooshed around him in a few swift, wide circles, and then disappeared as she fell into his arms.

Chapter 16

The cool water was chest deep in the channel through the reeds. He shifted his grip on Lowa so she was higher in the water. "My bow . . ." she moaned.

"Shush," he said, placing a palm gently on the back of her head.

He spotted Spring and Ragnall in the centre of the three-pace-wide water course. They reminded him of the seal cubs up north, whose little heads would poke out of the water expectantly, waiting for him and Brinna, and later Terry and Kelsie to swim over and play with them.

"Got her. She's all right. Let's—"

"Shhhhh! Behind you." Ragnall lifted a dripping arm to point.

He turned. Several log boats had launched from Mearhold and were paddling quietly towards them. There were three people in each boat, two paddling, one holding a torch.

"Badgers' cocks." Dug looked about. They were safe in their channel between the reedbeds for now, but any boat passing near would see them. If they tried to wade for safety, they'd be heard and overhauled.

"I can stand here," said Spring.

"Quiet," said Dug. They could try and tuck into the vegetation, but they'd surely be seen in the torchlight?

"Did you get my outfit?" Lowa was back in the land of the coherent.

"It's in my pack. But keep quiet. They're coming in boats from the island."

"We've got to get out of here." Ragnall's voice was shaking. Dug gave him the benefit of the doubt and decided it was the cold.

"But I can also crouch down under the water!" said Spring.

A bird squawked and dashed out of the reeds nearby. There was a shout, and two boats headed towards them, slowly, making sure their paddling didn't mask any sounds of escape. They were annoyingly proficient, these Maidun people.

"What weapons do we have? Can I stand here?" Lowa pushed herself out of Dug's grip. The water came to her neck.

"I have my hammer," he said.

"I gave my sword to King Vole," Ragnall offered.

"I've got a knife," said Spring.

"None of those are much use if they've got slings," said Lowa.

"Aye. And if we attack one, we'll bring all the boats on us." Dug looked about. What could they do? Thankfully the moon wasn't up, so it was darker than it might be. But the boats were coming closer, and they had torches. He might be able to hold his breath for long enough to stay submerged as they passed, but he doubted that the others could.

"I've cut some reeds with my knife," said Spring. "They're hollow. So I've got four hollow tubes. One each. They're quite sturdy."

"Spring, can you please be quiet," Dug whispered.

"But we can *breathe* through the tubes and hide underwater. The fishermen showed me how. You can do it to catch ducks. Slings are easier if you're going to eat them, but if you don't want to hurt them . . ."

The boats were maybe thirty paces away. "Well, hand them out!" said Ragnall.

"What?" said Dug.

"One end in your mouth," the young man whispered.

"One end above the surface." Ragnall edged back to the side of the channel and slipped underwater until only a short nub of his reed snorkel protruded. It looked like just another stem. Lowa followed and sank so close to him that Dug thought they must have been touching.

Spring sank too. Dug was alone.

"There's a channel here," said a low voice from a few paces away.

Dug backed to the channel edge next to Spring, took a huge breath, put the reed in his mouth, tilted his head up and crouched. He held the reed in a fist pressed against his lips, making sure to keep his hand below the surface but the top of the reed dry. The water was a pleasant chill on his face, the noisy noiselessness of underwater a familiar comfort from his days swimming and diving down in the sea. He puffed out a little breath and cautiously sucked one in, ready for a mouthful of water. Instead he got air. Reed-flavoured air, but air nevertheless.

He breathed out, then took a deeper breath. He stopped as firelight splayed out on the water, then danced more and more aggressively on the lightly rippling surface. The dark shape of the boat appeared. Spring gripped his arm. The boat came closer.

He didn't dare exhale. A paddle splashed down into the water, then up out again. He watched its trail drip towards him. It was going to be close. He could dodge, but surely they'd see the movement . . .

The paddle crunched into the end of his reed. The reed jammed into the roof of his mouth. He gripped it, crushing it. He heard a muffled voice above. The paddle went up and came down again, just missing his face. More voices.

The boat slid by. His reed was useless. He held his breath. His brain clouded, his lungs squeezed and an anxious inner voice demanded that he surface. But the boat was still far too close. Fortunately he'd spent plenty of his youth and early adulthood diving for shellfish and pleasure, and he knew that the trick of staying under for a long time was to ignore the panicky voice. He also knew a trick to silence it. He pictured Lowa's breasts. Was one bigger than the other? he pondered. He'd first seen them after the rainstorm . . .

The boat was past. He surfaced slowly. More boats were heading their way from Mearhold. Spring surfaced next to him. On the other side of the channel Ragnall and Lowa were still underwater.

"Can you cut me another breathing pipe, please?" he whispered.

Spring reached into the reeds. There was a *snick*, then another, and she handed him a newly cut reed. Dug leaned in to peer at her, to see why she hadn't delivered the reed with a quippy reproof for losing the first one. She was clenching her jaw tight to stop her teeth chattering. The girl was freezing. He crossed the channel and prodded Lowa. She and Ragnall emerged together,

"This is no good," he whispered.

Lowa looked from side to side. "Yes. They know I'm here. They might widen the search but they won't call it off. And we can't stay in the water. So we go through the reeds."

"They'll see the reeds moving from a mile off. We need to take a boat," whispered Ragnall. "There were three in that last boat, two with paddles at either end, one with a torch in the middle. If we can overpower them quietly while somehow keeping their torch, we'll look like another search boat and we should be able to paddle away unchallenged. But I don't know how we can take one . . ."

Dug looked at Lowa and nodded. The boy was right.

"Spring, give Ragnall your knife," whispered Lowa. "Dug, you have your hammer?"

"Aye."

"We're set then."

"What will you use?" Ragnall asked.

"I'll manage," said Lowa.

Dug tested the channel's bed with a foot. It was firmer at the edge and hopefully he'd be able to get some purchase. "You two go on the other side and get underwater. When they're on us, I'll surface first and take the middle one. That should turn the heads of the paddlers. Lowa, you know what you're doing. Ragnall, don't mean to patronise, but in case you haven't done this before, grab him or her by the hair, or even better get an arm round their head to muffle their mouth, and draw the blade across their neck with a sawing motion. Hard as you can, mind. Don't worry, you won't go all the way through. And grip the knife tight. Blood's slippery. I'll try to grab the torch, but if I miss don't let it fall in the water. Got it?"

"Sure." Lowa put the reed into her mouth and sank.

"Ye-es," said Ragnall, following her.

"You just stay under, aye?"

"Aye," said Spring.

Dug stood tall to look for boats. He didn't see any but he heard someone say, not far off, "What's that, in the reeds?"

The nose of a boat entered their channel. Dug sank, lower than before, not bothering with the reed. The boat glided through spangled torchlight into view above, the shadow of its nose, then the nose itself, then the first paddle . . .

Dug leaped like a salmon.

There were four in the boat. They all turned towards him. He whacked his hammerhead into the leftmost of the central heads, then into the right one, as if ringing a great bell. That was the joy of the hammer over other weapons. In group situations it was much more effective to whack than stab or slice. Blades could get caught in things; hammers tended to do their damage then bounce off. As the hammerhead cracked into the second head, a spurt of blood slapped into Dug's face and open mouth. He swallowed some and fell back gagging, then gulping marsh water to follow the blood. He

fought to get back on his feet, managing to grab the edge
of the boat and pull himself up, a nasty metallic taste in his
mouth.

His two were out cold in the centre of the boat. Ragnall's
was at the front, pouring black blood from his slit throat
and convulsing like a dying fish. At the back Lowa had hers,
a young man, by the back of the neck with one hand, strong
archer's fingers holding him in an eye-bulging, paralysing
grip. In her other hand she held the torch. *Ah*, thought Dug.
He'd completely forgotten about keeping the torch alight.

"Um . . . ?" she asked. Dug cracked his hammer onto her
captive's head. He felt the necks of his two: both dead.

"What's happening there!" shouted a gruff voice. The
shouter was close but shielded from view by the reeds.

"Squeeeeeee!" squealed Spring. They all looked at her,
bobbing in the water by the boat. "Squeeee?" she said.

"We startled some otters," called Ragnall in a gruff voice.
"Little bastards almost capsized us."

"Fucking otters!" said the voice.

"Yeah!" said Ragnall. "Fucking otters! We'll catch them
and make hats for everyone!"

"Ha ha! Nice one!" The boat paddled away.

Dug sat in the back with a paddle. Then it was Spring, Lowa
with the torch, then Ragnall on front paddle. They followed
the channel to the main river, then south past the hulking
shadow of Gutrin Tor, keeping to the edge to avoid detection
and to stay in the slackest part of the contrary current.

They saw only one of the Maidun attackers, a man on the
far bank.

"Any luck?" he asked.

"No!" Lowa replied. "You?"

"Not a sign. She's a slippery bitch, that one."

"She sure is."

Dug could see Spring's shoulders rocking in a silent giggle.

He leaned forward and pinched her. She started and slapped his hand away. Dug smiled and paddled on. Soon Gutrin Tor was a memory behind them. They were away, heading for Maidun Castle.

Out of the pan, thought Dug, but charging straight to the blacksmith's and leaping head first into the furnace.

Part Four

Maidun

Chapter 1

A metalled road ran from the south side of the great marsh, through the town of Forkton and on to Maidun Castle. It would have been two days' hard walking or a day's riding to reach Maidun on the road, but they couldn't risk it. Forkton was Zadar's town, so not only would the road have been thick with people who might have recognised Lowa, but there was a massive likelihood of meeting the force that had attacked Mearhold on its return journey.

So they travelled a few miles to the west, keeping to the woods. Dug and Spring scouted ahead with a tin whistle that the Mearhold hunters had given Spring. If they encountered anybody suspicious, the plan was for Dug to play the whistle and Spring to sing.

"Are you sure we'll hear that?" Ragnall had asked.

"Oh you'll hear me," Spring had said, then launched into song with a voice that was at least half scream.

"Aye." Dug interrupted her with a shout. "The giant beasts on the other side of the Great Ocean'll hear you too, and rip their own ears off and eat them so they won't have to hear any more."

Other than the odd forager and hunter, however, they saw nobody and Spring's song remained unsung.

Ragnall offered to take over the scouting a few times and Dug accepted, but Lowa pointed out each time that Dug had more experience with this sort of thing, and he'd be better at dealing with any trouble. So Ragnall stayed back with her. She couldn't scout herself, of course, since she was the fugitive. She was disguised to a degree, with her hair piled up into a leather hat taken from one of the dead on the boat, but anybody who knew her would have recognised her immediately.

The weather had cooled a little, mercifully, and the walking was easy. There was the odd fallen tree to negotiate, a few bogs to tussock-hop or circumnavigate and a small hill to climb every now and then, but there was nothing like the miles-wide sucking morasses, slippery, wet cliffs, aggressive wolf packs and easily upset bears that Dug had regularly encountered up north. In the busy south, the only wolves and bears left were those that had learned to avoid human contact. They did happen upon a large, disgruntled-looking wild boar, which stood on the track barring their way, but Dug put Spring behind him and stared at the beast until it ran off into the woods with a groink and a toss of its head.

"And that, Spring, is how you out-ugly a boar," said Dug.

"You're not ugly," said Spring.

Dug was happy in the girl's company. He told her stories and expanded on his theories about life. Talking to Spring was like plucking his thoughts from his head, laying them on the ground, sorting them and slotting them back in better order. She was, he thought, a unique girl.

Ragnall and Lowa seemed content too. Whenever he and Spring waited for them for a break or to discuss the route, they'd appear deep in conversation, or laughing together, or they'd just be sauntering along in happy silence like an old, devoted couple. In the evenings they would all talk together, but they usually covered subjects in which Dug had no interest and no view. So mostly Ragnall and Lowa talked while Dug listened and Spring slept.

The first night they sheltered in a derelict hut. With the animal droppings, bones and leaves swept out and a few branches interwoven across the door hole, it was cosy and secure. When it was time to sleep, Dug lay on the floor next to Lowa and put an arm over her. She rolled so she was facing away from him and was soon snoring softly.

The next evening they slept in the woods. Spring pleaded with Dug to lie so that she'd have him on one side and the fire on the other, so that any bears would eat him first and give her a chance to get away. He was, after all, used to being chewed by animals and she wasn't. He acquiesced and kicked the twigs and nutshells away from a spot next to hers, while Lowa found a place on the other side of the fire, next to Ragnall.

That second night Dug lay awake, listening to the cracks of the fire, the shrieks, barks, rustles and clicks of the woodland animals and Spring's porcine snufflings.

He couldn't sleep.

He couldn't ignore it any more. Lowa's apparent indifference towards him and her contrary interest in Ragnall was so heavy on his mind that he was having one of his very rare sleepless nights. When Lowa and Ragnall had laughed together earlier, their merry sounds had shaken him horribly and he'd had to admit to himself that he was jealous. He'd felt like this as a boy a few times, when he'd been achingly in love with a friend's mother or older sister and had to watch them enjoy the company of a lover who wasn't him. He remembered childhood emotions well – it perplexed him that most other adults didn't seem able to – but he'd thought this kind of infatuation had disappeared along with the belief that he was the centre of the world.

If he'd been talking to Spring, she'd have made him go through it in a detached way, as if he were looking from the outside rather than an irrational participant. He tried that. Yes, he'd found Lowa attractive, but he had by no means become obsessed like some old saddo. He'd been content with the traditional decent older man's undertaking of only ogling her when he was absolutely certain he wouldn't get caught. He'd never have tried anything. Then *she'd* kissed *him*. So, logically, she must have fancied him even more than he fancied her. Then that morning in Mearhold she'd leaped on him when he was half asleep. Then she'd suggested that they go for a "walk" with a saucy arch in her eyebrow. He hadn't gone, but it had been clear what would have happened if he had. Then, when he'd suggested a similar walk a few days later, she'd been busy with Ragnall. Since then there'd been nothing: no suggestion at all that she had any interest in him whatsoever, sexual or otherwise.

The training with Ragnall had seemed like a genuine excuse. Dug had been spending every day with Spring, so it had been reasonable for her to assume that he was going to do that again. And every night in Mearhold Spring had been there in the same hut. The two nights on the road, Spring and Ragnall had been there, in the hut and now by the fire. So she shunned physical intimacy when others were around. Nothing wrong with that. He wasn't mad on shagging in public either. Maybe, on top of that, she just wasn't in the mood. Women were like that. Brinna had been. Sometimes she'd been up for it every day – more than once a day at the beginning – and sometimes there would be long periods of abstinence, particularly for the few moons around the birth of the girls. In fact, he himself could go for days at a time without feeling like sex. Maybe, of course, it was her time of the moon. He wasn't squeamish about riding the red horse, but he knew some women preferred not to.

Aye, any objective observer would agree that he was being wet. If you were a lovesick young fool, Lowa's apparent indifference might reasonably upset you. But they were adults. He and Lowa were embarking on a lasting, adult relationship. They didn't need to shag ten times a day to prove their affection for each other. There'd be plenty of time for that once Zadar was dead.

That was another point. What he knew of Lowa's plan to kill Zadar – Drustan's plan – seemed plausible, but it was still terrifyingly risky, and he'd never heard how she was going to get away afterwards. With that on her mind there was little wonder she wasn't offering herself up like a seal in season. He must, he thought, talk to her about her escape plan. Killing Zadar was a noble goal and a useful one for the land, but it wasn't worth dying for. Nothing was worth dying for.

He felt happier. *But*, a nagging internal voice asked, *what about Ragnall?* He and Lowa did look good together. Their ages were much closer. And Ragnall had more in common with her than he did. But no. Lowa had pulled Dug, not the other way round. Like many women, she preferred older men. Ragnall was a friend, and it was good that she had friends, but he was far too young for her to find him attractive.

No, he decided, there was definitely no need to worry about anything. Besides, he'd seen her picking and eating wild carrot flowers that very evening when she'd thought nobody was watching. Wild carrot flowers stopped babies. She must be planning, he thought, to jump back on him as soon as the opportunity arose. That thought left him smiling peacefully up at the leaves above.

So he was surprised, still awake some time later, to realise that he was no longer listening to woodland groans and grunts, but to the sounds of Lowa and Ragnall having sex. He lifted his head quietly. Ragnall's white buttocks were carefully rising and falling. Lowa's gasps became louder and closer together until she came with a sigh. Ragnall pumped on a little longer, said, "Oof!" slowed down, stopped and rolled off.

Dug lay on his back, eyes closed. He pinched himself. He was definitely awake. *Big bald badgers' bollocks*, he thought.

Chapter 2

"Where *is* he?" Spring came back up the hill from the stream. "I've been shouting for ages. He's not down there."

Lowa looked at the distraught girl. She had twigs and leaves in her hair. "He's gone, Spring."

"Gone?"

"Headed off, on his own."

"I see. *Why?*"

"I don't know."

"It was you. You liked Dug then you changed to Ragnall. That's what's happened. You upset him and he's gone."

"No, Spring, we all like Dug." Ragnall raised a hand to comfort her, but the girl twisted away, turned and stared at him. Tears poured from her eyes.

"No! You can . . . fuck off! Fuck off! You fucking . . . rat's arse! It's your fault he's gone! If you'd never come he'd still be here, and we don't need you. You can't help kill Zadar. You can't even build a fire."

"I can do more than build a—"

Lowa held up a hand to silence him.

"I'm sorry, Spring," she said. "We'll find Dug, we really will. Don't blame Ragnall. He's lost Drustan, remember."

Spring stared back at her, hatred blazing through tears and snot. "Drustan! Drustan's a dried up old pile of seagull shit who told Zadar where we were! Who do you think sent the shout? Dug's a hero! We need him! And now he's gone . . ."

Spring fell to the ground and curled into a ball. She sobbed, then screamed, ripping at her hair and kicking her legs.

Lowa didn't know what to do.

"I'd have thought," said Ragnall, "she'd be too old for tantrums. On the Island of Angels—" He saw the look on Lowa's face and stopped. She looked at Spring, who, lying on her side, was pumping her legs as if running and driving herself round in circles on the forest floor. Lowa was amazed to find moisture springing to her own eyes. She turned away. Tears were streaming now. It must, she told herself, be deferred grief from her sister and her women being killed. She'd resolved not to grieve until Zadar was dead, but this minor upset had lifted the lid.

"Stay with her. I'm going to the stream."

Ragnall looked contrite. "I'm sorry. I didn't—"

"Stay with her." Spring was lying face down now, shaking, moaning and bashing a fist into the earth.

Lowa ducked under a tree and walked downhill to the stream they'd all washed in the night before. Dug had made a joke about pissing upstream. It hadn't been funny but Spring had laughed like a tickled baby.

Truth was, she felt shitty about Dug. She'd fallen for him, she really had. After she'd thought the Monster was killing him and been so relieved when he'd survived, she'd admitted to herself that she might just be in love with a man for the first ever time. She'd been so happy on Mearhold, waiting for him to recover. Then she'd gone off him. Just like that, so suddenly and completely it was impossible to remember why she'd been attracted to him in the first place. It wasn't her fault. The speed and depth of the switch in her affections had surprised her, but she'd learned a long time ago that people were weird and she was no exception.

What *was* her fault was how she'd dealt with it. Dug hadn't realised she'd gone off him and she hadn't told him.

And then he must have seen them shagging. She should have told him but had taken the coward's path. She stopped. This was what she'd wanted. She'd wanted him to work out what was happening and to slink off. That was why she'd had sex with Ragnall by the fire the night before. She'd *wanted* Dug to see and leave before dawn. By Bel, she realised, that was why she'd had sex with Ragnall *at all*. She'd used him to be rid of Dug. Well, that wasn't totally true, he was attractive and it was no hardship making love to him, but, she realised, her primary motive had been to upset Dug.

Was she that cold? No. It wasn't cold. It was best for everyone. Ragnall got a shag out of it, and she'd never heard a man complain about that, and Dug was gone, good and clean, bandage ripped from the wound. There would be none of the lingering "Did she really mean it?" agonising that she'd seen cause so much trouble at the end of romances. She had, in fact, done the decent thing. And of course she didn't need Dug for Drustan's plan. He had been useful and now he was out of the way. It was difficult to see how it could have worked out better.

She walked along the stream a few yards to a pool. On all fours, she looked at her face in the calm water and burst into tears. This time she didn't try to stop. She cried and cried until it was all out, then washed her face.

She *had* done a shitty thing to Dug. He was a good man, maybe even a great one. Spring could see it too. He didn't know it himself, but that was part of his greatness. He could see his own failings but not his qualities. If he hadn't been so strong, that blindness would have made him weak. It took such strength to be as kind and gentle as he was. And she'd done this to him. Massive shitting fucktwats, why *had* she gone off him? She shook her head and cried some more.

When she'd finished, she walked slowly back to the fire, reluctant to face Spring. The girl was still lying face down, crying gently. Ragnall was sitting on a log, watching her.

Lowa sat down next to the girl and pulled her into her arms. Spring resisted for a moment, then allowed herself to be hugged. Lowa rocked her.

Chapter 3

Ragnall bit his lower lip and watched Lowa sitting on the forest floor, holding the sobbing child in her arms. He felt a bit sick. He'd upset friendly old Dug and he'd betrayed Anwen. Worst of all he'd done it with magic like, very much like, the evil character in a tale. Recent events suggested that he really wasn't the man he thought he was.

But it wasn't his fault. One, he hadn't meant to. He really had not expected his spell, or whatever it was, to work. Two, it wasn't as if Lowa and Dug were gods-destined lovers. He was some older fellow she'd shagged a couple of times, probably just for something to do in the evenings. And a spell? Really? He was still deeply unsure about Drustan's fire-lighting feat. It really could have been a trick. He'd heard that people's principles slipped in times of strife, so wasn't that more likely?

Whatever it was, it had been worth it. He thought of the feel of Lowa's skin and her smell, and he smiled. As he did so, he caught Spring's eye. She had stopped crying and was staring at him with the sort of look that a cat might give someone who's just thrown water over it and laughed. He turned away.

Chapter 4

Dug stopped for the hundredth time and turned back. He'd imagined it. He must have imagined it. Lowa wouldn't do that, would she? She had. He hadn't imagined it. Those heaving buttocks were seared onto his brain for ever. Heaving boy buttocks on the girl that he loved. He chuckled. It was quite funny when you thought about it, he told himself. He turned and carried on towards Forkton.

Yeah, hilarious, he thought a few paces later. So very funny that he was heading for the nearest town to find the nearest inn and drink until rational thought troubled him no longer.

But there, up ahead on the road, coming towards him, surely that was Lowa? Definitely. Her height and her hair, if she'd tied it back. But how had she got there? No. No, he realised as the walker approached. In fact it was a boy of about fourteen, a bit taller than Lowa. And skinnier. With mid-length black hair and a twisted bronze torc around his neck that Lowa would never have worn. It was the third time that morning he'd thought he'd seen Lowa. He'd passed three people.

"Good morning!" said the boy.

"That, it is not," said Dug without breaking stride.

He stopped again. This was crazy. He'd banged a girl half his age. What had he expected? This wasn't twenty years ago. Twenty years ago people had principles about sex. It was different now. He should stop being so wet and head back. Maybe he'd get to shag her again once she'd tired of Ragnall. He started back towards the camp. She clearly wasn't too worried about who . . . But how *could* she? Right there, not more than three paces away? He turned again to Forkton, walking faster than before. He'd thought that he'd found a new Brinna. That he'd have new Kelsies and Terrys. He'd been a fool. He could feel Brinna and the girls watching him from the Otherworld, shaking their heads with disappointment. He'd betrayed them and made a fool of himself. His head throbbed, hot with shame and anger.

But no, it didn't matter. How could it matter? He was back where he was half a moon before, on his way to join Zadar's army with a quick stop to get pissed on the way. He'd have to steer clear of Weylin when he got to Maidun, but it was a big army, and if their paths crossed he'd just pretend to be someone else. He'd cut his beard off, perhaps.

Then he remembered Spring. He didn't want to leave her. He'd go back for her. And maybe find Ragnall gone and Lowa waiting for him . . . But he was nearly at Forkton now, so he'd just pop in for a quick afternoon's drinking – he owed himself that – then catch them up, get Spring, and go on to Maidun with her. He'd tell everyone that she was his daughter and let her call him dad.

Up ahead four men on horseback were leading a few trios of neck-shackled slaves towards him. But it wasn't four men on horseback. One was a woman. It was Lowa, wasn't it? But how could she . . . ? No, no, hang on. It was a bloke after all.

Chapter 5

Elliax Goldan's stomach was eating him from the inside. He was hungry. Starving. No, not starving, not really. Starving meant not eating at all, and he'd been eating enough to stay alive. Always meat. Vasin meat. He hadn't seen her for a while and he liked to pretend it was horse meat that he was eating. But he knew it was wife meat. He wondered which bit it was? Nothing too serious, he hoped.

He'd asked, he'd demanded to see her, but he'd been glad when they said he couldn't. He couldn't face those accusing eyes. But he'd only eaten what he really had to, to stay alive. Surely she'd understand? And it wasn't like she couldn't afford to lose some blubber. If they were feeding him her arse, well, he was doing her a favour. It couldn't be easy lugging that great big double ball of fat around the place.

And she'd forgive him when Zadar let them go and gave him his new position.

He'd decided that Zadar was going to make him chief quartermaster but was testing his loyalty and resolve first. Why else would he have brought someone of his skills back to Maidun? Why else would he have put him here, chained to railings at the side of his open-air court, if not so that he could see how things worked in preparation for joining in? Yes, soon they'd replace his leg irons with gold chains around his neck and give him a good hut, and he'd be quartermaster. And it wouldn't be long before he had the same arrangement as before. A payment overlooked here, a miscount there, followed by a plump young daughter delivered to his hut. With these happy thoughts he nodded into sleep.

IIe was woken by voices. Zadar was back on his throne across the courtyard. There was Felix, standing before him rather than sitting next to him as usual. The only other person around was an elderly man with a long beard and curly white hair next to Felix. The old man looked decrepit, leaning on a man-high staff bound with cloth at each end.

" . . . not so much a reward for me, as a benefit to you and Maidun and Britain," the old man was saying. "A druid school based here, administered by me, will soon surpass the Island of Angels. It will protect British culture while embracing Rome's."

Zadar looked at the druid, dead-eyed. Elliax shivered. "My druid has powers that will never be matched by you or any other druid that you train. Why would I need your school?"

If the old man was frightened, he didn't show it. "Outside Maidun's influence, where people have not yet learned to fear you, it is druids like me who hold sway. Ignorant, fearful masses listen to us because they think we talk for the gods."

Zadar nodded slowly. "And?"

"You want to rule the entire British island, united as it has not been for centuries. Nominally, it will be as part of the empire of Rome. In fact, you want power for yourself and intend to use the Romans' martial, logistical and administrative abilities to achieve it."

Zadar stroked his chin. These were brave words from the old man. Elliax had seen Zadar kill for less.

"Go on . . ." said the king in the same voice a child-killer might use to ask his prey to walk further into the forest.

"A druid school will provide you with a peaceful force to soften resistance before your armies advance, like dogs weakening a bear in your arena before a gladiator kills it."

"If I don't want a druid school in return for your information, what's to stop me torturing you to obtain it?"

The old man thought, standing in silence for much longer
than Elliax would have dared. "Two reasons. First, I have
seen how much you want to capture this woman. You want
to be certain that the information I give you about her is
correct. Promise what I want and keep me close, and you
can be surer of veracity than if you were to torture me.
Tortured men say what they need to say to make the pain
stop. Second, the druid school will be useful."

"Pain is only one form of torture." Zadar nodded towards
Elliax.

The old man looked over, seeing him for first time. Elliax
smiled at him.

"What are you doing to this wretch?"

"He is a toy."

"An educational toy," added Felix. "We are feeding his
wife to him, piece by piece."

"So he becomes his wife." The old man seemed interested,
not surprised or disturbed.

"Precisely."

"Interesting. The school would run experiments like this
if it pleases you, King Zadar."

"It pleases me."

"So you accept my proposal."

"I'll try it. Now tell me what you know."

"There is one more condition." The old man dared.

Zadar looked at Felix, eyebrows raised.

Oh, this was pushing it too far. Elliax rubbed his hands
in anticipation. *Nobody* gave Zadar conditions.

"Lowa Flynn may have a young man with her, a former
pupil of mine. He should remain unharmed."

"You may have the young man," said Zadar. "Now. Tell
me what you know about Flynn."

Chapter 6

Lowa, Ragnall and Spring walked for two more days through the woods and fields, keeping a good distance from the road. They were a subdued group. Ragnall and Lowa hardly spoke. When they did start to chat, about what they might have for lunch for example, Spring would interrupt, asking what they thought Dug might be having for lunch. "Some betrayal pie? Or a nice loaf of cheat bread?" she'd say.

The girl's tireless spite began to grate on Lowa. At first she tried talking to her, telling her that Dug's leaving was to do with adult issues that she couldn't possibly understand. Spring had replied that it seemed pretty clear and pretty childish to her. Next Lowa had tried ignoring her. That didn't work. Spring had an uncanny knack of knowing exactly when to mention Dug's name to the greatest effect. So when they finally turned west to join the main road and its steady trickle of soldiers, rag-clad refugees and driven slaves heading for Maidun, they were so deeply miserable that the role of poor farmers made homeless by bandits came to them easily. The guards along the road, undoubtedly looking out for Lowa, didn't give a second glance to the pissed-off hooded woman, miserable man and surly child.

"By Danu, Fenn, Toutatis and the lot of them," said Ragnall when they came over the rise and saw Maidun Castle for the first time, "I've heard the stories, but I never guessed . . ."

The great white hillfort shone like a beacon in the sea of brown town that had agglomerated around it.

"Yeah, yeah," said Lowa. "Built by giants and heroes."

"It looks like the gods built it."

"It's a shaved hill. Get over it."

"OK, but—"

"Where's Spring?" Lowa looked about. There she was, disappearing through the crowd. Lowa was off like a hound after a hare. The girl heard her coming and turned, and . . . it wasn't Spring.

Lowa looked up and down the road, scanning every person who could have been Spring. None of them was. *How could she have disappeared like that?* She went back to Ragnall.

"When did you last see her?"

"Just before we saw Maidun."

"She waited until we were distracted. I can't believe I didn't spot her slipping off. I must be tired."

"She's a clever one."

The road running downhill into Maidun was choked with people moving in both directions, spreading out into the delta of grubby huts, workshops and corrals that made up the town. There was no sign of Spring.

Chapter 7

"Who's that?" Jorth pointed at the new girl.

"That's Silver," said Miller. "She wandered in here this morning with a wondrous tale of woe, asking for work, food and lodging. Soft-hearted Mal believed her story, took pity on her and took her in. That about the size of it, Mal?"

Mal nodded reluctantly. His deputy knew him better than anyone with the possible exception of his piercingly perceptive young wife, Nita. Mal always seemed to be surrounded by people more intelligent than himself. He often wondered why they let him remain in charge of the yard.

Silver had convinced him that she was honest straight away, even though she was a far from convincing wastrel. By her looks and voice, Mal suspected she was high-born, and her story about her parents being eaten by wild horses that had drunk salt water and developed a taste for human flesh didn't ring true at all, but he found himself compelled to take her in. He didn't know why – he'd rejected many more experienced people looking for shelter and work – but there was something about this girl that made her impossible to refuse.

"Silver? What kind of name is that?" asked Jorth

"Yes, how did you get your name, Silver?" piped up Miller.

"How did you get yours, *Miller*?" replied the girl, looking around at the cart-building yard.

"My great-grandfather was a miller. As I might be. Perhaps I only work here occasionally? Perhaps I've popped in to chat? Don't judge a duck by its feathers, young Silver. So. How did you get your name?"

"My great-great-grandfather. He always sat on a stool in front of his hut on a busy road. Travellers started calling him Still There because he always was. That name came down to his son. Slowly it changed it to Sillthere, and then, you can see . . . "

"Yes. All right. Get back to your sweeping then."

"I've done it."

"Have you? That was quick. You can help Jorth."

"How did you get a name like Jorth?" Silver asked.

Jorth opened her mouth and looked at Miller.

"She has no idea, Silver. Like a lot of people round here, she doesn't know where she's from. Isn't that right, Jorth?"

"It's just my name."

"And," continued Miller, "she's not the type to make up a story about it." He winked at the new girl.

Silver smirked.

Mal looked from one to the other. Was he missing something?

Chapter 8

Ragnall and Lowa walked through the ever-growing town of Maidun Camp. Lowa wanted to avoid the castle gate – there'd be too many people there who knew her – so they were going the long way round to the whorepits. He'd thought she'd forgotten about Anwen but, after a brief and fruitless search for Spring, she'd suggested they search for his fiancée. He could hardly disagree.

The idea of seeing Anwen might have troubled him more if there hadn't been so much to look at. Possibly it wasn't as big a settlement as Bladonfort, but, with no tall buildings in the camp to block his sight, he had never seen so many people at the same time. There were so many, all looking as if they had parts to play . . . And, soaring over all of it, the castle! The walls were like great breaking white stone waves topped with the brown wooden surf of the palisade. He stopped for the tenth time to stare up at them. Tiny guards with spears looked down. To them he'd be just one more ant in this mass of ants.

"Can you stop gawking like a halfwit?" Lowa asked from under her hood, interrupting his wonder.

"Isn't gawking like a halfwit a bit more subtle than skulking along in a bandit's cowl?"

"Lot of cowls. Lot of skulkers. Not many gawkers."

She was right, as always. It was one of the many things that made him want to rip her clothes off. And yet they were off to find Anwen.

"Is that Spring?" she said quietly a few moments later, pointing at a child in the distance.

"No," said Ragnall. He was glad it wasn't. Life was a lot easier already without the brat's constant put-downs.

They rounded the eastern end of the hillfort.

"Those are the latrines." Lowa pointed down to the river. A long wooden building lined the nearer bank, with a door every pace or so. As they watched, a door opened. A man came out, stretched expansively and headed up the hill.

"People crap in a big hut by the river?"

"It's split into little rooms. Each room has a seat with a hole. The shit drops into the river and floats to the estuary and the sea. You scoop water through the hole to wash your arse."

"That's not a bad idea at all."

"Unless you live downstream."

"And here," said Lowa a little later, "are the whorepits."

Across a shallow valley, below Maidun's spectacular south wall, were two long wooden buildings facing each other across a narrow yard. High spiked fences linked each end of the sheds, with a ditch around the whole. It was essentially a little fort, its gate flanked by four guards, although open windows all along the spiked wall made the place look a little less formidable than the standard military stockade.

"Not pits as such, then?"

"No. Probably it used to be pits, or at least less spruce than now."

"It looks like the riverside shitter shed, with fewer doors."

"They were built at the same time. Same architect. And they're both places where men grunt and loose a load." Lowa smiled her not-smiling smile.

Ragnall laughed. "So what do I do?"

"Offer a guard three coins and ask to see all the women who have been brought in over the last moon. Hand over one of the coins and say you'll give her the rest when you're done. Say you're looking for your sister."

"They won't like that, will they?"

"They're used to it. Say you'll pay twenty coins for her

if you find her. Three coins is the going rate for a search, twenty will buy a girl's freedom. They won't be surprised."

Ragnall hooked three coins from the heavy purse Drustan had given him, put them in his pocket and handed the purse to Lowa. "You'd better look after this."

"OK. See you in a bit." Lowa walked up the hill a little and lay on the grass, eyes closed, face towards the sun. Ragnall looked at her for a moment. She'd been off-ish all morning, but then again she had a lot to worry about. He wanted to think that she was upset about him possibly finding Anwen, but he knew that the task ahead of her was much more on her mind. For some unknown reason, he reckoned that Spring running away was troubling her more that she would admit as well.

One of the guards, a small, smiling woman with a large head, no chin and a nose like a puffin's beak, greeted Ragnall's request to see if his sister was among the whores with all the surprise of a barmaid asked for a pint of beer.

"Although," she said cheerfully, "we like to call them sex smiths, not whores."

"Why?" said Ragnall. "Surely they are what they are?"

"If you wouldn't mind, we prefer it."

"Right. Sex smiths."

"That's it! Well, come with me and we'll see if your sister's a sex smith."

They went to the far end first, where a group of women was chatting and playing dice in a flower garden. They were all about as pretty and shapely as any women Ragnall had ever seen. He asked after Anwen, trying to keep his voice level and to focus on their eyes. They said they were sorry, but none of them had heard of her.

"I hope you find her!" said one as he walked away.

"Don't worry, sir, there's still hope. She might have used a false name," said the guard.

She knocked on doors and they met several more sex smiths, but no Anwen. Ragnall was surprised by the comfort and cleanliness of the place, and, more than that, that the women seemed to be happy, confident and relaxed. Their rooms, bright and airy from the open windows with a large clay vase of fresh flowers in each, were welcoming. They were more pleasant than the sleeping quarters on the Island of Angels.

Soon there was only one door left. They waited outside while the occupants finished.

"I am sorry if this isn't her," said the gatekeeper.

"No problem at all – not your fault," Ragnall replied, then found himself saying, "I must say, it's more homely in here than I thought it would be."

"Really? That's nice."

"I don't mean to be rude, I just thought—"

"That the whorepits would be a stinking, torture chamber of a place full of diseased, suicidal women who hated what they were forced to do and themselves even more?"

"Well, yes, pretty much."

The gatekeeper laughed. "Everyone thinks that. I suppose it's the name. But why wouldn't we make it nice? We're not trying to punish or torture the women. Far from it. It's about making money. The happier the girls, the happier the customers. And we like to work in a decent environment. Can you imagine if it really was a collection of pits? Who'd come here?" The guard put her hands on her hips and smiled. "Yes, best detail in Maidun, working here. It's safe, it's clean and—" the gatekeeper nodded hello to two passing women, who smiled back at her "—there are beautiful girls everywhere. Plus of course, the more money we make, the nicer we can make it, and the nicer we make it, the more money we make. It's a circle, you see. A happy little circle within the great circle of life."

"But the women are . . . captives?"

"Aren't we all, sir, aren't we all?"

"I'm not."

"Then you're lucky."

A happy shout interrupted them. Soon afterwards the door opened, and a small sharp-eyed fellow with a distinguished-looking cropped silver beard walked out, grinning. He tipped his cap at them and sauntered away.

Ragnall knocked. "Come in!" said a voice.

Was that Anwen's?

He pushed the door open. A dark-haired woman was facing away from him, bending to adjust her outfit.

Chapter 9

"Miller, Mal, would you come over here a minute and listen to Silver?"

Nita was standing in a hands-on-hips pose that meant her request wasn't a request. Miller and Mal looked at each other across the table, shrugged, stood, picked up their cups and walked over. It was nearing sunset and the first ciders after work were the best ciders. It was a shame to interrupt them.

Over at Nita's table the new girl was the centre of attention.

"Come on then, Silver, what were you saying?" Mal asked.

"Stuff."

"Silver was saying that things will be worse when the Romans come."

"Oh brilliant," said Miller. "Well done, Mal – you've found a rabble-rouser. You know how much Zadar likes trouble-makers . . ."

"I didn't say worse," said Silver, "I said different."

"It sounded worse to me." Nita's eyes narrowed. "They have weird gods; there are loads of rules about who can do what, and women can't own or do anything! Is it true, Mal?"

For years now the soothsaying druids had screeched and moaned so much about the coming of the Romans that everyone took successful Roman invasion as a done deal. Mal didn't know about elsewhere, but in Maidun, until recently at least, everybody said that the Romans' arrival would make life better for everyone. They'd eat better food, they'd live in houses that could be heated without filling with smoke, there'd be no more disease, everyone would have their own chariot . . . Mal was happy to accept this. He didn't care who was in charge as long as he could carry on making carts and living with the people he loved. And if he had a warm, smoke-free house and lived longer, that was no hardship. And who cared if the people who bossed them around looked and sounded a bit different? However he was hearing more and more rumblings, at the tavern particularly, that it was all lies. Zadar was going to sell them to the Romans as slaves. Families and friends would be separated. Some would be put to work making wine for strangers without being allowed to drink it themselves, others would be chained in great ships and made to row until their backs crumbled . . .

"It's not true," he said.

"Although of course there are many rumours," said Miller. "Not many of them are believable. I've heard that they eat rotten fish."

Everyone laughed.

"I don't know any rumours," said Silver, "I just know what it was like when I lived in Roman Iberia."

"You've lived under the Romans?" Miller sounded sceptical.

"Oh, it wasn't so bad. My parents and me worked in a big Roman villa – like a load of big huts stuck together and lived in by just one family and all their slaves. My mum and dad always said that being a slave under the Romans wasn't that different to living under a king's rule. We didn't like the beatings though."

"Beatings?"

"They beat us all the time – but not so we'd be really hurt. We were always able to work the next day, and we could have had it much worse. The Romans have these big mines in Iberia. Tens of thousands of slaves work at each one. The air at the mines is so poisonous that the slaves' skin turns white and any birds that fly overhead drop dead from the sky. The slaves don't live long either."

Her listeners made various amazed noises and somebody asked, "How did you get away?"

"Well first my dad died."

"How?"

"The Romans killed him."

"What for?"

"He was caught making cider."

Everyone at the table gasped, apart from Mal, who shook his head and walked away. He did not want to hear this.

Chapter 10

Lowa looked like she was asleep when he came back, but, standing over her, he saw that her eyes were open. Then he noticed her hand on her knife. One didn't creep up on Lowa.

"That wasn't what I expected," he said.

"She wasn't there?"

"No. Nor anyone who'd heard of her."

"I see."

"What does that mean?"

Lowa stood up and rubbed an eye. She *had* been asleep.

"Could be any of three things. She could have been taken elsewhere, most likely shipped across the sea, possibly to Rome. But if she's as beautiful as you say, it's possible that one of the Warriors has her up in the Castle, or she's in Zadar's harem up there, or . . ."

"Or . . ."

"Or she's dead."

"What do you think?"

"I think you need to ask around and find out. It's time we went our own ways for a while." She held out his purse.

He didn't take it. He stood on the green hill under the blue sky, feeling as if a trap door had opened under him. The whole world was whooshing into it and he was about to plummet himself.

"But, tonight . . . to get you into the fort, I need to make a . . . distraction?"

"You don't. It was never an integral part of the plan.

Chances are it'll make things worse. They won't divert any guards and you'll put them on a general alert."

"But?"

Lowa took him by the shoulders.

"Ragnall. Go back to the camp. Talk to people. Keep your eyes open. Go and see a show at the arena. You'll soon find out what happened to Anwen."

"And you?"

"I'm probably going to die very soon."

He'd never seen anyone look more beautiful.

"I hope to kill Zadar first," she said with a shrug. "If I do, the place will be in turmoil. There will be chances for advancement. You could do worse than stay here and join the army. You could easily make Warrior in a year or two. While you're doing that you'll probably find Anwen and discover whether she's still interested in marrying you. If she's not here, you should be able to discover where she went, then go on a well-informed quest to find her. Or just move on."

"But, Lowa . . ."

"Come on. Buck up. I'm only *probably* going to die. I might get away, in which case I'll come and find you. OK?"

"OK." He looked at his toe, which for some reason he was poking into the grass. He'd last felt like this as a child being upbraided by his parents for something he hadn't done.

"Now, go back that way." Lowa pointed west. "Nobody will ask anything. If they do, you've been to the whorepits."

"And you?"

"I'm going the other way. Goodbye, Ragnall."

"No. Lowa."

She stopped and turned. "Go, find Anwen and be with her."

"But—"

"Go."

Ragnall watched her walk away.

Chapter 11

Nita shook her head, took another swig of cider and carried on as loudly as before: "I bet she's right. She's been there. She should know."

Mal looked around apprehensively. There were too many people in the courtyard of Maidun Camp's biggest inn for this kind of talk. But he also knew better than to try to quieten Nita after a few mugs of cider.

"I've seen the way Felix looks at women when he walks through the camp. He doesn't like them. Stands to reason the rest of Rome will be the same. No women in the army. No professions for women. Can you imagine! No female smiths! Where would smithing be without women like Elann Nancarrow? And I'd like to see what Chamanca and that Lowa would say about no women Warriors."

"Excuse me?" A showily wealthy fellow called Ollic, whom Mal had never liked or trusted, leaned back from a nearby table. "Is this true, what I'm overhearing?"

"I *have* heard pretty much the same stuff before," said Miller. "From a man who'd spent many years in Rome. He said that woman are treated like animals. Like pampered animals, to be sure, but like animals all the same. They can't own property or coins. They wear jewels — better, bigger jewels than we have — but these are owned by their men and can be taken from them at a man's whim. There can never be a queen, only kings. Worst of all, all the women in each family have the same name."

"That *can't* be true!" Nita protested. "How would that work?"

"Say you and Mal had a daughter. Rather than getting her own name like, let's say . . . Chamanca Fletcher . . ." There were a few guffaws. "Yes, yes, calm down. Mal and Nita's daughter would be called Mallia. Just Mallia, not Mallia Fletcher. If you had two more daughters, they'd both also be called Mallia. Mal's mother would be called Mallia, because his dad would have been called Mal, and if he had any sisters they'd also be called Mallia."

"So the men get the same names too?"

"No. I didn't quite get it, but it seems they have three or even four names each. One, I think, is passed down the generations, but the rest are your own, including maybe a nickname. So my name here is Cheb Miller. Cheb's my name, Miller is my family name. In Rome I might be called Cheb Zadar Miller Most Handsome."

There were laughs and a few derisive comments.

"But my daughter would be just Millia, as would my sister, my mum, her sisters, her mum, her sisters . . . Women all just share the one family name."

Mal and everyone looked quizzically at Miller. Yet again Mal had no idea what Miller was talking about. "Can you say that again," he asked, "but so that people with just the one brain can understand it?"

"You idiots. The point is that women are thought of as objects in Rome so they all get the same name. If I have two dogs I give them different names. Roman women don't get that much respect. I'm pretty sure that's right, isn't it, Silver?"

The girl nodded.

"What about the lands they've conquered? What about the women there? They can't own anything?" asked Ollic.

"Same."

"But how do they get everyone to agree?"

"I can guess!" said Nita. "The men go along with it! They see the chance to double their wealth overnight. To shag that sexy little cousin they've always had their eyes on. They run the businesses, do all the fighting, make all the decisions and have all the fun while the women do the drudge work. That's about it, isn't it, Miller?"

"That is, indeed, about it."

"That's just the women," said Ollic, grinning. "We'll be all right, won't we, lads? Better off!" His friends laughed and clashed tankards.

"You'd think," said Miller, "but I've heard that it's not just the women who suffer. I've heard it said that everyone in the lands that Rome conquers, men and women, are slaves to the Roman soldiers, who treat them like curs with beatings, murder, rape, including male rape, by the way. Your Roman man loves a bit of male arse, apparently. For them, sex is all about power, rather than love or lust. So someone bold like you, Ollic, will need to be put in his place with a regular unwelcome bum-pounding. That's just the normal people of course. The kings and the rulers still have it all right, better even, which is why so many tribes go down without fighting. The kings tell their people that it will be fine, so they surrender. Then the people live like slaves and the kings live like, well, kings. That about right, Silver?"

Spring gave another big nod.

Ollic had nothing to say to that, which pleased Mal because he always liked to see a dickhead silenced, but this was dangerous talk. If any of the Fifty overheard, they'd all be heading for the arena. People had been killed for saying a lot less. He had to put a stop to it.

"You're wrong. We stay here under Zadar's rule and we're in a position of power like no Iberian tribe ever had. We can negotiate with the Romans to keep our way of life. A couple of minor things may change for the worse, but I'm sure that overall we'll be better off. They have better healers, heating in their huts and plenty of cheap wine!" There was a murmur of approval. "We'll have more comfortable lives. We'll live longer. Things will be better."

"Will we?" Miller looked sad. "Or will the well off simply become better off, while people like you and me sink?"

Chapter 12

Lowa Flynn slithered on her elbows through horse shit and grass towards the great white wall. The bundle containing her camouflage gear was tied between her knees, so her legs were splayed and of little use as she snaked along. She'd have liked to put the pack on her back, but it would have stuck up too much. Molehills were plentiful outside Maidun Castle, but none of them moved.

The path fifty paces to her right was thick with castle traffic. She was forty paces from the fort's outer wall. She stopped and lay still for a hundred breaths, moved half a pace forward, then lay still again and counted. This was Drustan's idea. People see movement, he'd said. After a hundred breaths – much longer than she thought necessary – any guard who thought they'd spotted her moving would decide that they hadn't and moved on. Face down and unoccupied, she noticed things: the smell of the ground, the feel of the wind, the dropping temperature as night approached. With plenty of time for her mind to wander, she found herself thinking more about Dug than anybody else. She kept trying to focus on the mission ahead but Dug kept strolling into her mind with his ready smile and his childishly expressive eyes. She kept picturing the moment when she'd walked up to him in the valley after shooting the dogs. He'd looked so happy to see her, so vulnerable yet so brave.

She realised she'd stopped counting, then decided she must have been still for a hundred breaths and squirmed forward another half a pace, ignoring the temptation to lift her hooded head. It was most odd, she thought. She wanted to look after Dug and be looked after by him. She wished that he was lying on the ground next to her. This mission would be so much more pleasant with him along. Everything had been better with him around, until she'd . . . She shook her head. Thoughts like this had never troubled her before. Maybe it was the danger? Maybe she'd eaten something unusual. She decided to stop being so soppy and get back to counting.

She reached the bottom of the first wall, where grassy earth gave way to hewn chalk. This was the first place she was very likely to be spotted and pummelled with slingstones. The first of many. She untied the pack from her leg and pulled out the white-wool top and trousers. She took off her brown outfit and slid on the white one, pulling the hood's white drawstring tight about her face. Her hair was near-enough white, but Drustan had pointed out that it might fly about in the wind.

She buried her discarded clothes in the loose soil of a molehill, tucked a coiled brown rope and its thin iron woolmuffled grapple into a white pouch on her side and looped the leather lanyards of the iron spikes around her wrists. She stood slowly and pressed herself into the white wall, arms spread, iron spike in each hand. She stayed there for a hundred breaths. The chalk wall smelled like flour, fresher than the soil.

No alarms and no surprises. She raised her arm, dug a spike into the wall, waited. No shouts from above. She raised the other spike. It was worryingly easy to jam into the soft rock but it seemed to hold firm.

Here goes, she thought, and ascended as elegantly as a spider. She was soon at the top, breathing heavily but quietly. She paused below the palisade and waited for a guard to pass. As soon as his or her footsteps died away – her, by the lightness of them – Lowa took out her rope and slung its padded grapple over the wooden wall. It landed between two spikes with a soft thud. She yanked. It held.

She landed two-footed on the walkway with a soft thump. The nearest guard was forty paces away, slowing as if about to turn. She gathered the rope, dropped over the inner edge of the walkway and slid, slowly, slowly down the wall. Mercifully, the inner side of the chalk-hewn wall was a little farther from vertical than the outer.

The base of the ditch was dark as a cave at night, but she stood still as she heard the guard pass overhead. She reached out and found two of the sharpened wooden stakes that lined the bottom of Maidun's ditches. The second wall was as steep as the outer wall and significantly higher. The first seven tenths or so were in darkness, but after that the starlight lit the chalk a silvery white. She readied the iron spikes in her hands, then frowned.

Drustan's theory that guards on a wall only ever looked outwards had seemed reasonable after a few ciders back on Mearhold. But the guards didn't stand looking outwards, they walked along the walls. So they *looked* along the walls a good deal of the time. So when she climbed the starlit section of the second wall, one of them would surely spot her.

A low growl interrupted her thoughts. It was a dog, no more than ten paces away. She heard it pad closer. She flung herself onto the wall and scrambled up. When she was certain she was out of paw's reach, she froze. Below her the dog barked, percussive shouts so loud she felt the air vibrate.

She clung to the wall. "Oi! What is it?" A man's voice from atop the second wall. "Outer wall?"

"All clear," came a woman's nasal voice.

"Can you have a look in the ditch?"

A pause. Lowa hung motionless. It felt as if the guard's eyes were boring into her back. Below her the big hunting dog barked and scrabbled at the wall. She pressed into the chalk. Stillness. Stillness meant invisibility. A beetle, spider or some other many-legged beast crawled onto her cheek and over her nose. She closed her eyes.

"I can just about make out the dog jumping about, but it's darker down there than Felix's heart. Could be an army of dragons hiding down there. But the dog's probably just found a squirrel or something. He's got form, that one. I climbed down once when he was barking and fell from halfway. I don't know how I missed the stakes. And what had he found? A dead robin. Trust me. It's probably nothing."

"Yeah, probably," said the man, "but last time I ignored a 'probably nothing' I was a hair's breadth from a bout in the arena. I'll lob a torch down. Lean right over and have a good look."

"All right."

Buggerfucktwats. Lowa pressed herself closer to the wall, willing herself to melt into it.

She felt the torch's heat flash past her shoulder. A yelp was followed by angry barking. Laughter came from both walls.

"You hit the fucking dog!"

"I know! Stupid bloody dog. It watched the torch fall! Why didn't it move? Is it alight?"

"Ha ha! He's barking at the torch now."

"And no armies down there?"

"Hang on . . ."

Lowa held her breath.

"No, just a deeply stupid dog!."

Lowa waited. Below her the dog yipped at the sputtering torch. Slowly, she began to climb again.

She reached the moonlit section. Up close it was so bright she was certain that if she went any further she'd be seen by one of the guards on the outer wall. She'd have to find another way.

A hundred paces away was a narrow wooden bridge. Like

all the bridges linking Maidun's walls it had two barrels of oil at its inner end. In the unlikely event of an attacker capturing the outer wall, these barrels would be emptied onto the bridge and the oil set alight. Her plan had discounted crossing bridges because each one had a permanent guard. However, below this bridge the wall was in shadow. She'd be able to climb unseen underneath it.

Even as she'd been deliberating, the glare from the rising moon had crept closer.

It was too far for her to traverse along the wall so she decided to go back down, walk along the ditch and head up under the bridge. She'd just have to dodge the dog and avoid or silence the bridge guard. She was wondering why she hadn't got to the bottom yet when there was a growl and a whoosh of air. Something clamped round her foot and pulled her from the wall. She landed on her back between two stakes. The dog leaped for her throat.

Chapter 13

In an inn in Forkton, Dug was interrupted. "Oi. What you looking at?" something said.

"Noverymush," he managed.

"What?"

Dug screwed up his face in an attempt to drag his eyes back from where they'd been spinning on the sides of his head. That was better, but still skew. He placed both hands on the table to find a horizontal horizon. That accomplished, he looked over to the next table.

There were four of them. The man who'd said "what" looked unhappy about something. He probably always looked unhappy, Dug mused. His round head, sprouting necklessly from fat shoulders, looked like a lump of meat that had been cut from the side of a massively fat sow, had most of the hair boiled off, then the nose, eyes and mouth gouged out by the thumbs of an apathetic and cack-handed workman as the third to last job of a busy day. Gold earrings the size of knuckles and a chunky bronze necklace showed that he'd had some success with something and thought it important that people should know.

His three companions were cut, thought Dug, from much the same sow. They were two men and a woman. The woman's anger-twisted, watery red, alcohol-melted face was topped by an incongruously fine and well brushed sweep of red hair.

"Garnish on a turd," muttered Dug.

"What?" said the man again, louder.

"I said—" Dug cricked his neck from side to side, then shook his head "—that I'm not looking at very much. I was listening to you lot earlier. What a lot of banal crap you spout." He put on his best southern accent: "*Don't you hate Mearholders? Yeah, they're lucky to be sent away as slaves; it's a better life for them. Don't you hate Dumnonians? Don't they all smell? Did you see the sport in the arena? Yeah, I did. Wasn't it good? Blah blah blah blah.*"

The four of them were staring at him, mouths agape.

"None of you think about what you're saying. You don't know if any of it's right. You're just repeating bullshit you've heard other people say. You might as well be sheep. The ability to speak is wasted on cunts like you lot."

Dug shook his head sadly and took a swig of cider. The man who'd spoken took a step forward. The other three stood.

Dug smiled and reached down for his hammer.

It wasn't there.

Big round badgers' nipples, he thought.

Chapter 14

Lowa drove the iron climbing spikes into the leaping dog's temples. It fell on her, dead. She heaved and squirmed out from under it.

If she left it, come sunrise the dog's body would be a beacon announcing her infiltration. She intended to spend at least a day hiding out in the fort. If the dog was found, they'd search all the sort of places that she intended hiding in. The ditches were kept clean of course, so there was no debris to cover the corpse. She decided to heft it onto a stake to make its death look like an accident. A totally freak, difficult to believe accident, but it would have to do, and surely no harder to believe than someone scaling the wall and killing it? They already thought the dog was stupid. She straddled it, squatted, thrust her hands under its shoulders and pulled with her whole body. It hardly budged. *Fuck it,* she thought. She was just going to have to find a good hiding place up on Maidun.

Feeling her way between the spikes, testing each step to avoid noisy surprises, head forward, peering into the darkness, Lowa crept along the ditch towards the bridge. Every little noise drifting out of the night sounded like a pack of dogs. An age later she was under the bridge. She climbed. Her arms were wobbling with strain by the top. That did not bode well for the third, even higher wall, she thought as she stood underneath the bridge on a supporting beam, panting silently.

Footsteps approached. They stopped above her.

"How's it going there, all right?" said the owner of the feet.

"Yeah, all good," said another voice from the outer wall, presumably the bridge guard.

"Did you hear about the dog?"

"Yeah. Stupid dog!"

"Yeah. See you later."

"Yeah."

Before the footsteps had fully faded, Lowa gripped the edge of the bridge and pulled herself up until her eyes were level with the walkway. A guard was standing on the outer wall, facing away from her. She twisted her head around. She couldn't see anybody else. She pulled herself quietly onto the bridge and lay flat. No sound from the other end. She crawled on her elbows across the walkway of the middle wall and slithered over its edge into the second ditch.

And gasped in horror. She jammed her spikes in to stop herself sliding and stared down, eyes wide. *What, for the love of Camulos, was this?* All along the chasm between the inner and middle walls, dotted between the forest of stakes, were small fires. Chained between the fires, every ten paces or so, were hunting dogs. Above them, lining the top of the inner wall every five paces were guards, all looking out, spears in hand.

Lowa had never seen the like. What had happened? Were they expecting an attack? Were they expecting her? Spring had said Drustan had betrayed them, but Lowa had dismissed that as the ranting of an angry child. But he could have done, and he knew the plan. For this level of defence, they must have known that *someone* was going to attempt to break in and they must have given a massive fuck about it. And, typically evil, Zadar had kept security light on the outer wall and allowed her to get this far, purely for the joy of building her hopes then crushing them.

She'd never get past this lot. If she climbed more than a

couple of paces down the wall, even in the shadow of the bridge, a dog would see her and she'd be target practice for slingers. If she tried to cross the bridge, half a hundred guards would spot her. But there was one way, if not into the fort, then very nearly into it. Maybe she could cross the ditch underneath the bridge, over the heads of the dogs, hanging from the walkway.

Lowa reached up, stuck her fingers through a gap between two planks and gripped. She lifted one foot, then the other, so all her weight was hanging from her fingers. It was sore but bearable. She reached for the next gap. It was narrower, but her fingers slotted through. After some experimentation she found that going backwards put less strain on her fingers. She turned, reached up and hung, legs dangling. She pulled out one hand and reached back . . . and realised the flaw in her plan. A few more planks along, and the guards on the inner wall would see her flailing legs.

Nothing, she thought, was ever easy. But maybe . . .

She flexed her arms, swung her legs up and jammed her toes into a gap between two planks, then hung for a moment in her upside-down crawl position. She felt ridiculous. Was she really going to do this?

She reached her left hand back past her head, felt for the next gap, poked her fingers through it and gripped. She lowered her right foot, scraped her toenail along the under-side of the plank towards her until it found the next gap and slotted her toes into it. She moved her right hand to the next gap. Then the next foot. Not so tricky. She was a whole plank closer to Maidun's interior. Now she only had to do that a hundred or so more times and she'd be across, with just the matter of fifty or so guards and the inner palisade to overcome.

A couple of times the gap wasn't wide enough for her fingers, and she had to traverse two planks in one go. When her arms began to shake with the effort, she rested. While resting, she realised how much her feet hurt. Blood trickled from her toes to her shins. She hoped it wouldn't drip. A dog barked. She hung still. Silence. She carried on, three paces, then a hanging rest, then three paces more. She turned her head when she thought it must have been nearly over. She was less than halfway. A ripple of fear shivered through her. Her shoulders were burning with effort. Her arms wouldn't take much more. Her inner thighs were horribly tight and felt like they might cramp any moment.

Lowa closed her eyes again and pulled a hand out. Her arm shook as she moved it to the next gap. She tried to focus on the feel of the wood, the smell of the air, anything to take her mind off the pain in her legs and arms. This had been a very stupid idea. She almost laughed.

She stopped. She couldn't go on. She hung, arms straight, legs as straight as they'd go. Her head twitched as her neck muscles jiggled involuntarily. She was totally fucked. She giggled quietly. Danu's tits, what an idiot she was. Left hand out, she reached for the next gap, but her muscles failed and her whole arm danced in flapping spasm then fell, useless. She held on, one hand and two feet jammed between the planks, panting. Cramp zapped into the arch of her left foot. She splayed her toes to ease the contraction, but that meant more effort from her leg to keep the foot jammed into the gap. Pain shocked across her lower back. She gritted her teeth and tried to ignore her many agonies.

She couldn't hold on. She was going to fall and land on a stake or a dog.

She pictured Aithne, looking at her, blood gushing from the gash in her neck. She pictured Zadar and Felix. She pictured Dug. She took a deep breath and heaved at her dangling arm. Slowly it rose. The strain was enormous. The tendons in her neck felt like they were about to snap. Tears rolled down her cheeks, dropping no doubt onto the dogs below.

Fuck. The. DOGS! she thought and with that last word jammed her fingers into the gap above. She toiled past the next plank, then the next.

She felt the footsteps on the bridge before she heard them. Surely they'd see her white digits poking up? She held her breath as they approached, then almost screamed when the walker kicked her big toe. Her foot slipped out of the gap. The walker stumbled . . . then carried on. Her left leg was dangling. She strained to lift it, but to no avail. She pictured Aithne. Still no good. She simply did not have the strength to raise her foot back to the underside of the bridge.

She looked around. Nearly there! She let both legs swing down, clenched her teeth and made a final effort hand over hand.

And she was there, past the prints where the support beams met the bridge. All she had to do was swing onto one and she could rest, thank Kornonos. She swung to her left, aimed her feet, missed and fell.

Chapter 15

Ragnall sat in the corner of the tavern outdoor corral. He was sure Spring hadn't seen him.

For as long as he'd been at the inn the girl had been driving the conversation that had the punters rapt. All the men and women there – gnarl-faced toughs who each looked like they could have beaten twenty Ragnalls in a fight, weasel-eyed shifters who might sell their children for whore money, morose mopers who looked like they'd failed in life and blamed everybody else for it – all had broken off their conversations to listen to little Spring. They sat, many with mouths moronically open, entranced by her sing-song proclamations.

It was something about Zadar and Romans, and how a real ruler would topple the former and defeat the latter. Ragnall would have marvelled more about how she'd gone from runaway child to some sort of super bard had he not been so consumed by his own misery. He'd heard that it was harder to dump somebody than be dumped. What an absolute crock of crap that was.

He felt angry, sad and, worst of all, worthless. She didn't want him so, one had to conclude, he didn't offer enough. Extrapolating the point, because her means of measurement had to be comparative, there must be men who offered more. Who were better than him. She wanted someone better than him and she was glad to be rid of him. Ragnall was not good enough for her. So he was worthless. When he remembered how she'd looked at him above the whorepits, pity on her face but a smile of relief in her eyes, it made him want to weep.

He pictured Anwen's loving look, grateful and joyful on the beach where he'd proposed marriage. He groaned with guilt. Anwen wanted him. He was enough for her. Could he forget Lowa, find Anwen and start again where he'd left off?

He decided to find somewhere to sleep. Perhaps things would be clearer in the morning. He stood, glancing over at Spring.

"A wise man called Dug told me," she said to her audience, "that an evil king tells his people that his evil deeds are for their own good. And they'll lie to themselves that he's right because that's the easiest thing to do. But soon the evil king will run out of enemies, and the people who helped him will become his victims. Then they'll regret it, but it's too late!"

Ragnall walked away.

Chapter 16

Lowa's feet hit the slope of the wall. She grabbed the support beam and wrapped her arms around it and managed to scrabble onto it. She gripped the beam. Her body was ruined. She would never, she decided, lift her shoulders or arms again. She'd just lie here until she died. Maybe she was dead already. She didn't mind at all if she was. As long as she didn't have to move.

Slowly she recovered. The dogs had stopped barking and she hadn't been discovered. Her impossible mission to kill Zadar, which was bound to fail at some point, hadn't failed yet. But she still had the final, inner palisade to negotiate. She raised her head. Down below, the dogs and the fires were undisturbed. She was convinced briefly that a dog was staring at her, but it turned away. Above her, where the bridge met the wall, there was scoop in the chalk – a mini cave. She climbed up into it. It was more than big enough to hide her, narrow and deep enough that she wouldn't be seen. She lay down and fell asleep.

Chapter 17

A huge dead dog had come to talk to Zadar. Even with its legs folded under it, it was the biggest dog Elliax had ever seen, big as a cow, and indeed others might have thought it was a cow, but he'd spotted its pert little ears and furry dog's pelt. No dead animal was going pretend to be a cow and fool Elliax! He giggled quietly.

The beast was prostrate in the open-air court, facing the king. Zadar was on his throne, Felix next to him as usual, the old man who'd turned up a couple of days before sitting on Zadar's other side, holding his bandaged staff. Elliax was famished. He knew Felix would soon offer him more "special meat" and he knew he'd say yes. Maybe it was the dead dog making him hungry. He liked a bit of dog. Although, now he thought about it, at least half the pleasure of eating dog meat back in Barton had been eating it in front of whoever's dog it had been.

The big hero with the limp bent over the dog, poking at it. Carden Nancarrow was his name – the man's, not the dog's. Elliax was trying to memorise the names of everyone important for when the test was over and Zadar made him quartermaster. People liked it when you remembered their names. It looked like this new old man, the one sitting by Zadar, was going to be important. He'd have to learn his name too.

Carden stood, pushed back his long dark hair and eyed his king darkly from under his overhanging brow. Here, thought Elliax, was a powerful man   physical strength-wise. Perhaps Elliax might be allowed him as part of his quartermaster's bodyguard? It would be some compensation for suffering this hideous test. He missed his guards from Barton. Although they'd been bugger-all use when he'd needed them most, come to think of it.

"The dog was killed by strikes with a thin knife – most likely two thin knives – to either side of its head," said Carden.

"Or iron climbing spikes?" said Felix.

"Possibly," said Carden.

"The dog was found between the gate and the nearest northern bridge, in the outer ditch?"

"Correct."

"So she came," said Zadar. "Where is she now? Drustan?"

Drustan. That was his name.

Drustan paused for a long time before saying, "The ditch has been searched?"

Zadar looked at Carden.

"Thoroughly," said the Warrior.

"Hmmm," the old man continued. "What will you do with her if you find her?"

"The arena," said Felix.

Drustan nodded as if that made good sense, then spoke slowly, as if taking care to get each phrase just right. "She scaled the first wall successfully. She killed the dog at the bottom of the first ditch. She climbed the second wall, came over the palisade. She saw the inner ditch's guard and realised she could get no further. There she had three choices. To hide and wait, to return to Maidun Camp to plan an alternative approach, or to abandon her scheme and flee. Which did she do? That is the question."

Felix rolled his eyes. "Yes. We'd managed that much."

Elliax rather agreed with Felix. This Drustan fellow had taken a long time saying what they all already knew. He wouldn't be around for long if he carried on like that.

Zadar looked at Carden. "Go. Take the Fifty into the camp and search for her. Torture people if you need to."

"I won't need to torture anyone," said Carden, not quite managing to meet Zadar's gaze.

It was possible that something flashed in Zadar's eyes, but his big sulking fish expression didn't change. Felix, however, leaped out of his chair like a wasp-stung weasel. "You will do what Zadar tells you! Go to the camp. Find Lowa Flynn, Dug Sealskinner and the child Spring! Now!"

"Sure." The Warrior was unimpressed by Felix's rage.

"The child is nine years old, pretty, with long mousy hair. Dug is around forty, big and northern. You will find them."

"Got it." Carden turned to go.

"A moment. As I was about to say, I know where she is," said Drustan.

"Yes?" Felix looked at him as if daring him to lie. Zadar lifted an eyebrow.

"I'd like Carden to show me where the dog was found."

"What could you *possibly* see that a search team hasn't?" Felix's forehead wrinkled above his unimpressed sneer.

Drustan looked at Zadar. The king nodded. Felix shrugged. "All right. Carden, take the druid to the wall and show him where the dog was found. When he doesn't find her, search the camp."

Drustan strode out with Carden limping behind. Elliax wondered if Drustan even needed that staff. Zadar and Felix remained, quietly talking to each other.

Elliax could hear Zadar's low voice but not what he was saying. He heard Felix's reply though: "I'm sorry, finding people is not my . . . speciality. I tried with a full sacrifice and got nothing. It's almost as if something is stopping me, or shielding her, although that would be impossible. But having failed once with a full sacrifice, I don't think it would be wise to try again."

Zadar spoke, again inaudibly. Felix listened, then nodded, stood and came over to Elliax.

"Are you hungry?" he asked.

"I am."

"Good. Can you hear that?"

Elliax listened. He heard a *yelp* from one of the huts behind where he was chained. He swivelled around. There was another yelp. It came from the third hut along, he thought.

"I can hear a woman."

"Yes. Do you know who she is?" Felix's eye widened.

"No." He did know.

"She's your wife. We brought her here while you were sleeping."

He looked at his feet.

"Are you still hungry?"

He nodded.

"Good," Felix said soothingly.

Chapter 18

She woke at dawn in her tiny cave at the end of the bridge. She felt like a lump of meat that a blind but mighty blacksmith had mistaken for an iron ingot. She peeled and ate the two boiled eggs she'd brought, then found that her water skin had split. Very soon she was so thirsty it hurt. She found a flint nodule and sucked it. That helped, but she didn't know how she was going to make it to sunset. Danu curse summer's long days, she thought.

She listened to the sounds of business as usual in the camp and castle. She could hear the clang of iron on iron from workshops, the odd whinny of a horse and, from closer by, the movements of the wall guards, one of whom had a death-heralding cough. The smell of frying pork wafted into her hiding niche, making her stomach rumble so much she thought someone above must surely hear it.

It reminded her of being ill as a girl, lying on her parents' bed in their hut, hot and thirsty, troubled by muffled everyday village noises from outside. How could things carry on with such insulting normality without her, she'd wondered. Now she wondered if this was how things sounded from the Otherworld – familiar but muted and intangible? She was likely to find out soon enough. She remembered that she wasn't meant to believe in an Otherworld. Was being near death persuading her that there might be one?

The guards above changed. The new lot spotted the dead dog. It started calmly enough with people calling to each other about some stupid dog asleep in an inconvenient place.

Swiftly though they realised it had been killed – "Murdered!" shouted one hysterical fool. There was a flurry of commotion.

A short while later, she heard Carden's voice on the bridge. Her mind was flung back to being held by him while her friends and her sister were killed in front of her. The urge to emerge from her hiding place and stick him with her climbing spikes was strong. But she held back, and even smiled a little when she realised from his irregular tread that he was walking with a serious limp.

She heard Carden say her name and knew for certain that they were looking for her specifically, and that she had been betrayed. Could it have been Drustan? She'd been pretty free with her conversation on Mearhold, discussing her plans with several people she had no reason to trust. Any of them could have shouted to Zadar that she was at Mearhold and reported her plans. It wasn't necessarily Drustan. Next time I plot to kill a king, she thought, I'll share the details only with people I've known for longer than a day.

Carden directed a search, during which Lowa found a worm and ate it. She needed the moisture and she'd need energy later. The hunt continued and she heard dogs barking along the ditch below her. It was slightly satisfying that all this effort was for her. She didn't expect to be found. Her little niche was invisible from any distance and deep enough for the soil to mask her smell. The search dwindled away, everyday sounds returned and she lay and waited, planning her route that night.

Zadar would know that she'd tried to break in. How would he react? Surely he'd think she'd given up on seeing the second ditch and buggered off? Surely the security would be laxer that evening, and she'd be able to nip over the palisade? She had nothing to do but wait and see. She looked around for another worm, as much for something else to think about as for sustenance. The previous worm had been the first one she'd ever eaten. It hadn't been awful, but she couldn't see why badgers went quite so nuts for them.

She heard voices above and froze.

"So, assuming she climbed up over there, as you reckon—" it was Carden Nancarrow again, standing on the bridge almost directly above her "—she would have dropped over the palisade about there and seen our welcome. At that point, options were to commit suicide by carrying on, to commit suicide by staying put or to retreat. She's gone. I know her. She's not stupid. She'll have left the camp too."

I am stupid.

"Have you searched inside Maidun?"

That was Drustan's voice! She was certain. That traitorous old fucker. He must have sent the shout and told them her plan. The shit. Why? Well that wasn't hard. He'd done it for selfish reasons, the same reasons anybody ever did anything. The person loved by Zadar was fortunate and he wanted some of that love. Why not? She'd basked in it for long enough.

"We have. Although she didn't get past the guards."

There was a long pause.

"Yes. I think I know where she is."

Do you, you old twat?

"She would have taken two hours to approach the first wall and scale it." There was a long pause.

"And?" Carden's voice, impatient.

"You cannot rush genius, boy."

"Nor senility," Carden muttered. They really were right above her.

Another pause. A sneeze crept into Lowa's nose. She pinched her nostrils.

"She spotted the lone dog in the first ditch, dropped down from the outer wall onto it and killed it."

Well, you got that wrong, genius.

"But by then the moon was too bright. Do your guards walk the walls constantly, as they're doing now?"

"Most of them."

"Yes. There was a flaw in my plan."

"Don't you mean her plan?"

"No. It was my plan."

"Right."

I'll do my own planning from now on.

"The flaw was assuming the sentries always look outwards. Walking along, they have a peripheral view of the inner wall."

"Yes . . ."

"So, given the brightness of the moon, Lowa would have been seen as she scaled the upper part of the wall. She would have realised this and looked for another way in. So. Let us have a look at the outer ditch."

Their footsteps faded, Carden's limping, Drustan's accompanied by the thump of a cloth-bound walking stick. The stick was new. Perhaps he'd been tortured? That would excuse him spilling the plan – everybody broke under torture – but not his happy complicity now. Carden and Drustan stopped at the other end of the bridge. They were still talking, but she couldn't make out what they were saying. After a few minutes they wandered back.

"And this," Drustan said, "is therefore as far as she could have got. What is under here?"

Oh fuck.

"A ditch. Stakes."

"No. directly under here."

"The underside of the bridge."

Drustan sighed. "I'm glad you weren't my pupil. You! You! You!" Lowa heard people running over.

What would Dug have said? *Badgers' cocks*, she decided.

"Over there, facing this way, slings ready."

"What?"

"Do it," said Drustan. "You, fetch a crowbar. Elann Nancarrow will have one."

The problem with very good hiding places, thought Lowa, is that they also make very good traps.

"And you and you, stand guard here."

"Guarding what?" Our bridge has a troll."

Lowa wriggled out of the little cave. She'd been found and she had to come out. Not to fight – she didn't have a chance – but to save some face. Better to climb out than to be discovered curled in a pathetic ball with worm juice on your chin.

Chapter 19

Consciousness crept over Dug like a regretted but persistent bedfellow. He refused to open his eyes and he'd be buggered by a horse before he lifted his head off the pillow.

He remembered that he was staying at a tavern in Forkton. He remembered that he wasn't with Lowa any more. He remembered fragments of the night before as if somebody was holding up blocks of wood etched with pictures of his evening and whacking his head with them.

Lots of cider, a failed pass at a girl, then lots more cider and becoming increasingly annoyed by the casual ignorance at the table next to his. Then, what? A fight, no doubt.

He let his arm fall off the bed. His hand found his hammer. So he still had that. *Good*. He tried moving both legs and the other arm. It wasn't fun, but they all worked. He probed his face with his fingers. Nothing broken there.

He screwed his eyes more tightly shut. It was probably too early to start drinking again yet. He'd try to sleep until it wasn't.

Chapter 20

"Hello." The woman chained to the other wall had waited until the soldiers had gone to speak. "Who are you?"

Lowa yanked at her chains, then gave them a long hard pull. No good. Here they'd made less effort to disguise the hut's metal frame, the iron uprights standing out from a thin, broken wattle and daub. A short, heavy chain linked her ankle shackles.

"My name's Lowa Flynn."

"I'm Vasin Goldan. Of Barton. You're the one they were looking for that night they took Barton. The night they took me and Elliax."

"Yes."

The two women were quiet for a while. They were in one of the Eyrie's large holding cells. As cells went, it wasn't too bad. Being chained to the wall wasn't exactly comfortable, but there was a slops bucket, and two large holes in the roof high above let in plenty of light and air. Not so great in winter, Lowa thought, but OK for now. And there was no way she was going to live until winter.

"Have you got any food?" said Vasin. It sounded to Lowa like it had taken a while for her to suppress her dignity enough to ask. Her skin was sallow and her eyes shone with pathetic pain, but she held her chin high.

"Sorry, I haven't."

"They don't give me any food."

"I'm sorry."

"They cut me as well." The woman held up a bandaged

arm. "They do clean the wounds, but that's only to keep me alive for longer. I suppose we must be grateful for small things."

"That's one way of looking at it."

"Yes. They moved me here yesterday. It *is* much better than where they had me before. Funny, how one's expectations change. If you'd told me a moon ago that I'd think of this cell as an improvement in circumstances, I would have laughed in your face." Vasin looked up, blinking back tears.

"I really am sorry."

"That's kind, but it's hardly your fault. And it looks like we're in the same boat now. Same cell, anyway." She smiled grimly.

Lowa felt tears at the corners of her eyes. Suddenly she felt very heavy. Here was one more of the thousands whose lives Zadar had ruined, all in the name of preparing Britain for the Romans. But that wasn't why he did it. He did it because he could. And people not only let him do it, they helped him because they got something out of it. And few had helped him more, and got more out of it, than her.

"You mustn't look so worried." Vasin interrupted her thoughts. "My mother always used to say that where there's life, there's hope. And we are alive."

Wow, thought Lowa. *I think I hate myself.* "I'll get you out of here, Vasin," she said.

"That would be kind, dear. I don't like it much here."

"I will get you out."

Lowa sat and thought. Her mission to kill King Zadar was short-sighted. She had to free everyone, not just Vasin. She needed to undo the chaos she'd helped Zadar wreak. That meant taking control of Maidun's tribes and its lands, restoring wealth and health to the people, and preparing to repel the Romans rather than welcome them. Yet her girls were all dead. She'd driven Dug, Ragnall and even Spring away. She was caught and chained. An objective observer might argue that she wasn't in the best position to conquer and succeed a popular, powerful tyrant who commanded an army of thousands.

Chapter 21

The wheels had arrived, finally, so they had a hard day
ahead of them attaching wheels to axles and axles to
carts. The day would be all the more difficult because the
wheels weren't nearly as well made as had been promised
and paid for. It was as if Will the wheelwright had put all
his effort into making sure that no two were the same size.
Perhaps that's why it had taken so long. It was less a case
of pairing up the most similar, more a job of finding the least
different.

Silver and Jorth were sorting the wheels into size order
when Miller arrived.

"They're here!" he said, rubbing his hands.

"They might as well not be. This is the worst batch yet.
That's why they dropped them off in the middle of the night.
Nita's headed over to Will's now to get some money back."

"Good luck to her."

"Good luck to Will the wheelwright."

"Yes." Miller caught sight of Silver and grimaced. "Mal,
we need to have a word." He took Mal's elbow and directed
him to the far side of the yard.

"What?" said Mal. There was much to do, and if this was
one of Miller's amusing observations . . .

"You have to be rid of her. Immediately."

"What? Silver?" Mal looked over at the girl. Jorth was
carrying the wheels from place to place while Silver sat on
the fence directing her.

"Of course Silver," said Miller. "The tavern last night . . ."

"That was just pub banter. The cider talking."

"And the beer. But I've never heard everybody damning Zadar's rule so openly and loudly. We've seen people do it more closed and quietly though, haven't we, and we've seen them die in the arena. Remember Torok? Eenfill? Anstees? Simac? By Bel's breasts, Simac put up a fight, didn't he?

"But they were ringleaders."

"As Silver was last night.' But she was even worse than them because her points made sense and they were well argued. Most dangerous of all, I think she was *right*. They'll think she's too young to have thought of all that herself, and so, my chum, you are in serious peril."

"Miller, she might be young, but she is freakishly intelligent."

"Yes, we know that, but they won't. They'll assume that it all came from you and Nita. Do you know that Nita and Silver went over to Crabtree's place after we'd left last night and carried on with the rant?"

"She's not even ten."

"Exactly my point. They'll be *certain* that her views came from you and Nita. You might already be doomed. Me too probably, just for knowing you. You have to get rid of her, now."

"She's a little girl!"

"Mal, your kindness is a great gift, but she'll get us all killed if she stays."

"I'll ask her to keep her views to herself."

"Does she seem like the type to follow orders? And anyway, she'll be fine anywhere else."

They looked across the yard. Jorth was carrying a large wheel, back bent, with the quick short steps of someone at the limit of their weight bearing capacity. Silver was looking at seagulls flying overhead. As they watched, Silver looked down and noticed Jorth.

"Roll it along the ground, don't carry it," said Silver.

"Good idea! Thanks!" said Jorth, putting the wheel down.
Silver looked back up to the seagulls.

"You have a point," said Mal.

"I do. Send her away. It may already be too late. Tadman
and some of the Fifty might be on their way here right now.
At least if she's gone, you can say that you heard about her
bad-mouthing Zadar and told her to leave."

"You're right, but it shouldn't be like this. We should be
able to think and say what we like."

Miller laughed. "Yes! And winters should be warm, boars
should be plentiful and Chamanca should be on her way
here right now to ask me to bed her . . . Come on, Mal!
Things don't change. All that happens is people like you
and me get put in the arena for saying that they should."

"Maybe things should change."

"Mal, you have a young wife. A business. Jorth. Me!"

Mal shrugged. "I suppose you're right. I'll get rid of Silver.
But not until this afternoon."

"Why wait?"

"Nita will be back any moment. This afternoon she'll be
over at her mother's for a few hours. By the way she was
talking about Silver when she got back last night, she won't
let her go without a fight."

"Fair enough. I'd pick the arena over an angry Nita any
day."

Chapter 22

The open-air court filled quickly. Elliax hadn't seen it so popular since they'd killed that boy Weylin. So it looked like there was going to be another killing! That was good. He liked a bit of murder. He particularly enjoyed watching Chamanca go about her work. If he ever had to be executed himself, he thought with a slimy grin, he wanted Chamanca to do it. Nice and slowly. But he wasn't going to be executed. Any moment now Zadar would tell him that the test was over, he'd passed, and he'd be freed. In preparation for his position-to-come he went through the names of the most important people who'd gathered that morning.

There was Atlas, the bandage finally off his face. The wound looked odd on his nearly black skin, like purple wax had bubbled out of his mouth and set. People said that dark-skinned southerners were skilled fighters, but somebody had clearly got the better of this one. Unless of course his face had been ravaged by some exotic southern disease. They had diseases in the hot lands, the bards said, that made your insides liquefy and leak out of your holes.

Carden was next to Atlas, looking manly as usual, then there was a pretty girl whose name he hadn't caught yet. Next was Felix the oily Roman druid, Tadman the huge bodyguard, King Zadar of course, and Drustan the new old druid. Chamanca wasn't there.

Ah, here she was. She was pulling an iron rod and walking backwards out of one of the cell-huts – the one they had Vasin in, if he wasn't mistaken. At the other end of the rod was a collar fixed around the neck of the blonde woman that Carden and Drustan had brought in earlier. The woman shuffled forward, head bowed. A heavy chain linked her ankles. A lighter one held her wrists behind her back. She was wearing dirty white winter pyjamas.

Chamanca drove her forwards on the rigid metal leash. She was a marvel, Chamanca. She seemed even more vibrant than usual, next to her plodding captive. She bounced with every step, vital as a young deer. Her white pointy-toothed grin was ablaze with the joy of being alive. It was too much to hope that Zadar might give him Chamanca for his body-guard when the test was over.

The blonde straightened and faced the king. She may have been through a rough time, but she stood straight-backed and prideful, raising a pert chin and bringing cool blue eyes to bear on her captors like a heroine levelling her sword at a clutch of demons. Elliax liked to think that he cut a similar figure: down on his luck but full of spirit and ready to rise again.

"Hello gang," said the chained woman. "Good to see you, Drustan. Haven't seen you since Mearhold. You must be feeling pretty good about repaying the people who saved your life with betrayal and death? All those children. You must be proud of yourself." She winked.

Zadar looked at her with the same bored, superior stare he treated everyone to.

Felix laughed his fake laugh. "Well done yourself, Lowa. I think that that might be the most hypocritical statement that anyone has ever made."

Lowa seemed not to hear him. "And Carden, Atlas, you've both recovered since the evening you murdered your friends."

The big African and the large black-haired Warrior looked back at her, then at each other.

"What happened to you? You used to be decent. There was some honour in both of you. Where did that go?"

Felix laughed again. "All this from the coldest killer I've ever seen." His eyes narrowed. "Chamanca, quieten her."

Chamanca smiled and twisted the rod. Lowa fell to her knees with a choked gasp.

"Stop." Zadar raised a hand. "Let her speak. Let her amuse me one last time."

"Going somewhere are you, Zadar?" Lowa managed as Chamanca loosened her grip.

Zadar's mouth smiled at Lowa, but his eyes didn't.

Lowa looked at the girl next to Carden, seemed to pause for a moment, then fixed her gaze on Felix.

"And you, Felix," she said calmly, "are the most odious glob of mucus-streaked shit that was ever squeezed out by a diseased formori. I don't know what you've got on Zadar, or what he owes you, but you're more responsible than anyone for the amoral depravities handed out daily by his evil army."

Felix looked at her pityingly. "You're a brainless soldier, Lowa. You can't understand the complexities of preparing Britain for Rome's rule. Sacrifices must be made. And you've hardly held back in making them. How dare you lecture us?"

"You've enslaved half the south and murdered the rest. The sacrifices have been the poor and the weak – our own poor and weak – and for what? To prepare for Roman rule you say? That's self-serving bullshit. If you used this army to unite the country rather than destroy it, we could repel Rome."

Felix shook his head. "You haven't seen the Roman army, have you? It's a shame you never will. But let me tell you, Lowa, the Romans will destroy any resistance like a herd of boar ripping up a flower garden. The *only* way this island can survive is by bending and absorbing their onslaught like tall grass in the storm. Your bow won't penetrate Roman shields. The Romans have bows so large they need to be mounted on wheels and pulled by horses. Where is your bow, by the way, Lowa?"

"The Roman army is made of men, Felix, and men can be killed. With our numbers, our knowledge of the land and our iron, we can beat any army. But we need to prepare now, not destroy ourselves to save them the job." Lowa looked from person to person like a bard trying to engage a whole audience. Her eye even caught Elliax's. "The point is that Felix and Zadar are disingenuous. The motives that they tell you are not their real motives. They are not enslaving, killing and raping for the sake of Britain. They're working purely for their own—"

Zadar raised a finger at Chamanca. The Iberian lifted the collar pole, forcing Lowa's chin onto her chest, cutting her off mid-sentence.

"You are becoming boring, Lowa." Zadar leaned forward, chin on steepled fingers. "Now, for injuring Atlas and Carden for the murder of at least ten other Warriors, you will be punished."

Elliax rubbed his palms together in anticipation.

"You will repay the Maidun army for weakening it by entertaining it. You will fight in the arena until you are killed. Take her away."

Elliax slumped in his chains. He could hear the fights in the arena every afternoon, but he couldn't see them.

Chamanca hefted the slave pole. Lowa had to jump to her feet.

"Wait!" she managed. Chamanca walked around her, forcing her to turn, and pushed. Lowa stumbled. "Wait!" she choked again.

Chamanca pouted questioningly at Zadar. The king shrugged assent. The Iberian swung Lowa around to face him.

"If I'm to die, I'd like to know why. Why did you kill Aithne and the others?"

Zadar sighed. "For all you've just said, Lowa. For betraying me, and Maidun. I liked you. And your women. But my likes and dislikes must take second place to Maidun and the land I'm bound to protect. I can't have someone of your charisma and popularity speaking out against me."

"I was loyal! I did nothing to undermine you."

"No, but you were going to. You've never been a pack animal, Lowa. You're a loner. You're not a soldier, you're a leader. We need only one leader. You know what decided it for you and your women?"

Lowa shook her head.

"When we lined up before crushing Barton, I ordered nobody to look at them. You did."

"That was it?"

"That was it."

Chapter 23

If he'd spent their whole year apart trying, Ragnall would never have guessed that this was how he'd see her next. She was opposite him, across the arena. He was sitting on a rough bench with the masses. She was in the best seats, the ones that you could only access down the wide wooden steps from Maidun Castle's outer wall. She was only a few seats along from Zadar, next to a large, magnificent-looking Warrior. It was hard to be sure at this distance, but it looked like her hand was on his leg. Ragnall felt the same feeling deep in his gut that he'd had when they'd run from the soldiers in Mearhold. He was glad they hadn't met face to face, because he was pretty sure he wouldn't have been capable of speech.

Somebody jostled his arm.

She looked so beautiful and sad. She probably had no choice. The Warrior said something to her and she laughed. It was the fresh natural laugh that he recognised. The real laugh.

The jostler took Ragnall's arm and forced him to turn.

"They say she tried to kill Zadar!" It was a cheery older fellow, maybe Dug's age, with a cloud of sandy beard below a peaked leather cap and the ruddy, broken-veined skin of a man who'd spent many hours piloting a boat or a horse in a high wind and was used to a drink or three when he got home. He finished off in a loud whisper: "When they were *driving the pork cart to salmon town.*"

"Uh?" managed Ragnall.

"Her! Lowa! Come on, keep up!" The man pointed. "Tried to kill Zadar while they were, you know, hiding the stoat, playing snakes and snake-holes, putting the goose's neck into the fur collar?"

"Ah, OK, I get it."

A door opened in the arena wall opposite them, ten paces below Anwen. Lowa walked out onto the reed-strewn circular arena floor, blinking in the sun. She was dressed in the grubby white shirt and trousers she'd been so pleased with on Mearhold, holding a robust wooden stick topped with four regularly spaced blades and a spike. Ragnall wasn't sure if it would be called an axe or a mace. She was barefoot, with a shackle around one ankle attaching her to a thin chain that ran back through the doorway she'd emerged from.

Her name rang out all around the arena and thousands of men, women and children applauded, jumped and cheered. Standing out among the jollity, the people in the elite seats remained still and stony-faced.

"Here, get your shouting gear round this!" Ragnall's neighbour pressed a bulging bladder towards him. "It's water," he said with a huge "it's not water!" wink.

Ragnall took the skin and sniffed. It smelled strong and disgusting. Some sort of rancid wine perhaps? He took a big swig. It tasted like it smelled, but it felt good.

"Thanks," he said, handing back the skin.

The man smiled and nodded, then offered a hand. "I'm Rollo."

"Ragnall." Rollo had a surprisingly sure, dry grip.

"Should be a good one today. That Lowa, they say she bested Atlas Agrippa and Carden Nancarrow hand to hand *at the same time*. I wouldn't believe it, but I've seen her with a bow, and if she's half as good with a mêlée weapon as she is with her bow, well . . . But sorry, you probably already know all this?"

"I don't. What's going to happen?"

Rollo looked at Ragnall. "You've never been before?"
"Nope."

"It's always different. Well, it's almost always fighting."
Rollo took another swig from the skin and handed it to
Ragnall, who did likewise. "But the fights vary. There are
four basic types of fighter. Most common are captives, or
slaves you might call them. Useless mostly, but you get the
odd good one. Next are criminals. They vary massively. They
might be children, who are not very good at all. I don't much
like watching the children being killed, but you might? Each
to their own!" Rollo smiled broadly but sadly. "But most of
the criminals are adults, and some of them are really quite
good. I saw one kill a Warrior once. She was freed. I think
she *became* a Warrior after that. Zadar is true to his word.
But I'm getting ahead of myself. Forget Warriors for now.
So you've got your captives, your criminals and . . . Oh look,
that's Tadman Dantadman."

The biggest man Ragnall had ever seen was walking across
the arena, small shield in one hand, a stout sickle in the
other. A few were cheering, more were jeering.

Lowa walked to meet him, her bladed weapon at the ready.

Tadman stopped. Lowa came forward slowly, then looked
back. She was nearly at the end of her chain, and there
wasn't enough left to get to the big man. She stood, smiling
her confident, sarcastic smile. It looked like Tadman was
talking to her, but Ragnall couldn't hear a thing over the
cheers.

"He always does that," said Rollo. "Always stands there.
Sometimes they charge at him, reach the end of the chain
and trip. That's usually hilarious, but I'm glad Lowa didn't
fall for it."

"I guess she's seen the show before?"

"Probably. Although, now you mention it, I've never seen
her in the posh seats, which is where she would have sat.
Anyway, there's always a bit of a gap while Tadman talks to

the fighter, so I'll carry on. Next after captives and criminals are animals. They can be great. It depends mostly on the type of animal and how many there are. We had something called a tiger once. From the east. It was amazing. They let it go on some children. As I said, I don't like seeing children in the arena, but these were all seriously nasty little shrew-faced guttersnipe thieves, the type who'll bump into you in the street and laugh, and steal anything that's not nailed down . . . and I've never seen anything like it. It was like a fox with chickens.

"Next up from animals, best fighters of the lot, are Warriors like Tadman. They don't fight very often, and actually they're not the best entertainment because they almost always win. They're better fighters and they're given superior armour and weapons. It's unfair. But some of them are really good at using their imagination and stretching out the kill. There's one woman called Chamanca. Oh, she's a wonder. I saw her take an hour to kill a man, and it wasn't dull for a heartbeat!"

"What will happen to Lowa? Could she get out alive?"

Rollo shook his head. "A top-end criminal *and* Warrior like Lowa? No. They won't waste her. They'll send in a few she can handle for our entertainment, but her fights will get progressively harder until they send in someone or something she can't beat."

"Like what?"

"Dunno. But it'll be something good."

Ragnall tightened his lips. What, by Kornonos' knobbly knees, could he do?

Chapter 24

"I won't kill them." She felt like a child, looking up at the towering Tadman. She'd thought he was going to attack her, but instead he explained, with plodding glee, that she was to take on five captives from Mearhold.

Tadman breathed a short laugh through his big nose. "You will kill them."

"I won't."

"They and their families will be freed if they kill you, so they will try to kill you. So you'll have to kill them."

"No, I'll have to stop them from killing me."

Tadman smiled a knowing smile and backed away.

A door at the side of the arena opened and a man walked out. The crowd cheered, jeered and shouted insults based on his appearance. He was a tubby, white-skinned, dough-faced fellow in his late teens or early twenties. He wore leather shorts and an armless leather waistcoat. Bright orange hair fanned out from a plain iron helmet. His short spear had a leaf-shaped iron head. Lowa didn't recognise him from Mearhold, but he nodded at her as if they'd met. He walked towards her. The cheering crescendoed, then subsided in anticipation.

Lowa took a few steps back so she had more play with the chain. He didn't look like much, but you never could tell. The retreat earned her howls of delighted derision from the crowd.

The man stopped and said: "They say I'll go free if I kill you. And my wife and daughter – I mean they'll go free too, I don't have to kill them." He shrugged.

"Well, that's a plus."

"Yeah. I don't want to kill you, but . . ."

"We all have our burdens."

"They say you're good, but I'm pretty good with this too." He hefted the spear.

"It should be quick then."

"It will be, don't worry. I'll try and make it a clean kill."

"Thoughtful. Shall we then?"

The man roared, the crowd roared, and he charged.

Lowa dropped her mace, skipped to the side, grabbed the shaft of the passing spear and drove a punch into the Mearholder's kidneys. He folded around her fist and collapsed, leaving the spear in her hand.

The crowded cheered and shouted advice, most of it suggesting that she kill him.

She put down the spear and reached out a hand to help him up. The crowd booed. He took her hand and pulled hard, trying to launch himself at the spear. The crowd cheered. Lowa let him come at her, tripped him and jumped onto him, knee on the back of his neck, hands holding his wrists.

"I could have killed you with the punch. I held back because I don't want you to die," she said. "But I'm not going to let you kill me."

"Seems we have a problem then," growled the Mearhold man into the sand, "because they'll kill me if I don't kill you."

"Hmmmm."

Lowa looked around at the crowd. An odd sensation. There must have been . . . she had no idea how many. Thousands of people? Ten thousand? They were almost all shouting at her. Her eyes came to rest on Felix and Zadar. They weren't shouting. Zadar looked bored. Felix's lips were curled in a nasty little smile. Carden . . . Carden looked pained, as if unhappy with proceedings. He nodded at her with what looked like respectful support and raised a hand in some annoying we're-all-Warriors-together gesture. She narrowed her eyes at him in disdain. If he wanted, he could ease his conscience by pretending he wished her well, but she wasn't going to go along with it.

She looked back to the struggling man under her knee. What could she do? She could let him kill her. She was going to die in this arena whatever happened, so it might as well be at his hand. But she didn't want that. She could kill herself? That would take the ox from their cart. But also hers, in a more permanent and severe way. Really cutting off her nipples to spite her tits.

The thing was, she didn't want to die. If she stayed alive, maybe she'd get a chance to escape. Maybe they'd send her someone who needed killing, like Carden or Chamanca, although how she was going to beat anyone like that in an open fight without her bow . . . So what to do with the Mearholder? If she didn't kill him, surely they'd sell him as a slave? No point in killing a healthy adult when you could trade him for booze or coins.

She stood off him and kicked him in the arse as he got up.

He scrambled away and turned to face her. He looked round her at the spear, which lay behind her on the arena floor. He looked back to her. The crowd watched, quietly curious.

"You're a bit better than me," he admitted.

"Sorry. Fighting's my job. It's all I've ever done."

"Ah. I'm a weaver by trade."

"There you go. I wouldn't know where to start with weaving."

"Yeah. Maybe we could get them to change the format? Duelling looms might be a real crowd-pleaser?" The man's sad smile collapsed into misery. "But I'll never be able to beat you, will I?"

"I don't think so."

"So you'll kill me?"

"I won't."

"Not even if I attack you again?"

"No."

"So what do we do?"

Lowa looked down at her chain. "I stay here. Why don't you walk away and see what happens."

"They told me. They'll kill me and my family."

"I don't think they will. You'll make a few coins as slaves."

"A slave . . ."

"A weaving slave. Might not be too different?"

"I'm proud of being a weaver." He was strangely angry, given the situation.

"Sorry. I didn't mean to insult your trade. I just meant that being alive has to be better than being dead. And really, you spend the day weaving. What's the difference if you do that as a free man or a slave?"

"All the difference! I trained for six years under—"

"Look, the point is, with luck they'll keep you with your family. Families of slaves sell for more than the sum of the individuals. You can slave a few years then buy your freedom."

The ginger-haired man seemed to deflate. "OK, OK, I'll try. Good luck in here."

"Thanks."

He walked away, back towards the gate he'd emerged from. The crowd booed.

"And where do you think you're going?" shouted Tadman, loud enough for the crowd to hear. The Mearholder tried to run, but Tadman caught him easily, holding him by the neck of his waistcoat. The giant Warrior lifted his long-handled curved blade in one hand, the Mearholder in the other. The waistcoat strained, but its toggles held as Tadman lifted him a good pace from the arena floor, his muscles rolling and swelling like a draught horse's, the Mearholder's arms and legs waving like a gassy baby's. The crowd cheered.

Tadman, soaking up the crowd's admiration, turned slowly.

When his slab of a back was towards her, Lowa picked up the spear. It was short, with a heavy head – very much not a throwing spear. She took aim and launched it anyway. It missed by a good three paces.

Tadman turned, smiling at her.

"You have to kill them Lowa, or I kill them."

Tadman let go of the man, pushed him stumbling away and swung his blade. The back of the Mearholder's knees sprang open with a double spray of blood and he fell onto his face with a scream. He struggled onto his elbows and tried to slither away.

The giant raised his bloodied weapon for another cheer, walked over to the crawling man and knelt next to him. He scrunched the back of the man's waistcoat in one hand and lifted him onto all fours. With the other hand he lifted his weapon. Slowly, all the while smiling at Lowa, he pushed the blade into the man's anus then pulled it out. The Mearholder shrieked, then bellowed.

"All right, Tadman, I'll kill him," Lowa shouted.

"You had your turn. Now it's mine."

Lowa picked up her mace. She made to throw it at Tadman. He ducked behind his victim, then emerged grinning. He pushed the blade halfway into the Mearholder, withdrew it to the tip, then thrust it back, harder and deeper. Then out again. Then back in.

The Mearholder waved his head, screaming. His helmet tumbled to the arena floor and his long ginger hair swung from side to side.

Most of the crowd went wild with adulation, but there were also yells of horror and shouts of "Stop!"

Lowa put down the mace and yanked her chain two-handed. No joy there. She picked up the mace again and aimed a throw. Tadman ducked behind the screaming Mearholder again. This time he carried on working his blade, his arm bloody to the elbow and becoming bloodier as gore squirted with every thrust. Lowa took aim and threw the mace. It spun through the air and lodged in the Mearholder's head. The screaming stopped and the man went limp. Some cheered, but most of the crowd booed.

Tadman pulled out his blade and stood. He grabbed the shaft of the mace, yanked it from the Mearholder's head and tossed it back to land by Lowa's feet.

"You kill them or I kill them. It's up to you. Next!" he shouted.

Lowa looked over to the door that the ginger man had come from. A woman no more than seventeen years old – a girl really – came stumbling out of it as if pushed. She had a long dagger in each hand.

Roars of joy drowned out the few cries of "Shame!"

The girl looked around wide-eyed.

"*Please* don't kill this one," said Tadman, "because I would absolutely love to. And I won't be nearly so gentle next time."

Lowa looked up at the blue sky.

Come on gods. Do something good for once.

Chapter 25

"King Zadar, I've come from the gate. There's a girl who wants to see you. She says you know her," said the soldier.

Zadar nodded. "It's Sabina, or Spring as she's calling herself."

"I don't think so. Her name's Ing-bo, Ang-bo, Icky Icky Wang Bo Bing Bo Bong Bo Bong Bo. She made me memorise it." The soldier scratched at his beard. It looked like he'd had a difficult morning.

Still damp from an earlier rain squall, Elliax was shivering. It was cooler than it had been for a long time. Zadar had come to his throne earlier, on his own, and sat. It had looked like he was thinking. Elliax had wanted to say something but couldn't summon the courage. Instead, he sat on the ground next to his holding post, clasped his knees to his chest and rocked, trying to warm up. He'd had some more special meat that morning and vomited nastily. He was unwell and unhappy, yet his mind was more with him today. He wished it wasn't. He'd spent Bel knew how long convinced that this was all a test and he'd be freed any moment. Now he knew he was going to die as Zadar's plaything. Not even his plaything, just a decoration that would be discarded like dead flowers.

He looked at Zadar and hated him. How could the gods allow one man, one such twisted man, to have such power? Because the gods were either indifferent or, more likely, they revelled in human misery as much as the crowds he heard baying in the arena. Or perhaps they were as different as humans, complicated combinations of good and bad? Perhaps the fact that people like Zadar and, let's face it, himself, were in the ascendancy at the moment reflected a similar shits-in-charge situation among the gods?

He thought of Vasin. Almost every word she said and everything she did had made him wince for a good few years now, but he'd loved her. And he'd been eating her. He should have refused. But it was so easy to pretend it wasn't her. Even now they'd moved her nearby and he could hear her cries, he was still eating her. He just pretended the screams were someone else's.

"Hi, Zadar!" The chirpy voice shook him from misery. He looked up. A pretty young girl tripped in, ahead of a soldier. Age-wise she was at the younger end of the honeys Elliax had enjoyed at Barton when life was better. He'd seen her somewhere before though . . .

The girl stood there, beaming.

Zadar looked at her levelly. "Leave us," he said to the guard, beckoning the child closer. "Sabina."

"It's Spring."

"So I heard. And Silver. It makes no difference to me what you have others call you. Here you will answer to the name I gave you."

The girl shrugged. "Did you miss me?"

"Had any of my other children absconded at your age, I would have expected them to die. I would have been disappointed if you had."

"Why?"

"Because ever since you could talk, perhaps even before – you weren't brought to me until you could – you have displayed charisma and intelligence. You may be protected by magic and may even be able to use it. I suspect that you will rule Maidun, and probably much wider lands, under the Romans."

"I won't ever rule."

"Oh? And why not?"

"I've seen what your rule does. I was in Barton before you destroyed it and killed them all. The people were good even though they were poor, and they were only poor because you took away their riches.

That was it, Elliax remembered. Little Spring. She'd been part of Ogre's gang. He'd done good business with Ogre, back in his other life. He'd noticed Ogre's new little girl just a few moons before, but the earless bandit had threatened him when he'd asked to rent her for an hour.

The girl continued: "Ogre told me that after you came to Barton their king went mad and you put a horrible little weasel-druid in charge, who took their food, raped their daughters and ruined a lot of lives."

Zadar nodded towards Elliax.

Spring looked at him. Elliax looked back at her. His throat constricted. Horrors – his horrors – flashed into his mind. He saw hungry families and crying girls. He saw the girl who'd died in his hut. He hadn't meant her to! He saw Vasin cowering as they came in to cut her again. He saw the Maidun cavalry surging over the weak Barton line and the horrible massacre of innocents that was all his fault . . .

Spring looked away. The visions cleared and Elliax slumped, sobbing.

"Yes, that's him. I don't know what he's doing here and I don't know why he looks so ill, but I am sure that even he doesn't deserve what you're doing to him."

Elliax opened his eyes. The girl was facing her father, hands on hips. "And Barton didn't deserve what you did. I saw the battle. But it wasn't a fight between two sides. You were like mad boys slaughtering a field of geese. That was the worst I saw, but everywhere where you rule I saw miserable people. *Everyone* said that you had made things worse. Almost all the good people were poor and miserable and the bad people, men like Elliax and Ogre, were happy and rich. As soon as I left the lands that you ruled, it was all fine. Kanawan and Mearhold were clean and nice and how towns should be. But then you came along and destroyed both of those too! Why?"

Zadar looked long and hard at his child. She gazed right back, unafraid.

"I'll tell you," he said eventually. "Come and sit down here." He patted the chair that Felix usually sat on.

"I don't want to sit next to you."

Zadar breathed in and seemed to grow a little. Elliax had seen that happen before, usually just before he ordered someone's death.

"All right. Stand. Obedience can come later. The first thing you have to understand is that the Romans are coming. Disputes in Rome have delayed them and a slave revolt put them back a year or two, but the delays will not last for ever. They are surely coming. All the druids agree."

"Druids are liars and fakes." Spring glanced at Elliax. It was like being slapped. He cowered. How could a little girl affect him so powerfully?

"Most of them are, but, as you'll learn, some aren't. The Romans *are* coming."

The girl looked as if she was thinking. Elliax could swear the air was vibrating around her. "All right, maybe the Romans are coming, with endless ships and strange beasts, but we'll fight them."

"Did you just . . . ?" Zadar leaned forward. It was the first time Elliax had seen him look interested in anything.

"What?" The girl looked confused.

"Never mind." Zadar sat back. "They are coming and we cannot fight them."

"Why not?"

"Who wins in a fight between a squirrel and a bear?"

"A bear. Unless it's a giant squirrel with a bear spear."

"Let's assume normal-sized, unarmed squirrels for the sake of this analogy. How about a bear against a hundred squirrels?"

"The bear."

"Indeed. Now the Roman army is a like a hundred bears to Britain's one squirrel. You saw the battle at Barton. That was a small part of my army, and we were outnumbered ten to one. Yet we obliterated them with no injuries to any of my soldiers because we're well armed, well trained and well led, and they weren't. The difference between the Roman troops and my troops is greater than the difference between mine and Barton's. Their skills, weapons and tactics are immeasurably superior to ours. We cannot hold the land. They will invade, and they will invade successfully."

"Yes, but that's like being in a running race against someone you know is faster. You can't not race. You *might* win. You have to try."

"Not if you're going to be killed for losing and there's another option. We have to survive. I am not the wanton tyrant that I appear to be to those who cannot see. I am ensuring the survival of our people. The British people. We may be many tribes on this island, but really we are one people bound by the sea. I am saving all of us."

"By killing us and selling us as slaves to Rome? That *saves* us, does it?"

Zadar sighed. "Your mother – Robina, was she not?"

"Yes."

"A good woman. I was sorry when she died."

"Me too."

"She took you to the beach in the summer?"

"A few summers ago, yes."

"And you saw the tide. It comes in, it goes out."

"It does."

"Did you build sand forts?"

"We did."

"What did the tide do to those forts?"

"It destroyed them."

"And when the tide rolled back, what was left of them?"

"Nothing."

"No trace at all?"

"Nothing."

"Well, Sabina, the Romans are the tide. They are coming, and we cannot stop them. But they will ebb away like the tide. Empires never last for ever, but a people can. Britain is a nation of sand forts. Have you heard of Carthage?"

"The tribe who won loads of big battles against the Romans? Yes, my mum told me about them."

"The Carthaginians did win a battle or two. They almost finished the Romans at the battle of Cannae, but almost wasn't good enough. Do you remember the end of the story?"

The girl looked at the ground.

"The Carthaginians were obliterated. Their huge city of Carthage – imagine fifty Maidun Castles built of cut stone rather than hewn rock – was ground into the soil and its people slaughtered. When I was a boy I met an old sailor who'd seen Carthage a few days after its destruction. The horrors that he described – mountains of hacked-apart bodies, hordes of lions, vultures and other beasts feeding on flesh – have stayed with me. He said that the worst of it were the dead dogs and horses piled up in the rubble with the human remains. The Romans had killed every living thing in the city. But the greater horror for me is that the Romans obliterated an entire culture."

"So what? We'll fight them and beat them."

"No. Since then, they have greatly improved their armies. Around the time you were born, hundreds of miles from Rome, a Roman general called Lucullus marched a small force into the lands of a king called Tigran. Tigran had a mighty army and thought he was invincible. He'd conquered four other huge tribes and made their kings into his personal slaves. They had to run behind King Tigran's horse wherever he went and take it in turns to be his chair and his footstool whenever he sat. When Tigran saw Lucullus' little force marching towards him, he joked that it was too big for a deputation but too small for an army."

"What happened?" asked the girl, clearly as interested in the story as Elliax. He liked the sound of this Tigran.

"Lucullus attacked," said Zadar, "and defeated an army twenty times the size of his with almost no loss to his side. Tigran fled."

"Hmm," said the girl.

"Sabina, the Romans are unbeatable. If they had come ten years ago, before I'd bolstered Maidun, they would have washed over the land and wiped out our people, leaving no trace of our stories, our songs, our ways – what makes us *a people*, rather than just *people*."

"And now?"

"Let's go back to your sand forts. What if you'd built them on rock, out of boulders?"

"They'd have been knocked over by the waves."

"Bigger boulders."

The girl pouted and Zadar continued.

"A boulder fort would stand, and remain when the tide retreated. And that, Sabina, is what I am doing. I am making Maidun and the land around it into a fort of boulders. The Romans will come, they will wash around and through us, but we will stand. When they go, the British people will still be here."

"What about everyone who isn't in your boulder fort?"

"They are like the bees that die so that the queen bee and the hive live on."

"The rest of Britain suffers so that Maidun can thrive?"

"Yes."

"That's unfair."

"It's not. The best come to Maidun, more and more every

day. They are welcome. It is only the weak, the unwell and the stupid who suffer."

"But those people are just as important. Everyone is as important as each other."

Zadar looked genuinely amused. "Do you really think that, Sabina?"

"Yes."

"Who *have* you been talking to? The idea that all people are equal is for wool-headed druids who are given everything they need and don't see or live in the real world. Compare an oak tree to a dandelion. They're both plants but they are hardly equal. There is that much difference, and more, between people. Do you know why the best hunting dogs are from Britain?"

"No."

"We take the strongest and most intelligent dogs and breed them with each other. The lesser ones we kill."

"But that doesn't mean the lesser ones have any less value."

"It means exactly that. What *value* is a small, weak hunting dog? And humans are just animals, like dogs. It is no more difficult to separate the weak from the strong, the useless from the useful. If we're going to become stronger as a people, in order to protect ourselves from this stronger breed called the Romans, we cannot support the weak. This is not a new idea. A Greek druid called Aristotle said centuries ago that the greatest inequality comes from trying to make unequal things equal. If Maidun accommodated the weak and ineffectual from Barton and places like it, we might well move towards some sort of equality, but only by weakening the strong. We'd become less as a people and ripe to become an inferior race under the superior Romans. I'm amazed that the self-evidence of this evades you. I thought you were better than the smug, unaware, ideology-stuffed blowhards they produce in places like the Island of Angels."

"A king isn't a god to decide who is weak and strong.

Why are so many people sad, sick and dying? Why does everyone hate you if what you're doing is right?"

"Sabina, as you'll discover, a king must be like a parent to his people, not a lover. My duty isn't to be *liked*. My role is to make us all stronger, to provide an environment in which we can thrive. I am a great king because, for the greater good, for the future of our people, I make decisions, force changes and enforce rules that go against the people's will but are good for them. I will be remembered for ever as the great king who saved the land of Britain."

"You'll be remembered for ever as a smelly badger's dick!"

Zadar's already bulging eyes widened. "Spring, you've been with weak people and their bleatings for too long. You have been blinded. Everyone who follows me – everyone – has more because they follow me."

"What about everyone else?"

"They don't matter."

"But they do! You say it's all because the Romans are coming, but you'll destroy your stupid boulder fort on the sand by making everybody Roman before they even get here. Coins are a Roman thing. I saw a town full of people in togas because of you. And why the Roman names? *I've* got a Roman name."

"Those are all surface things. We remain British inside. The Romans will leave Maidun alone, but only if we convince them that they *can* leave us alone. They must think that we are already part of their empire. We'll continue to send them slaves, to use Roman names and dress like Romans. We'll look Roman but we'll stay British. We'll keep our stories and our gods. We will survive."

Spring stared at her father, her fists clenched at her sides. Tears bulged in her eyes, then burst to flow down her cheeks. "Badgers' balls!" she yelled. "Big sweaty itchy badgers' balls! You're wrong! We should be helping everybody, not just ourselves! The strong help the weak. *That* is how it should be! I *know* that is how it should be!" The girl stormed away.

"Chamanca!" Zadar called.

The Iberian melted out of the shadows. Elliax had had no idea she'd been near. She caught the fleeing girl like a hawk grabbing a mouse. Holding her by the shoulders, she marched her back to Zadar.

"I'm sorry, Sabina," said Zadar, looking a long way from sorry. "You cannot go. You will be a danger to me."

"Like Lowa?"

"I hope you'd be a much greater danger than the little archer woman."

"So you're going to kill me?"

"No. You're my daughter. I'm going to keep you by my side. You'll soon see the reality of the world and come to agree with me."

"I'm sure I won't. And do you know what?"

"What?"

"A squirrel could beat a bear if it jumped down its throat and choked it."

Chapter 26

The crowd's cheers were higher-pitched today, and they sounded less lascivious, more enthusiastic. Lowa blinked in the afternoon light. The arena's seating was full, as it had been the day before, but there were many more women and fewer men. That explained the change in the noise they were making, but posed a new question. Why so many women?

Tadman was standing in the centre of the ring, arms raised, the short spear from the day before in one hand. In the other was a wooden carving of a fish. Spotting Lowa, the crowd began to shout: "Lowa! Lowa!" It wasn't a bad feeling, several thousand people shouting one's name. She felt a small smile creep onto her lips and stifled it. She had no right to be proud. She'd executed five Mearholders and a few semi-capable bandit types yesterday, all for Zadar. Despite everything, she was still killing innocents at his behest.

She looked to Zadar's seat. He wasn't there. Drustan had taken his spot, with that staff he'd affected to carry propped up behind him. Atlas sat next to him, then Carden. No sign of Anwen. The three men were talking quietly to each other, not looking at her.

"Today is animal day!" Tadman shouted. The crowd cheered. "What will we give Lowa to fight with? Spear?" Tadman waved the spear. "Or . . . Fish?" He waggled the wooden fish.

A deep-voiced chant started: "Fish! Fish! Fish!" but a higher-pitched counter-chant: "Spear! Spear! Spear!" overwhelmed it.

"Silence!" shouted Tadman. "I think you said . . . Fish!"

There were cheers and boos.

Tadman chucked the fish to Lowa. She picked it up. It was solidly carved from wood, about half a pace long. Actually not that bad a weapon. She also had the chain attached to her ankle. It depended on what they sent at her, but the chain might be useful too.

When she looked up again, Tadman was climbing a ladder out of the ring. He pulled the ladder up after him and stood on the ring's side "Are you ready, Lowa?"

A small cheer.

"Come here and you'll find out!"

A huge cheer.

Tadman smiled. "Open gate one!"

Lowa heard bolts shift. She turned.

A large bear lumbered out and spun round, hollering hatred at whoever had just jabbed it out of its cage. The door swung shut. The bear surveyed the baying crowd and roared again. Probably, thought Lowa, angry from lack of food. It would have been starved for long enough to make it ravenous but not long enough to weaken it.

The chain would be no use against a raging bear fifteen times her weight. She looked at the wooden fish in her hand, then at the bear. It had seen her. It was looking at her, nose out, sniffing. Bears, they all said, ate your face first, then your liver, maybe while you were still alive but with a wet bubbling hole where your face used to be. And she had a wooden fish.

The bear took a step towards her and growled, showing its teeth.

She hefted the fish from hand to hand. Could she jam it in the bear's mouth? Who was she kidding? She was fucked.

A flash caught her eye. A short iron sword landed on the arena floor a few paces away. She picked it up and looked into the crowd for its source. Atlas, sitting between Carden and Drustan, nodded back at her.

The bear charged.

Chapter 27

"I can make you some eggs or something?"

"Um?"

"To go with your cider. It'll make you feel better?"

Dug looked down at the little barmaid. She really was tiny. Not a dwarf with a disproportionately large head, more like a woman who'd shrunk in the rain, or a child with an adult's face and body. Quite a nice body. What was it about hangovers? It felt like bright light would make him vomit, but he was overrun by a base, shag-anyone horniness that the most dedicated of sex pests would consider a little over the top.

"You're kind, hen, but just the cider will do," he managed. "Maybe in a few pints' time I'll have the eggs."

"That's what you said yesterday."

"Is it?" Dug searched his memory . . . Nope, yesterday had gone. "Aye, well, I agree with me." He was still well enough to speak, but he knew the hangover would really kick in if he delayed any longer.

"What's the damage for yesterday, by the way?"

"You didn't fight last night and you're all paid up for the night before. It looked like you were going to start something at one point, but you all ended up singing together. Remember?"

"Aye," he lied.

"Hold the cider," said an educated young man's voice that Dug knew and disliked. He turned slowly.

"Ragnall."

"Dug, you've got to help. Zadar's got Lowa."

"Left you already, has she? I'm sure they'll make a lovely couple. Sorry for your loss."

"He's making her fight in the arena. She may be dead already. You've got to come. I can't do a thing, but maybe you—"

"No, sorry, can't help." He looked back towards the barmaid. "Make that two ciders."

"I don't want any cider," Ragnall said.

Dug didn't look up. "And? They're both for me."

"He's got Spring too."

Dug turned. They were the same height, but somehow he towered over Ragnall.

"You let them take Spring."

"You left Spring."

Dug raised his fist. Ragnall cowered. Dug lowered his fist.

The light outside the tavern was like knives in his eyes. The world swung towards him like a great weight on a rope and . . . aye, there you go. He spun round, hunkered down against the tavern wall and quietly vomited an evil bright green liquid, tending, towards the end, to orange. Recovering, he blinked and looked around. It was quite a cloudy day, thank Toutatis. Who knew what unfiltered sunlight would have done to him? So this was what Forkton looked like. He hadn't noticed it on the way in and he hadn't left the tavern since.

It was like a crap version of Bladonfort, with ramshackle single-storey wooden buildings surrounding a market. There was a burned-out, jagged-timbered gap on one side. The odd clean-shaven, toga-wearing man and a few women with hair in ringlets looked with wrinkled noses at the man who'd disturbed the peace with his chundering, but most of the people staring at Dug looked British – leather-clad, hairy and unscrubbed.

Ragnall was untying a couple of horses from a rail next to a water trough.

"Out the way, I'm going to dunk my head."

"Actually I was thinking the river might be better? You smell quite bad . . ."

Dug looked at Ragnall. Ragnall took a step back.

"All right. River. But I'll do this as well or I won't make it that far." Dug plunged his head into the water.

Chapter 28

Nita returned from the arena at the head of a gang, most of whom were women. Mal didn't like the look of it. Nita peeled away from the throng, waving goodbye and shouting that she'd see them at the tavern in a heartbeat or two.

"She was amazing." Nita's eyes were ablaze.

"She?" Mal asked.

"Amazing. They sent in three huge bears. I don't know where Tadman got them from. He must've been saving them. They didn't stand a chance though. It was like she was dancing. Tadman looked lost. He obviously thought it would last a while but it was over in seconds. They put on a couple of dogs after and drummed up some captives from somewhere, but they were clearly an afterthought. They went even quicker than the bears. She is *amazing*."

"She's still alive then?"

"They'll never kill her."

"Oh, they will." That was Miller, walking into the yard.

"Were you there?"

"I was. Part of the ever dwindling male audience."

"Men aren't going?" asked Mal.

"They're trying to, but there are so many women clogging the stands that it's tricky getting seats. They love Lowa. And that's why she'll die tomorrow,"

"Who's going to kill her?" asked Nita. "You?"

"Nita, I like her too. But they have to kill her. She's become the unwitting head of a fermenting rebellion."

"What rebellion?" asked Mal, dreading the answer.

"The one that started at the inn, with little Silver. This idea that everyone – women particularly – will be treated badly under the Romans. People are questioning Zadar crapping on everyone else and letting the Romans come. There's a lot of talk, a lot of very dangerous talk, that we should be bringing the Murkans, Dumnonians and all the rest into line and preparing to defend ourselves."

"But that will mean war. It's a stupid idea."

"Maybe not. A lot of people have been talking to merchants and sailors. It seems that Silver was right. They all say that women are treated little better than animals in Rome and all over its empire. In fact, they're saying that, bar a few at the top, everybody in the conquered lands is treated like shit, has to bow to Roman laws, follow the Roman gods . . . So pretty much everyone is speaking out against Zadar. I have some sympathy. But supporting Lowa and talking in the taverns is not the way to do things. We should choose someone to talk to Zadar ask him to reassure us that we won't take on Roman ways. As it is, people are getting excited and angry, and that's coalescing as support for Lowa in the ring. But you should have seen her today. She killed three bears with a sword like they were lambs, then they took the sword off her and she killed two wolves with a wooden fish. After that the captives never stood a chance. She can fight like Makka's own. Plus I daresay she'll be filling a few men's thoughts for the days to come, if you know what I mean. If the people are ever going to unite behind anyone to oust Zadar, it'll be Lowa Flynn. These are dangerous times and Zadar knows it. Someone needs to talk to him before he takes it out on the people."

"But you reckon tomorrow will be the end of it?"

"I hope they'll hold off suppressing the people, kill her tomorrow and end this insane anti-Zadar movement."

"They won't kill her. They won't be able to. I'm off to the tavern. See you later!" Nita left, hips swinging.

Miller looked around as if to check that nobody was listening. "Mal, sorry, I don't think that sending Silver off was enough. You have to talk to Nita. If killing Lowa doesn't quieten the people, then they'll be after the ringleaders. And Nita has very much become one of the ringleaders."

"Oh no."

"It's not too late. She's one of many. If you can persuade her not to go to the arena tomorrow and to stop spreading anti-Zadar talk, then I'm sure she'll be fine."

"I'll try to talk to her. Come on, let's both go. We'll catch her at the pub."

"Are you sure? She'll be with her friends."

"Yes, but later she'll be pissed. We're best off catching her sooner."

Chapter 29

Despite it all, Lowa slept until dawn.

She lay on the bed as light chinked through the gaps around the edge of the door, looking up at the brightening ceiling. This would probably be the last day. That was a shame. She wished she really did believe in the Otherworld. To think she'd never wake up again was quite poignant. Almost frightening. Tears threatened, but she blinked them back. The thing was, she liked being alive. Even now, in the arena. Perhaps especially now.

She was buoyed by the adoration of the crowd, but more than that, much more than that, the life of a captive fighter thrilled her. She could rage and kill. In fact she was meant to. She didn't have to think of others or watch her temper. She didn't have to sneak and plan, or find food and shelter. All she had to do was kill and kill again. It was why she liked battle. Proper battle, when the plans had all gone to shit and it was fight, fight, fight. She loved nothing more. That was one reason she was so good at it.

She looked around and found that someone had been into her arena-side cell. That was disconcerting. First Spring had crept into the hut in Kanawan, and now this . . . She was getting old. Now in her mid-twenties, she was no longer the super-scout who woke at the sound of a mouse's cough. Perhaps it was her time to die.

Whoever had been had left two buckets of water, a bowl of eggs fried with mushrooms, nettles and salt – strangely enough exactly the same dish that Spring had cooked the morning after she'd rescued them in Bladonfort – some bread, a short but well made iron sword and some leather garb: a pair of shorts, laced-to-the-knee sandals and a thick band with four thongs at one end and four holes at the other. They clearly expected her to tie the band around her chest. Her first reaction was that she wasn't going to go out there dressed like an unimaginative king's harem's fantasy fighting girl, but then she thought, *Why not?*. Her fort-breaking camouflage outfit hummed with a multi-layered reek of her own varyingly aged sweat and others' blood. And, she thought with half a smile, she'd look pretty good in a leather two-piece.

She ate, stripped and washed, then squeezed into the outfit. The shorts fit well but the chest band was tight. Which was fine. Movement was fine, and if her boobs were a bit squeezed, so be it. She washed her trousers and top and laid them on the bed to dry. Maybe, she thought, she could sleep in them that night. She stretched in preparation for the fights to come as feet began to tramp into the wooden arena, first like distant drums, then like rumbling thunder. Finally, as she sat cross-legged on the floor bending over one knee, preparing for battle, her cell door swung open. Bright light and the roar of the crowd flooded in. She stood, picked up the sword and walked out.

If anything, the cheering was louder than the day before. There were perhaps ten thousand shaggy-haired shouting faces in the stepped terraces around her. Spectating on the spectators were the armoured and armed Warriors of the Fifty, plus members of the elite cavalry and charioteers, stationed regularly along the top of the arena wall. Interesting, thought Lowa. The crowd hadn't been policed like this on the previous two days. It looked like Zadar had become unsure of the mob's loyalty. Or maybe he thought women were more trouble? An even higher proportion of the noisy throng today were female – shouting, screaming, even ululating. There were plenty of male voices too though,

providing a bass rumble and threading a vein of wolf whistles and "phwooaarr" noises through the encouraging cheers.
Lowa spread her feet, lifted her chest, raised an arm and
stretched out her right flank. The male shouts trebled in
volume, which was satisfying.

She turned to see who was in the posh seats above her
cell. Ah, this isn't good, she thought. They contained a less
ecstatic crowd. That shit Drustan sat smugly, plus Carden,
Atlas, Anwen, Chamanca, Keelin, Felix and Zadar. Even the
snivelling captive from the Eyrie was there. And there was
a child next to Zadar . . . Spring! The girl jumped up and
waved frantically when Lowa caught her eye. Zadar pulled
her back into her seat.

So Spring had gone back to her dad. Lowa couldn't blame
her. With Zadar as a father, Spring would have a life of ease.
Assuming he stayed in power, which seemed likely, Spring
could do whatever she wanted – lead a band of mercenaries,
make pretty pots, travel to mysterious lands, sit around
getting fat, whatever. Lowa would have gone home if she'd
been Spring.

Zadar looked at her, dead-eyed. He was unchanged. She
hadn't dented his rule, let alone brought him down. She hadn't
even spoiled his day. That was annoying. But what had she
expected? He was King of Maidun, she was a lone soldier.
Try as much as you like, you can't change the world on your
own because, no matter how important and clever you think
you are, there's so much more to it than just you. She was
like one starling splitting from a huge flock. Nothing was
going to change and it didn't matter to any of the other birds.

When they were no more than Spring's age and wandering,
she and Aithne had gone through a phase of killing sheep.
If they came across an unguarded flock, the rule was that
you had to fire an arrow as high as you could, angled slightly
to come down among the grazing animals. Every now and
then they hit one. The rest of the flock might be startled for

a moment, but soon after Lowa or Aithne had finished off the unlucky sheep, the others would go back to munching away at the grass as if nothing had happened. Today Lowa was the unlucky sheep. Fate's arrow was zooming down out of the sky, straight for her. Wasn't her fault, nothing she could do, and nobody would really give a crap afterwards.

She turned back to the crowd. Wave after wave of cheering buffeted her like a warm sea. There were no boos. It felt good. Even if she was about to die. Now, she thought, who – or what – was she going to be killed by?

As if in reply, two big bearded men in leather garb appeared from the door that Tadman usually swaggered out from. One had a nasty-looking hammer, the other some sort of short, vicious stabbing weapon. Lowa checked that she had enough play on her chain and waited. She didn't recognise them, but they were tough-looking bastards, perhaps newly recruited, probably superbly skilled with their weapons. When they were five paces away she raised her sword two-handed and crouched with her weight on her back leg, ready to spring.

"Danu's tears, stop!" shouted one, holding out a hand. "We're here to take your shackle off." He nodded towards her ankle and held up a thick chisel.

The other waggled his hammer. "That's all, princess, I promise!"

"All right." Lowa proffered her chained ankle. "But don't call me princess."

"All right, but that's what they're calling you."

"Who are 'they'?"

"People."

"Why?"

"Cos they reckon you'll be queen soon."

"I'm going to be dead soon."

"Yeah, more people are saying that."

"Thanks for the boost."

The men got to work. Once they'd finished, unseen hands dragged the chain back into her cell. It snaked back jingling across the ring.

"Hang on," said Lowa as the men turned to leave. "Leave your tools."

"But . . ." They said in unison. Lowa waggled her sword at them. The blacksmiths looked at each other, shrugged, put the hammer and chisel down on the reed-strewn arena floor, and jogged away accompanied by the laughter and jeers of the crowd . . . which changed to cheering as a wide gate opened and a horse cantered into the ring, followed by an adapted war chariot. The vehicle had a light chariot's frame but the bulkier wheels and, more noticeably, the pace-long wheel blades of a heavy chariot. The driver was a slight, long-haired, bum-fluff-bearded boy of maybe sixteen whom she'd never seen before, but she recognised the Warrior.

Dord Chandler was a bald, round-headed, dark-skinned man with a large, powerful frame, stiff black moustache and an attractive twinkle in his eye. Lowa had spoken to him a few times and found that he wasn't nearly as interesting as he looked. He talked only about chariots and fighting from the back of them. Try to change the subject, and he'd relate it to chariot warfare. "Eggs? Yeah, I like a good yolk but I prefer the new triple wood yoke that Elann Nancarrow and me . . ." And so on. She hadn't taken to him. Still, the obsessives were usually the best, and his reputation was strong. So was hers, of course, but only as an archer, and she didn't have her bow.

So, finally, they'd sent a name against her. She wasn't meant to walk away from this one. Lowa was mildly surprised. If she'd been organising, she would have spun her death out over the morning – maybe some lions or a better-armed group of captives. Zadar obviously wanted her dead quickly. She turned to the king and waved. He looked back impassively. She changed her wave to a V-fingered "fuck off" gesture. Pretty pathetic, she thought, but the people seemed to like it, going by their noise. She bowed, turning as the crowd cheered some more. She might as well, she thought, enjoy this.

The charioteer steered the horse into a gallop around the periphery of the arena. Lowa picked up the chisel and stood in the centre, sword in one hand, chisel in the other, turning to follow the chariot's progress. She had an insane plan. Her head told her that it would never work, but the battle lust fizzing in her blood told her head to stay the Bel out of this one. She smiled.

In the chariot, Chandler took a sling from his belt, fitted a stone, swung it about his head and loosed at her.

Lowa pulled her sword back, swung and whacked the stone out of the sky with a *spang!* The stone sailed off into the crowd, who roared their approval.

In front of the castle, below the king's seats, the chariot turned for the centre.

Lowa ran away from it in a straight line.

"Go to the side! Dodge!" she heard people shouting above the increasingly loud thundering of the horse's hooves. She reached the wall and veered left. She heard the chariot turn behind her. She sprinted along beside the wall. The chariot closed on her, fast.

She turned to run across the centre. Before she was halfway across she could hear and feel the horse no more than a pace or two behind. She knew Chandler's shot was coming, so she jinked her head from side to side. A slingstone stung her ear. She saw the horse's head in her peripheral vision and tossed her sword away, keeping the chisel in her left hand, then sprung into a leap that would have cleared a small man's head.

At the apex of her jump she drove the chisel down at the horse's neck.

The charioteer saw her plan and jerked the reins. The

horse twisted. Her chisel glanced off a bronze fitting and sliced a short gash in the horse's shoulder. Lowa fell.

The horse's flank thumped into her legs. Her arse went up as her head came down and she was falling upside down, the wheel blade flashing towards her face.

Elliax was watching but not seeing. His mind wasn't on the fight. They'd put him between Drustan and Felix, only one away from Zadar himself but with his feet bound to his seat and his hands bound to each other. What did it mean? When they'd walked him down to the royal section he'd thought that maybe he'd been right before, and they were going to give him some position of power – perhaps they were going to announce it to the thousands in the arena that very day! And then they'd tied him up. What, by Cromm Cruach's many tentacles, was going on?

Everyone around him was focused on the action. In the ring Lowa, brave but stupid woman, threw her sword to one side and attacked the horse with the spike that the blacksmiths had left. The crowd screamed in excitement, then cried a communal "Whooahhh!" as she completely missed her mark and fell onto the spinning blade of the chariot wheel.

The arena quietened, dust drifted down and he could see her lying prone. Elliax expected her to be in two pieces – those blades were heavy and probably very sharp, and at that speed . . . But no, she stood. There were massive cheers, including a scream of delight from Zadar's daughter, sitting on the other side of the king. The clamour subsided as Lowa tried a step and almost fell, one hand going to her right butt cheek where the blade must have hit. The leather of her shorts had deflected it. Good leather that, he thought.

"It must have been the flat of the blade," said Felix, sounding appalled.

"Do you think so?" said Zadar.

Felix turned to the king. "You don't think . . . ?"

"Probably not. But be ready."

What the Bel was that about? thought Elliax.

Back in the arena Lowa staggered over to pick up her sword. She was badly injured, by the way she was walking. It looked like she was beaten.

The chariot circled the ring. The charioteer climbed forward to stand on the horse, which won him some applause. He put the reins in his teeth and danced a jig, which wasn't, to Elliax's mind, particularly good, but it plucked a few whoops from the audience. While the driver capered, the passenger whirled his sling and loosed. It was a good shot, but Lowa dodged it somehow.

The Warrior said something terse to the driver and he climbed back in. *Quite right*, thought Elliax, the show-off jackanapes had work to do. He pulled the chariot in a tight curve back towards the centre, directly at Lowa. She waited, sword in one hand, spike in the other, bouncing from toe to toe. At the last moment she dived. The charioteer was ready. He pulled the reins in the same direction. Lowa hit the ground. She went under the blade, almost clear, but the iron-rimmed wheel ran over her calves, throwing her into a spin. She came to a crumpled stop and immediately a slingstone from the Warrior whacked into her back. She arched in pain.

The chariot turned.

Elliax was distracted by an animalistic squeak from Drustan next to him. Strange noise for a man like him to make, he thought. The druid was bent forward, staring at Lowa, muttering, with his hands inside his robe, working away at his groin. *Yuck*, thought Elliax.

He looked back at the action. Somehow Lowa had stood up, but she was all twisted. The chariot picked up speed, hurtling towards her. She dropped her sword. It looked like she didn't have the strength to hold it any more. The chariot was paces away. She wasn't even looking at it. It was going to be messy.

Chapter 30

"Badgers' tagnuts! They said it was big, but . . ." Dug pulled at the reins to stop and have a proper look. There it was, Maidun Castle, gleaming colossal and white under a blue sky. Despite what it symbolised, despite Lowa's plight, despite his lurching, poisonous hangover, the sheer majesty of the hillfort made his chest swell in appreciation.

"It's just a shaved hill. Get over it," said Ragnall. "Come on, they'll have started by now."

As if to prove his point, a distant cheer drifted from the direction of the fort.

"Let's go!" shouted Ragnall. He kicked his horse into a gallop.

Dug looked after him for a moment, tempted to stay where he was, even to shout, "Bugger off, you horrible wee jumped-up woman-stealing kludge-bucket!" at his back, but he sighed and remembered Lowa and whacked his heels into his mount. It jerked forward unpleasantly, and Dug was bouncing down the hill, past the first outlying tents and sheds of Maidun's sprawling camp.

There was another cheer. It sounded like Lowa was still alive, so, theoretically, they could still rescue her. There was just the matter of a several-thousand-strong army in the way. Some kind of plan would have been comforting.

Chapter 31

Lowa spun to a stop. Before she could get up, a slingstone cracked into her back, right on a vertebra. She yelped. That shit Dord Chandler. She pressed her shoulders together to squeeze the pain out, and it dissolved. She wiggled her back. Chandler must have held back with that stone, she thought. The Makka-cursed rat wanted to kill her slowly. She reached down to her calves, where the wheel had run her over, expecting to find her feet at least half-severed by the metal rim. They weren't. It must be a very light chariot, she thought, if the leather sandal thongs had saved her from injury. Probably Chandler had found a new kind of wood or a way of hollowing out struts that he'd been busy boring the crap out of everyone by describing.

Lowa stood. She tried her legs and arms. The worst pain was in her right buttock where the blade had hit her. A touch with her fingers revealed that she wasn't bleeding, which was a surprise. Everything else worked too. She wasn't exactly winning, but where there was life . . .

The chariot was coming at her again. Looking ready for it last time had been a mistake. She hung her head, dropped her sword and waited. And time slowed. She felt energy surge. She could hear the *boom boom* of her heart. She was looking at her feet but knew where the chariot was. She could tell how far it was by its *smell*. Now it was a pace away. She leaped, pleased to see surprise in the charioteer's eyes. He pulled the reins. *Too late this time*, thought Lowa. Without looking, she sensed the gap between the horse's shoulder blades and smashed down with the chisel. It drove in to the hilt. She pushed on it, adding thrust to the momentum of her jump.

Her feet came up over her head. She thrust on the chisel with both hands so powerfully that she felt the horse begin to collapse under her. She released, flinging herself up and back, somersaulting over horse and chariot. Two faces, looking up open-mouthed, flashed underneath, then she was over.

She landed square on two feet as if she'd practised the move for years. The horse ploughed into the arena floor. The draught poles dug into the ground and the chariot flipped up, over and smashed onto the arena floor in an explosion of wood, blades and limbs. The boom was loud enough to wake the dead, but it was immediately overwhelmed by the ear-bursting roar of the crowd.

"By Danu," said Drustan.

The girl Sabina had jumped up and was pumping her fists in the air. Zadar was looking at the carnage below. His expression hadn't changed, but Elliax could feel his rage. Elliax realised that his own mouth was open. He closed it and shook his head. That, he thought, was the most amazing thing he'd ever seen. One small woman beating a chariot. Not with luck, but with the most elegant, stylish, effective . . .

"Cromm Cruach," said Felix, then turned his head to look at Drustan as if Elliax wasn't there.

"You!"

"If that is a question, you will need to flesh it out a bit," said Drustan.

"But I saw . . . I didn't see. You don't have . . . ?"

"Carden, Atlas." Zadar's calm voice cut though Felix's enraged gibbering. "Detain Drustan. Ensure he cannot use his hands. Check his person for animals."

"Animals?" Carden asked from his seat behind Drustan.

Zadar looked back at him. Carden swallowed any further questions, leaned forward, grabbed Drustan's shoulders in two massive hands and lifted him back, over his seat.

"Be ready with plan two," said Zadar.

"I'm ready." Felix turned and winked at Elliax. Elliax felt as if centipedes were scurrying up his back.

"I found a freshly dead rat, nothing else," Carden called out.

Lowa looked at the destroyed chariot. She bounced on her toes, still thrumming with the energy of a forest fire. Then, suddenly, the power poured out of her like wine from a tipped amphora. She almost sobbed. *What the Bel?* A moment ago her body had zinged with the force of a god; it had seemed like anything was possible, and she'd almost burst into song with the joy of it all. Now she felt about as zippy as seaweed at low tide on a cloudy winter's day. What was going on?

She shook to try and dispel her lassitude. She walked around the twitching horse. The men were no longer part of the wreckage, recognisably human. It looked as if a butcher's cart had been pulverised by a giant hammer. For some reason Chandler's and the boy's deaths filled her with chills. She shook her head and pulled at a wheel. The sling and its stones might be useful, if she could find them. Stifling through the debris, she heard the crowd go quiet. She didn't want to know why yet. Then she heard an Iberian voice ring out: "Cooo-eeee! Stop playing with the dead! It's time to play with me!"

Chamanca.

Lowa's stomach fell. She couldn't beat Chamanca. Not without her bow. Although she'd had her bow on Mearhold and Chamanca had still bested her without breaking a sweat. And now, as if to ensure she had no hope whatsoever, this bizarre weariness had come over her. It was a strain to lift her head.

"Who's dressed like a blind whore now?" asked Chamanca as she sashayed across the arena in her usual skimpy armour. She had her ball-and-chain mace in one hand and a fine-looking iron sword in the other.

"We both are," said Lowa, swivelling her eyes to look for her own sword. "But I didn't have a choice."

"Ha ha! So clever with words." Chamanca smiled to show her filed teeth. "But such a heavy and clumsy fighter. It's a shame to kill such a clever girl. Go on. Get your sword, clever girl. It won't help you."

Lowa walked over and picked up the weapon. She raised it, lifting the other hand for balance. She bent her knees and shifted from the ball of one foot to the other. The torpor was falling away, normality returning. She knew the basics of fighting with mêlée weapons. In fact she knew some fairly advanced stuff. However, compared to Chamanca, she knew nothing. She turned to face the Iberian.

"Those *are* my clothes you're wearing," said Chamanca, cocking her head. "Somebody must have stolen them!"

"I'm sorry."

"Never mind. I will take them back in a moment."

"I don't suppose we could ally against Zadar? Slutty dressers take on the tyrant?" Lowa tried.

"No, Lowa. Today you die. I'm going to enjoy killing you."

The Iberian came at her, lithe as a liquid. The crowd chanted: "Lowa! Lowa! Lowa!"

From a swirl of limbs Chamanca's sword flashed at Lowa like a bolt of lightning. Lowa parried. As their swords jarred together, she felt something crunch into her ribs. The ball mace. She hadn't seen it coming. Her left side was paralysed with agony and she fell. She climbed up onto one knee, but the pain overcame her and she flopped onto her face.

"Do not let Drustan move!" Felix commanded Carden.

Carden nodded, tightening his grip.

"In fact, knock him out."

Carden pinched the druid's neck with a mighty thumb and finger. The old man sighed and went limp.

That looked fake, thought Elliax, turning back to the fight.

Lowa half lifted herself, but her hand skidded out and she crashed down in a wave of hurt. I'd hoped to do a bit better than that, she thought. She felt arms curl around her head and pull her up. Her broken ribs screamed in protest, but she was helpless. Chamanca dragged her across the arena towards Maidun's finest and the soaring castle wall.

"Kneel, shrimp," Chamanca snarled.

Lowa tried to resist as Chamanca pulled her up and kicked her legs into a kneel, but she was powerless. In the stands, Felix was beaming. Zadar looked unconcerned. Chamanca's arms tightened around her neck and harbinger clouds of unconsciousness bloomed through Lowa's head. She closed her eyes.

"No! No!" she heard the crowd shout.

Chamanca let go of her neck. Lowa considered leaping up and spinning round with a high kick, but her limbs were limp and incapable. She was pulled to her feet. She saw Zadar's face at the centre of a swimming mass of faces. Her hate gave her no energy.

Chamanca's arms encircled her arms and chest, and squeezed, hurting her injured ribs. "Now I'll eat you, my pretty."

She felt Chamanca's tongue lick from the top of her back to her ear. Lowa expected the tongue to probe her earhole as it had on Mearhold, but instead the Iberian bit into the lobe.

This is no good. Lowa gathered her energy for one last struggle, tensed her shoulders and pulled back her leg to stamp, but before she could carry out her move, Chamanca flung her grip open and punched her in the small of the back. Lowa felt her legs become useless. She would have fallen had Chamanca not gripped her again, all the tighter.

"No, no. You don't fight. You're a shrimp, remember. I bite your head off."

Lowa felt the teeth pop through the skin on her neck. Not this again, she thought. The scabs were only just healing from the last time.

"Noooo!" the crowd howled.

So this is it, thought Lowa. She thought of Dug, Ragnall, Zadar, little Spring, Aithne, Seanna, Realin, Cordelia, Maura, her bow . . . and came back to Dug. Big Dug whom she'd treated so appallingly. That was a big regret. That, and not killing Zadar a long time ago. And, now she thought about it, Felix could have done with an arrow in the face too.

The sound of Chamanca gulping her blood became louder and the roar of the crowd quieter. The pain in her ribs and her back dissolved as consciousness slipped away.

It wasn't a big deal, dying.

She thought of the top and trousers that she'd cleaned, drying on her bed in her cell, waiting for her return. Somehow that was the saddest thing of all.

Chapter 32

Ragnall and Dug pushed through the packed masses outside the arena. The wooden stairs tacked onto the wall – the only way up to the terraces that Ragnall could see – were so thick with people that they'd never have got up them, but that was a moot point since the crowd was so dense that they couldn't get anywhere near the bottom of the stairs anyway.

"Noooo!" A great shout, the loudest yet, came from within the arena.

"I do not like the sound of that! Get out the way!" Dug heaved, people stumbled. Ragnall swallowed an urge to apologise for him.

"There's no need to push, chum," said a prim young chap with a vast bush of a beard. "We're all—" Dug's fist crashed into his face. He crumpled. Dug looked for the next person to hit.

"Dug." Ragnall grabbed his arm. "You can't punch your way in."

"I can try!" Dug swung again and another man fell.

"No, no. There must be another way. Come on, over here." Ragnall grabbed his arm and pulled.

Chapter 33

"Lowa." She heard a voice through the crowd's tumult. It sounded like her mother, calling quietly into the hut to see if she was awake. Maybe it *was* her mother. Maybe there was an Otherworld after all.

She opened her eyes. Blood was flowing over her stupid little leather top and over Chamanca's arms, which were still gripped around her ribs. Her blood. She felt foolish. "Lowa." The voice insisted. She looked up.

A mass of blurred shapes and muted shouting whirled in a dizzy dance of noise and colour. The dance swirled into a spinning maelstrom. Slowly burning in the centre of the whirl, more and more brightly, until it outshone everything else, was one face. Spring. She was looking calmly at Lowa with bright eyes and a peaceful smile. Lowa had never seen anything more beautiful than the little girl with the overbite and ball-fungus nose. Spring dipped her head, as if to say *Well, go on then*.

It felt as if someone had come into a damp, abandoned hut and put a torch to the huge cauldron of oil that had waited there for years. Lowa exploded out of Chamanca's grasp. She spun. Chamanca was already coming at her, swinging her mace. Lowa ducked easily and drove a left then a right fist into the Iberian's stomach. Chamanca fell forward. Lowa slammed an uppercut into her face. Chamanca flew five paces and landed heavily on the arena floor, where she lay still.

Lowa had once stood under a waterfall. The noise from the crowd sounded and felt like that. She raised her arms and turned around and the cheering became even louder. And then it quietened as, from the arena walls, twenty or so of the Fifty dropped, all heavily armed. They walked towards Lowa like a team of spiders heading across a web towards a fly. Behind them, a door burst open in the arena wall. A huge man clad in preposterously thick plates of iron armour stamped out. The blades strapped to his forearms and shins were so large they looked more like farming equipment than weapons. *Tadman*, Lowa thought. Only he could walk in that get-up.

She looked about for Chamanca's sword. This time the tiredness hadn't come after the explosion. She felt ready. She'd never beat twenty of them, let alone the iron giant, but she was going to give it a go. She'd die fighting with all her wounds in the front. Unless they got behind her of course, which was likely . . .

There was a *thwack* behind her. She flicked round. A bow lay on the arena floor. It was her broken bow's twin, made at the same time by Elann Nancarrow. She smiled as a quiver of arrows slapped down next to it. Carden and Atlas were giving her the thumbs up. Drustan, standing between them, was smiling.

She dived at the bow and whipped up the quiver. Her attackers saw what was happening and charged. No matter. She reached up, grabbed an arrow, strung, three-quarter drew – at this range there was no need for a full pull – and released. The nearest Warrior fell. Lowa's arms pumped. Grab, nock, draw, release. The next attacker went down, then the next and the next and the next. The poor fools had brought mêlée weapons to a projectile fight.

By the time she had emptied the quiver, there was only one Warrior left in the arena. And Tadman, still lumbering towards her, but he hadn't crossed even a quarter of the ring. Lowa unstrung the bow and brandished the thick stave.

The last Warrior held up his hands in submission and walked away.

"Yahhhhh!" jeered the crowd.

The waddling, iron-clad Tadman approached.

"You faithless *shits*!" Felix was purple, staring at Atlas and Carden. "How dare you!" Elliax was peppered by gobs of spittle from the druid's uncontrolled bellowing.

"Calm, Felix." Zadar sounded like he was dealing with a tiresome child who was spoiling a family outing. "Use the contingency. Detain them, kill Lowa."

The purple drained from Felix's face and he smiled. "Good idea, my king." He turned to Elliax with a look on his face that Elliax did not like at all.

Felix's left arm lashed out, whumping into Elliax's chest. Elliax thought he was just being moved out of the way, but the hand stayed there and something horrible happened. He looked down. Felix's hand was inside his shirt like a boy's hand inside a girl's blouse at a dance, but it was also inside his chest . . . squeezing, if he wasn't mistaken, his heart. He heard himself moan like a grief-stricken goat.

Felix pointed at Drustan, Carden and Atlas. All three fell and lay immobile, apart from their eyes, which widened, pupils darting from side to side.

"Few things more useful than a life force as twisted as yours, Elliax. Especially after what we've put you through," whispered Felix. "And you, Drustan! You thought you could compare to me. You dared to challenge Zadar . . ."

As the rant continued, Elliax smiled to himself. He may have been in an unenviable position, having the life squeezed out of him by an evil druid, but he was still managing to feel a little smug because he knew something that Felix didn't. While the king and his dark druid were focusing on Drustan and his accomplices, they were completely ignoring their real problem: the little girl sitting peacefully on the other side of Zadar.

*

Mal had insisted that he and Miller come to the arena with Nita, hoping to temper her burgeoning hooliganism. He'd been surprised when he'd seen Silver with Zadar, but apparently Nita had known she was Zadar's daughter all along.

"And her real name is Weasel-biter," she'd said with that strangely great pleasure that she took from knowing something he didn't. Miller had said he wasn't surprised. Hadn't he said that she looked high-born?

Despite his misgivings about challenging Zadar, Mal had enjoyed himself greatly. When Lowa had destroyed the chariot, he'd found himself on his feet with everyone else, roaring with pure pleasure and excitement. Now half the Fifty were falling under her bow, he was clapping enthusiastically. There was an invincible-looking, iron-skinned man mountain waddling towards her too, but he was so slow and unwieldy that Mal couldn't see her being caught. No, the real worry, he realised as the second-last of the Warriors in the ring fell and Lowa ran out of arrows, were the rest of Zadar's elite forces who were guarding the crowd.

He was about to voice his concerns to Nita when she put her hands to her mouth and shouted, "Now!"

With a swish of iron on leather, all around the arena hundreds of swords and knives were pulled from their sheaths and brandished at the soldiers. Most surrendered immediately. A few refused and were hacked apart. Nearby he saw a bloody hand raised, before a bleeding Warrior was pushed off the stand to thump soggily onto the arena floor below.

"You three, tie him up! You – you're with us or you're dead! You there, help them! No, not them, *them*!" Nita pointed and shouted as Mal gaped at her aghast. He was going to say something, but instead he sat down, closed his eyes and hoped that everything would be better when he opened them.

*

There was some kind of trouble in the crowd. The people were attacking Zadar's remaining guards, Lowa saw with relief and confusion. Out of arrows, she wasn't looking forward to taking on any more of the Fifty. At the centre of the rebels was a square-jawed, tawny-headed woman brandishing a hatchet. Lowa caught her eye. The woman raised her weapon in salute and shouted, "Lowa! Lowa!" Lowa nodded back her gratitude.

The crowd took up the chant. "Lowa! Lowa!" Her name crashed around the arena as she turned to face Tadman. He was approaching with the noise, speed and grace of an iron cart full of iron ingots pulled by reluctant iron oxen. There was a particularly loud *clang!* as one of his arm blades whacked his leg. It was a wonderful suit of armour, and it might have been some use against a massed enemy hemmed in on a battlefield, but here . . . He was slowing down. It looked like fatigue was going to stop him even getting to her. If he did reach her, she'd move.

Was that it then? She looked around. Chamanca was stirring, so she cracked her on the head with the unstrung bow and she collapsed. She considered following with a windpipe-crusher but realised with a pang of surprise that she actually quite liked Chamanca, or at least that she didn't want to kill her. Weird, she thought.

Instead she picked up her sword. She might as well, she thought, go and see if there were any gaps in Tadman's armour through which a blade might be stuck.

Elliax was still sucking in breaths. He tried to raise his arms to pull Felix's hand from his chest, but he couldn't. He felt himself being shifted around as Felix turned his attention to the action in the ring. The druid lifted a finger and pointed at Tadman.

There was a massive clang then a series of bangs. The iron-clad giant leaped into the air, crashed his massive arm blades together, then sprinted at Lowa. It was as if the impossibly weighty armour had suddenly become light as the finest cotton and Tadman had gained the springiness of a fifteen-year-old acrobat. Lowa felt her mouth open in dumb wonder. She clamped it shut, crouched and readied her weapon.

He was there in moments, massive arm blade sweeping. She dived, rolled and ran. The strange but joyful power was still coursing through her limbs. She'd never run so fast, even down the slope of Barton when she'd first escaped Zadar.

Lowa looked over her shoulder. Unbelievably, he'd already turned and was coming after her like a multi-limbed mobile metal mountain. More unbelievably, he was catching up. She didn't even have speed on her side.

He was on her.

She leaped, stabbing her bow at his exposed face, planning to leap clear over his head to get behind him.

Tadman turned his head. She whacked thick metal. Something grabbed her foot. Her trajectory changed with a jolt and she was flying in the wrong direction. The crowd flashed by in a blur. He was swinging her around his head. In among the blur she was sure she saw Felix's smiling face.

He let go. She was in the air for an age, time enough to wonder whether she should land with her arms out, which might break her arms, or tuck her arms back and land on her head, which would . . . She came down on her hands, sprang from a handstand onto her feet – How was she doing this? – spun round and—

He was already there. He kicked with his bladed shin. She dodged. His arm swung and she ducked, driving her bow at the gap where his leg plate met his groin. He shifted, she missed, and his iron-gloved hand smashed into her head. The flat of his blade cracked across her body and she spun away stumbling, then falling.

She was on her back. She'd lost her bow. She opened her

eyes. Tadman's huge iron boot crashed down onto her chest like a rockslide onto a village. He lifted his arms in victory. She punched at his iron-clad leg ineffectually. With a huge heave, she achieved absolutely nothing. He raised both arm blades high into the air, then swung them down together, to scissor through her neck. She closed her eyes.

Mal opened his eyes. It hadn't got any better. Not only was his wife a rebel rabble-rouser, but the intended head of the rebellion was about to be killed. It would mean doom for them all. Mal could already see the future. Without a popular leader the rebellion would certainly fail, they'd have to flee, they'd be hunted down, probably by dogs . . .

In the arena it was all but over for Lowa. It looked like she was out cold after that mighty whack. The iron giant ran up, raised his foot, pinned her to the ground and lifted his blades. She pounded at him weakly . . . But what was this? Tearing across the ring, faster than a hare with its tail on fire, faster than anyone had a right to be running, especially one as stocky as this fellow, was a bearded man brandishing a hammer.

Hang on a minute, thought Mal. To his massive surprise, he recognised him. It was Dug Sealskinner. Mal had soldiered with him in the north, years back. Nice guy, he remembered. Big fan of boozing, not so keen on training, marching or anything that required effort, although he was surprisingly frenzied if you could persuade him to join a battle. He'd saved Mal's life once and nearly killed him a couple of times despite being on the same side. And here he was. This was turning out to be a very strange day.

As the blades came down, Dug launched into the air like a hound leaping for a stick. He flew helmet first into the giant's chest, knocking him backwards off Lowa. The blades swished together, missing her nose by a whisker. Dug fell onto his back, sprang up, grabbed Lowa by the leather chest-guard and flicked her away across the ring. Already the giant's blade was coming down, but Dug parried with his hammer. The other blade fell, and Dug parried again. The giant smashed his blades up and down like a mushroom-demented bard beating a drum at Beltane, but Dug blocked and blocked and blocked.

Mal found himself involuntarily blowing out a low whistle. It was a sight to see. They were big men – Dug was perhaps shoulder height to the giant – but both were moving with the agility of young wildcats. Where had Dug got this from? He'd been good, back in the day, but not gods-powered amazing.

The giant stopped his aerial assault and kicked with one of his bladed shins. Dug melted to the side, swung his hammer back, under and up and *spang!* into the giant's groin. The giant staggered.

"What the fuck," asked Zadar, "is happening?"

"I don't know. There must be another druid. A capable one." Felix sounded more perplexed than worried. "Perhaps it's the man with the hammer, but I doubt it. There's a druid channelling power into him and he could be anywhere in the arena."

Elliax smiled even though he was dead. The secret druid wasn't a he. He knew who it was. While everyone else cheered and booed and ooed, one was still. Perhaps only he could see the shimmering river of power flowing from her to the bearded man in the ring because he was dead and nobody else was. He was pretty sure he was dead. His heart was crushed but he didn't feel any pain. That sounded like death to him.

There was a great "Ooooooo!" from the crowd as the iron giant retreated. The Warrior followed up with hammer blow after banging hammer blow, forehand and backhand to the giant's flanks as Tadman flailed his arms, trying to regain his balance.

"Felix. You must win this fight," said Zadar. Was that a note of concern in his voice?

"Let's add a moral sacrifice to our amoral one then," said Felix. He reached out towards Anwen with the hand that wasn't in Elliax's chest. She flew over from where she had been bending over the prone Carden and was spitted on Felix's outstretched limb. She gasped.

It's always easier to have someone else in the same predicament, thought Elliax, especially someone as lovely as Anwen. He tried to say hello to the gulping girl, but his mouth didn't work, which wasn't a surprise, him being dead and all. No matter. He looked back to the ring. The giant had regained his balance, and the blades attached to his arms had burst into flame.

That's clever, thought Elliax.

Dug whacked away the flaming blade. The other one came closer before he could knock it back, and he felt his face blister, but that didn't matter so much. He'd never felt better. He leaped in a diving headbutt at his large opponent's face, the only exposed part. He felt his helmet crunch bone. He leaped back. The giant, blood in his eyes, flailed at him blindly with his flaming swords. Dug dived, rolled, came up behind him, jumped and slammed his hammer down two-handed onto Tadman's head.

Lowa stood. The lethargy was on her again. She shook her head to clear it and met Tadman's eyes just as Dug's hammer crashed down. The German's thick helmet bent almost imperceptibly out of shape, his pupils widened and his jaw bulged. Dug leaped and brought his hammer down again. A tooth and a squirt of blood jetted from Tadman's pursed lips. Dug jumped and hit him again and again, like a determined madman malleting a post into rocky ground. The helmet crumpled, whack by whack. Lowa watched, fascinated, as

Tadman's face collapsed into pulverised teeth, bone and brain.

"Felix?"

Zadar turned to his henchman, but Felix was staring past him, slack-jawed, at Spring, who was sitting happily as if waiting for a favourite bard to begin, as if she'd been absolutely nothing to do with the carnage in the ring.

"You!" Felix pointed at the girl.

Finally, thought Elliax.

The girl didn't respond. She was focused on Dug.

"Zadar, you must kill Sabina now," said Felix through tight lips.

If the idea of killing his own daughter caused Zadar a moment of internal debate, it didn't show. He whipped out a blade and slashed it across the girl's throat.

Chapter 34

"Are you all right?" His brown eyes bulged with concern as if her well-being was the most important thing in the world. It was an awful lot more than she deserved.

"Dug. I'm sorry."

"Don't fuss, Lowa. Things happen. Are you injured?"

Lowa reached her hand to her neck then looked at it. It was covered in blood. She showed her bloody hand to Dug with a questioning eyebrow.

"Aye. OK. Are you injured badly? Are you going to die if I don't get a druid to you immediately?"

"No, I'm all right for now."

Nita looked about herself and nodded. Mal followed her gaze. Yes, she and her followers had subdued all the Warriors who'd been guarding the crowd, but they were just a fraction of the troops that Zadar commanded. What would come next? What had she done, by Toutatis? And surely, whatever it was, she could have involved him in it a little more? At least told him *something* was going to happen.

Ragnall climbed the arena wall. As he'd watched Dug defeat Tadman it had struck him yet again that he was hardly the hero. Dug had defeated the giant. He had fetched Dug and found the service route into the arena, so he had been useful, vital even, but in the bard's tale of the day he'd appear as sidekick at best. Not even that probably. Useful ally perhaps. Quirky friend.

And now it was time to face Anwen.

When Raynall reached the top of the wooden wall, he saw a small man with receding hair holding Anwen by the chest with one hand and a skinny man in the same way with the other.

To the left was Zadar and, next to him, Spring.

"Anwen!" he shouted.

She didn't respond.

He started up towards them.

The small man said something to Zadar.

A blade flashed into Zadar's hand and he lashed out at Spring, slashing the blade across her neck. Spring didn't seem to notice. Zadar looked at his hand. Where the dagger had been was a long, brown duck feather. He threw it away and looked disgustedly at Spring. Spring looked back at him, enough disappointment for a hundred lifetimes on her young face.

Zadar turned to the small man, said something, and the latter . . . disappeared. One moment he was there, the next he was gone. The man he had been holding and Anwen collapsed, thumping down onto the seats.

"Anwen!" Ragnall cried. Next to her, Drustan and two large Warriors struggled to their feet.

She was face down on a bench. He turned her over. Her eyes were open and beautiful and sad and dead. He felt her neck. No pulse. Ragnall stared at her, waiting for the tears to come. They didn't. He called on the gods to breathe life back into her. Nothing happened.

"Hold Zadar!" he heard Drustan say. The Warriors pushed past him.

"The bleeding's stopped. Nothing vital nipped." Dug stood back and looked at Lowa expectantly. She felt very tired. She did not want to fight any more.

She looked up at the posh seats. Drustan and Spring were

smiling at her. Atlas and Carden were holding Zadar by one arm each. He looked calm as ever. Felix was nowhere to be seen. Keelin was standing next to Spring, looking from the captured Zadar, to the crowd, to Lowa, in open-mouthed wonder.

"Dug," Lowa said, "would you mind . . ."

"Looking for these?" He held the bow, strung, in one hand, a bloody arrow that he'd pulled out of somebody in the other.

"Yes. Thanks."

She took the bow, nocked an arrow and tried to draw. She couldn't. She was spent.

Zadar looked back at her, contempt shining from his eyes, as if, somehow, after all he'd done, he couldn't see what an evil shit he was. He still thought he was better than her, better than her sister, better than her girls, better than everyone. She held his gaze and felt power flow into her limbs. She drew a full draw and loosed.

Zadar looked down at the little feathery rosette protruding from his chest, and died.

The crowd cheered. Lowa raised one arm and turned slowly as the chant – "Queen Lowa! Queen Lowa!" – washed over her like storm waves.

"Dug . . ."

"Got you," he replied, putting an arm around her as she fell against him.

Chapter 35

Spring caught up with Dug on the north road near where she'd run away from Lowa and Ragnall. He was silhouetted in the silver light of the waning moon, a small pack on his back, valuables bag and hammer hanging from his belt. The night was so still she could hear the tramp of his feet on the road ahead and, from behind her, the shouts, squeals and music from Maidun Castle.

It was Lowa's coronation and the end-of-Zadar party. Spring had been looking forward to it but then hadn't enjoyed it at all because Dug hadn't been there, and she'd left the moment Ragnall told her he'd seen Dug heading away. She'd kicked herself for being so stupid. Of course he'd been planning to leave during the party when she wouldn't notice and try to stop him. That was why he'd tried to give her Ulpius' mirror earlier, and insisted she look after it for a while when she wouldn't take it.

"Hi," he said when she caught up to him, without looking down or slowing his stride.

"Where are you going?" She took his big rough hand in hers. She pulled on it a little. She'd slow him down without him realising.

"North. Back home."

"That's silly. All your friends are here."

Dug stopped and crouched down in front of her so their heads were level. He took her shoulders in his hands. He smelled of warmth and beard. His eyes shone with a thousand years of sadness. He looked up behind her, as if thinking what to say.

"There's a lot to be done here," he said eventually.

"So stay and do it."

"It's not my sort of place. I thought it might be, but—"

"It's Lowa, isn't it?"

"Maybe. A little."

"Dug." She felt tears swell. "It was my fault. On Mearhold—"

"Don't be silly. I loved our fishing and our hunting. I wouldn't change a second of it. Spending time with you didn't make Lowa—"

"No, but *I* did it. I made her go off you."

"What do you mean?"

Did he look angry? She hoped he wouldn't be angry. He had every right to be angry. She shouldn't have done it.

"You know what I did in the arena?"

"I really don't, but, by Makka—"

"I don't know what I did either, or how. But I know I did it, and I know that I did the same thing to make Lowa go off you."

"What?" He let go of her shoulders. He was angry.

"I didn't do it on purpose. I didn't think it would work. But I told her to go off you. It was the same as when I helped you and Lowa in the arena, the same feeling. But I didn't think it would work! I was just jealous and I didn't like her after she wanted to leave me behind in Kanawan and I didn't think she was good enough for you and I *swear* I didn't make her like Ragnall instead. I really didn't! I didn't think she was good enough for you, and I was jealous. I'm sorry. But I didn't make her full for Ragnall. That wasn't me! I'm *so sorry*."

"I see." Dug nodded, not angry any more. He looked disappointed but accepting, as if a thatcher who'd let him down before had just told him he couldn't do his roof repairs that moon as promised.

"I didn't mean it to happen!"

"It wasn't you, Spring, even if you thought it was. These things happen. Love is complicated. Sometimes it's not love, it's just physical. And people do go off people they liked before, immediately and irreversibly. It's annoying when you're on the wrong side of that, but it happens and you have to accept it."

"I *know* it was me. And it's good that it was, because it's worn off! I've seen the way she looks at Ragnall now, and you! It's back to how it was! You can come back and I won't do anything this time! I *promise*. I like Lowa now. I didn't like her because it was her fault that they were after us in the first place, and her friend Farrell was a total dong, and it was her fault you had to fight the Monster and I was *so* worried you'd die and—"

"Shush." Dug smiled. "Spring. I'm grateful for what you're telling me."

"So you'll come back?"

"I will not."

"But I need you!"

"You don't need anybody. They need you. Lowa faces some big problems. She'll be a good queen, but there's trouble in the west, there's trouble in the north, Danu knows what in the east, and all the druids say that the Romans are coming . . ."

"They are coming."

"How do you—?"

"I don't know. But they are coming. Won't you stay and help?"

"Spring, I'm just one man. I'm old. I've been fighting for so long. Before that I lived off the sea. I'm ready to go back to that. I can't do anything here. But you could be the difference between defeat and victory."

"I'll come with you!" She'd dreamed of wandering from place to place with Dug, getting into adventures and helping people in trouble. There wasn't anything she'd rather do.

"I'd love that, I really would, but you're needed here."

"So are you! I need you!"

She was frustrated that he wouldn't believe her about Lowa, but she could understand. She knew for certain that she'd killed Lowa's love for him, but she wouldn't have believed her if she'd been him. She also knew, if she was honest with herself, that he had to go. She told herself to grow up and accept it.

Dug closed his eyes and opened them. It must have been her imagination or a trick of the moonlight, but his eyes looked wet.

"You don't need me," he said. "You'll come to see that you don't. I'm going. You're staying. Goodbye, Spring."

He stood and turned and walked away.

Spring watched him go, being grown-up about it for about four heartbeats, but then tears burst from her treacherous eyes and her shoulders heaved with sobs. He disappeared over the next rise and she was still crying. And he was gone.

After a long while, she decided that standing on her own in the night crying wasn't helping anyone. She pressed a thumb into each nostril, blew out snot, wiped her eyes, turned and headed back to Maidun Castle. She'd help Lowa, kill all the Romans, and then she'd find Dug.

She was almost at the western gate when she heard the shout. It was still a good four shouters away, so it was too faint to make out. She stood still to listen to the next one. The words were clear this time: "Dumnonian army. One hundred thousand strong. Three days from Maidun."

One hundred thousand Dumnonians. What had Lowa said Maidun's army was? Twenty thousand? One hundred thousand against twenty thousand. Like ten against two. That didn't sound too good.

"Big badgers' bollocks," she said, quickening her pace.

Historical Note

Because the British Celts didn't write, and because the period was followed by four hundred years of Roman occupation, almost nothing is known about the British Iron Age. That is why the period is rarely taught in schools, and why most people couldn't even tell you when the Iron Age was (800BC to 43AD), let alone what took place during it.

Pre-historians' descriptions of life in the Iron Age are based on four sources: archaeology, comparison with other Celts at the time, comparison with modern primitive cultures and a few written sources from the Romans and Greeks. The most important of the written sources is Julius Caesar's primary account of his invasions in 55 and 54BC. However, basing our history of Iron Age Britain on Caesar's diary is like basing our history of Germany's last thousand years on the account of a xenophobic Englishman who travelled to Germany in 1951 to see a football match which England lost, and who was beaten up several times, yet claims that he had a marvellous time and that England won the game 10-0.

The archaeological sources—hillforts and pottery, mostly—have been analysed by fine historians like Barry Cunliffe and Francis Pryor, and from such men and women we do have a picture of what an Iron Age Brit ate, what he or she wore and what their homes were like. However, it is just a picture. Very few man-made objects have survived from the Iron Age. For example, historians are certain that Caesar did lead two huge invasions into Britain in 55 and 54BC though there is no archaeological trace whatsoever of either invasion.

While we're not certain about how they dressed and other details, we have absolutely no clue at all about what they actually did. We know nothing of their kings and queens, love affairs, wars, intrigues, disasters and so on. It's slowly emerging that Iron Age Britain was much more sophisticated than previously believed, with towns and roads established well before the Roman invasion. Historical population estimates vary, but it's likely that the population in 61BC, when *Age of Iron* is set, was about the same as it was in 1066 (between 1.5 and 4 million, depending on what you read). So Iron Age Britain was a busy, thriving place, with a lot going on. But what?

I became interested in the Iron Age when writing an article for the *Telegraph* about a management consultant called Allan Course who makes Stone Age tools (it's on my website, guswatson.com, if you're interested). He took me to Cissbury Hill, a Stone Age flint mine that became an Iron Age hillfort. Standing on this hill's Iron Age ramparts, you can see another hillfort. It struck me for the first time that Britain's hillforts were linked. I'd seen loads of these massive fortifications all over Britain, and briefly pondered what people might have got up to in them, but I'd only ever considered then individually.

Now you can look at, for example, Warwick Castle, as an individual building and it's pretty interesting. But it's much more fascinating if you consider *why* the thick-walled, multi-towered edifice was needed, how it fitted in with the rest of Britain, and what adventures took place there, both known and unknown.

So I began to research the Iron Age. I got another article commissioned in the *Telegraph,* this time on Iron Age hillforts directly, and went off to meet Peter Woodward, prehistorian and curator of the Dorset County Museum (this article is also on my website). As we walked up Britain's finest hillfort—Maiden Castle, just outside Dorchester—I asked him flippantly whether the Iron Age was like Conan the Barbarian. Was it a time of lone warriors raiding temples and rescuing women from snake cults?

"Yes," replied Woodward in all seriousness. "Some of the visuals in films like *Conan the Barbarian* are as valuable as any others."

I decided that moment to write a novel set in the Iron Age, based around Maiden Castle (which became Maidun Castle in the book, as you may have worked out).

Over the next couple of years I worked out the story and the characters, and the book became a trilogy.

It is, of course, a fantasy story, not intended to be serious history. However, the history in it is generally accurate. I've made up the tribes and the characters, but all details—their homes, the towns and villages, clothes, industry, farming, flora and fauna, weapons, etc.—are as correct as they can be. One exception to this is Lowa's longbow, which doesn't officially appear in history until over a thousand years after the events of the book, but I think it's conceivable that the secret of Lowa's longbow lived on through her or Elann Nancarrow's descendants in Wales before surfacing again for the Hundred Years War.

As for the magic, sixty-two years after this book is set, according to a lot of people, a chap was born who could bring people back from the dead, multiply fish and so on. Is it that much of a stretch to believe that he wasn't the first person who could drum up a little magic?

End of Book One.

The story continues in book two
of the Iron Age trilogy:

Clash of Iron

Acknowledgements

Thanks foremost to my wife Nicola and her tireless and unfailingly cheerful support. Despite being a high-flier in a serious career, she has always listened attentively and compassionately to my gripes about writing a non-serious book, even when she knows that while she's been in board meetings and on conference calls with New York, I've spent the afternoon in the bath, reading history books.

I'd also like to thank my brother Tim for his ideas about the plot, my agent Angharad Kowal for taking me on and finding me a book deal, and my editor Jenni Hill at Orbit for her enthusiasm and excellent editing.

extras

orbit

meet the author

Nicola Watson

In his twenties, Angus Watson's jobs ranged from forklift truck driver to investment banker. He spent his thirties on various assignments as a freelance writer, including looking for Bigfoot in the USA for the *Telegraph*, diving on the scuppered German fleet at Scapa Flow for the *Financial Times* and swimming with sea lions off the Galapagos Islands for *The Times*. Now entering his forties, Angus is a married man who lives in London with his wife Nicola and baby son Charlie. As a fan of both historical fiction and epic fantasy, Angus came up with the idea of writing a fantasy set in the Iron Age when exploring British hillforts for the *Telegraph*, and developed the story while walking Britain's ancient paths for further articles. You can find him on Twitter at @GusWatson or visit his website at www.guswatson.com.

interview

What was your favourite part of Age of Iron *to write, and why?*

The interaction between Spring and Dug. The first book may be ostensibly centred on the love affair between Lowa and Dug, but I think the platonic relationship between Dug and Spring is more interesting and important.

If people are interested in the Iron Age, where should they look to find out more?

There's a good museum in Dorchester, Dorset, and there are various books (see Historical Note for authors). However, it takes about ten minutes to find out ninety-five per cent of what's known about the Iron Age (which you can probably do on Wikipedia) and after that it's pretty much all just analysis of pottery samples. So the best thing to do is to walk up to your local hillfort, stroll around and imagine what might have gone on there.

Was there anything that surprised you about researching the Iron Age?

I was disappointed when I discovered that the history in Asterix the Gaul books, particularly Asterix in Britain, is far from spot on.

extras

What prompted you to start writing Age of Iron?

I'd always wanted to be a novelist. After ten years' travelling and mucking about, then ten years of writing features, I hoped the time was right. I came up with the setting while on a hillfort, but made up the characters and the outline of a story on a long bus journey in France in 2009. I started writing the book as soon as I was back at my desk.

Who are your biggest influences as a writer?

Aged about eleven, I would read parts of *The Hitchhiker's Guide to the Galaxy* by Douglas Adams to anyone that would listen, particularly the passage about the filing cabinet with a sign on it saying "Beware of the leopard". That was the first book I remember loving, alongside *Watership Down* by Richard Adams. I've read those two books more times than any others, so daresay they are the strongest influences. I also read a lot of James Herbert and Sven Hassel as a child. Their influence just may have made itself heard in my gorier passages. Since then, Joseph Heller, John Irving, Thomas Hardy, William Boyd, Iain Banks, George MacDonald Fraser, Patrick O'Brien, Carl Hiaasen and Joe Abercrombie have probably all changed the way I write. I was lucky enough to interview Iain Banks once. He was an excellent man, genuinely interested in the novel I'd just started. That fact that both he and Douglas Adams died so young has not helped to dispel my atheism.

Talking of that sort of thing, my parents both died before I reached my teens. That changed the way I thought about everything, and so I'm sure has had a massive effect on my writing. I can't say I recommend early parental death, but I don't think the effects were all bad.

I also should mention the Asterix the Gaul books by Goscinny and Uderzo, which are set just a couple of years after

Age of Iron and should be compulsory reading for everybody (although, with apologies to Uderzo, they haven't been quite so good since Goscinny died in 1977).

You started writing as a features journalist for national newspapers—what's the strangest thing you've ever been asked to write about?

Freelance features writers usually come up with ideas themselves and propose them to papers. An article I wrote about the noise ducks make when they land was voted *Guardian* readers' favourite feature one year. It was good that Dug got to enjoy the same noise on the island of Mearhold. I like putting things in my books that people who know me will spot. Writers probably aren't meant to do that.

What do you do when you're not writing?

I read a lot more since I've been writing for a living because I can justifiably call it work. Years ago I pioneered the afternoon working bath (i.e. reading in the bath), and have been perfecting it ever since.

I love video games, particularly the *Elder Scrolls* and *Fallout* games. I'm also a keen photographer, serious enough that I have several lenses and process every shot with Photoshop. That processing now takes all the time that I used to spend playing video games. Photos are a more productive hobby, but I do miss the virtual world excitements of storming fortresses and finding slightly better swords than the one I've been wielding for the last ten hours of gameplay

Do you sympathise at all with the bad guys you write?

Completely, since most of the good characters I've created have bad sides and most of the bad ones have good sides.

Weylin, for example, could have been a perfectly decent fellow in different circumstances and with better role models.

The totally bad ones, like Zadar, I respect and understand, rather than sympathise with. Listening to right-wing radio in the USA, I've heard intelligent men articulately and persuasively flummox left-wing callers by explaining right-wing views that I find abhorrent. I don't like these men much, but I do respect their minds and the way they make me challenge my own beliefs.

While I'm on the subject, I think that as soon as people define themselves as left wing or right wing, they put on blinkers and lose about twenty IQ points. Both sides have their good points and their really dumb ones. Right or wrong should be the focus, not right or left.

What were the challenges in bringing this book to life?

I was lucky not to have to work in an office or factory or similar while writing the book. I can't write when I've spent most of the day working on something else—I just don't have the brainpower or energy. Beyond that, I think the biggest challenge was the constant nagging suspicion that what I was writing was a stinking pile of crap that nobody will ever want to read. A book is a very long project and you're very lucky if there are any points during it when someone says, "That's good; you should carry on with it." As I write, I've just finished the first draft of the second novel in the Iron Age trilogy. It's been well over a thousand hours' work, and nobody else has read a word of it. What if it's rubbish and those hours were wasted? Thoughts like that might keep me awake at night.

extras

What advice would you give to budding writers?

Go on a course. You may think it can't possibly improve your marvellous writing and it may even stifle your wonderful style, and you can't teach genius, but that's all crap, and, if nothing else, a writing course will get you to start writing. That's the other piece of advice—start.

What are you reading at the moment?

I'm reading *Dune* by Frank Herbert, which I'd been meaning to do for ages. I'm enjoying it so far. I like older fantasy books (like the Conan series) because they're great stories, but also because they tell you about the time that they're written in. I'm also reading a book on North American history, because I'm planning to set my next book or series of books there (after the third Iron Age book). My book will be set in prehistoric times, but F11 probably get some plot and character ideas from post-Columbian America. I find the USA fascinating and spend quite a lot of time there, usually staying in Las Vegas and taking photographs of the Mojave Desert. You can see these pics on my anonymous Twitter account @LasVegasHood (followers currently 52).

The people in the book have some quite modern characteristics. What made you write about them in this way?

I think there's a bizarre kind of prejudice about people from the past. We think of them as less than us and one-dimensional. But, of course, they were just as full of playfulness, jealousies, wit, passion and so on as we are.

Women and men have something like equality in your version of the British Iron Age. Is that a nod to political correctness?

No. I don't like tokenism. There are strong women in the book I guess because I've known a lot of strong women and

537

I do believe that women are equal to men (and everybody's equal to everybody, for that matter). I'm not trying to court a female readership or be right on. Similarly there's a guy from Africa, not because I thought "ooh, better have a black bloke", but because his origin is exotic and interesting, just like Chamanca's (Spain), Lowa's (Germany) and Felix's (Italy).

Are you trying to get any messages across in your book?

The book is stuffed full of messages. If readers notice any of them, fine, if they don't, also fine. There's no need, for example, to work out that Tans Tali is an anagram of Atlantis or see the parallels I'm trying to draw between Atlantis, other flood stories and climate history to show that there were definitely vast, forgotten civilisations, with who knows what levels of technology and sophistication, which were obliterated ten thousand years ago at the end of the last ice age when the sea level rose three hundred feet...

What's coming next for Dug, Lowa and Spring?

Their immediate problem is to consolidate their victory over Zadar. They're going to face attacks by more powerful tribes in Britain, and something pretty terrifying that they'd never imagined from across the sea to the west. On top of that, they've got the invincible Romans to worry about. Ragnall's life is going to change a lot, and some other characters from the first book will go to Gaul to see what they can do to halt Caesar's relentless march north to Britain.

introducing

If you enjoyed
AGE OF IRON
look out for

ARCANUM

by Simon Morden

*Rome was the center of the most powerful empire
the world had ever seen, but that didn't stop it falling to
Alaric the Goth, his horde of barbarian tribesmen and
their wild spell-casting shamans. Having split the walls with
their sorcery and slaughtered the inhabitants with
their axes, the victors carved up the empire into a series
of bickering states which were never more than
an insult away from war.*

*A thousand years later, and Europe has become
an almost civilized place. The rulers of the old Roman
palatinates confine their warfare to the short summer months,
trade flourishes along the rivers and roads, and farming
has become less back-breaking, all due to the magic,
bestowed by gods, that infuses daily life.*

*Even the barbarians' gods have been tamed: where once
human sacrifices poured their blood onto the ground, there
are parties and picnics, drinking and singing, fit for
decent people and their children.*

*But it looks like the gods are going to have the last
laugh before they slip quietly into ill-remembered obscurity…*

Chapter 1

As Peter Büber climbed, he left spring behind him. The mountain peaks, stark and blinding, immense and razor-edged, made him feel the most insignificant creature that ever dragged itself across the land.

The valley behind him, narrow, deep and shadowed, was nevertheless showing the first flush of green. Ahead of him was nothing but white snow that stretched from summit to summit and covered everything between.

Büber stopped and planted his walking-stick in the ground. He pulled on a pair of fur-lined mittens, sat a furry hat hard over his shaved scalp, and took up his stick again. The wind was tearing loose snow from the exposed upper slopes and trailing it like cloud in the blue sky. The higher he went, the colder and more open the terrain became.

He aimed for the first cairn of rocks, a couple of stadia uphill—snow stuck to its top like a crown, but its flanks were dark and clear. His boots crunched through the crust of ice with every footstep, leaving a trail of holes through which poked the first moss and tough alpine grasses of the year.

He reached the cairn breathing hard. He needed to slow

down; it had been months since he'd been up this high. His rough stubble was already coated in moisture, and it was threatening to freeze. So he wiped at his scarred face with his sleeve and leant back against the cairn, letting the weak sun do its best.

Recovered, he set off towards the second cairn, using a more measured pace. He planted the end of the stick, listened to the soft crush as it landed, then moved his feet, left and right. Repeat. There was a natural rhythm to his stride now, one that let him walk and breathe easily.

Past the second cairn, and on to the third—simple to find as only black rock against white snow can be, but he knew from bitter experience how hard it was trying to keep on course when the clouds descended and the precipices shrouded themselves in fog. Not today though. Today was glorious, bright and clean, and it was a pleasure to walk to the top of the pass and check the snow depth. It didn't even need to be clear, just shallow enough for the carts and wagons to wade through, and the short route to the Mittelmeer would be open again.

Büber, thinking contentedly of olive-skinned women, missed the first rumble of sound. He caught the echo, though. He stopped mid-stride, as frozen as the air.

Avalanches were common this time of year. He'd seen trees, buildings and people swept away and entombed in suddenly rock-hard snow that fell from mountaintops like a flood. They started with a crack and a whisper, then built like an oncoming storm to be the loudest thing he'd ever heard.

The last of it faded away, and he couldn't see the tell-tale sign of a plume of snowy air rising from the slopes. Everything was quiet again, the sound of even the wind muffled and distant.

It was said that there were foolish hunters and old hunters, but never foolish old hunters. Büber wasn't old, not yet, but he had every intention of living long enough to prove both his friends and his enemies wrong.

He stayed still for a while, scanning the east and west slopes with a practised, hand-shadowed gaze, but there was nothing he could spot. Perhaps it had been something in the next valley along, then, reverberating from peak to peak.

More cautiously, pausing at every cairn to listen, he walked higher and higher. The gradient wasn't that bad—the Romans who'd used it a thousand years earlier had picked out the route and built one of their wide roads south to north. Büber's ancestors had made the reverse journey, on their way to crack Rome's walls and set its temples ablaze. But up near the head of the pass, there were no smoothed stones or compacted gravel left. The via had worn away to soil and rock, just as it once was, and probably always would be.

He looked behind him. The line of cairns stretched away into the distance. Looking ahead, he could see three more before the slope took them out of sight. Almost there.

He trudged on. The snow rose over the turn-downs on his boots, and almost up to his knees. Not much, considering how high it would have been piled at Yuletide; warm air from the south helped clear the pass sooner. Difficult to walk in, all the same.

Difficult to run in, too.

The ground started to dip away to the south: he was there.

He plunged his walking-stick down, pulled out his knife and bent low to notch the wood. His breath condensed about him as he marked the snow level, not as proof—any idiot could stand at the bottom of the valley and guess—but for tradition. He'd been shown how to do it by a man now five years dead, and at some point he'd have to show some other rough kid from the mountains that this is what happens when you want to declare the pass open.

The flake of wood he'd cut fell to the snow. By the time he reported to the prince and the first ceremonial wagon was rolled up the via, even this covering would be little more than slush.

When he straightened up, he saw them.

They were in the far distance, coming down from the very top of the Aineck and almost invisible against the background: three large—and one of them was really very big—figures. They cast long black shadows that rippled against the contours of the snow, moving purposefully towards him.

There wasn't much meat on him, but giants weren't particularly picky about their choice of game. If they caught him, they'd eat him: quite how they'd spotted him at such a distance was a mystery left for later.

Time to go. If he turned around now, he'd just about beat them to the lower slopes, and at this time of year they wouldn't venture much below the snow line. While one man out on his own was prey, a crowd of them with spears was a predator. Giants were just smart enough to care about the difference.

Büber jerked out his walking-stick and took a last look around, just in case he'd missed something obvious. He was about to turn and follow his footsteps back when he saw a pack slowly sway into view. Then the ass it was strapped to. Then the man driving the ass on with a switch.

It wasn't him who'd attracted the giants' attention. It was this idiot.

And it wasn't just one idiot, because as Büber ran forward, his boots sinking deep into the snow, he could see a whole line of men and beasts snaking up the pass from the south.

He stopped again and stared. Maybe twenty donkeys, each with a pack tied high on their backs and roped together, and a dozen men at intervals down the chain, encouraging their charges to climb.

"Hey!" Büber waved his arms. "Hey, you!"

The lead driver raised his clean-shaven chin from his chest and looked uncertainly at Büber. He kept on coming though, switching the ass's hindquarters as it struggled upwards with its load.

"Giants," called the huntmaster. "Over there." He pointed.

The driver looked behind him and shouted something in a language that sounded like Italian. Büber didn't understand a word of it.

"Ah, fuck it." Büber squinted at the flanks of the mountain, but the snowy slopes were clear. "Fuck!"

He knew he should have kept the giants in sight. They could be anywhere now: together, split up, ahead, or coming over the ridge behind them.

"Giants," he said again. He mimed their size by lifting his hands as far over his head as he could and stamped the ground. What was the word? Stupid foreigners: why couldn't they speak German like civilised people? "Gigante. Si. Gigante."

Now he had their attention. The driver relayed the message down the line, and he definitely said "gigante" at some point. One man in particular took notice and slogged his way up the rise to Büber.

His clothes showed he was rich in a way Büber would never be. But then again, Büber wasn't about to see a substantial portion of his wealth eaten by giants, which was exactly what was going to happen if this man wasn't careful.

"Greetings in the name of the Doge, signore."

"Yes, that. Prince Gerhard, Carinthia, welcome. Giants, you Venetian cretin. Three of them, over to the east, though gods only know where they are now." Büber looked very carefully at all the places a creature twice his height might hide. "You have to get off this mountain now. And what are you doing here anyway? Didn't anyone tell you the pass is closed?"

"Pah. You Carinthians. You do not own this pass."

"Yes. Yes, we do. We open it and we close it and between times we make sure that people like you don't get butchered up here." Büber's head snapped around at something he thought he might have heard. "Save what you can and get ready to run."

"There are no giants," said the Venetian, warm beneath his furs. "Are you sure it was not dwarves you saw?"

"Oh, I'm sure." The donkeys plodded on. The first one was past him, the second one going by now. Their breath made little clouds and frost sparkled on their brown coats. They were making too much noise, and even he could smell them. Their scent must be driving the giants into a frenzy.

"You are a prince's man?"

"Yes." Büber's hand dropped to the pommel of his sword. It would be mostly useless against a foe whose reach was far longer—he carried a Norse-style blade, short and broad—but he felt better knowing it was there. "I'm the master of the hunt, and you need to listen to me."

"You wish for me to turn back because you think I should have waited for your permission."

"You should have waited until it was safe." Where were they? Giants usually just waded in, fists swinging. One blow was enough. What were they waiting for?

"Your ploy will not work. Besides, we have a little insurance of our own." The Venetian nodded at a man walking by. Dressed head to toe in a long red hooded cloak, it was only the tip of a nose and a sly, confident smile that Büber saw. "You Carinthians do not have a monopoly on magic."

"No. We just have the best." Büber had had enough. He'd seen the giants, he'd warned the merchant. He couldn't force them to turn back, or to abandon their cargo, or to sacrifice half the donkeys in order to try and save the other half, and themselves into the bargain. And besides, magicians gave him the fear in a way even a fully grown dragon didn't. "I've got my duty to do, and it's not to you. Good luck."

With all that donkey flesh available, the giants weren't going to bother with him, just as long as he got clear. When it was all over, when he'd got back down into the valley and made his report, he could come back with a squad of spear-armed soldiers and a hexmaster or two. And there might be something of the merchant's cargo worth salvaging.

The line of the train occupied the lowest point of the valley, so Büber turned perpendicular to it, and scaled the lower slopes of the mountain on the west side. He could keep them in sight, and put them between himself and the giants. Who were still nowhere to be seen. It concerned him that something that big could hide in plain sight. He had a commanding view over the whole of the upper pass.

He hadn't imagined them. He'd swear any number of oaths, to the gods, on his honour, on his parents' graves, that he'd seen those three long shadows shambling down towards him.

The lead driver tapped his jenny onwards towards the next cairn, and suddenly, from over the brow of the hill, came an immense rushing. When they wanted to, giants could move fast, using their long, tree-trunk-sized legs to devour the ground. Snow, knee-deep for a man, was simply kicked out of the way. They came in an arrowhead, the biggest one in the lead, the smaller two flanking.

The driver was rooted to the spot for far too long, and started running far too late. He was enveloped in a blizzard-like wall of white, along with his charge. He re-emerged, flying, limbs tangled, propelled like he'd been shot from a catapult. The donkey went straight up: giants did that, throwing their victims high in the air so that they would land, broken, behind them.

The animals were still tied together. The second one in line was jerked over and dragged before the rope snapped. The giants didn't stop. They thundered down the now-static formation, smashing their hands down like hammers and stamping on anything fallen.

And there was nothing Büber could do to help. The men at the back of the line ran more or less in the same direction, back to the south. The merchant, screaming uselessly at the wanton destruction of his property, and equally pointlessly for his guards to stand and fight, was knocked casually aside with enough force to shatter his ribcage, even with the cushioning effect of all his fine furs and padded coats.

The only one who looked like he was going to take the giants on was the Venetian sorcerer. He'd dodged to one side to avoid the initial onslaught: now he planted his feet and lifted his arms.

Three donkeys remained, still tied on to at least four or five of their dead or dying stablemates. They panicked and brayed and pulled, they rolled and twisted. The first giant slowed to a walk and reached down with its horny fingers splayed wide, catching a donkey's head and crushing it by making a fist.

With the animal still in its grasp, it turned to look at the magician.

The man had crossed to Büber's side of the valley, so the hunter had a good view, and despite both the urge to run and a clear path to take now the giants had gone past, he hesitated.

If this red-cloaked magician was any good, Büber might not have to run after all.

The giant dropped the donkey in a wet heap, and bared its long yellow peg teeth. It opened its mouth wide, wider than it had any reason to go, and roared out a geyser of white breath, spit and green mucus. The other giants—a female with pendulous dugs, and a juvenile already her height—stopped tearing chunks of bloody flesh and slippery entrails to view the scene.

The man in red rocked back on his heels and steadied himself. Büber had never seen such confidence, and he waited for the fireworks to begin.

The big giant was ugly even for its kind. Its face was more battered and scarred than even Büber's, and its hair was matted and growing in tufts. Old and angry, it glared down with its coal-black eyes at this weakling stick-thin figure that had the temerity to defy it.

The magician raised his hands, and the ink of his tattoos started to flow.

Nothing happened, and the giant charged.

It took a mere four steps to close the space between them and a perfectly timed duck-and-lift to scoop the man into the air. The cloak billowed as he flew: arms and legs flapped hopelessly against his useless scarlet wings.

He landed at the giant's feet, spreadeagled and on his back. He looked more surprised than hurt, but only because his surprise was very great.

The giant raised its foot, and a vast pale slab with curling toenails the colour of bone broke free of the snow. It brought it down hard on the magician, and then leant forward to apply extra pressure.

Büber heard the crack, and suddenly realised he was alone, up a mountain, miles from home, with only three pissed-off giants for company.

"Shit."

Now he started running.

There was a moment when he thought one of them would chase him: actually several moments, because every time he glanced fearfully over his shoulder, the baby of the group was looking at him even while it gathered up another handful of donkey—or man, he couldn't tell and didn't want to tell—and crammed it into its already red-stained maw.

When he thought he was far enough away, he slithered down the icy slope to the line of cairns, and kept his pace up until his lungs burnt, his vision swam and he could taste blood.

He leant his back against a cairn, hauling thin alpine air, and coughing like he had the plague. The sweat started to freeze on him, chilling his body and making him shiver. He knew what that would mean: he had to keep moving, but he still gave himself a few more moments to rest his hands on his knees as he tried to get his breathing under control.

There was a sound, stone on stone. Not right behind him, but too close all the same. He crouched down in the lee of the cairn and slowly, slowly, drew his sword. He stayed as still as he could, trying to trust his abilities to keep him hidden, but after a while, the waiting became unbearable.

He leant out ever so slightly. The giants' child was at the next cairn along, dragging some bloody morsel behind it, but searching for him. Büber ducked back, and prayed to the gods he hadn't been seen.

When he looked again, the giant had gone, and just a circle of red-spattered snow marked where it had been standing.

Büber hurried away, down the slope, to where spring was waiting for him.

introducing

If you enjoyed
AGE OF IRON
look out for

MALICE

The Faithful and the Fallen: Book One

by John Gwynne

The world is broken...

Corban *wants nothing more than to be a warrior under
King Brenin's rule—to protect and serve. But that day will come
all too soon. And the price he pays will be in blood.*

Evnis *has sacrificed—too much it seems. But what he wants—
the power to rule—will soon be in his grasp. And nothing
will stop him once he has started on his path.*

Veradis *is the newest member of the warband for the
High Prince, Nathair. He is one of the most skilled
swordsman to come out of his homeland, yet he is always
under the shadow of his older brother.*

*Nathair has ideas—and a lot of plans. Many of them
don't involve his father, the High King Aquilus.
Nor does he agree with his father's idea to summon
his fellow kings to council.*

*The Banished Lands has a violent past where armies of men
and giants clashed in battle, but now giants are seen, the stones
weep blood and giant wyrms are stirring. Those who can
still read the signs see a threat far greater than the ancient wars.
For if the Black Sun gains ascendancy, mankind's
hopes and dreams will fall to dust...*

...and it can never be made whole again.

Prologue

Evnis

The Year 1122 of the Age of Exiles, Wolf Moon

Forest litter crunched under Evnis' feet, his breath misting as
he whispered a curse. He swallowed, his mouth dry.

He was scared, he had to admit, but who would not be?
What he was doing this night would make him traitor to his
king. And worse.

He paused and looked back. Beyond the forest's edge he
could still see the stone circle, behind it the walls of Badun,
his home, its outline silvered in the moonlight. It would be so
easy to turn back, to go home and choose another path for his

life. He felt a moment of vertigo, as if standing on the edge of a great chasm, and the world seemed to slow, waiting on the outcome of his decision. *I have come this far, I will see it through.* He looked up at the forest, a wall of impenetrable shadow; he pulled his cloak tighter and walked into the darkness.

He followed the giantsway for a while, the stone-flagged road that connected the kingdoms of Ardan and Narvon. It was long neglected, the giant clan that built it vanquished over a thousand years ago, great clumps of moss and mushroom growing between crumbling flagstone.

Even in the darkness he felt too vulnerable on this wide road, and soon slithered down its steep bank and slipped amongst the trees. Branches scratched overhead, wind hissing in the canopy above as he sweated his way up and down slope and dell. He knew where he was going, had walked the path many times before, though never at night. Nineteen summers old, yet he knew this part of the Darkwood as well as any woodsman twice his age.

Soon he saw a flicker amongst the trees: firelight. He crept closer, stopping before the light touched him, scared to leave the anonymity of the shadows. *Turn around, go home, a voice whispered in his head. You are nothing, will never equal your brother.* His mother's words, cold and sharp as the day she had died. He ground his teeth and stepped into the firelight.

An iron cauldron hung on a spit over a fire, water bubbling. Beside it a figure, cloaked and hooded.

"Greetings." A female voice. She pushed the hood back, firelight making the silver in her hair glow copper.

"My lady," Evnis said to Rhin, Queen of Cambren. Her beauty made him catch his breath.

She smiled at him, wrinkles creasing around her eyes and held out her hand.

Evnis stepped forward hesitantly and kissed the ring on her finger, the stone cold on his lips. She smelled sweet, heady, like overripe fruit.

"It is not too late, you may still turn back," she said, tilting his head with a finger under his chin. They stood so close he could feel her breath. Warm, laced with wine.

He sucked in a breath. "No. There is nothing for me if I turn back. This is my chance to..."

His brother's face filled his mind, smiling, controlling, *ruling* him. Then his mother, her lips twisted, judging, *discounting*.

"...matter. Gethin has arranged a marriage for me, to the daughter of the poorest baron in Ardan, I think."

"Is she pretty?" Rhin said, still smiling, but with an edge in her voice.

"I have only met her once. No, I cannot even remember what she looks like." He looked at the cauldron on its spit. "I must do this. Please."

"And in return, what would you give me?"

"The whole realm of Ardan. I shall govern it, and bow to you, my High Queen."

She smiled, teeth glinting. "I like the sound of that. But there is more to this than Ardan. So much more. This is about the God-War. About Asroth made flesh."

"I know," he whispered, the fear of it almost a solid thing, dripping from his tongue, choking him. But exciting him, too.

"Are you scared?" Rhin said, her eyes holding him.

"Yes. But I will see it through. I have counted the cost."

"Good. Come then." She raised a hand and clicked her fingers.

A hulking shadow emerged from the trees and stepped into the firelight. A giant. He stood a man-and-a-half tall, his face pale, all sharp angles and ridged bone, small black eyes glittering under a thick-boned brow. A long black moustache hung to his chest, knotted with leather. Tattoos swirled up one arm, a creeping, thorn-thick vine disappearing under a chainmail sleeve, the rest of him wrapped in leather and fur. He carried a man in his arms, bound at wrist and ankle, as effortlessly as if it were a child.

"This is Uthas of the Benothi," Rhin said with a wave of her hand, "he shares our allegiances, has helped me in the past."

The giant drew near to the cauldron and dropped the man in his arms to the ground, a groan rising from the figure as it writhed feebly on the forest floor.

"Help him stand, Uthas."

The giant bent over, grabbed a handful of the man's hair and heaved him from the ground. The captive's face was bruised and swollen, dried blood crusting his cheeks and lips. His clothes were ragged and torn, but Evnis could still make out the wolf crest of Ardan on his battered leather cuirass.

The man tried to say something through broken lips, spittle dribbling from one corner of his mouth. Rhin said nothing, drew a knife from her belt and cut the captive's throat. Dark blood spurted and the man sagged in his captor's grip. The giant held him forward, angling him so that his blood poured into the cauldron.

Evnis fought the urge to step back, to turn and run. Rhin was muttering, a low, guttural chanting, then a wisp of steam curled up from the cauldron. Evnis leaned forward, staring. A great gust of wind swept the glade. A figure took form in the vapour, twisting, turning. The smell of things long dead, rotting, hit the back of Evnis' throat. He gagged, but could not tear his eyes away from where two pinpricks glowed: eyes, a worn, ancient face forming about them. It appeared noble, wise, sad, then lined, proud, stern. Evnis blinked and for a moment the face became reptilian, the eddying steam giving the appearance of wings unfurling, stretched, leathery. He shivered.

"Asroth," whispered Rhin, falling to her knees.

"What do you desire?" a sibilant voice asked.

Evnis swallowed, his mouth dry. *I must take what is owed me, step out from my brother's shadow. See it through.*

"Power," he rasped. Then, louder, taking a deep breath. "Power. I would rule. My brother, all of Ardan."

Laughter, low at first, but growing until it filled the glade. Then silence, thick and heavy as the cobwebs that draped the trees.

"It shall be yours," the figure said.

Evnis felt a trickle of sweat slide down his forehead. "What do you want in return? What is your price?"

"My price is you," the swirling figure said, eyes pinning him. "I want you." The lips of the ancient face in the steam twitched, a glimmer of a smile.

"So be it," said Evnis.

"Seal it in blood," the ancient face snarled.

Rhin held her knife out.

See it through, see it through, see it through, Evnis repeated silently, like a mantra. He clenched his teeth tightly together, gripped the knife, his palm clammy with sweat and drew it quickly across his other hand. Curling his fingers into a fist, he stepped forward, thrusting it into the steam above the iron pot. Blood dripped from his hand into the cauldron, where it immediately began to bubble. A force like a physical blow slammed into his chest, seemed to pass through him. He gasped and sank to his knees, gulping in great, ragged breaths.

The voice exploded in his head, pain shooting through his body.

He screamed.

"It is done," the voice said.

Chapter 1

Corban

Corban watched the spider spinning its web in the grass between his feet, legs working tirelessly as it wove its thread between a small rock and a clump of grass. Dewdrops suddenly sparkled. Corban looked up and blinked as sunlight spilt across the meadow.

The morning had been a colourless grey when his attention first wandered. His mother was deep in conversation with a friend, and so he'd judged it safe for a while to crouch down and study the spider at his feet. He considered it far more interesting than the couple preparing to say their vows in front of him, even if one of them was blood kin to Queen Alona, wife of King Brenin. *I'll stand when I hear old Heb start the handbinding, or when Mam sees me*, he thought.

"Hello, Ban," a voice said, as something solid collided with his shoulder. Crouched and balancing on the balls of his feet as he was, he could do little other than fall on his side in the wet grass.

"Corban, what are you doing down there?" his mam cried, reaching down and hoisting him to his feet. He glimpsed a grinning face behind her as he was roughly brushed down.

"*How long*, I asked myself this morning," his mam muttered

557

as she vigorously swatted at him. *"How long before he gets his new cloak dirty?* Well, here's my answer: before sun-up."

"It's past sun-up, Mam," Corban corrected, pointing at the sun on the horizon.

"None of your cheek," she replied, swiping harder at his cloak. "Nearly fourteen summers old and you still can't stop yourself rolling in the mud. Now, pay attention, the ceremony is about to start."

"Gwenith," her friend said, leaning over and whispering in his mam's ear. She released Corban and looked over her shoulder.

"Thanks a lot, Dath," Corban muttered to the grinning face shuffling closer to him.

"Don't mention it," said Dath, his smile vanishing when Corban punched his arm.

His mam was still looking over her shoulder, up at Dun Carreg. The ancient fortress sat high above the bay, perched on its hulking outcrop of rock. He could hear the dull roar of the sea as waves crashed against sheer cliffs, curtains of sea-spray leaping up the crag's pitted surface. A column of riders wound their way down the twisting road from the fortress' gates and cantered into the meadow. Their horses' hooves drummed on the turf, rumbling like distant thunder.

At the head of the column rode Brenin, Lord of Dun Carreg and King of all Ardan, his royal torc and chainmail coat glowing red in the first rays of morning. On one side of him rode Alona, his wife, on the other Edana, their daughter. Close behind them cantered Brenin's grey-cloaked shieldmen.

The column of riders skirted the crowd, hooves spraying clods of turf as they pulled to a halt. Gar, stablemaster of Dun Carreg, along with a dozen stablehands, took their mounts towards huge paddocks in the meadow. Corban saw his sister

Cywen amongst them, dark hair blowing in the breeze. She was smiling as if it was her nameday, and he smiled too as he watched her.

Brenin and his queen walked to the front of the crowd, followed closely by Edana. Their shieldmen's spear-tips glinted like flame in the rising sun.

Heb the loremaster raised his arms.

"Fionn ap Torin, Marrock ben Rhagor, why do you come here on this first day of the Birth Moon. Before your kin, before sea and land, before your king?"

Marrock looked at the silent crowd. Corban caught a glimpse of the scars that raked one side of the young man's face, testament of his fight to the death with a wolven from the Darkwood, the forest that marked the northern border of Ardan. He smiled at the woman beside him, his scarred skin wrinkling, and raised his voice.

"To declare for all what has long been in our hearts. To pledge and bind ourselves, one to the other."

"Then make your pledge," Heb cried.

The couple joined hands, turned to face the crowd and sang the traditional vows in loud clear voices.

When they were finished, Heb clasped their hands in his. He pulled out a piece of embroidered cloth from his robe, then wrapped and tied it around the couple's joined hands.

"So be it," he cried, "and may Elyon look kindly on you both."

Strange, thought Corban, *that we still pray to the All-Father, when he has abandoned us.*

"Why do we pray to Elyon?" he asked his mam.

"Because the loremasters tell us he will return, one day. Those that stay faithful will be rewarded. And the Ben-Elim may be listening." She lowered her voice. "Better safe than sorry," she added with a wink.

The crowd broke out in cheers as the couple raised their bound hands in the air.

"Let's see if you're both still smiling tonight," said Heb, laughter rippling amongst the crowd.

Queen Alona strode forward and embraced the couple, King Brenin just behind, giving Marrock such a slap on the back that he nearly sent his nephew over the bay's edge.

Dath nudged Corban in the ribs. "Let's go," he whispered. They edged into the crowd, Gwenith calling them just before they disappeared.

"Where are you two off to?"

"Just going to have a look round, Mam," Corban replied. Traders had gathered from far and wide for the spring festival, along with many of Brenin's barons come to witness Marrock's handbinding. The meadow was dotted with scores of tents, cattle-pens and roped-off areas for various contests and games, and *people*: hundreds, it must be, more than Corban had ever seen gathered in one place before. Corban and Dath's excitement had been growing daily, to the point where time had seemed to crawl by, and now finally the day was here.

"All right," Gwenith said. "You both be careful." She reached into her shawl and pressed something into Corban's hand: a silver piece.

"Go and have a good time," she said, cupping his cheek in her hand. "Be back before sunset. I'll be here with your da, if he's still standing."

"'Course he will be, Mam," Corban said. His da, Thannon, would be competing in the pugil-ring today. He had been fist champion for as long as Corban could remember.

Corban leaned over and kissed her on the cheek. "Thank you, Mam," he grinned, then turned and bolted into the crowd, Dath close behind him.

"Look after your new cloak," she called out, smiling.

The two boys soon stopped running and walked along the meadow's edge that skirted the beach and the bay, seals sunning themselves on the shore. Gulls circled and called above them, lured by the smell of food wafting from the fires and tents in the meadow.

"A silver coin," said Dath. "Let me see it."

Corban opened his palm, the coin damp now with sweat where he had been clutching it so tightly.

"Your mam's soft on you, eh, Ban?"

"I know," replied Corban, feeling awkward. He knew Dath only had a couple of coppers, and it had taken him moons to earn that, working for his father on their fishing boat. "Here," he said, delving into a leather pouch hanging at his belt, "have these." He held out three coppers that he had earned from his da, sweating in his forge.

"No thanks," Dath said with a frown. "You're my friend, not my master."

"I didn't mean it like that, Dath. I just thought—I've got plenty now, and friends share, don't they?"

The frown hovered a moment, then passed. "I know, Ban." Dath looked away, out to the boats bobbing on the swell of the bay. "Just wish my mam was still here to go soft on me."

Corban grimaced, not knowing what to say. The silence grew. "Maybe your da's got more coin for you, Dath," he said, to break the silence as much as anything.

"No chance of that," Dath snorted. "I was surprised to see this coin—most of it fills his cups these days. Come on, let's go and find something to spend it on."

The sun had risen high above the horizon now, bathing the meadow in warmth, banishing the last remnants of the dawn cold as the boys made their way amongst the crowd and traders' tents.

561

"I didn't think there were this many people in all the village and Dun Carreg put together," said Dath, grunting as someone jostled past him.

"People have come much further than the village and fortress, Dath," murmured Corban. They strolled on for a while, just enjoying the sun and the atmosphere. Soon they found themselves near the centre of the meadow, where men were beginning to gather around an area of roped-off grass. The sword-crossing ring.

"Shall we stay, get a good spot?" Corban said.

"Nah, they won't be starting for an age. Besides, everyone knows Tull is going to win."

"Think so?"

"'Course," Dath sniffed. "He's not the King's first-sword for nothing. I've heard he cut a man in two with one blow."

"I've heard that too," said Corban. "But he's not as young as he was. Some say he's slowing down."

Dath shrugged. "Maybe. We can come back later and see how long it takes him to crack someone's head, but let's wait till the competition's warmed up a bit, eh?"

"All right," said Corban, then cuffed his friend across the back of the head and ran, Dath shouting as he gave chase. Corban dodged this way and that around people. He looked over his shoulder to check where Dath was, then suddenly tripped and sprawled forwards, landing on a large skin that had been spread on the floor. It was covered with torcs, bone combs, arm-bands, brooches, all manner of items. Corban heard a low rumbling growl as he scrambled back to his feet, Dath skidding to a halt behind him.

Corban looked around at the scattered merchandise and began gathering up all that he could see, but in his urgency he fumbled and dropped most of it again.

"Whoa, boy, less haste, more speed."

Corban looked up and saw a tall wiry man staring down at him. He had long dark hair tied tight at his neck. Behind the man were all sorts of goods spread about an open-fronted tent: hides, swords, daggers, horns, jugs, tankards, horse harness, all hanging from the framework of the tent or laid out neatly on tables and skins.

"You have nothing to worry about from me, boy, there's no harm done," the trader said as he gathered up his merchandise. "Talar, however, is a different matter." He gestured to an enormous, grey-streaked hound that had risen to its feet behind Corban. It growled. "He doesn't take kindly to being trodden on or tripped over; he may well want some recompense."

"Recompense?"

"Aye. Blood, flesh, bone. Maybe your arm, something like that."

Corban swallowed and the trader laughed, bending over, one hand braced on his knee. Dath sniggered behind him.

"I am Ventos," the trader offered when he recovered, "and this is my faithful, though sometimes grumpy friend, Talar." Ventos clicked his fingers and the large hound padded over to his side, nuzzling the trader's palm.

"Never fear, he's already eaten this morning, so you are both quite safe."

"I'm Dath," blurted the fisherman's son, "and this is Ban—I mean, Corban. I've never seen a hound so big," he continued breathlessly, "not even your da's, eh, Ban?"

Corban nodded, eyes still fixed on the mountain of fur at the trader's side. He was used to hounds, had grown up with them, but this beast before him was considerably bigger. As he looked at it the hound growled again, a low rumble deep in its belly.

"Don't look so worried, boy."

"I don't think he likes me," Corban said. "He doesn't sound happy."

"If you heard him when he's not happy you'd know the difference. I've heard it enough on my travels between here and Helveth."

"Isn't Helveth where Gar's from, Ban?" asked Dath.

"Aye," Corban muttered.

"Who's Gar?" the trader asked.

"Friend of my mam and da," Corban said.

"He's a long way from home, too, then," Ventos said. "Whereabouts in Helveth is he from?"

Corban shrugged. "Don't know."

"A man should always know where he's from," the trader said, "we all need our roots."

"Uhh," grunted Corban. He usually *asked a* lot of questions—too many, so his mam told him—but he didn't like being on the receiving end so much.

A shadow fell across Corban, a firm hand gripping his shoulder.

"Hello, Ban," said Gar, the stablemaster.

"We were just talking about you," Dath said. "About where you're from."

"What?" said the stablemaster, frowning.

"This man is from Helveth," Corban said, gesturing at Ventos.

Gar blinked.

"I'm Ventos," said the trader. "Where in Helveth?"

Gar looked at the merchandise hung about the tent. "I'm looking for harness and a saddle. Fifteen-span mare, wide back." He ignored the trader's question.

"Fifteen spans? Aye, I'm sure I've got something for you back

564

here," replied Ventos. "I have some harness I traded with the Sirak. There's none finer."

"I'd like to see that." Gar followed Ventos into the tent, limping slightly as always.

With that the boys began browsing through Ventos' tent. In no time Corban had an armful of things. He picked out a wide iron-studded collar for his da's hound, Buddai, a brooch of pewter with a galloping horse embossed on it for his sister, a dress-pin of silver with a red enamel inset for his mother and two sturdy practice swords for Dath and himself. Dath had picked out two clay tankards, waves of blue coral decorating them.

Corban raised an eyebrow.

"Might as well get something my da'll actually use."

"Why two?" asked Corban.

"If you cannot vanquish a foe," he said sagely, "then ally yourself to him." He winked.

"No tankard for Bethan, then?" said Corban.

"My sister does not approve of drinking," replied Dath.

Just then Gar emerged from the inner tent with a bundle of leather slung over his back, iron buckles clinking as he walked. The stablemaster grunted at Corban and walked into the crowd.

"Looks like you've picked up a fine collection for yourselves," the trader said to them.

"Why are these wooden swords so heavy?" asked Dath.

"Because they are practice swords. They have been hollowed out and filled with lead, good for building up the strength of your sword arm, get you used to the weight and balance of a real blade, and they don't kill you when you lose or slip."

"How much for all of these," Corban asked.

Ventos whistled. "Two and a half silvers."

"Would you take this if we leave the two swords?" Corban showed the trader his silver piece and three coppers.

"And these?" said Dath, quickly adding his two coppers.

"Deal."

Corban gave him their coin, put the items into a leather bag that Dath had been keeping a slab of dry cheese and a skin of water in.

"Maybe I'll see you lads tonight, at the feast."

"We'll be there," said Corban. As they reached the crowd beyond the tent Ventos called out to them and threw the practice swords. Instinctively Corban caught one, hearing Dath yelp in pain. Ventos raised a finger to his lips and winked. Corban grinned in return. *A practice sword, a proper one, not fashioned out of a stick from his back garden. Just a step away from a real sword.* He almost shivered at the excitement of that thought.

They wandered aimlessly for a while, Corban marvelling at the sheer numbers of the crowd, at the entertainments clamouring for his attention: tale-tellers, puppet-masters, fire-breathers, sword-jugglers, many, many more. He squeezed through a growing crowd, Dath in his wake, and watched as a piglet was released squealing from its cage, a score or more of men chasing it, falling over each other as the piglet dodged this way and that. They laughed as a tall gangly warrior from the fortress finally managed to throw himself onto the animal and raise it squeaking over his head. The crowd roared and laughed as he was awarded a skin of mead for his efforts.

Moving on again, Corban led them back to the roped-off ring where the sword-crossing was to take place. There was quite a crowd gathered now, all watching Tull, first-sword of the King.

The boys climbed a boulder at the back of the crowd to see

better, made short work of Dath's slab of cheese and watched as Tull, stripped to the waist, his upper body thick and corded as an old oak, effortlessly swatted his assailant to the ground with a wooden sword. Tull laughed, arms spread wide as his opponent jumped to his feet and ran at him again. Their practice swords *clacked* as Tull's attacker rained rapid blows on the King's champion, causing him to step backwards.

"See," said Corban, elbowing his friend and spitting crumbs of cheese, "he's in trouble now." But, as they watched, Tull quickly side-stepped, belying his size, and struck his off-balance opponent across the back of the knees, sending him sprawling on his face in the churned ground. Tull put a foot on the man's back and punched the air. The crowd clapped and cheered as the fallen warrior writhed in the mud, pinned by Tull's heavy boot.

After a few moments the old warrior stepped away, offered the fallen man his hand, only to have it slapped away as the warrior tried to rise on his own and slipped in the mud.

Tull shrugged and smiled, walking towards the rope boundary. The beaten warrior fixed his eyes on Tull's back and suddenly ran at the old warrior. Something must have warned Tull, for he turned and blocked an overhead blow that would have cracked his skull. He set his legs and dipped his head as the attacking warrior's momentum carried him forwards. There was a crunch as his face collided with Tull's head, blood spurting from the man's nose. Tull's knee crashed into the man's stomach and he collapsed to the ground.

Tull stood over him a moment, nostrils flaring, then he pushed his hand through long, grey-streaked hair, wiping the other man's blood from his forehead. The crowd erupted in cheers.

"He's new here," said Corban, pointing at the warrior lying senseless in the mud. "I saw him arrive only a few nights ago."

"Not off to a good start, is he?" chuckled Dath.

"He's lucky the swords were made of wood, there's others have challenged Tull that haven't got back up."

"Doesn't look like he's getting up any time soon," pointed out Dath, waving his hand at the warrior lying in the mud.

"But he will."

Dath glanced at Corban and suddenly lunged at him, knocking him off the rock they were sitting on. He snatched up his new practice sword and stood over Corban, imitating the scene they had just witnessed. Corban rolled away and climbed to his feet, edging slowly around Dath until he reached his own wooden sword.

"So, you wish to challenge the mighty Tull," said Dath, pointing his sword at his friend. Corban laughed and ran at him, swinging a wild blow. For a while they hammered back and forth, taunting each other between frenzied bursts of energy.

Passers-by smiled at the two boys.

After a particularly furious flurry of blows Dath ended up on his back, Corban's sword hovering over his chest.

"Do—you—yield?" asked Corban between ragged breaths.

"Never," cried Dath and kicked at Corban's ankles, knocking him onto his back.

They both lay there, gazing at the clear blue sky above, too weak with their exertions and laughter to rise, when suddenly, startling them, a voice spoke.

"Well, what have we here, two hogs rutting in the mud?"